The Devil's Road

The Devil's Road

A Group Novel About America's First Serial Killer

by U.S. Five

(Bob Stanton, Sandi Branum, Gary F. Izzo,
Dedra Torelli & Nina D. Wade)

CREATIVE ARTS BOOK COMPANY
Berkeley • California 1999

The Devil's Rood is published by Donald S. Ellis
and distributed by Creative Arts Book Company

For Information contact:
Creative Arts Book Company
833 Bancroft Way
Berkeley, California 94710
(800) 848-7789

ISBN 0-88739-220-2 paper
ISBN 0-88739-221-0 cloth
Library of Congress Catalog Number 98-89651

Printed in the United States of America

To Jacksonville University

The Devil's Road

ME

Call me Lucky. In the past eleven months I've lost my birth name, Luther, and a solid middle name, Lincoln, both of which used to appear together in my syndicated column in this city's loudest newspaper, CT. My surname, Rust, was the most appropriate of the names, but I didn't know that then, the time when I had a job, a family, and a good middle-class life in America's busiest city, Chicago. Between then and now I've become The Loser, for losing became the main and then the only activity in my now homeless life.

But not more than a month ago, on Christmas Eve, 1995, I climbed into an almost abandoned building, breaking a window to do so, on the corner of Sixty-Third and Wallace. Not wanting to share a near-empty bottle of whiskey with other no-names there, I looked for a stairway going down and found it fast.

Even in the basement I couldn't escape my peers who grunted and groaned and cleared their throats in their troubled sleep. So I sought relief among a junkpile of office machinery, including typewriters probably not twenty years old, but certainly obsolete in a world gone crazy with computers. Anyway, I began to build up a low wall of metal and plastic typewriters, adding machines, and broken monitors, making a space just large enough to lie down, where I could finish off the whiskey and then sleep on an old blanket I keep rolled up on my back.

But then, when almost done clearing away the machinery, I felt with my foot a slight indentation in the floor's dark surface. If I hadn't had a big hole in my shoe, I probably would never have known. Curious, I got down on my knees to explore the floor with my free hand, the other still gripping my bottle, and soon found what later proved to be a trapdoor, complete with an opening big enough for my index finger to enter.

It was too dark to make any further explorations, and I wanted to get that whiskey into my belly before doing anything else. I literally slept on the trapdoor.

The next morning I pulled up the door and found an old wooden staircase leading down into total darkness. Never fond of spiders, rats, roaches, and other anti-human things, I decided to find a source of light first.

The best I could find was a book of matches lying next to an old sleeping man wearing a heavy black shoe on one foot and a red sneaker on the other.

Slowly, I descended the wooden steps, each creaking loudly with age. About ten feet down, I stepped onto the ground and then lit a match. The last thing in the world I expected to see was a skeleton stretched out on a large dis-

secting table. I moved immediately back up the stairs and banged the door shut. But five minutes later I was staring at the skeleton again.

The room had other things: old rusty saws, long knives, and other cutting instruments hanging here and there from the walls of the cellar. I found a hurricane lamp still holding oil near the skeleton's head. Soon I had it working, producing a constant light, and even some welcome heat.

I found several bottles of chemicals, some red-splashed rags, and a box of women's underwear. I found a giant furnace, too. And inside the furnace I found a large metal box. Locked.

My hope, at that time, was to open up the box and find a few thousand dollars, enough to buy a large supply of alcohol and maybe six months of a nice room where I could finish it off. At first I was disappointed when I found a pile of hand-written letters, numerous newspaper clippings, some bank savings books, several insurance policies, and other kinds of legal documents.

But I'm lucky because my old newspaper instinct had not completely died. One part of me, the disappointed part, wanted to move on toward the next bottle, even a used bottle of stale beer; the other part, the lucky part, was growing curious about the contents of the box.

Hell, one thing I have in abundance is time. And lucky loser me had found himself a story—or at least the materials to put a story together. I didn't know that then, of course, but I know it now. The box held the materials for the story of a pathological madman, a devil named Herman Mudgett, also known in his time by more than a hundred different names. But I'm moving too fast. I need to start at the beginning.

The contents of the big box had been organized into separate bundles, each tied up with rope. Although the room was large, the only furniture was the dissecting table; so I carefully moved the skeleton to one side, leaving plenty of space for the bundles. Using a pair of women's underpants, I swept the thick layer of dust and cobwebs from the table, finding it stained with old dried-up blood. Not having anywhere else to sit, I sat next to the skeleton, my back up against a stone wall.

I untied the bundle of letters, and the first letter, dated June 1, 1896, was addressed to me:

To the finder of the box:

Holmes asked me to tie up his letters and all the crap written about him. Before he died, he got all his wives to give him all their letters about him, even those they sent to others. May sound a bit mad but these ladies were crazy about him. Dr. Holmes was born in 1860 and died May 16, 1896. The papers says he went like a man and I believe it. He werent afraid of nutin, even what people in the future might say. Hes now buried in a few tons of

cement in Philly, near the place where they hanged him. I did my best to wrap up these things like he told me. The body on the table once loved him—and he loved her. He told me to tell you to do what you wanted with his things, so I guess I done my job.

His friend and Castle caretaker,
Patrick Quinlan

*I*looked at the skeleton but couldn't tell whether it was male or female. I then spent half an hour reading the letters before going out to beg for some money. It was Christmas Day—and even two cops felt sorry enough for me to reach into their pockets and give me their change, a buck eighty-one in all. I made about thirty dollars that day in two hours. In a deli I bought two six- packs of Milwaukee's finest, a small jar of mayo, some boiled ham, and a loaf of French bread. In a supermarket I bought some wicks, oil, and a big box of matches to keep the lamp burning. Then I went back to my rent-free room to eat, drink, and read.

Because of my drinking problem, I need to beg almost every day. You might think I could have gotten a job sometime during these past eleven months, but after the paper "downsized" me I couldn't find any other hack work and our savings disappeared into paying the bills for having lived beyond our means. We soon lost our cars and then our house on the city's north side. To get welfare payments for our two children, I had to go onto the streets. Somewhere along the line, I found help from alcohol. Without a permanent address, without a phone, without a meaningful life, I became a beggar, the only thing I could do without becoming a criminal.

Needing at least two hours to beg each day, it took me more than a week to read all of the material Quinlan had bundled up for me. Sometimes I found myself talking to the skeleton, telling it what I thought about Holmes and his victims. Often I asked Miss Bones to tell me her real name, but I was obviously quite drunk at those times. Still, I think that the nature of the material and my talking to a skeleton gave me some ideas on the best way to present the material to you. My primary concern as a writer is to keep you entertained as readers. But I don't want to mislead you. We are dealing with a real killer here. And everyone else mentioned in my account was also real. So I want to keep the reality of the story intact.

After some sober thinking about my aims, I decided that much of Holmes's story will come directly from himself, America's first serial killer, who wrote several letters to a Dr. Frank Noland at the Norristown Insane Asylum in

Pennsylvania. And to give balance to Holmes's overpowering revelation of his hideous misdeeds, I have given his victims and others a right to speak through my analyses of the many newspaper accounts I have read. To do this, I made use of the Victorian device of dramatic monologue, so that you will sometimes feel as if you're overhearing a one-sided telephone conversation.

And so, like Ralph Ellison's Invisible Man, I have been staying below a basement since Christmas, doing what I can to give birth to my own life by giving birth to a mad murderer who probably took a hundred lives or more in his mean, cold-blooded way. I used some of my begging money to buy a ream of paper, but the typewriter is free.

If really lucky, I will find a publisher for this unusual discovery and be back with my wife and children by next Christmas. If not, this kind of life will kill me in fewer than five years.

1857

Congregational Church   Saturday, *October 31*
Gilmanton, New Hampshire

Theodate Mudgett:

I only have a few minutes to talk so I'll get right to the point. You might want to sit down for this.

I'm pregnant.

Yes, I'm sure.

I know. I didn't expect this either, but now that's it's happened, I've come to talk.

Been thinking about it for a couple of weeks and I've decided I don't have much choice about what we can do.

No, nothin' like that.

Listen to me. I'm going to have this baby just like nothing is wrong, and after the little one is born, you're going to take it to the hospital in Peterborough and leave it on the doorstep. We'll write a note sayin' I couldn't take care of it and we want it to go to a good family.

I'll tell Levi it died.

Of course he'll believe me.

No, Luther, I can't keep it. You know my oldest is 17 now and always in trouble, and my youngest is a handful.

My life's a constant struggle keepin' Levi's belly full of buttered biscuits, tryin' to stay out of the way of his backhand, and holdin' my tongue when he screams at me. I don't want to bring another child into this world just to feel the sting of Levi's hickory stick.

I know, but it's the truth. Everytime I'd look at that little baby, I'd see your eyes looking up at me. I'd be constantly reminded of what might have been. It's hard enough now just knowin' that we've decided not to see each other anymore. I'll miss you so much.

Yes, I really think we've made the right decision—it has to be. You know Levi would kill us both if he ever found out I was sneakin' around seeing the Congregational minister.

So, there'll be no argument. For sanity's sake, I will have my way at this.

Confessional Booth, St. Paul's Catholic Church   Wednesday, *December 23*
Concord, New Hampshire

Pastor Luther Stanton:

Father, forgive me for I have sinned. I am not a Catholic, but I am a man of the cloth even though I no longer deserve to hold that title.

Yes. I'm a minister of the Congregational Church.

I'm here because I can no longer stand the pain. I've done a terrible thing and I want to know that God forgives me. Your faith has such a concrete method for absolution, and since I am no better than a common thief or murderer, I need someone to hear my confession. I need to feel better.

It all started very innocently. I became friendly with a family in my township and talked several times with the wife about problems she was having with her husband—all without his knowledge, of course. He was very strict and abusive, and my heart went out to her. She's young and attractive and before I knew what was happening, I was more involved than I intended. Well, one thing led to another and suddenly we were meeting behind the barn when the husband was working out in the fields.

Yes, I made love to this woman many times... and...and she got pregnant.

Oh, it was mine. No doubt. Anyway, the husband continued to beat her throughout the pregnancy. So, on the day the baby was born, she told him that the baby had died during the birth. She lied and said she buried the baby behind the barn so as to save him the trouble. And you know what he did next? The bastard booted her out of the bed and made her prepare his dinner. He told her he'd had a hard day and needed to eat, that he was hungry.

No, there's more, I'm afraid. I was with her when she gave birth and as much as I'm ashamed to admit it, I'm the one who drove the baby in my wagon to Concord. I left him, my own son, outside the door of the hospital with a note attached to his little blanket. I still can't believe I did such a thing.

Father, I feel awful. My heart is heavy. So much guilt is unbearable.

I wanted her to keep the baby, but she'd made up her mind to get rid of him, saying it would only remind her of me. And, what kind of life would the child have with that idiot thinking it was his? And, what if he should find out?

What a mess I've made of our lives. I still love her, but she won't have anything to do with me now—won't even see me. I should never have gotten involved. The worst part is I'll never know my son, and he'll never know his real parents. Do you think God can ever forgive me?

1858

Mudgett Farm
Gilmanton, New Hampshire
Theodate Mudgett:

Saturday, June 5

Oh, God, please forgive me for giving my baby away. I can't believe I did such a horrible thing. He was so innocent—poor little boy. What did he know? Who did he ever harm? Nobody. Ooooh...I'm a terrible mother and deserve all your wrath. I promise to endure any punishment you deem appropriate. I really deserve to burn in Hell for what I've done. My poor baby— the one child I could have loved, and I had to give him up. How could I have made such a bad choice?

Oh, Levi, I was just saying my prayers. Leave me alone for once and let me pray in peace.

Ooooww...all right, I'll get in the bed. Just don't hit me again.

Oh, Levi, not tonight. Please...please...Ooooww

1860

Mudgett Farm
Gilmanton, New Hampshire
Theodate Mudgett:

Oh, that's right, little Herman. Go ahead and cry! Scream all you want. I'll feed you when I'm good and ready and not a minute before.

Yeah, yeah, yeah. Drive me crazy with your cryin', you *little* devil. I'll give you somethin' to cry about.

How do you like that? I'll show you who's in charge here. You'd better shut up or I'll have to pinch you again.

Oh, be quiet. Put this in your mouth and suck it. That's right. Get your fill. You'll be the death of me, anyway.

What have I gotten myself into—what kind of life do I have? It's a hell we live in. Oh, life would have been much kinder had I not given Luther's child away. *You*, my dear son of Levi, never should have been born.

Not again! Herman, you stink. Now you're *really* gonna get it!

1875

The Mudgetts' Farmhouse Kitchen   *Saturday, January 23*
Gilmanton, New Hampshire

Levi Mudgett:

Give me the second cup, now, Theodate.

The fence needs mending, snow or no snow, with or without the help of boys who are too good to be doin' work with their hands.

More butter! You know I can't eat dry biscuits.

They disappear when work must be done. Hiding on me, I bet. When I was a boy in our beloved Bulgaria, Father never had to look for me, never had to shout, "Levi, Levi, where are you?" Not once, not even once did I not do what I was told. He would break my face if I didn't have those damn cows fed by sunrise.

Here, give me more butter!

What are you thinkin' about? Always the face, always the mouth turned down. Soon your lips will touch the earth.

I say you try too hard to please.

Yes, you do.

We must do business with them, yes, but must we break bread with them or kneel down in their unholy temples? Next thing, you will be baking cakes for their church socials.

Yes, you will, and on Saturdays, too. Maybe even today you'll be out cooking for them in the snow, for damn Jesus followers.

It's bad enough you must teach their children. But on Saturdays you must stay home. I need you here.

Housework, plenty of housework to do.

And watching those boys. I can't be a mother, you know.

Lift the mouth, if you can. Always the face.

Someone must keep their eyes on the wicked boys, especially our Herman, who spends too much time doting on the female Gentiles. Last week he was buying candy for one of them at Martin's store. Martin told me—the boy actin' like he owned the store.

When I find him, I'll beat him. Between you and the boy, we'll soon be sharing our table with the pig-eating Christians.

Martin's wife told you that?

Martin, a Christian? No, not Martin!

His whole family? In the Congregational Church?

No, we won't go. Now we will be the only Jews in Gilmanton. We must be strong.

Yes, strong like bulls.

The mouth, the mouth, must you always walk 'round with the face?

The Gilmanton Library Steps   *Saturday, January 30, mid-morning*
Gilmanton, New Hampshire

H. H. Holmes:

This is some hick town, ain't it, Herm?

Can't even keep the library open in winter. Turn around and look at the sign—
closed till spring!

Are you listenin' to me? What's wrong with you lately?

Are you still moping over her? The world is full of Claras...and, even more
depressing, Gilmanton is covered with snow.

Special in what way? Does she have three breasts or somethin'?

You're too serious 'bout her. I say throw her on the ground and jump on her.
Then see if she's so special.

Okay, I'll be quiet, but the face, Herman, always the face!

That's better. Come on, let's go find Tom and warm our wet asses at Martin's
counter.

The Loverings' Parlor   *Sunday, February 7, mid-afternoon*
Gilmanton, New Hampshire

Clara Lovering:

Father, why couldn't Herman ride with us to church this morning?

But he was so happy when I invited him. I felt horrible telling him we didn't
have room in our carriage.

He was *not* filthy...he had on his best suit.

I have *not* been seeing Herman too much.

Well, occasionally I see him at Mister Martin's store, where we're surrounded
by people. It's not like I'm sneaking off to see him. Herman wants to court me.

He won't always be a farm boy.

I'm not exactly sure. That's why *you* should talk to him and find out.

He's the perfect age for me. I'll be fifteen next year. Please, listen to me—I want
to marry Herman.

It's not too soon. I've loved him since I was nine.

He'll be able to provide for me. He's a hard worker and willing to do anything
to move ahead. One day, he'll be as rich as you are. Besides, I don't care about
that. All I know...

You did *what*, Father?

Who's Derek Courtney?

A bank clerk? Why would you invite *him* to dinner?

And just how *old* is Mister Courtney?

Thirty? That's ancient. We'll have nothing to talk about.

That's nice, but I still don't see why *he's* allowed to dine with us and Herman isn't.

But, Father...

Yes, sir. I'll wear the peach dress and be especially charming to *your* guest.

Loon Lake   *Sunday, February 7, mid-evening*
Gilmanton, New Hampshire

Herman Mudgett:

I'm hot and sick of skating. Let's stop.

I've got to see her, H.

Now. Walk me to her house?

H, why does her fat father hate me so much?

But I don't practice the religion—wearing the funny hat and all that.

So how difficult can it be to become one of them? At least they use words any idiot could understand.

English, not Yiddish. I don't even like the word "Yiddish." It sounds like something from Mars. And I can't stand to see the old man rocking back and forth as if he were on an invisible horse. He spits when he talks, too.

Look, her light is on. Let's go see what she's doin'.

The Loverings' Front Porch   *Monday, February 8, late afternoon*
Gilmanton, New Hampshire

Clara Lovering:

Herman, what a surprise! I wasn't expecting you.

No, we'd better stay here. Mother's tired, and I need to stay nearby. Would you like some lemonade?

Here—now what's the matter? You can tell me anything. I know you're upset about something.

Please, Herman...

Why did you do that?

Oh, he's just some bank clerk named Derek Courtney. He's nice, but not very exciting. Then again, that's the kind of man Father wants me to marry.

There's no reason for such an outburst. I won't marry Derek.

He told me to call him that.

Nothing happened between us.

This is a ridiculous conversation. There's no need to be jealous. I have no control over the people my father invites for dinner. If I did, you would have been there.

Herman, you're the only one I want. I love you. And I know my parents will come to accept you. Besides, why would I marry an old man like him? I don't always do what Father says.

I've got to go. Mother's calling.

The Mudgetts' Cow Barn   *Tuesday, February 9, late afternoon*
Gilmanton, New Hampshire

Herman Mudgett:

I'd like to squeeze someone's throat rather than this cow's tits.

Some fat asshole, a big slob named Derek.

Derek Courtney, a bank clerk, probably thirty years old. I'll stick my head in a tub of shit if I'm a bank clerk at thirty.

He's dating my girl.

Clara.

Yeah, Clara Lovering. Know her? Get me another pail, will ya?

Thanks.

Old Derek has the permission of Clara's father to see her. I'm not good enough, of course.

Nineteen.

I am so. Why?

I've known her all my life. There's no way he'll ever get to know more than the feel of her hand. The day he tries to go further will be his last.

No, I'm not kiddin'. She's mine, all mine.

Right, no matter what it takes.

Dearest Diary,

I no longer know what to think. Herman has only been by to see me a few times since I told him I loved him. Did I do wrong? Perhaps I was too forward, but I thought he loved me also. I know he hasn't come out and said so, but I thought it was just because he was scared or shy.

The few times I've seen him have been anything but wonderful. He's always talking about leaving Gilmanton. What will I do? If he leaves, he'll probably fall in love with some worldly woman—everything I'm not. Maybe I'm worrying for no reason. He's promised to send for me after he moves. Should I go?

This isn't the way I planned our future when we saw each other again. I thought Saturdays would be spent together down by the lake—it's always been Herman's favorite place, even when we were children. Instead, I am here at home with Mother and Father.

Father still hasn't relented. He says Herman's never going to be good enough for me because he's Jewish. How can he compete against Father's opinion? I don't have any answers, so I still have dinner with Derek, even though I don't love him. He's nice and safe, and I'm sure he would be a good husband, attentive and caring. But Herman stirs my soul.

Did you know Derek has already told me he'll be asking Father for my hand? This happened last night when he tried to kiss me. Of course, I told him not to kiss me and being the gentleman Derek is, he didn't. If it had been Herman, I'd have said yes. Not that I would've let him do more—Pastor Stanton says it's sinful to do anything else before marriage. Luckily, Herman understands how I feel about that and he's willing to wait. Though it's hard because I would like to feel his lips on my cheek again. They were so soft that one time.

I can't wait until Herman and I are man and wife. Will that day ever come? What should I do about Derek? If only I didn't love Herman so.

Clara

Wednesday, April 14, 1875

Loon Lake   *Saturday, August 7, dawn*
Gilmanton, New Hampshire

Herman Mudgett:

You're right, H, we're gettin' too old for this town. Even the fish know who we are. Any bites yet?

Yep, no money here. No one has money here. And my father's a lunatic. Sometimes I want to stuff his mouth with those white worms we find in cow shit. At least I'm too big for that bastard now. Next time he whacks little Ira and Joel around I'm gonna tear into him.

Right, our talents are going to waste in this dinky place. I'll never become a doctor if I don't break away. What are your plans?

Tomorrow? Well, I've got those experiments I'm doin' with mice—that will take another week. And I'm waitin' to see how much longer those birds will live without their legs.

Right, the old roads heading west are gettin' awful dusty. I don't know, H.

Don't know if I can leave Clara.

Sure, she'll think better of me if I make a life for myself. The thing is, where should I go?

With you? What could I do there?

That doesn't seem too sanitary to me, H. Are you just havin' fun with me?

Clara's Parlor   *Thursday, August 12*
Gilmanton, New Hampshire

Clara Lovering:

Mother, have you heard...Herman's disappeared!

But he promised he wouldn't do this to me.

I don't know where. All I know is...he's...left me. Please...hand me your handkerchief. Mother, what did I do wrong?

I know, I know. I must accept the truth...Herman no longer...loves me.

Why should he come back? My love isn't enough for him. I feel so used.

No, I would never do that—at least not until after marriage. I always thought it would be me and Herman who...

I'll be fine, I think. It just hurts so bad. I loved—still love him so much.

That's easy for you to say. You married the man you loved. I don't know,

maybe Father's right about Herman. I guess I'll have to forget...him.
Derek? Tonight?
Yes, ma'am. I'll dry my eyes and go change.
You're right, Derek would never leave me.

1876

Gilmanton, New Hampshire   *Wednesday, January 19, 1876*

My dearest Herman,

I'm so thrilled to finally receive a letter from you. I was afraid you had left Gilmanton forever and had forgotten all about me. Yes, you are for-given for not writing sooner. How could I not forgive you?

How do you like teaching the younger children? I'm sure they enjoy having you as their teacher. You're fantastic with children of any age. You'll make a good father one day.

When do you think you'll come to visit, dear? I miss you more every day. I had hoped you would become partners with Mr. Martin. We could have been seeing each other almost all the time. Also, I think you would make a successful businessman. Father would like it better if you were a businessman rather than a teacher. He thinks you're wasting your talents right now. However, if it makes you happy, then I wish you the best. Just think, you could become a headmaster one day.

Herman, I must make a confession. I'm still seeing Derek, which pleases Father. But now that you've confessed your love for me, I'll stop seeing him. Of course, it will take time since I don't want to hurt his feelings. I promise, Herman, I'm yours. I'll wait for you to decide when we can finally be together. I only pray that it will be soon.

I better stop writing so I can post this letter. May God keep you in his care.

> *With all my love,*
> *Clara*

A Prostitute's Room   *Friday, April 21*
Nashuah, New Hampshire

Herman Mudgett:

Clara, that's your name tonight.

Right, I'm payin' for it.

Now listen to me close, Clara Bitch. You're not to see other men. See one more man and I'll cut your pretty face into a thousand pieces.

Are you seein' someone now?

No?

You sure? No one?

You're a lyin' bitch, Clara. You're still seein' that big air bubble, Derek Courtney. Can't get enough of the old fart, can you?

Oh, no? Well even your father puts the boots to you, doesn't he? Even your goddamn father rides your ass, you worthless whore. A good beating and some good hard kicks will straighten you up.

Scream all you want, slut! I'll make you pay for betraying me.

Scream! Scream! I love to hear you scream, I love to see you bleed! I love it! I love it!

Gilmanton, New Hampshire   *Saturday, September 23, 1876*

My dearest Herman,

How are you doing? Mother and Father are fine. I, however, seem to tire easily. I think it's because of the Indian summer. I pray this letter reaches you because it has been several months since I heard from you. Why haven't you written? I miss your letters and I want to know what you're doing.

I've been busy lately. Mother has been taking me to all the church teas. You would never believe how boring those afternoons have been—the old women sniffling and fanning, for none of them thinks to open a window. I have managed to survive those times by sitting and day-dreaming of you and when we'll be together all the time. Even your mother thinks we would make a beautiful couple. However, so much time has passed since I last saw you. Your handsome features, especially your smile, are starting to dim in my mind. Please, Herman, come home soon.

My nights have also been full, but only because I'm trying to escape the loneliness. Derek has been escorting me to the fall dances. Now, don't get upset—he's only a friend. The only forward thing he has said is that he can't understand how you could leave me for such a long time. His question does make me wonder why you haven't come for me.

Please hurry home. I need to know you still love me.

> *With all my love,*
> *Clara*

Lake Candlewood   *Saturday, December 23, 2:00 a.m*
Brookfield, Connecticut

H. H. Holmes:

Give me a hand, Herm. She's a lot heavier than she looks.

Not yet. You know we need to throw in the stone at the same time. Like we used to do at Loon Lake.

Ready?

Now we need to row back to shore and see if the owner of this boat is still asleep. If not, we'll need to make another trip out here.

1877

3838 Rose Street
Akron, Ohio

Saturday, February 10, dawn

Herman Mudgett:

I can't do too much more of this sellin' stuff, H.

I've been tryin' to do everything you say—it just doesn't work for me. Maybe you should do the talkin', and I'll hang around and study for medical school.

I'm not a lazy bastard! You're the one with the gift of gab. I'll never make us rich, so what's the use?

The Loverings' Front Porch
Gilmanton, New Hampshire

Monday, June 18

Clara Lovering:

Oh, Herman, I'm so happy to see you. The roses are beautiful, and you even remembered to get red ones. When did you get back?

Hehehe. Your mustache tickles.

I wish I had known you were coming. I'm a mess.

You really think so? Well, you look very sharp yourself. Is that a new suit? I didn't realize teaching posts paid so well.

What other jobs have you been doing?

I'm just curious, that's all. I've missed you and I guess I want to know...

But a year is so far away.

I know, but so much can happen. Are you at least moving back to Gilmanton?

Why not?

Don't you realize I get tired of waiting?

Herman, that's not what I said. I do love you. I only want to spend more time with you.

No, I'm not complaining. By the way, how long are you staying?

Tomorrow morning? Can't you stay longer?

Then we should be grateful to have this afternoon by ourselves.

Herman, you know I can't. Besides, Derek is coming over tonight.

Father wants to discuss some business with him. You should really meet Derek. You would enjoy his company.

All right, let's forget I mentioned him.

What did you have in mind?

I would love a walk down by the lake.

It's tempting, Herman, but a swim just wouldn't be right. Come, take my hand.

The Mudgetts' Kitchen,   *Saturday, September 22, mid-morning*
Gilmanton, New Hampshire

Levi Mudgett:

You're sayin' I have to be a Christian to be the postmaster?

Martin, I can't do it. Here, have more bread. Theodate made it just for you.

Just change books? Give up the Old Testament for the New? That's it?

Make the change at Christmas?

Wipe your mouth.

Crumbs.

Join the Rotary?

Shave my beard?

Take my hat off on Sundays!

Stop beating the boys? Martin, I don't think I can do it.

1878

The Congregational Church, Choir Loft   *Thursday, January 31*
Gilmanton, New Hampshire

Clara Lovering:

Herman, why did you ask me to meet you here? It's so eerie, and what if Pastor Stanton should come by?

No, I shouldn't sit beside you.

Please don't touch my hand.

Because I'm engaged to Derek, remember?

That's not fair! What was I supposed to do—wait around forever while you wandered from town to town, having fun?

Of course it's my father's argument, but it makes sense. No, Herman, don't kiss me. Why haven't you written? Why haven't you visited?

I think that's wonderful! You'd make such a great doctor. When do you start your practice?

I didn't realize it would take so long. Have you thought about setting up here?

I am being serious. What are you doing?

Mmmm, your kisses are soft—I'd forgotten—but you mustn't. Derek...

But the wedding plans are already in motion. No...don't...oh, Herman, if only *we* were getting married.

We can't. Father would never approve of you. Oooh, you shouldn't do that.

I'm not trying to drive you mad—it's just...

Yes, I do love you. I always will.

Show you? How?

No! We're in a *church*.

Please let me go before I...

Mmmm...oh, Herman...*what is that?*

No! I don't want to touch it!

I don't know. Are you sure we should be doing this?

Yes, it feels good, but...

I want to be with you forever, too.

Herman, I can't fight you any longer. Oh! Ohhhh...yes, there...do you mean like this?

I want you so much...ohhhhhhhh......please touch me again...ahhh, Herman...yes, yes...I love you...oh, God...don't stop, not now...oh, my God...wait...

That's it?

Burton's Funeral Home
Albany, New York   *Sunday, April 7, just past midnight*

H. H. Holmes:

Here, let's put old man Burton on the floor. By the time he wakes up—if he ever does—we'll have tasted the fruits of his labor.

I'll pull down their sheets while you open the top curtains—I like doin' it in silver moonlight.

Wow! It's a field of paradise, ain't it, Herm? There must be six or seven of 'em.

Yeah, they're all fresh as autumn apples, just ripe for the pickin'. Let's start with the young one over there, the pretty boy with an erection.

The Mudgetts' Front Porch
Gilmanton, New Hampshire   *Sunday, June 23, mid-morning*
Levi Mudgett:

Hurry, Theodate, the pastor will include us in his sermon if we show up late.

Hold your horses, Martin! We're looking for our Bibles!

Hurry, Theodate, the Martins will jump off their buggy and march in here like Confederate soldiers in search of Grant. Get a move on, woman!

The Lord will forgive us, I know, I know, but the Martins and the pastor will not.

The Loverings' Dining Room
Gilmanton, New Hampshire   *Sunday, June 30*

Clara Lovering:

No, Father, I don't know where Derek is. He was supposed to be here by now so we could take a stroll before dinner.

I'm not sure. He's never been this late before. I wonder if he tried to walk here. Perhaps he's sitting by the side of the road, resting.

I'm not saying anything bad about Derek. It's just that he's getting older and can't move around quite as quick as he used to.

I'm sorry. I didn't mean that. Can we please start eating, Mother?

He probably decided to go home and change before coming over and accidentally fell asleep. He even yawned a couple of times during the church service this morning. Once he wakes up, he'll come running over here.

Well, I only hope he isn't this late to our wedding. Mother, what happened to the roast? It's all shriveled and dry.

I'm not blaming Derek. I know he's the *perfect* man, even when he's messed up a good meal.

I *am* worried, Mother, but Derek's a big boy. He can take care of himself.

The Gilmanton Iron Works   *Sunday, June 30, almost midnight*
Gilmanton, New Hampshire

Herman Mudgett:

Mike, old man, I've a nice fat gander of love on my wagon. It's yours if you'll roast it for me in one of your hot fires tonight.

Freshly plucked, yes, even fresher than that young man I brought you last year, the one you said was as sweet as August corn.

But the other one was too thin. This one is plump and was happy eating all his life.

No, I haven't had him myself—I was saving him for you.

He was never married, no—maybe a virgin.

Mike, I don't have all night. Want him or not?

Good, mind if I watch?

I can have a go at him after you? Mike, you're a real pal!

Loon Lake   *Tuesday, July 2*
Gilmanton, New Hampshire

Herman Mudgett:

Nice night, yes. The lake is aptly named, filled with the sound of crazy loons. Tomorrow I'll be singing louder than they.

A tip on the fairgrounds race.

A horse called Chicken Wings. I'll make a small fortune on that bird.

Clara, I love you. I can't live without you.

Darling, Derek is a filthy louse.

He's a crook, ran off with over a thousand dollars two days ago. You haven't heard?

The night smells wonderful, yes, but you're trying to get me off the subject. Your fat friend is long gone—will never be seen again. He didn't even take the time to close the door to the bank vault.

Our friend George is the new security guard. He told me. Clara, Derek's a rude, selfish pig.

Dearest, look me in the eyes. Marry me. I'll never leave you.

We'll elope. Say yes.

Dearest Diary,

I finally did it—I went against Father's wishes and married Herman. I still can't believe Father expected me to wait for Derek after he embezzled that money from the bank. But there are times I wonder if Father wasn't right about Derek being framed, especially since he has completely disappeared.

Enough about them. This is my honeymoon. It has taken three years, but now no one can ever part us. Herman's smiling in his sleep. He told me earlier that Father will forgive us. Yet, somehow, I don't think we'll be forgiven. Father's too stubborn. Oh, well, I am now married to a man who will love me forever. I'm almost afraid that I will never experience another night as incredibly romantic as last night—but with Herman who knows?

Our wedding took place in a Justice of the Peace's study in Louden. We even had dinner with Mr. Westingbrook's family. At first I was worried that it wasn't legal, but Herman showed me the license. He said everything was right because no one would ever take me away from him again. I'm not sure if he was talking about my father or Derek, but it didn't matter. I only wish we could have done this sooner.

We arrived at the hotel after ten. I was very nervous. The one time we had made love was over too quickly. In fact, it didn't really seem worth it, at least for me, but not this time.

Once the door shut behind the bellboy, we were alone. Herman was so thoughtful and understood my shyness. Thank goodness that didn't stop him. He's obviously learned some new tricks since January. He took my hand, stared at me, and said I was the most beautiful woman he'd ever seen. Then he slowly caressed the skin peeking out from the open neckline of my dress. His hands shook slightly as his thumbs rubbed across my breasts. Then he leaned closer, his breath fanning my hair when he exhaled. He kissed my earlobes, sucking on them. I thought I'd faint when he licked my lips but wouldn't kiss me. I asked him why and he said I would have to kiss him first. I did and became dizzy when he slipped his tongue into my mouth. I felt I couldn't stand and gripped his shoulders tightly. I wanted him then as much as he wanted me.

We made love on the floor, our clothes beneath us. I could feel the buttons burrowing into my skin, but I didn't care. By this point, we were possessed. He moved in and out without slowing, and I could feel the tension inside me building, straining to be released. As my nails dug into his back, Herman pushed once more and I shivered. Finally, I eased my body back onto the floor. He lay on top of me, both of us drained.

I didn't think it could get much better, but I was wrong. After a while, he stood up and threw back the coverlet. Then, he picked me up and I saw the entire bed covered with rose petals, their fragrance filling the room.

Of course, we made love many more times. It's only now in the day-light that I wonder if I did the right thing. I know once he wakes up and reassures me, I'll feel better. I will write a letter to Mother later today and pray that Father will let her have it.

Well, I had better go. Herman is stirring.

Clara
Friday, July 5, 1878

1881

Alton, New Hampshire   *Sunday, July 31, 1881*

Dearest Mother,

How are you doing? I hope you have finally gotten rid of that summer cold. How is Father? Has he even started to forgive me, yet? Even though the years have been a little rough, Herman and I are staying married. But enough about that. I'm not writing this letter to bring up past hurts and memories.

I wanted to let you know the wonderful news. I have given birth to a son—Harold Herman Mudgett. Herman wants to call him Harry. Oh, Mother, you should see him. He's so tiny (you never told me babies could be so small) and has the cutest little hands. His fingers are long and grasp anything close to him. Every now and then, when I'm nursing him, I'll stroke his cheek and I swear he smiles at me. He's got blue eyes like the color of those wildflowers I used to pick. His feet are small with tiny toes. He's completely bald, so he looks like Father. Harry was born a few days after our third anniversary. I know I should have written sooner, but I have been so busy with him.

I need to hire a nurse, but Herman is in-between jobs right now. In the past few months, Herman has been gone for weeks at a time, hunting for a business to buy or a good job. He hasn't found anything yet. Right before I went into labor, Herman came back home. Mother, he has been better than any nurse I could hire. He brings me flowers every day and even cooks some of the meals. While I'm nursing, Herman stretches out on the bed and watches, occasionally stroking the top of Harry's little head. I've never seen a more attentive husband and father. I don't know how I will manage when he does find steady employment.

I truly wish you could see your grandson. I think he could even melt Father's heart. Do you think it might be possible? Herman has agreed to let me come home and visit as long as I return quickly. I would so much like to see you and Aunt Margaret.

Well, I must close this letter. Harry's crying—he has the appetite of his father. Mother, please think about what I've said. If you think Father will let me and Harry visit, please write soon and tell me. Even though I will greatly miss Herman, he needs the time to find some work. Take care.

With all my love,
Clara

1882

The Mudgetts' Bedroom
Alton, New Hampshire

Sunday, August 13

Clara Mudgett:

Mmmm, that feels so good. Oh, Herman, we need more time for each other.

I know, darling. It's just that I miss you when you're gone. Little Harry misses you, too.

Okay, turn over. Do you want me to use some of that lotion you bought last week?

I love the smell of this. Your back is so tight. Try to relax. How's that?

Tell me something, dear, have you heard from that last interview?

Oh, well, you'll find something.

Herman, why are you bringing Derek up after all this time? I married you and I'm happy. We have an adorable little boy who is becoming more like his father every day.

Mail? Why do you ask?

I didn't even know the University of Vermont had a medical school. When do you start?

That soon...but there's so much to pack, and we'll have to sell the house. I don't know of anyone looking for a small house, but surely it won't take that long. Also, I'll have to write Mother and...

But, darling, I want to come.

I promise Harry won't be a distraction. Besides, you'll need me.

But, dear...

I don't want to live apart from you. According to the Bible, my place is with you.

Why didn't you tell them you were married?

They don't? That's not fair!

Of course it's a great opportunity. I guess we can manage for a few years, but you have to promise me you'll come home every chance you get. Herman, what are you doing? I can't reach your back if you turn over.

The apple or cream?

Here you go. Oops, let me wipe it off.

Lick it off? You can't be serious?

How's this?

Mmmm...

Harry's crying. I have to go.

There's no need to get angry. He may have fallen. I'll be back in a minute. Please, let me make sure he's not hurt.

But...

You don't need to get up. I'll only be a moment. Once I've calmed him down, we'll finish what we've started. I promise.

Herman, please come back.

The University of Vermont   *October 8, 1882*
Burlington, Vermont

Dear Clara,

Enclosed is ten dollars I earned selling a drug to an addict. I should be able to send you more if I can find more slaves like him.

I hope all is well with you and Harry. Maybe I'll be able to get home for the December holidays.

My studies are going well, but I do find the lectures a bit boring. The professors are old and have no idea that they are putting most of us to sleep. They just go on and on talking, not at all caring whether we ever get their point. Darwin is the rage—or rather the roar—up here. Did you know that your father's ancestors ate bananas in trees?

I'm in a special program that allows me to observe the work of doctors in the Burlington community. The more I get involved in this profession, the more I might want to become a funeral director. The regular family doctors have to spend much of their time collecting money from patients who don't pay their bills. Unfortunately, the University doesn't offer any course in preparing people for their graves, so I'll just have to fight against my peers to get my share of money from the old rich farts hanging on forever to their useless lives. It's depressing, but true.

I'll write again as soon as possible.

> *Love you,*
> *Herman*

1884

University of Michigan   June 3, 1884
Ann Arbor, Michigan

Dear Clara,

Well, I'm a medical doctor now, a real M.D. Sometimes I don't know
how I ever did it, especially when I was caught with that dead woman
last year. I know, you want to scold me for not telling you. But I didn't
see any need to worry you. I had my friend Holmes talk to the dean in
charge and in a matter of three weeks I was back in school. (That's the
time I sent you the little pile of twenty dollar bills, remember? Holmes
and another student at the University worked out a way to earn some
money from an insurance company—and I have learned never to question the ways of Holmes.)

Holmes wants to take a trip out to the Chicago area, and I've agreed to
go with him just for a week before I take up my new position.

Oh, yes, my dear, I've landed a position as an assistant doctor in
Mooers Fork, New York. Sorry for giving you another surprise, but it's
a good one! The name of the place sounds familiar to you because I was
a teacher there for a few months two or three years ago. I'm pretty sure
I wrote to you about it—if not, now you know!

I'll be helping an ageless doctor, but when he dies I'll probably step into
his practice. At least, that's the understanding. The money is horrible,
so I won't be able to bring you and Harry out to join me yet.
Meanwhile, Holmes and I were recently able to provide a Michigan
doctor with a handsome cadaver that brought in $40. I'm enclosing
$13 for you and the boy.

> Love to you,
> Herman

Mooers Fork Hospital   November 15, 1884
Mooers Fork, New York

Dear Clara,

I just assisted in an operation where our patient, a young girl with
inflamed tonsils, died from a slip of the old doc's hand. He cut open her
throat. That means we'll never get any money from her parents.

People want medical help for nothing. It's tougher to get money out of
these farmers than to find a cure for consumption.

Doc Killer will not give up the knife either; so unless the profession

takes steps to kick him out of the office, I'll be an assistant well into the next century.

I'm having second thoughts about this career. If things don't get better soon, I'm going to follow Holmes into some business adventures.

Wish me luck.

Love to you,

Herman

The Main Street Hotel   December 4, 1884
111 Main Street
Cleveland, Ohio

Dear Clara,

The old doc and I had a big shouting match, so my career as a man of medicine is over in Mooers Fork. I will never again work in a small burg for as long as I live. I may never work as a doctor again—I like the curious study of flesh and blood, but I don't want to live a dog's life, begging for money instead of bones.

So it's off to see the world with Holmes. He has a genius for making money, and I have an unquenchable thirst for it.

Wish us luck.

Love you always,
Herman

P.S. I enclose $2, all I can afford for now.

1886

CHICAGO TRIBUNE   SUNDAY, JULY 18,
1886
HELP WANTED
MALES

WANTED-A FIRST CLASS gardener .
Married, no children; wife must understand care of dairy. Apply on Tuesday
at 11 o'clock, No. 23 East 26th St.

WANTED-ASSISTANT FOR well established,
busy drugstore. Must be familiar with mixing
of medicinals and capable of taking charge of
store. A permanent place for the right young
man. Inquire Holton's Drugstore, 63rd and
Wallace, Englewood.

WANTED-BRIGHT, ACTIVE boy from 18 to 20
years old for night work; one living with his
parents preferred. Apply in Tribune's editori-
al rooms after 1 P.M.

WANTED-STENOGRAPHER One who thoroughly understands his business and a good
penman. Address. J. M.W., Box 203, Tribune
Office.

Mrs. Holton's Drugstore   *Thursday, August 5,* early evening
Englewood, Illinois

H.H. Holmes:

Just let me take care of everything, Missus Holton. It's been a long day and you
look really tired.

I know.

Yes, too much work and too few hours to do it.

Say, Missus Holton, would you mind terribly if I took out some small insurance
policies on you and your husband?

Two thousand.

Each.

Well, Missus Holton, it's one way you older people can be a great help to

younger people. I was able to attend medical school because of insurance I had on my grandmother.

One never knows, right. So you don't mind?

Thanks.

Now go home and get some sleep or you'll keel over dead before I'm able to take out a policy on you.

'Night.

Dear Diary,

I met the most extraordinarily wonderful man on planet earth today and have been completely swept off my feet! I've known him —Harry H. Holmes (even the name is magical)—for less than 8 hrs., and already I just know he's the perfect man for me. God, I hope I'm not being a romantic fool.

Me and Shelly were fooling around on the piano when this good-looking stranger entered my life—forever? He disarmed me with his smile, and I was spellbound by his speech. It was a few moments before I realized he had ducked into the music shop to get out of the cold and ask directions. Without thinking, I was offering to walk him back to his hotel. (Poor Shelly later said she felt completely ignored.)

When he offered me his hand, our handshake seemed to last for hours—and those eyes—they looked right through me. Shelly said I blushed 14 shades of red!

Well, anyway, I can't wait until tomorrow. He asked me to the opera. Christmastime has always been so magical. Goodnight, Diary. I'll let you know how things go.

Myrta
12/23/86

Dear Diary,

Merry Christmas, and what a wonderful Christmas it is!

Harry was the perfect gentleman last night—from the moment he came calling—to his polite goodnight kiss. I really think this is the one.

Mother and Father were none too pleased that I was going to be spending most of Christmas Eve on a date. But after promising them I would be home in time to go with them to Midnight Mass, they relented. Because of this, I think my parents, especially Father, were overly critical of Harry. But Harry did his best to charm them, and I

was finally able to get Mother to admit he was handsome. Ah, my Handsome Harry!

The concert was grand, and more than one neighbor's eye turned when they saw me enter the theater hand-in-hand with this elegant stranger. To be perfectly honest, I missed much of Handel's Messiah because I kept staring at the face of this man who has taken my breath away. I think it's his eyes and his smile that has me so enraptured.

Although Harry wanted to take me out for a late dinner, I insisted he take me home so I could fulfill my promise to my parents. Ever the gentleman, he complied, although I did take him on a less than direct route back home.

When we got to the porch, Harry never asked if he could come in. Instead, he bent down before I could react and brushed my lips ever so lightly with the sweetest goodnight kiss a girl could ask for. I've been floating on clouds ever since. He's the greatest Christmas gift I have ever received in all my 19 years.

Harry has to leave town for a few days on business (didn't I tell you, he's a most successful businessman in Chicago!) but promised to call me when he gets back. He asked me to accompany him to the Norwegian Hotel for their New Year's Eve party. I can hardly wait!

Myrta

12/25/86

1887

Dear Diary,

Things are moving way too fast—at a dizzying, breathtaking pace. Can I keep up? Should I keep up? He has me mesmerized, Diary. I feel ashamed and yet exhilarated. I am powerless under his gaze...it is frightening beyond my wildest dreams. Perhaps this is all a dream.

Last night was the wildest yet. What a way to bring in the New Year! Do I dare put down on paper what happened? I believe I must, for he told me this morning before he left (after I told him about you) that I must write about last night's experience—and write it to him. So, I'm yours, Dear Henry—read on.

Who are you and what are you doing to me? These were my last willing thoughts as you approached me on the settee, watching your confident stride bring your captivating smile ever closer to me.

You took my hand in yours, kissing, nibbling, softly licking my fingers. Then, continuing to hold and caress my hand, you brought it softly to my cheeks, touching me with both our fingers, then down to my chin, to my lips, to my tongue. Slowly, ever so slowly, our fingers were back on my chin, running down my neck. When you took us inside my bodice and stiffened my nipples, I became paralyzed and nearly lost consciousness.

I was breathless (as I am again now) and nearly gasped when I realized we were traveling up my thigh, and then you were there. I knew I was supposed to be screaming and fighting you off, but I also knew I was yours and was experiencing feelings that I never knew existed. You knew it too.

Your tongue was on my neck, my ears, my eyes, while your hands removed my clothing. Then your hands and tongue were back on my neck, my breasts, my stomach, my legs...first teasing, then exhilarating. When you finally entered, I shuddered.

Time no longer seemed to exist. Our bodies moved in rhythm. Everything seemed so natural. It was as if I had left my body and was watching us from above. The chiming of the clock was what finally brought me back. I was shocked to see it was midnight. Two hours seemed like 10 minutes. I was exhilarated, yet exhausted and couldn't believe it when you brought "it" to my mouth. You were in me before I realized it, and you made such a dirty act seem so natural and enjoyable. The thought of putting that in my mouth would have been so repugnant to me two days ago. But as I write this now, I feel that aching again between my thighs.

You have turned my world upside down, Handsome Harry. I no longer know right from wrong. I'm confused—are you angel or devil? All I do know is that I need you—I'm on fire!

Myrta

1/1/87

Lake Harriet at Lyndale Park
Minneapolis, Minnesota

Saturday, January 8, near midnight

Herman Mudgett:

She's damn heavy, H. Why did you want to kill this rich old bag?
I'm pullin' her! Are we going to cut off the feet before we throw it in?
Ring finger? What for?

Dear Diary,

He did it! He asked me to marry him last night. I must be the luckiest girl alive!

He's coming over tonight to ask Father for permission, so I must get my thoughts together before he arrives. But before I do that, let me tell you all about it.

I knew something was up when he arrived at the house 20 minutes late. Arm-in-arm we strolled to the street, and he helped me into a waiting carriage. Around Lake Hiawatha we rode, a light snow starting to stick to our collars. Harry had already opened a bottle of some expensive French champagne and proffered a toast to "us." I kept trying not to be too giddy, but I must admit I kept hoping he would "pop" the question, not just the cork.

Throughout dinner at Moll's, he kept me blushing with sexual comments between bites of trout and wine. At one point, he even put his hand between my thighs. I almost stabbed him with my fork, I was so embarrassed.

After dinner we rode through the park before riding back to the lake. Here, Harry slipped the driver some money, and before I knew it, we were all alone. The sky was now crystal clear, and the moon glistened on the freshly fallen snow. Magic was definitely in the air. My heart was racing as Harry took me in his arms and held me close.

"My lovely Myrta," he said, stroking my hair. "Why do you love me?" The question caught me off guard. There isn't one reason or even a dozen reasons why I love this man. There must be a thousand reasons— and no reason at all. It seemed to please him that I just looked into his eyes, unable to speak. And then he laughed that Handsome Harry laugh of his and, taking my hand in his, said, "Well, I'll give you one good reason anyway." With that, he slipped a 2-carat diamond ring onto my finger.

The moon never seemed so bright as it sparkled inside my diamond.

Harry was brushing the tears off my cheeks, and then we were hugging and kissing. I was so overwhelmed by the moment that before I knew it, I had him unbuttoned and in my mouth.

I think Harry likes it that way best. I know I'm beginning to enjoy it myself, especially doing it outdoors and with the coachman nearby. But it's okay now because we're engaged! Mrs. Harry H. Holmes—I think I'm used to it already.

    Myrta
    1/10/87

Minneapolis, Minnesota   *1/12/87*

Dear Kate,

Sit down and prepare yourself for some news out of the blue.
I'M GETTING MARRIED TO THE MOST WONDERFUL MAN IN THE WORLD!
No, you did not misread that. Yes, Miss Myrta "I'll never get married until I'm 30" Belknap has said yes to Mr. Harry "the World's Best Catch" Holmes. He proposed to me two nights ago at Lake Hiawatha in the most romantic setting imaginable. I'll have to tell you all about it when you come here to be my Matron of Honor. You will be able to make it—oh please say yes, Kate. I know it is such short notice—the wedding is set for the 28th of this month—but you always promised me that no matter when or where, you would be there. Just in case you can't make it, I have asked DeeDee to be my Maid of Honor. But really, Kate, I would just die if you couldn't make it. The wedding is set for St. Stephen's at 2:00 p.m., and the reception will be at the Norwegian Hotel. Father Murphy is doing the ceremony.

I know what you're thinking—that this is all so sudden, and who is this guy anyway? Well, you're right, it is sudden. He swept me off my feet just two days before Christmas when he happened into the music shop, looking for directions. One thing led to another, and we spent Christmas Eve, Christmas, New Year's Eve, and New Years together. By then, we both knew we were meant for each other, and then he proposed Monday night.

He's from Chicago, Kate, and that's where we are going to live! And get this: he is originally from a little town in New Hampshire called Gilmanton, which just "happens" to be in a county called Belknap. Can you believe that? Belknap! I tell you, it was fate from day one. He's 27, a doctor, a teacher, a pharmacist, an inventor, and a first-rate businessman. He's incredibly smart, Kate, and incredibly good-looking (5-

10, 165 lbs., black hair, piercing blue eyes, SMART dresser). In fact, I call him "My Handsome Harry." There's one other thing that he is: fantastic in bed.

I know, I know. After Gary, I swore I would never have sex again with any man until after I got married. But like I said, things have happened so fast, and well, it has just seemed right and natural with Harry. I'll tell you all about it when you come.

Another thing I have been thinking about is when you and Bob do your annual summer trek back here, you can stop by, either on your way to or back from Penn. (Or maybe even stop here both on your way to and on your way back.) That way, we could both tour Chicago and shop like we used to dream about back in high school. Can you believe it? I, Myrta Z. Belknap, am finally not only going to Chicago, but I am also going to be living there—and with the man of my dreams! Oh, Kate, I do hope you can make it here for the wedding.

Well, I best be going, as I have so much to do (as you can well imagine). I trust all is well with you and that you and Bob are finally settling down in Omaha. I promise to get out there someday. In fact, I promise right now that if you do make it for my wedding, then I will visit you in Omaha (if you're still there), by the end of this decade. Deal?

Give my best to Bob, and do let me know right away. Hope and pray to see you on the 28th.

> *The soon-to-be happily married,*
> *Myrta*

69 Minnihaha Avenue   *Wednesday, January 26, 10:00 p.m.*
Minneapolis, Minnesota

DeeDee Davidson:

Myrta, hurry up. Get your nightgown on and sit down here on the bed. I'm dying to know.

You know what. You promised to tell me about Harry.

Yes, I want to know the juicy details.

Like...you know. Oh, come on, Myrta. Tell me quick, what's he like in bed? How is he?

Really? That big?

What do you mean like an icicle? Because it's cold or is it stiff?

How can that be?

Okay, you're telling me it stays cold the whole time he's doing it?

You must be making this up. I've never heard of such a thing.

Yes, I believe you. I just have a hard time imagining how it must feel and after some of the wild stories you've told me, I'm surprised you haven't found some way to melt that thing.

God. Some women have all the luck, Myrta. A man with an insatiable appetite who can poke all day with an icicle that never melts—I should be so lucky to find one like that.

The Triangle Hotel   *Wednesday, January 26, 10:00 p.m*
Minneapolis, Minnesota

H. H. Holmes:

I can't come in her, Henry.

Turn around. I'm not talkin' to you, bitch! Just keep your face in the pillow, and I'll take care of the fuckin'.

No, I'm not gettin' all goofy over Myrta. Hey, bitch, didn't I tell ya to stop lookin' at us!

You have a go at her then. Too many women wrappin' their legs and teeth 'round me this month.

Yeah, call the bitch Myrta if ya want. When you're done, I'm gonna walk Miss Myrta here down the block to the Saint Anthony Falls.

For the nice view, sure.

Dear Diary,

Well, the time when I officially become Mrs. Harry H. Holmes has arrived. My big day is tomorrow. I'm so excited, I doubt I'll sleep a wink tonight.

Harry has been such a gentleman. The night he asked Father for my hand, he also told me that we would abstain from any more sex until our wedding night. He said that abstaining would make my day (and night) all the more special. He's so caring and loving. I know how hard that must be for him, a man with his sexual appetite.

Tonight my parents had a dinner here for us and our wedding party. The only damper on the evening was when Harry confided to me through misty eyes how for the first time in years he could finally say how much he really missed his parents, and how he wished they were still alive so they too could enjoy the most important day of his life.

Harry has never spoken much of his parents—or his upbringing, for that matter. It just pains him to talk about that period of his life. Could it be he has a few skeletons in his closet? I suspect we all do, some more than others. What are his deep, dark secrets? Perhaps I'll never know.

But enough of that for now. Tomorrow, at 2 p.m., I will become Mrs. Harry Holmes. Saturday we leave for Niagara Falls on our honeymoon! I can't believe it's been over two weeks since our last romantic interlude. I must admit that I've been missing him in that way and the sensations he provides. When he left tonight he whispered to me that tomorrow night will be an evening I will never forget. We've rented a suite on the top floor of the Norwegian for after the reception.

What evil thoughts are lurking in the mind of that sex fiend? I can't wait to find out!

Myrta

1/27/87

Dear Diary,

Whew! What a ride!

Harry's finally asleep now. We didn't get to the hotel until almost midnight, and then of course Harry said we had to "christen" the room. Honestly, I don't know where the man gets his energy.

I'm sorry I didn't get a chance to write to you before tonight, Diary. I thought for sure I'd get a chance on the train, but, well, let me tell you all about everything.

Father Murphy performed a beautiful ceremony, and everyone said I was the most beautiful bride they ever laid eyes on. I must admit they were right. Kate and DeeDee also looked pretty in their pink chiffon dresses and were great bridal attendants. Mom, of course, was a total wreck, but then pulled herself together in time for our vows.

The reception at the Norwegian was elegant. The food, from what everyone said, was delicious. I, of course, couldn't eat a thing—my stomach was tied in knots all day. It wasn't until shortly before we left the ballroom and Harry had plied me with plenty of champagne that I finally began to relax.

As we walked up the grand staircase to our room, butterflies replaced my knots. My heart began to race when Harry swept me off my feet and carried me over the threshold. I swear I felt like a schoolgirl when he began undressing me, first with his eyes, then with his hands. I felt myself blushing when he sat down on the bed, leaving me

standing there with just my undergarments on. But I knew what he wanted me to do, and so I slowly slipped off my chemise. I could feel my nipples stiffen as my fingers moved down my stomach....And there I was, completely naked, unable to move. I never wanted him more in my life, and yet he just sat there, looking me up and down for an eternity.

Finally, while standing there in front of him, he slowly and gently nuzzled his face into my scent, as his hands caressed my buttocks. My legs buckled when his tongue found me, sending waves of passion through my entire body. My fingers moved through his hair, and I pulled him tighter to me, my breasts framing the top of his head.

I think I caught Harry by surprise when I fell on top of him, unable to stand any longer. We lay like that on the bed for a few minutes, Harry stroking me as my body continued to convulse, my heart pounding inside me.

When I finally caught my breath, Harry told me I was a naughty girl and needed to be punished. Before I could react, in one motion he had me across his lap and began spanking me. At first, his slaps were almost like pats, but as I became more aroused, the stings became sharper. Soon his fingers were inside me while he continued his spanking. When he commanded that I not orgasm again, I had the most intense one of my life and fell to the floor.

Laughing, Harry stepped over me and poured us two glasses of champagne. He sat down beside me, lifted my head into his lap, and brought my glass to my lips. "Cheers," he said. "Here's to us, Mr. and Mrs. Harry H. Holmes."

I must say, the champagne never tasted sweeter—all my senses were tingling. And that's how it went all night, Diary. I could go on and on. I suspect we set a record for the number of times we had sex. I never dreamed there were so many variations.

Before I retire for the night, I do want to mention the train ride here—ah, the train ride. It was nearly midnight when the train rumbled through Indiana. Harry and I had a late dinner, then enjoyed our coffee while we watched the moon and stars race along with us. There were about a half-dozen others in the diner, none paying much attention to anyone else.

Without going into great detail, Harry sat me on his lap and entered me right there in the dining car! The best part about it was we never had to move. The vibrations of the train on the track allowed Harry to penetrate deep inside me. I can't believe an Episcopalian, Midwestern girl like me can get such a thrill by having sex in public, but it seems that I do—it was sensational! The hardest part was trying

to keep quiet. Harry had to put his hand in my mouth—poor thing, I almost drew blood. But that seemed to set him off as well. I must say, after all was said and done and I came to my senses, I was quite embarrassed. I kept looking around to see if anyone had noticed. If they did, they didn't seem to mind.

Well, Harry's starting to stir. God, I hope he doesn't wake up. I'm exhausted. Goodnight, Diary. I can't wait to see the Falls tomorrow.

Myrta
1/30/87

Englewood, Illinois   2/8/87
Dear Mom and Dad,

Can you believe it has already been more than two weeks since we were married? First off, thank you both again for giving me such a fabulous wedding. I know that must have cost you a fortune, Dad, but do know it was very much appreciated. I love you both dearly.

The train ride to Niagara Falls was long, and at times exhausting, but Harry had a way of making it go quicker. The Falls, as you could see from the postcard, was breathtaking. It is hard to imagine such power. God is truly wonderful.

Harry, too, has been wonderful. He is such a romantic, yet very respected by his business associates here in Chicago—actually, Englewood. The drugstore he owns (we own!) sits on the corner of two main streets here in town—63rd and Wallace. Harry is eyeing property across the street for a larger establishment where he can rent out to businesses and individuals. As for this store, it has two levels. The downstairs is just like Harry described it—large and always bustling. The upstairs is even nicer than Harry made it out to be, although I do need to do something about the furniture. Harry says I can refurnish it however I want and not to worry about the cost. He says he knows where he can get some really good deals. Isn't that something? How many husbands would tell their wives not to worry about the cost of furniture? I honestly don't know how he does it.

As you know, Englewood sits just below Chicago proper. What you might not realize is how well-to-do it really is. This is where all the rich people live, many of whom take the train into Chicago (it's only a 30-minute ride to "The Loop," the center of activity—Mom, you would love it). It's also only a 15-minute ride to Lake Michigan. You should see Lake Michigan! It makes Hiawatha and Nokomis look like ponds—maybe even puddles. And it's deep, too. I forget how deep Harry told

me it is, but there are some parts he says where the bottom still hasn't been found!

Harry wants me to get to know the area before I start working with him in the store. I suspect this will be a bit different than the music shop. I really did enjoy working there, selling and playing—especially playing. Harry says I can get a piano, too. After I sign off here, I'm going to take a stroll around town and start doing some serious furniture shopping. I'll also check out some stores in Chicago itself.

Well, I best be going. Thanks again for everything. You're the best parents a girl could ever hope to have. I really do wish you all can come here in the very near future. I miss you all very much. Give my best to all and let DeeDee know I'll be writing her soon.

Love & Kisses,
Myrta

Dear Diary,

Well, I finally got the furniture I wanted, but I'm really having mixed emotions about it all. Harry insists that it's just one of the ways of doing business in Chicago, but I know it's wrong. Yet, I must admit it was a thrilling experience.

Harry told me I could get anything I wanted, but I had to get all the furniture from Gibson's, and have it delivered on Saturday after sunset, telling them I was Jewish and honored the Sabbath.

When the three movers showed up, Harry sized them up and asked two of them if they could come upstairs with him first to help him move some files into a closet. While they were up there, he "accidentally" locked them in the closet and then told them he would get them out as soon as he could get a locksmith, since he did not have the key.

When Harry came downstairs with that smile of his, I knew it was my turn for phase two. Dressed as a "Lady of the Evening," I enticed the third mover, who was supposed to be guarding the furniture, behind the store. The way I was looking, I doubt any man could have resisted my charms, and I knew none of my neighbors would recognize me the way I was made up.

While I went into the back alley with the poor boy, Harry got into the carriage and secured it into our storage area. Then he put on a police uniform. When I saw Harry turn the corner, I pulled out the boy's penis and started to yell for help. When the boy saw a "cop" running toward us, he ran like he had seen a ghost. Harry and I

couldn't help but laugh as we saw him struggling to put it back in his pants as he ran away. We knew he wouldn't return.

With the plan working so far to perfection, I could see that glint in Harry's eyes. My heart was still racing from touching another man, even if he was still a boy, and from pulling off my part of the scheme. "As long as you're dressed the part..." Harry said, slipping a $20 bill between my breasts. Then, firmly pushing me to my knees, he said, "Undo it, darlin', and make it fast." It was exhilarating—me dressed like a hooker, outdoors, Harry in my mouth, and a scheme only half complete. He erupted in seconds.

Back in the house, the two movers in the closet were yelling. I went to our room, and Harry quickly got out of his uniform. Suddenly, I could hear him making a commotion downstairs and then heard him running upstairs, shouting to the movers that someone had just stolen the furniture, that he was going to get the police, and that a locksmith would soon be there.

As I waited in my room, I still wasn't sure if Harry was going to pull this all off. Granted, the movers weren't very smart, so when Harry miraculously found the key and let them out of the closet, they bought his story completely. Harry told them he saw the young man who was supposed to be guarding the furniture running down the alley. After he started to give chase to see what was the matter, he heard a commotion in the street, came back, and saw everything gone. Harry said he thought maybe the young man was in on it, and the two movers agreed as they really didn't know him all too well.

Harry told them he was sorry he had accidentally locked them in the closet, but he was also upset that all of his furniture was missing. He said he would "talk with the Mrs. about the whole thing" and get back with the store owner on Monday.

I kept my "outfit" on, knowing that Harry would be ready to go again after the excitement of the evening. It was a good decision on my part.

Myrta
4/17/87

CHICAGO TRIBUNE   SUNDAY, APRIL 17,
1887

New Furniture Stolen

ENGLEWOOD.— It was reported a whole houseful of new furniture was stolen yesterday while being delivered to the 63rd and Wallace residence of H.H. Holmes. The furniture, according to witnesses, was in a delivery wagon parked in the alleyway behind Mr. Holmes' drugstore. During the time the deliveryman pulled the wagon up to the backdoor and went inside to collect money for the delivery, the wagon was stolen. Two men were seen jumping on the front seat of the wagon and quickly driving the wagon out of the alley, according to Mrs. Holmes.

1888

Dear Diary,

I'm devastated and at a loss for words. Tears have already stained your pages – my world is coming apart. I found my Harry, my Handsome Harry, in the arms of another woman. My life as I know it is over. How could he? Why would he? What will happen to me, to us?

I know I need to get away for a bit. In a day or two, when I can compose myself, I'll write my parents and let them know that I—just I, will be coming to spend a week or two. I won't tell them why. I'll give them some excuse as to why Harry cannot be with me. That will be easy enough. I'll tell them he's on a business trip of some sort. There, the lies are becoming easier and easier. It's as if my whole life has turned into one big lie. Oh, Diary, what has he done to me?!?! It's as if someone has plunged a knife deep inside me, and now it's being twisted and pulled. I'm in such pain, such agony.

What gets me the most is I even noticed those two making eyes at each other for some time now but convinced myself that Harry would never do that to me. My God, we've only been married a year. Why, just last night we were laughing and joking, making love—the BAS-TARD—and doing the little bitch right here in MY HOME, in MY BED!

I can't see through the tears, Diary. I must stop for now. It's all too much. Everything is out of control. Oh God, Harry, why for God's sake, WHY?!?!?!?!

Myrta
3/10/88

The Parlor Room   *Thursday, March 15*
The Castle

Myrta Holmes:

Don't touch me, Harry. We're not finished.

Look, Harry, I already said I understand the male need. But that still doesn't mean that I have to put up with it in *my* home, in *my* bed.

For God's sake! Can't you understand I just don't ever want to catch you with that little tramp—or any other whore for that matter—ever again? Now I told you, buy me that house in Wilmette and the matter will be dropped.

That's right. I'll be there, and you can do whatever it is you *have* to do here. Just don't ever let me catch you again—stop that—I mean it, Harry. I just don't ever want—God, you're hard...

Bedroom of Holmes   *Sunday, April 8*
The Castle

Myrta Holmes:

Well, thank you, Mister Holmes. You weren't too bad yourself.

Oh, my Handsome Harry, let me brush all those worry lines off your face. You've been working and worrying too much lately.

Jesus, Harry, for the size and location, fifty grand was a darn good deal. And besides, I know of a place where we can get some pretty good furniture for practically nothing.

Yeah, not bad if I do say so myself. Seriously though, there's now another reason why we need that house.

Well, now just lay still. Remember how last month I was still mad at you about...when I was still mad at you, and told you to stop...well, now I'm a full week late, and I've been feeling sick in the morning.

Now, there's no way to stop you when you get like that. Besides, I'm not even sure I am pregnant. Still, I've set up an appointment with Doctor Ripton for next week.

I'm so glad you said that. I wasn't sure how you would take the news. But just think, a miniature us running around the house. She'll have your eyes and mouth, and my hair and nose, and...

OK, then, *he'll* have your eyes. But really, Harry, I do think it will be a girl.

I don't think it quite works that way. But if you're ready...yeah, you're ready. Honestly, how do you do it?

Englewood, Illinois   *5/1/88*

Dear Mom and Dad,

Stop the presses! Boy, do I have some GREAT news for you.

Guess what? I'm pregnant! I just got back from the doctor's, and he has confirmed what I've known for the past few weeks—I'm due around the middle of December. It'll be an early Christmas present. I hope you will be able to come visit us over the holidays.

Once again, everything is happening so fast. Just like me, isn't it? Last month I write you about buying a new home, and now a baby. It's been like this ever since I met Harry. Everything happens so fast, I scarcely have time to catch my breath.

These are such wonderful times, and Chicago is a wonderful place. I

can't wait until you come visit. I know you were planning to come this summer and we were going there for Christmas, but obviously this changes things a bit. We're still not sure if Harry can get away this summer, but even if he can't, I'll come visit you around July 4th. Hopefully, you'll come here for Christmas.

Well, Harry's calling me, so I better run. I'll write you again in two weeks, after we move.

> *Love & Kisses,*
> *Myrta*

P.S. Tell Tom I said hello. Do let him know he is also welcome to come visit for the holidays. I really miss you all so much.

Boston Conservatory of Music   *Tuesday, June 5, 1888*

My Dearest Annie,

I suppose by now you've received the telegram about Uncle Herbert. It's sad knowing he's really gone. Who would ever have thought a fall from his horse would have killed him? He was so strong and resilient—he'd been thrown so many times before that this one really shocked me. Well, he died doing what he liked best—riding like the wind.

You know Uncle Herbert was like a father to me. I feel like I owe everything to him. After all, he not only raised me after Mamma and Papa died, but also paid for my schooling here at BC. He was such a good, sweet man, who treated me kindly and always protected me like I was something precious and delicate. He really treated me special. It's a shame you never got to know him like I did. I guess we can both consider ourselves lucky to have been taken care of by such good, caring relatives. After all, Uncle Charles raised you and he is just as good and kind a soul as Uncle Herbert was.

Well, I just wanted to let you know that I am doing well, under the circumstances, and am preparing myself for graduation tomorrow. I'm really sorry you won't be here to see me accept my diploma. Imagine...me with a degree in music and elocution! I'm ready to begin a new life, something exciting and adventuresome. However, I'm still not sure exactly what my plans will be after graduation, so let me hear from you soon. Maybe we can get together before I step out into the world.

Hugs and kisses, miss you, and as always...

> *Love,*
> *Minnie*

Jack's Bar   *Wednesday, July 4, 11:00 p.m.*
Chicago, Illinois

H. H. Holmes:

Say, bartender, I've got a deal for you.

Just a glass of milk, please. Don't like to upset my stomach before going to bed. Did you hear what I said? I've got a way we could both make some easy money.

Thanks. Here's what you do: Take out a ten thousand insurance policy on an old relative, someone you don't like too much. I'll give you a thousand for the policy the day after you get it approved. Then, when the relative dies, you let me know and we'll go down to the insurance office to collect the money. After they turn over the ten thousand to you, we split it down the middle and you go your way, I go mine. Good deal?

Right, you end up with six thousand and I get four.

I'll pay all the premiums after the first one.

Good. Here's my card. Write me when the policy's in your hands.

Parlor Room
38 North John Street   *Sunday, July 15*
Wilmette, Illinois

Myrta Holmes:

Oh, Harry, we had a wonderful time. I just wish you could have come with me. Minneapolis never looked so beautiful.

Well, on the Fourth we had a family picnic at Lake Hiawatha. Everyone was there, including the little cousins. Even Aunt Jo made it. You remember her. She's married to my Uncle Marion, the farmer from Rochester?

Yeah, her. Anyway, everyone brought a dish to pass, we played cards, even a few of the kids brought a bat and a ball. I know some of them play that here, but that's the first time I recall seeing anyone playing that back home.

Let me finish. I haven't gotten to the best part yet. This was the first time I was back at Hiawatha since you proposed. Right before we all left, I took a walk over to the spot where we were the night we got engaged. When I closed my eyes, I swear, Harry, I could smell you for a moment, standing there by the water's edge. It was the strangest sensation. I was almost afraid to open my eyes. I was half expecting to see that coachman walking back toward us.

Do you always have to be so crude? Here I am, relating a romantic moment.... Do you always have to bring your *thing* into it?

Ah, you just wouldn't understand.

Oh, the usual stuff. Went to Henniger Plaza for some shopping. Took a ride with the folks on the Mississippi. You know, I haven't done that since I was a little girl. Why is it we just get so used to things around us that we stop taking advantage of them and don't even notice them until they're no longer around?

Well, I'm not going to do that anymore. I'm going to start appreciating everything. Every moment I have—starting right now with you.

Mmmm—my, I've missed him. By the way, how was your Fourth?

Kitchen
38 North John Street   *Saturday, September 15*
Wilmette, Illinois

Myrta Holmes:

It's so good to see you, Kate. I hope you had a good night's sleep. Coffee?

Well, I wasn't sure how much you remembered from last night. That's the most I've drank since...well, probably since the last time you were here.

I'm telling you, Kate, it's really easy. I'm almost embarrassed by some of these furniture clowns. I'm just not sure if I've gotten that good, or if it's becoming easier because of my obvious pregnancy. I suppose I'll know the answer to that one in a few months.

My pregnancy? As I told you last night, it really has been—knock on wood—incredibly smooth. I haven't been sick in ages, and I've only gained weight in my stomach, thank God. My doctor says everything is going according to plan, and I should be delivering in mid-December.

We really have gotten all those problems behind us. I'm almost embarrassed to remember how out-of-control I acted back in February when I caught Harry with that harlot. This new home has been a Godsend. When Harry is here, our lives are full of bliss. When he's in Englewood or away on business, I tend to other matters, like this furniture business.

I don't think he's seeing anyone. Perhaps I did overreact a bit.

Oh, Harry's probably right; a man's needs are different from a woman's. When I went home this past summer, I told Mama what happened and she just laughed—she said Daddy did the same thing. She says all men are like that.

Still, I'd better never catch him again!

Oh, Minneapolis was wonderful! I got to see the folks, most of my relatives, Shelly, Missus Claiborne, Mister and Missus Steele...gosh, has it already been over two months?

C'mon, Kate, stop changing the subject. I want to tell you about this fur-

niture business. I can't believe what fools people are. Harry says people like me and him were born to run things. He says there are basically two types of people, the fools and the leaders. I must say, he certainly seems to be right.

It's as easy as baking pie, I tell you. Harry buys a home with little or no money, promising the balance in a few days. Then I go to a furniture store— I had no idea how many there were in Chicago—and using the name Lucy Burbank, I describe to the owner the home and tell him how I want to furnish it completely.

I've really been playing up the pregnancy lately to get them to knock a few more dollars off, which really clinches the deal. They figure if I'm fightin' so hard to get more money off, it must be legit. Then I promise them the money only upon delivery, but I always have it delivered on a Saturday.

That way they think they'll get paid on Monday. But of course, by Monday, the furniture is long gone.

Why, mainly we use two or three different distributors. Half the time, they have the furniture sold off before even getting it out of the house.

Sometimes I'm not even home when it's delivered. I just tell the owner if I'm not home, I'll leave the door unlocked and just leave it. When I do that, I tell the owner I never received it. Other times, Harry sells the house as soon as the furniture is delivered. Then he tells the furniture people that the new owner also bought the furniture.

I know it sounds unbelievable, Kate, but we have worked this at least two dozen times over the summer, and I don't see any end in sight. In fact, last week Harry had the house torched right after we got rid of the furniture, and we're now in the process of having the insurance company give us a check for not only the house—ten thousand—but also twenty-five thousand for the furniture!

Well, that's where you come in. Harry is always looking for a different name or two to use on his mortgages.

I promise you there's nothing to it. And Harry will give you a pretty nice sum for your efforts.

That's it! All you have to do is sign your name, take your money, and not worry about it again. By the time you're back in Omaha, two other people will have owned it, honest.

Oh, Kate, I knew I could trust you to do the right thing. Harry'll be so happy to pay you instead of someone he hardly knows. He'll be up in a few minutes to fill you in on all the details.

All right, how many eggs do you want?

First National Bank   *Friday, October 12*
Chicago, Illinois

Bank Teller Brian Cowan:

Good afternoon, Missus Belknap, you're looking fine. How much longer?

Boy, I'll bet you can't wait. Now, how can we help you today? Another deposit?

Let me count it...twenty-five, twenty-six, twenty-seven, twenty-eight, twenty-nine, three thousand. Now, that's twenty-five hundred in your joint account and five hundred in your account, right?

Take care of yourself, Missus Belknap. I trust I'll see you again before the blessed event?

Very well. Enjoy the rest of the afternoon. There won't be many more like it before ol' man winter settles in.

Good afternoon, Mister Huber. How can we help you today?

Dear Diary,

I can't write much tonight. I'm exhausted. Our little Lucy Marie came into this world at 10:15 yesterday morning. She's the prettiest little girl there ever was—all 19 inches and 7 pounds of her. What a lovely Christmas present.

Harry has been absolutely wonderful these past several days, staying by my side right up to the delivery. After spending so much time the past few months with his new building, he's promised to stay by my side through the holidays. He even helped Dr. Ripton with the water and towels. And while I was sleeping on and off today, Harry was holding Lucy. I've never seen a man so gentle and natural with an infant. In fact, as I write this now, Harry is softly cooing to Lucy, rocking her ever so gently.

Well, Diary. I must sign off for now. I can barely keep my eyes open, and my parents are scheduled to arrive tomorrow night. I promise to write much more about Lucy in the morning.

Good-night.

Myrta

12/21/88

1889

Holmes' Office
The Castle

Kate Durkee:

You know they're going to catch up with you sooner or later.

Don't play coy with me—you know what I mean. Myrta's told me all about you two and your shenanigans. You make a pretty good team, but even the best get caught.

Well, you just better keep your eyes open, that's all I can say. Especially since I'm involved.

I certainly appreciate the opportunity to make a little money, and I also want to help out an old friend. But I don't want to end up in jail.

Is that supposed to make me feel better? Could get a little crowded, couldn't it, with you and Myrta and me?

Harry! I can't believe you said that. Myrta might not appreciate that very much.

Of course, I'm flattered. You are a very sexy man, as I'm sure you know, but so is my husband. Besides, Myrta is my best friend.

I'm not admitting anything. Maybe, if things had been different, who knows?

This is not funny, Harry. Please remove your hand right now. My God, Harry, do you do this sort of thing often? Does Myrta know?

Well, I may be a lot of things, but this isn't one of them.

What I *want* to do and what I *will* do are two different things.

I think the best thing we can do is forget this ever happened. I'm not going to tell Myrta about this little episode, and I suggest you do the same.

You are a devil, Harry, but I like you anyway. I'll see you later.

Pharmacy
The Castle

Ben Pietzel:

Hi. I'm Ben Pietzel and I'm here to answer that ad for a carpenter. Is Mister Holmes in?

Thank you.

Mister Holmes, I'm...

Well, it certainly is a pleasure meeting you too, sir.

I can be back here by lunch time, if you need me.

Whatever you say, Mister Holmes. You won't be sorry. I can do any job. I guess you could say...

One o'clock it is then. Good-bye, sir.

Pietzel Kitchen   *Tuesday, November 5*
Chicago, Illinois

Ben Pietzel:

I tell you, honey, this is the shot in the arm I needed. Alice, pass Daddy the potatoes.

H-o-l-m-e-s. Henry Holmes. About my age, and very well-educated.

Smart dresser, too. I really think you'll like him.

Enough, Carrie! Can't we ever have one meal in peace?

Well, if you would just stop nagging, and for once have some faith in me. I wouldn't have to yell, and the kid wouldn't be cryin'.

I'll drink as many beers tonight as I Goddamn well please. This is supposed to be a celebratory meal, for Chrissakes.

Thank you. I'm sorry too, honey. It's just that...hell, Carrie, I really think things will be different this time. I've always enjoyed construction work. I think it helps sweat the meanness outta me. Besides, it's good money. Twenty-five bucks a week, not that you've even asked.

I thought you might like that tidy little sum. That's almost five bucks a week more than I made doing that thankless dick job in Saint Joe's. With this kind of money, we'll be able to have meat more than just Sundays. And Dessie can finally get those new shoes.

Yes, pumpkin, we'll get both you and Nellie some new shoes, too.

A dress and a winter coat? Ha-ha-ha. Now, Alice, what would you need a new winter coat for?

Outdoors   *Sunday, December 22*
The Castle

Ben Pietzel:

Christmas?! This here ain't no charity affair Mister Holmes is runnin'. Ya' want money for you and your crew, ya' do the job you been axed ta do.

I told ya, I don't give a flyin' fuck if it's Christmas, New Year's, or my Goddamn birthday.... Either ya do the job right, or ya don't get no coin. Now, Mister Holmes says you and your crew ain't worth a shit. But

because he's so kind-hearted, if you wants to make amends, come
back next week and do the job right. Otherwise, take your stinkin'
half-assed crew and get da fuck outta here.

Try me, asshole.

Yeah, you're smarter'n ya look. That woulda been the last swing you
ever took. Now get the fuck outta my face and don't ever let me
catch you or your shit-can workers here again.

1890

Office of Holmes
The Castle

Ben Pietzel:

Hell, I think ten bucks for runnin' off these yokels is great money. It's just that it's becoming more and more dangerous. Why just last week...

Jesus, Harry, he even drew a gun. If he hadn't blinked, I might be dead as we speak.

Very funny. I'm not saying a ten spot on top of my salary is chicken feed for running off a crew. What I am saying...

Pat who?

For Chrissakes, I've done everything you've asked. Now don't be gettin' all bullshit on me, Harry. And don't be shovin' some potata-pickin' 'grint down my throat, neither. I've been nuthin' but honest and true to you. I'm just sayin' this bizness is gettin' more dangerous, that's all, 'kay?

'Preciate that. Look forward to meetin' him. If he's half as good as you say he is...

Great. See ya in the mornin'.

The Castle

Pat Quinlan:

So, youse da Peetza-man? Mista Holmes tells me all 'bout ya.

Yeah, I answered 'n ad, too. I'm da jan'tor now, but Mista Holmes promises bigga tings down da road. An' get dis—he's promised me ten bucks a week ta start out!

Sofie. We've knowed each udder since we wuz kids. Got married 'bout ten years back. Jes' one kid so far, but Lord knows we ain't got more fer lacka tryin'. Anyways, she's stayin' with her folks up on da Nourt Side 'til I get set up down here. An' wid ten bucks a week, it shouldn't take too long. How 'bout you? How much youse gettin' paid?

Well, fuck you very much, Peetza-man. Ol' Patty Q'll 'member dat one 'til da day he dies.

Yeah, well like you, Mista Hot Shit, I only got one person 'round here dat I gots ta worry 'bout, and dat sure as hell ain't you. Now gets outta da way. I gots more 'portant tings ta do den ta sit hear listenin' to your shit, PeeeeetZA-man.

38 North John Street   *Tuesday, April 1*
Wilmette, Illinois

Myrta Holmes:

Well, it's good to finally meet you, Mister Ben Pietzel. Harry speaks so highly of you.

Thank you...you're making me blush. This is our little Lucy. Lucy, can you say hello to Mister Pietzel?

That's very kind of you to say. Harry, take his coat for God's sake, and go on in. I'll fix us all a drink. Dinner will be ready in one hour. You did bring an appetite, didn't you, Ben?

Now, Harry, don't start discussing the plan without me. Has he mentioned any of it yet to you, Ben?

Oh, I tell you, he's ingenious.

Well, thank you, Harry, but I learned it all from you. Now, let me get those drinks. I can't wait to get started.

Pietzel Bedroom   *Thursday, April 17*
Chicago, Illinois

Ben Pietzel:

Well, what'd I tell ya? He's a prince, ain't he?

Aw, come on, Carrie. Holmes charmed the socks off ya, and you know it! And look how the kids acted. It took us fifteen minutes just to settle 'em down after he left. He had 'em laughin' and singin' and dancin'. Why, I can't remember the last time we all had such a grand time.

Jesus, I only had six beers tonight. Besides, he drank a glass of wine himself.

Yes, dear, that was very nice of him. I told him not to bring anything. But instead he brings a top-notch bottle of vino and a little somethin' for each of the kids. Didja see Howard's face light up when he gave him that rubber snake? He even took it to bed with him tonight after tryin' to scare his sisters with it before dinner.

He did? Good Lord, Pigeon, now tell me that's not impressive. Imagine that, a five-dollar bill. I can't believe you're not sold on him. Who else has ever given any of us anything, huh? No one, that's who. I tell ya, we're all very...

You're kidding me! When?

And on the lips? I'm sure it was nothin' more than him just showin' his 'fectionate ways—that's all it was and nuthin' more! Don't be gettin' me goin'; not now, not again tonight, Goddammit!

Well, if you didn't want me wakin' up the kids, then you shouldn't be sayin' stuff like that 'bout Holmes. He may be a bit shady 'bout some things, but not when dealin' with me and my family. 'Specially my lil' Carrier Pigeon.

That's my girl. Now come here and I'll show you what a real kiss is like.

Hmmmm...ah, to hell with the kids...

63rd and Wallace   *June 3, 1890*
Englewood, Illinois

Dr. Frank Noland, M.D.
Norristown Insane Asylum
Norristown, Pennsylvania

Dear Dr. Frank Noland:

It's me, your old "assistant," the one you thought was always Dr. Herman Mudgett. But you must write to me, as I know you will, as Dr. H. H. Holmes, my Chicago name.

On second thought, let's drop the "Doctor" titles between us. Okay? I feel more comfortable calling you Frank, as I used to do when we worked among our looney friends. Is Miss Turner still talking to her shoes? And old Mister Bill, is he still finding bats in his soup?

Frank, I want to open myself up fully to you. In fact, because of the special relationship that developed between us, you're the only person I dare take into my confidence.

After all, I helped you in ways you don't want revealed to anyone else. I can still smell the sweet sweat you and I produced in giving our patients their "afternoon therapy." Those were the good old days when you were quite the stallion among the goofy boys and girls. So I won't tell on you if you don't tell on me.

Frank, I finally built the perfect place in which to live and work. When we first came to Chicago, Herman and I got on some street trollies and rode around looking for our future residence. We found it here on the corner of 63rd and Wallace, an Englewood location complete with several railroad crossings, where the trains stop and go over a hundred times a day. Lake Michigan is nearby and the city provides easy access to gas and water. The remarkable thing is that the area still has numerous pieces of property that lie undeveloped. The place was truly ripe for making a fortune once the good sleepy people of Chicago woke up from their wind-filled dreams.

Two years ago I was able to buy two lots of land for next to nothing. Then the fun began. Our plan was to build a place where I could make some easy money, Herman could conduct his chemical and medical experiments, and the rest of us could fulfill our different desires. As you might imagine, the place we finally built is a mixed bag of eclectic curiosities.

People in the neighborhood call our creation "The Castle" because its design makes use of several impressive turrets. Like any other castle, ours has a secret dungeon, where Hatch hides his torture rack and dissecting table. Howard has some secret hideouts, small dark rooms where he can curl up and hope to die. We had fifty bedrooms built so I could make my money and Henry could make our roomers. Herman, of course, has his Frankenstein lab. My special place is a bedroom closet where I am able to control gaslines to all the bedrooms and to a large walk-in vault big enough to hold a curious woman.

Since the fall of '88, I have taken my creditors to the cleaners, bankrupting a few along the way. It amazes me that most people will do work—and plenty of it—on just the promise of payment. And so I made promise after promise, becoming a great expert in creating stories—sometimes right on the spot—on why I would only need a week or two more to provide payment for work that "had to be done immediately" on the building. I had an entire room built by the crew of a kind and gentle soul, never paying a penny to him or his help. They worked like dogs while I urged them on day after day for five weeks until the entire room—a wooden floor that stretches for thirty feet toward an entire wall of interesting closet space—was completed. I even tried to get them to start on a second room, telling them that the money for the first room would be in their hands in a matter of days. Instead of taking their anger out on me, the crew blamed their kind-hearted boss and beat the hell out of him. He's still in the hospital, and I'm now making some extra money on renting the room out to a family traveling on its way from New England to California. It's just not fair!

All kidding aside, Frank, America is a great place for smart go-getters like us. With just a slight bit of luck I'll take over all of Englewood some day and master its pretty women as I pile up riches for both myself and my children. We really enjoy the act of taking things from others: money from reluctant business people, moist pants from fast-breathing women—especially if they're married— valuable land from the unimaginative, power from those not bold enough to use it, and life itself from anyone who screams to hold onto it just as a sharp knife draws its first drops of blood from his or her quivering neck. Have you ever taken the life of someone, Frank? Amazingly, without any help

from me, my cold, pointed dick shoots a large jet of hot sperm every time I do it. Think of the world's surprise if I could tell them that murder is the greatest aphrodisiac, a cure for impotence!

Frank, old boy, I am the most fortunate human on earth, for I have found success where others fear to tread. I have come to the fountain of manhood, the core of maleness, its violent yet sacred center.

But you can't know of what I speak. You play the game of life cautiously and therefore will never know what it is to risk everything one has—his entire being—for a brief moment of exquisite existence. I have known those exquisite moments, Frank, but you and most others will never know them—you are not fully a man, Frank, but perhaps more a woman with a beard rather than a true naked man.

"Enough! Enough!" you yell, not wanting to hear more of my superiority over you and your gutless peers.

Okay, so let me tell you of things you can easily understand, like making lots of money. Frankie, dearest, I'm going to make a killing—in every sense of the word—in the upcoming World's Columbian Exposition, better known as the "World's Fair" here in Chicago. Old Ben Harrison signed a bill a few months ago designating Chicago as the Exposition site. Think of all the young lambs coming to the marvelous slaughterhouse, curious about all the modern wonders, and looking for a place to lay their empty heads. And I, of course, shall provide the innocent sheep with soft pillows of death. But before I do, dear Franklin, I will get them to enjoy the taste of their own blood, maybe even getting a thank you from them moments before I slice open their throats.

Do I scare you, darling? I am,

Yours truly,
H. H. Holmes

Ground Floor
The Castle

Thursday, June 5

Myrta Holmes:

My God, Harry, it's enormous! I had no idea that what I saw last year would turn out like this. I still can't get over the fact you were able to pull this off without paying anyone hardly anything.

Well, let's start from the beginning. I want the grand tour.

Oh, Harry, the store is wonderful. And that fountain—it must have cost a fortune.

Of course, silly me, what am I thinking? How much would it have cost?

Five grand? You got to be kidding. Well, if they ever demand it back, dear, let them have it. It's nice, but five thousand?

It's a pleasure to meet you, Mister Quinlan. I'm sure I'll be seeing you around. Who was *that*?

Jesus, Harry, I wouldn't trust that guy for nothing.

He's creepy, that's all. Just keep him away from me. Now Ben—I really do enjoy him and his family. That Carrie's so sweet.

Quinlan is married? You've got to be kidding. Who in God's name would marry a creep like that. I swear, Harry...just keep him away from me, okay?

I want to see your office next.

God, the stairwell is dark and drafty. I wouldn't show too many people this part of the building.

Gosh, that's a long hallway and nearly as dank as the stairwell. I sure hope your living quarters are...wow, now this is more like it.

Like it? I love it. And look at that safe—it's huge. Why, I bet you could fit a dozen people in there at one time.

No, no, let me open it, please-please-pleeeze! What's the combination?

Four-eighteen-eight. Jesus, Harry, it's immense. Why would you need a safe this big?

Is it safe to go inside? Gosh, Harry, I just don't think it's wise of you to have this monstrosity in here. What if you were inside this thing and the door closed?

Just be careful. Better yet, why don't you have El Señor Creepo put a knob on the inside, just in case.

Mexican, Mick, what's the difference? I tell you, I wouldn't step one foot inside that thing, even if there were a knob on it.

What are you looking at? Oh, for God's sake, Harry. At two o'clock in the afternoon?

Well, why not? We might as well christen this place, too—but not in the safe. I know, let's use your desk—I've always fantasized about doing it on your desk while you were at work. Have you ever thought of that?

63rd and Wallace   *June 20, 1890*
Englewood, Illinois

Dr. Frank Noland, M.D.
Norristown Insane Asylum
Norristown, Pennsylvania

Dear Frank:

Yes, you write to me, H. H. Holmes. You used to see me as Herman in the hospital's lab now and then, but I don't know if you knew it. Herman is the scholar among us, a modern scientific hermit. He was a boy wonder, always experimenting with dead plants and animals. He seems fascinated by dead people, too, but he won't admit it.

You want to know more about Herman, Henry, Howard, and Hatch. You say they're different sides of me, but I don't fully agree. It's true that my relationship with the four of them is far more intimate than my relationships with others. We seem to know each other very well, but how do you explain that I, H. H. Holmes, can see and hear Herman as Herman, Henry as Henry, Howard as Howard, and Hatch as Hatch? They have their lives and I have mine. We have different interests, different likes and dislikes. Different ambitions, ideas, and experiences, too.

You used to call us Dr. Mudgett, or Herman, depending on whether you were working in the lab or screwing around in your office. But I saw Herman, also. I used to see both of you bent over microscopes or test tubes while you were talking to him. But in your office I saw Henry bent over human bodies whereas you saw Herman. Henry let you call him Herman because it increased the fun of his reckless activities.

I was not amazed that you called me Herman, too. People have done that most of my life. We look alike.

"Good morning, Herman," you would say with a wink as we went into the breakfast area. I wouldn't answer you, then, just smile. And while I was thinking about ways I could turn the asylum into a profitable institution, you would carry on a loving conversation with Herman, who sat between us.

The point is, how can Herman or Henry or anyone else be really me if I can see that person just as clearly as you can? Frank, I have had round-table conversations with Herman, Henry, Howard, and even Hatch in the same hotel rooms all over America. It's one thing for me to be Herman at one time and Henry or someone else at the next. But how can I be five different people at the same time? It's not possible, is it?

It's true I have not always known Henry, Howard, and Hatch. However, I first started to know Herman when we were both five years old. He would be beaten by his insane father and then come running to me to complain. I would calm him down as much as a five-year-old could, and then we would play with things. Herman would study them and I would think about how wonderful they were as things in and of themselves. One idea that has ruled my life completely is that no two things are totally alike. Every thing is unique. By the time I was ten, I wanted to collect and make use of anything I could get my hands on. The value of life, as far as I'm concerned, is in one's experience with different things. The more you experience the quality of difference, the more you experience the secret of life itself.

Herman convinced me that the next step beyond the experience of getting to know something is the step of preserving it—to freeze its difference in time—and thus to possess it, to make it come under one's domination and therefore to be used as one sees fit. A living thing is always attempting to change, to be free of domination. It resists the threat of standing still for all time. But it is such resistance that I enjoy engaging. When I stop things in time, I experience an immediate thrill of pleasure, taking on the life of my new possession. It's as if a flash of lightning jumps from the body of my victim into my own. Instantly, we then become a bolted marriage of two lives brought into being from the sacrifice of a third life. It's all very Godlike—a Trinity—isn't it?

But how can you or anyone else understand what I have just revealed to you? You probably think I'm mad. Well, what do I care? I don't seek anyone's approval of my doings. In fact, my actions are those of a true patriot, in line with the American cliche, "It's a free country, ain't it?" I'm just enjoying my sweet share of the American apple pie.

Henry ran into my life within seconds of Tom losing his. Tom had been Herman's only friend in Gilmanton. He was a wild sort of kid, but we both like that wildness. He was insightful, too, and knew the difference between Herman and me—calling us "Hermit" and "H. H."

The three of us had agreed to explore an abandoned barn sitting three miles east of the center of town, just across the road from the 1777 cemetery. Tom, as usual, took the lead, taking us up a tall ladder until we reached a solid standing place at the top, where we could look at the dirt floor about thirty feet below us. Earlier, Tom had gone to the barn and placed a twenty-foot piece of lumber between two thick beams, one of which was our standing place.

"I'll go first, Hermit, and then you follow."

"Okay," Herman said.

But before Tom had reached the halfway point between beams, I

pushed Herman aside and jumped on our end of the plank. The quick movement caused the whole plank to rock, and Tom fell to his death.

Herman and I looked down on Tom's broken body—he had gone down head first—and both of us were unable to move. Then someone appeared suddenly, from where I don't know. He seemed to come out of the blackness that lay up against the walls of the barn. He walked over to Tom, bent down, and took our friend's wrist into his own hand to check Tom's pulse. A moment later, the one we would soon call Henry was looking up at us, Herman's face as frozen as my own. Henry's face, however, was that of a mad joker. He had broken into an odd peal of laughter, creating such a shock of surprise that Herman almost fell to his death himself.

A week later, depressed Howard appeared, slumped on a chair in young Herman's room. He has been with us ever since, never saying much with words, but speaking loudly with his miserable frown.

Hatch, the only man I dread, is also a quiet one; he joined us about thirteen years ago, first entering my dreams for several months before showing up in the flesh one night, jumping right out of a nightmare I was having. It's his way to appear suddenly, always unexpectedly. I hate it when I find him standing over me, looking sternly down upon me with eyes as cruel as Herman's father's. Henry or Howard must let him into my bedroom because I'm careful to keep the door locked—too many criminals in the world.

I fear Hatch. I know that he has done terrible things to people and means to do me great harm. I can't prove it, but I feel sure he has something to do with the bodies of two dead girls I found in my cellar last week. Someone beat them black and blue, broke their necks, and then threw them like ragdolls against the walls. To protect myself, not Hatch, I cut up their bodies and stuffed them into the furnace.

You need to help me deal with Hatch. He is trying to consume me. He's definitely out to get me, and I'm at a loss on how to escape from him. He's been killing people to get to me, trying to scare me into his trap, whatever it is. His eyes are full of arrogance, his mouth smirks. He thinks me a fool. Worse, he thinks me worthless. Next to my father, Hatch is the darkest thing in my life. He's my death. Frank, can you help me?

All for now,
Holmes

The Castle   *Saturday, June 21*

Pat Quinlan:

That's it, ya lil' bitch. Now which hole ya wan'it in?

Good choice. Now take ya medicine like a good lil' girl. Open wide.

Wider—that's it—hhh-hhh-hhh—swaller ev'ry las drop, ya Goddamn slut — whooooh—hahhhh—hahhh—hahhhhhhhh—God, ya good.

I'll get ya hands; untie ya feet y'self. I'll get us a cup'la beers.

Drag? Jesus, Lizzie, youse da only one dat gets 'ol PattyQ off like dat.

Yeah, I calls it da Dragon 'cause I uses it ta slay, heh-heh-heh.

Your tongue? Lizzie-Lizzard, da Dragon Slayer! I loves it, heh-heh-heh.

One last smoke 'fore I put it out?

Your skin—your body's so tight—I could just stroke ya all night. An' look at dem dere tits, wouldja? Mount Ev'rest'd be proud of dem suckers. Smoooooooch.

Ya know I luvs ya. Youse da best lay I's ever had.

Sheeet! I'm, tellin' ya, me and da misses are a ting of da past, we is. I gotta go back up dere a few more times for business, but I'm tellin' ya, we's done over wit', we is.

Now where ya goin'?

Oh, for Chrissakes. C'mon, Lizzard, I'll even let ya slay da dragon tonight.

Your way? Ah, why da hell not?

The Castle   *June 27, 1890*
Englewood, Illinois

Dr. Frank Noland
Norristown Insane Asylum
Norristown, Pennsylvania

Dear Frank,

I'm one step ahead of you on the guilt explanation. I'm sure I have many things to feel guilty about—if a hell exists, I'm going there—but I don't feel anything that resembles the definition of guilt.

I feel anger, loneliness, fear, greed, envy, and the other deadly sins: lust, gluttony, sloth, and an enormous sense of pride. But I don't know what it's like to feel bad about what I'm doing. I don't regret the things I've

done. For example, I always have taken advantage of people's stupidity. The result is that they have hurt themselves while I, on the other hand, have benefitted from my ability to manipulate them. They have brains to protect themselves, but perhaps my brain is more effective because I don't wash it in the thick waters of guilt. Most people are only servants; a few are masters. I'm one of the masters, a great man.

I don't have any problem in recognizing my greatness, no guilt in my superiority. Little people don't like to hear what I'm saying, but that's their problem—not mine.

I think the thing setting me apart from the masses—are you aware that Alexander Hamilton said the masses are asses?—is that I don't have any soft feminine spot you find in most women and, to a lesser extent—but still there—in most men. In fact, I don't feel too much for anything, including myself.

I remember one time a young girl advised me to drink a supposedly "nice" bottle of wine she had bought to make me more "romantic." She was trying to bring out my feelings, especially any warm ones I might have for her. Well, I drank the whole damn bottle but still didn't feel one degree warmer toward her. In fact, Henry raped the little bitch and told her he would break her neck if she ever told on him. I was so indifferent to the whole thing that I just sat and watched Henry having his good time with the girl. She left us in tears. Later, Henry got dressed and left me alone without saying goodbye.

The truth is, I don't have any warm spot, but I do have a giant cold center. For better or worse, that center dominates my emotional life and will probably determine my fate. So be it.

    Sincerely,
    Holmes

The Castle   July 4, 1890
Englewood, Illinois

Dr. Frank Noland
Norristown Insane Asylum
Norristown, Pennsylvania

Dear Frank,

Yes, I'm unable to control any of what you call my "intimate friends." When young Henry hungers for a female, for example, he can't be stopped. Part of his pleasure is for me to watch his domination of girls

and women—the more married, the better. Even if I'm not in the mood, Henry's lust spreads like melted butter on a hot pan, and so I often find myself standing naked and erect at the edge of a brass bed, waiting for Henry's nod of approval to share one of our skirted roomers with him. Aside from my wives, I haven't had sex on my own for many years.

Herman and Howard lack full sexual lives. They're both thinkers: Herman of anything that exists in solid form, Howard of darkness and death. Obviously, I prefer Herman's company and avoid Howard and his eternally bleak moods as much as possible. But I'm unable to carry on conversations with either one. They talk to me, self-absorbed, neither one listening to my views.

I'm only free to be myself when I'm doing business with others. If not for me, my companions would probably starve. I get far more satisfaction out of the manipulation of other people's money than I do of their bodies. I can manipulate everyone but my so-called intimate friends. My inability to deal with Hatch is especially troublesome because I know he does horrible damage to all people, including us.

I tell you, Frank, no one is safe when Hatch is near. One afternoon a Mrs. Holton, a fragile woman who lost her family's drugstore to me, came back to spit out her natural disgust for what I had done to her miserable life. She huffed and puffed while I calmly used a white cloth with gilded edging to wipe off an expensive countertop of marble once owned by her. She lifted her head high—an absurd gesture for one in her position—to inform me that she had filed a lawsuit against me. I looked at her as if I were frightened by her action, as if I hadn't faced similar lawsuits a hundred times before. I had to concentrate hard to keep myself from yawning; but to annoy her, I silently rubbed my fancy cloth of white and gold round and round on the bright slab of stone that stood between us.

Suddenly, Hatch came out of a corner, approached Mrs. Holton with a concerned look in his eyes, and tipped his hat to her. Completely fooled by him, she soon had her arm in his and lifted her nose to me as if to say that at least one gentleman knew a lady when he saw one. A moment later they both walked out of my store, and she into oblivion.

When questioned by the police, I said she had gone to Michigan to live with relatives. I have no idea if she really did have relatives, but Darwin says we are all probably related to fish; and so I meant her relatives in Lake Michigan, not the state of Michigan. The police, earnest in everything they do, searched everywhere in Michigan for her and her relatives until I told them she had also mentioned a sister in California. They're probably still cutting down the Redwoods looking for them.

You asked if I'm married. Like a Mormon, I have two wives and looking out for more. Marriage is good for doing business. My second wife, Myrta, is almost my equal in creating imaginative ways to get money out of tight pockets. She and my first wife, Clara, are the mothers of my children—a boy from the first marriage, a girl from the second. The state of Illinois does not think that marital bliss should be experienced in my particular way, but I never intended to lead a comfortable, safe life as sanctioned by bureaucrats and priests. I was not born to live with one woman only, especially since they're so easy to get. Promise marriage to a single woman and she will turn down your bed covers and hop naked into your arms the first chance she gets. Having learned this lesson many years ago, I have promised marriage to hundreds of women, always gaining sexual pleasure for Henry and me immediately after each proposal. Mr. Hatch, a true devil if ever there was one, gets rid of those women who insist we make good on my promise. I don't know how he keeps their bodies down on the black floor of our nearby famous lake, but somehow the bastard does. Speaking of the devil, he's with me now.

Enough,
Holmes

Examination Room

The Castle   *Wednesday, July 30*

Rebecca Carroll:

Good mornin', Doctor Holmes.

Oh, that's right...Henry then.

Not very good. I'm still breathless at times, and the room seems to close in. I've been taking those pills you gave me at least five times a day...sometimes I take an extra few like you suggested, especially when I feel myself starting to get faint. Be honest with me. Do you think I will ever get better?

Isn't there anything else I can try?

But I am desperate. I'm tired of having to stay in bed most days, and I never get to go anywhere. My husband buys everything I wear 'cause I can't handle the crowds in the department store.

You do? More pills?

Yes, sometimes I feel like I'm walking around in a daze. How much will this cost?

I don't know. That's a lot of money.

No, I'm not saying that. I'm just afraid Mister Carroll is going to question that amount. He says I already spend too much when I come to visit you. Are you sure it will work?

But aren't you going to explain it to me first? Then I can let Mister Carroll know what's happening.

He came with me today. I felt too weak when I awoke this mornin' to come by myself. In fact, he's waiting for me in the outer room.

Very well, if you must. I'll follow Nurse Hart's instructions. Oh, Herman, you will explain everything to me when you get back, won't you?

Hello, Miss Hart. Doctor Holmes said you would tell me what I need to do.

Do I have to? There's so many buttons, and I just know I'll be tired by the time I manage to take it off.

There's two more below the waist. So tell me, how long have you been working for Doctor Holmes?

That's not very long.

My underthings, too? I don't know...

Well, a massage sounds wonderful. Do you have a sheet I can use?

Thank you. Where did Doctor Holmes hear about this treatment? Has it worked on anyone else?

Really? How fascinating. And you've helped him each time?

Ouch!

No, it hurts. I have very sensitive skin.

That's much better. Mmm, it feels good. I sure hope Mister Carroll will agree to pay for the new treatment. Oh, Miss Hart, are you sure you're supposed to be rubbing that low?

All over? And how is this going to help?

Okay, if that's what Doctor Holmes ordered. Ahhh, that is nice.

Turn over?

Yes, I've always thought they were rather large. Perhaps that has something to do with my problem, what do you...Oh!

No, I just wasn't expecting you to do that. Uh, Miss Hart, are you sure you're supposed to massage them like that?

What are you doing now? Oh, Miss Hart, you...must stop...your mouth's so...warm...yesss...and the other one?

Ahhh...that feels sooo...wonderful...where are you...down there?

Oooh, I don't know...ohhhhhhhh...yes...oh my...Miss Hart...oh, you must stop...I'm losing...my breath...oh yes!

Oh, Doctor Holmes, when did you...come...please, help me...she

won't...ohhhh...I feel faint...oh, yessssss...harder...your tongues...yes, that...ahhh...please do it...don't stop...oooohhhh.
Please...Doctor Hol...why are you stopping? What...did my husband say?
He'd only pay half? Can't we...finish the treatment? I'll pay you the rest. Honest!
I'm beggin' you. Pleeease...I'll pay you double on Friday.
I promise, I'll get him to agree to at least four more treatments.
Yes, that's it.... Oh, thank you, thank you....

The Castle   *August 8, 1890*
Englewood, Illinois

Dr. Frank Noland
Norristown Insane Asylum
Norristown, Pennsylvania

Dear Frank,

I'm not really at The Castle, but visiting with my wife Myrta in Wilmette. She and our child are asleep, a nice breeze is blowing through a room we call my study, and I feel comfortable enough to address some questions you raised in your most recent letter to me. By the way, I'm burning it now; I don't keep your letters.

You ask about my upbringing. I remember my father's anger and just barely recall my mother. I remember Herman's parents far better than my own. Levi and Theodate Mudgett were Jews from Bulgaria. Like most other people in a new country, they soon found it profitable to become like the natives. So they eventually dropped their Jewish rituals and became Congregational Protestants, just like everyone else in the small New Hampshire town of Gilmanton.

Gilmanton is a town for Christians. It has a large New England common that's still used in winter for skating. Hills run north, south, and east of town; so everyone has sleighs with horses. A big event in town was the December day the mayor judged the best looking sleigh-and-horse combination: the owner of it would receive a new set of Christmas bells and lots of red ribbon for the horse. All the houses are white, just like their owners. It's just an ideal place for tilling the soil and praying to bright blue skies.

If you were different, as Herman and I were, you ran into problems

with small-minded Christians, especially the town bullies three or four

years older and six inches taller than you. One day three or four of them got hold of Herman and dragged him through mud, making him squeal like a pig. Another time a group of hooligans locked him up late at night in a funeral parlor with a man and woman who had died in a train accident. The absolute silence of the place was more horrifying than the sight of their torn-up bodies.

To get away from the Christian barbarians, Herman and I spent many hours at the town's Loon Lake, where we fished and swam by ourselves. Herman was fascinated with lily pads, the sound of frogs, and the eternal mist and dark corners of the water. There I learned to accept myself as a free thinker, a true poet of the American ideal of independence.

Another place of greater interest to me than to Herman was the Gilmanton Iron Works, a factory of giant furnaces. Its lone proprietor at midnight was someone we called Old Iron Man Mike, who kept the fires burning, sometimes with human bodies. I became a child of light there, my soul consumed in flames, leaving me with the cold, empty center that in turn has consumed my life.

Our best youthful experience was meeting Tom, a red-headed American beauty. Tom was our inspiration to break out of dead Gilmanton and be adventurers searching out the wonders of the world. Tom and I were great friends, but we were always in competition for gaining the attention of girls and for playing tricks on people. Tom was difficult to beat in both competitions—I always brooded over each of his victories.

One day, I began to think, I'll pull a trick on Tom he'll never forget. The next thing I knew, Tom was walking on that plank he had placed in that abandoned barn I already told you about. Tom was laughing, trying to show that he could do something I couldn't do. But Tom underestimated me, like most people do, and he paid with his life. Let's just say I'm doing my best ever since to rid the world of ignorance.

Suddenly, I'm tired.

> *Good night,*
> *Holmes*

The Castle   *August 28, 1890*
Englewood, Illinois

Dr. Frank Noland
Norristown Insane Asylum
Norristown, Pennsylvania

Dear Frank,

I turned 30 a few months ago. To celebrate the new event in the world's history, I rented some rooms in Turner's Hotel downtown for my partners and me. Henry ordered a bottle of Jack Daniels for Howard and himself. The rest of us don't drink.

Within an hour we had a wild, dark-haired prostitute in the bedroom. Herman, Henry, and I took her; sometimes we shared different parts of her body at the same time. Howard continued to drink in a small sitting room while Hatch sharpened a knife for the young woman's throat.

My life is so different from others that I think people will be reading about me in the next century. I would like to read the book myself, if only to correct the mistakes that will be made. I hope no one writes a biography of me because the author of someone else's life story will never be able to determine the truth about his subject's real thoughts and feelings, an impossible task even for the subject himself.

When we were boys, Herman and I would read books gathering dust in the Gilmanton Library. We both liked books on science, but the greatest reading experience I ever had was of Herman Melville's MOBY DICK. The moment Ahab pounded his wooden leg on the ship's deck, I could see myself in him—the captain, not Ishmael, a common sailor. Ahab was consumed by his need to possess the whale and everything it contained: its great strength, its power over all other creatures in the sea, and its strange connection with god. Ahab wanted the whale and I want the world. And on a higher level than Ahab, I want the world to love me as I conquer it, America first. In a way, I want to rape the world and receive its thanks as I'm doing it. Is this such an unreasonable request from someone as great as I?

Yours,
Holmes

The Castle   *Friday, October 31*

Pat Quinlan:

Jeezus, Mista Holmes, I jes' can't help me'self. I luvs da lil' wench, I do. Deres sumtin' 'bout her—she's jes' so Goddamn weird and kinky – and she wants it all da time.

Of course I luv da missus, too. It's jes', y'know, diff'rent.

In da spring. Mista Holmes, we been over dis time 'n time a'gin. Look, ya know how it is, what with all da dames ya bed. Dis is my only one—and she's a knockout. Ya haven't seen me wife yet. She ain't like yours at all. An' besides...

All right...so da damn pregnancy does fuck tings up but good. But if ya jes' give her some of dem pills.

I dunno—mix it up in her food, can'tcha?

I'm tellin' ya, she jes' won't listen ta reason. She tinks if she has it den I'll for sure dump da missus.

Well, tanks a mill, Mista Holmes. Dats all I can do. I'll keep workin' on her, and you keep on doin' da schemin'. Dats ya specialty anyways. I'm trustin' ya ta figure dis one out.

60th and Pulaski Street   *Saturday, November 15, 4:30 p.m.*
Chicago, Illinois

Julia Connor:

Ned, you're back...good...dinner will be ready in about thirty minutes. So, tell me, did you get it?

You don't even have to say. I can tell by the look on your face...you got the job, didn't you?

He wants you to manage the shop? Oh, this is wonderful...what about the salary?

Twelve dollars a week...and room and board, too? This Doctor Holmes sounds very generous.

Oh, Neddie, we've struggled much too long—no money for clothes or even food at times. But, no more. Maybe now we can buy Pearl that new winter coat she needs. So, tell me about our new benefactor.

Well, he really sounds too good to be true. Darling, I think this Doctor Holmes has just changed our luck.

Connor Suite, Third Floor   *Wednesday, December 10, 7:00 p.m*
The Castle

Julia Connor:

Gertie, why are you so upset? I think you should be flattered to have a man like Doctor Holmes interested in you.

He actually told you he wants to divorce his wife?

Ned, I'm not trying to force your sister into anything—it's just that Doctor Holmes is such a good catch.

Oh, don't be such a silly goose. You're not really planning to go back to Muscatine now, are you, Gertie?

I think you need to be more mature about this. He must be in love with you if he plans to divorce his wife. Why, I'd jump at the chance....

Oh, Ned, don't be such a fool! Of course I meant if I weren't already married.

1891

Drugstore
The Castle

Julia Connor:

Oh dear, I'm sorry, Mister Holmes. It's really tight behind this counter.
No, I don't mind at all. It actually felt kind of nice.
I don't care. I'll do whatever I want.

666 East 63rd Street
Englewood, Illinois

Monday, March 9, 1891

Dear Beverly,

Sorry I haven't taken the time to write since Ned took the new job here in Chicago, but I was sure you'd understand. After all, you've been my closest and dearest friend since the third grade, when we cornered Jimmie Beltzer in the coat closet and beat him up for trying to ignore us on the playground. Remember how he refused to tell on us because he was ashamed to admit two girls had given him the black eye? I think Mrs. Dubrowski suspected us, but we were really good at keeping secrets, weren't we? Anyway, I have something I must tell you now just to get your advice on what I should do about a very confusing situation.

Do you remember when I told you about a Mister Holmes, the man who hired Ned, and that I would be working in his drug store? Well, this Mister Holmes is not only successful but also very attractive. He's much better looking than Ned, but then again, who isn't? I don't know why I ever married him. Well, anyway, Mister Holmes stares at me all the time. He even looked me up and down the first time I met him. Then, he just stood there staring at my breasts. He didn't seem to mind that Ned was right there beside me. Of course, Ned said nothing...the little mouse.

Anyway, I've caught Mister Holmes looking at me with that glare in his eyes—the one that says I want to bed you, now. Anyway, I'm beginning to think I'd like him to take me. He makes me ooze, and you know what that means. I've been through this before and I'm always ready for anything. Besides, Ned doesn't excite me anymore.

To top everything off, today, when I had to ask Mister Holmes to help me find something under the counter, he slid in behind me, put his hands at my hips, pulled me against him, and then actually rubbed himself back and forth against me so that I could feel his hardness. It felt so good, I was immediately wet and wanted him to take me right there.

I don't even remember what I said to the man. I was so weak I think I just looked at him and sighed. I'm sure he knew how I felt because after he stopped rubbing me, he said as he left, "Anything else I can help you with, Mrs. Connor?"

Lulu, I liked it. What's wrong with me? I'm married and yet I want this other man. I want to watch him pant like a dog while I undress for him and I want to wrap my legs around him and hold him there until he comes inside me three or four times.... Oohhh, I think I'm in trouble. Should I pursue this man's advances or do I play the dutiful wife to someone I can't stand? You know I've been through this once before, and even though it's exciting, we know it can be devasting for a marriage. Help! Write soon.

> *Julia*

The Castle   *March 15, 1891*
Englewood, Illinois

Dr. Frank Noland
Norristown Insane Asylum
Norristown, Pennsylvania

Oh, Frankie!

I'm still excited by what happened less than an hour ago, when I took possession of my drugstore clerk, a Mrs. Julia Conner.

Before I tell you all the dirty details of my success, I'll begin with a brief mention of failure. For almost a month I lusted after an 18-year-old virgin, the sister-in-law of the woman I left panting for more sex on my bed.

I wanted to be nice to the virgin Gertie, but the little bitch wouldn't let me press my hot hand between her cool thighs. Her modesty was no match for Henry's aggressiveness, though. He got her pregnant, and then I sent her home with an abortion medicine that will kill more than the baby if she takes it as prescribed.

In November, 1890, I interviewed a jeweler, Ned Conner, to see if he would be willing to set up his sparkle display in a cozy little nook in my store. I didn't like him, but I did like the physical descriptions of his wife and sister. So I agreed to pay him twelve dollars a week if he brought along Julia and Gertie to help us do business.

The first time I squeezed Julia's hand I knew I would be squeezing a lot more before I was done with her. Today I squeezed every inch of this six-foot giant while I shifted her into every imaginable position to make her scream with pain and pleasure. I asked her to scream, to scream as

long and loud as possible, all the while both of us knowing that old Ned was tinkering with watches in their bedroom located just above my own. It absolutely thrills me to be taking Julia away from her husband, especially since he knows that I'm screwing her but can do nothing about it.

She wants to do it again—now!

> *Be good,*
> *Holmes*

Connor Bedroom   *Saturday, March 28, 8:30 p.m*
The Castle

Julia Connor:

Oh, it's you.

No, Ned, I wasn't expecting someone else. You just startled me when you came through the door.... I didn't hear you coming up the stairs and I thought it might be Pearl wanting to say goodnight again.

Yes, I've already put her to bed and I'm also tired, so goodnight now, too....

No, Ned, don't bother me. I really don't feel like talking about anything now.

Well, we don't talk any other time, so why should we start at this late hour?

I just told you I'm tired, and that's why I want to go to sleep.... I've been on my feet all day. You know how busy we were to....

But, Ned, I just told you, I....

Well, what about him?

Okay, so he's my lover. You're just finding this out?

I don't really care how much more you know. It doesn't matter. You'll never be the man he is. Henry treats me like I belong to him, and he wants me all the time.

No, you brought this up and you're going to hear this. So sit there and squirm. Henry's been touching me for weeks, now. He only has to touch my hand and my loins ache.

Yes, that's right, you heard us in his bed. He makes me scream and he's noisy and rough like a man should be. He knows what to do between my thighs.

Oh, what a fool. You're not half the man he is. You couldn't satisfy me even if you knew what to do with it. Do you really believe *that* little thing could make a woman like me happy?

I don't need you, Ned. I have Henry now and he'll have me in his bed anytime I want it. Now, get out of my sight, you disgusting little worm—you make me sick.

Kitchen   *Sunday, March 29, 7:00 a.m.*
The Castle

Julia Connor:

Good morning, my darling.

I feel wonderful today, Henry—no more problems.

Why Ned, of course. He left last night.

Don't look so shocked.... This is what we've been waiting for. I'm a free woman now, free to marry you, my darling, free to make love with you all the time.

I'm sure we'll get a divorce now. I told him we were lovers and I made sure he knew how disgusting I think he really is. Oh God, I can't stand the thought of him.

Henry, let's not talk about Ned anymore. Let's celebrate my freedom from that weasly little worm and our future union by having a little dessert before breakfast. How does that sound?

We'll have to hurry though—Pearl will wake up soon. Just put it right here on the table. Ooooh, Henry, that looks delicious.

The Castle   *Wednesday, April 1*

Pat Quinlan:

It's a boo'ful lil' lass, Jess'ca's her name. My God, Peetza-man, what's gonna happen to me?

She won't let me git near 'er. She don't want no parta me. And Holmes, he done really fuck me over good dis time. He promised me he'd kill da damn ting at birth—I was really hopin' he'd git 'em both. But look at him in dere now with dem two, smilin', cooin' ta da kid, rubbin' da bitch's forehead. Whadafuck'm I gonna do?

Y'know, Peetza-man, sometimes ya ain't all dat bad. But I still don't git why Holmes' doin' what he's doin', whatever da hell it is he's doin'. He told me he'd git at least one at birt'—and he said it with dat damn satan look o' his. Now he looks like Saint Mutter Marie herself in dere.

I tell ya, dis is nuttin' but bad news—bad news, I tell ya. He's got sumt'in' up his sleeve, he does. And whatever it is, it spells bad news for ol' PattyQ. Sofie's due here at da end of da month. How'm I 'spose to pull dis off? I gotsta git her outta here, and she says she ain't leavin'. Says she can't wait ta meet da misses. Ya gotsta talk ta Holmes fer me, Ben, ya jes' gotsta.

You're a real pal after all, ain'tcha? I don't give a rat's ass what da utters say, heh, heh. Today you're da PRINCE-man, dats what ya' are. Now hurry up and git talkin' wit' him, 'kay? I'll be awaitin' in me room.

Office of Holmes, Second Floor
The Castle

Julia Connor:

Excuse me, Henry, are you busy?

I'm sorry, dear. I realize you're working on your books, but actually that's what I wanted to talk to you about.

Thanks. I'll only be a few minutes, and this really is important.

No, there are no customers out front now. It's still raining, and I'm sure the downpour is keeping everyone at home where it's warm and dry. Besides, I can hear the door opening if anyone comes in.

Well, like I said, this is something I've been meaning to discuss with you for some time, and now with Ned out of my life I'm actually free to help you in your business dealings.

Yes, I'm serious. I've watched you slave over those books night and day and I know that I'm intelligent enough to handle your bookkeeping. I could take a six-week bookkeeping course at Lafayette. I've already checked into the dates and time—a new class begins a week from Monday. I could register tomorrow.

Henry, I'm not trying to meddle in your business. I just want to spend my time doing something more challenging than working as a drugstore clerk the rest of my life.

Be reasonable. This is something I really want to do to help you. Just think of all the free time you would have for your other business ventures.

Oh, you can always hire another clerk. You don't need me out there anymore. And besides, darling, working back here in the office allows us to work together side-by-side.

My, my, doesn't this desk looks like an interesting place to....

The Castle

Pat Quinlan:

Hiya, Mista Holmes. Lil' Lizzie 'n me is here ta git da bond. Can we come in?

Yeah, it is enormous, ain't it? Ya sure ya don't want Mista Holmes ta hold da kid?

Awright, awright, Lizzard—don't be gittin' your tit caught inna ringer. Can't we least be civ'l ta each utter on our last day? It should be right inside da vault. Can we go in, Mista Holmes?

Whatsamaddah? Ya ain't never been inside no vault 'afore? Da bond's up here on dis shelf. Here, five hunderd smackers like we said. Oh, 'n as an extry

bonus, ta prove 'ol PattyQ ain't da bast'ad like ya says he is, back dere on da bottom shelf's a few hunderd bucks fer y'self.

Satisfied? I can't believe ya makin' me a part of dis. Why couldn'cha've jes' finished 'em off three weeks back when she was dumpin' out da kid? Now it's like I've just done sold me soul ta da devil—and I tinks da devil is sittin' right dere at his desk.

Holmessss! I don't like dis one bit. Der givin' me da willies. I can't take da screamin'!

Holmes! Godammit, didja hear me!?!? Da noise's drivin' me insane!

Would'ja put da fuckin' cards down 'n list'n ta me? Put 'em down, Goddammit! I can't believe you're playin' Goddamn solitair' while dem two is in dere screamin' der fuckin' heads off.

Holmes, ya gotta either give me da fuckin' combination or ya gotta let me leave. I'm tellin' ya, I jes' can't take it!

How da hell can ya jes' sit here playin' cards? Would'ja say sumtin'?!?!

No, I honestly tink she'da tak'n da money 'n run.

Sheeeet, dere ain't no guarantees 'bout nuttin', but I woulda tak'n da chance. Anyting beats da shit outta listen'n ta dese two hollern' away like dat.

Well, I see dis is bodderin' ya a bit, too, huh? I've never seen ya take a swig of da hard stuff 'n da afta'noon. So da man of steel ain't so solid after all, is he?

Tanks, I needed a swaller' me'self.

Jesus, dis is jes' killin' me. How much longer ya tink dis is gonna go on?

Now wha'da fuck ya doin'? You're one of da sickest men I knows, Missssta Holmes. I can't believe ya. What in God's name ya writin' now, wit' all dis death screamin' goin' on?

Hey, ya finally hear dat? Silence. D'ya tink it's over?

Honest? Ya really gonna let me go? T'anks 'lot, Mista Holmes, y'know I jes' couldn't stand goin' in dere now—hey, what're ya gonna do wit' 'em? No, never mind, I don't wanna know nuttin' else 'bout dis whole mess. No, 'ol PattyQ'll jes' pick up his hat 'n walk out dat door now, if it's all da same.

Sheeeet, Holmes. Who da fuck ya t'ink I'm gonna tell—Sofie? No, sir, dis here goes ta me grave, dats where dis goes. May God have mercy on da both of us.

Train Station
Englewood, Illinois

Pat Quinlan:

Hey dere, Sofe. Howya doin'?

'N me lil' Corker. How's me utter gal?

Here, lemme git ya bags. Where's da res' of 'em?

Holy shit, Sofie! Did'ja hafta take ev'ryting now? Hell, we'll leave 'em here. I'll git one a Mista Holmes flunkies ta pick 'em up later.

Dats what I been tryin' ta tell ya. We be shittin' 'n high cotton now'days. And why jes' da utter day, da boss-man gives me a whole two dolla' raise. Dats twelve bucks a week, plus a mighty fine place ta stay.

Let's jes' say he was rewardin' me loy'lty.

Ain't dis jes' great? Da Quinlans takin' a Sunday stroll together on a bee-yoo-teeful spring day. I tell ya, Sofe, we be done havin' our hard times. From here on out, it's you 'n me 'n baby make t'ree. We're gonna have da best times, we are, and startin' right now. See dat? Dats our humble home.

Well, say sumtin'—looks like your ma can't talk, Corky, whaddaya say? Look at da two of youse, your eyes'r wide as saucers, heh-heh-heh. Ain't it ev'ryting I said it was? Jes' wait'll ya see our livin' quarters. We gots t'ree whole rooms, plus our very own bat'.

Here, lemme git da door. Ah, dere's Mista Holmes now.

Over dere wit' blondie. He's got a way wit' da womenfolk, y'know. Now 'member, Sofie, he's da reason we're a fam'ly a'gin.

Good afta'noon, Mista Holmes, dis here's me wife, Sofie, and me lil' girl, Cora. Can ya say hi ta Mista Holmes, honey?

Heh-heh-heh. Yeah, she's jes' a tad on da shy side—kinda takes afta' her ma dat way.

Well, we had ta leave a few back at da station. I was wonderin' if either Doug or John were 'round ta go fetch 'em while I git da mizzes and Cora here freshened up a bit?

Oh, dat'd be jes' great, Mista Holmes. For dat, even I'll freshen' up a wee bit, heh-heh-heh. We'll be down at five sharp, and wit' our appetites.

Lafayette Business School   *Tuesday, May 5*
Chicago, Illinois

Julia Conner:

Tonight's class was such a big help. I think I almost understand that last chapter now. You do have an interesting teaching technique.

Another technique? Why, whatever do you mean, Mister Kozinski?

In private? Hmmmm...why, I'd love to see this special technique of yours—in private, of course.

This may come as a surprise to you, Mister Kozinski, but I've been watching you, too. You're a very attractive man for your age, you know.

Oh, I didn't mean to imply that you're an *old* man. I just meant to say that your grey hair gives you a very distinguished look. You possess the charm and looks a woman finds very attractive in a man.

Ooooh, your hands...that feels nice.

I'd like to get to know you better, too. Perhaps, we could go to your office where you can give me some *private* tutoring?

Connor Suite, Third Floor   *Wednesday, May 20*
The Castle

Julia Connor:

Oh, you startled me! What are you doing here?

Darling, I told you I had to stay late tonight. You know I have private tutoring after class.

What are you talking about? Of course we were studying. What else would we be doing?

You're imagining things, Henry. Your accusations are ridiculous.

Oww, that hurts...don't! You're hurting my arm...let me go!

No, I'm not fooling around with Mister Kozinski. The class is over soon, anyway, so there's no need for you to get upset over something as absurd as this.

Third Floor Hallway   *Monday, June 15, 8:30 p.m*
The Castle

Julia Connor:

My God, what are you doing? Henry...Emily van Tassel, you little tramp, get away from...oh, I can't believe this...right out here in the hallway. Henry, how could you?

A tour? Oh, that's a good one. You *look* like you're giving her a tour—maybe a tour of your trousers.

Don't even try to explain. I know what I see. I know you better than you think. I'm sure your next move was to shove it in her right here, you bastard.

No, Henry, I won't lower my voice—I'm not finished with the little slut yet. That's right, Emily, you better lower those eyes if you know what's good for you. Your tour is over, so get your sashaying little ass outta here. I never want to see you anywhere near this place again.

Henry, how could you? She's only sixteen.

Try another story, Mister Holmes; I'm not stupid. There's nothing wrong with my eyes. And besides, from the glazed look in your eyes, I can tell you were about to take her right out here in the hallway!

I don't want to hear any more lies. I thought you loved me....

Well, what was all that about then? No, stay away from me and don't touch me. I need time to think.

Drugstore   *Saturday, June 27*
The Castle

Julia Connor:

Good morning, Henry. Sleep well last night?

I'll bet you did—in whose bed?

You're lying. You were not in your bed last night.

It is my business and I'll *not* shut my mouth. We've been through this before, and I'm getting pretty tired of watching you flirt with anything in a dress.

I'm not exaggerating. You were with that little tramp again, weren't you?

Emily van Tassel, that's who. I hate the little whore. She just won't leave well enough alone, will she?

Don't *you* tell *me* to calm down. I don't care who's coming in the door...

Oh, damn, it's that old hag, Granny Tisdale...

Good morning, Missus Tisdale. So good to see you again. You're certainly here

bright and early—our first customer this morning. You look like you're in pain, though. Is your gout acting up again?

Well, I'm sure our *kind* doctor would be more than happy to fill your prescription. Wouldn't you, Doctor Holmes?

And how is that corn on your foot, Missus Tisdale? Don't you need to discuss that with Doctor Holmes while you're here?

No, he's not busy—he'd love to check it for you. Why don't you take your shoe off right now and show the good doctor your foot?

Oh, no buts about it, Henry, she would love to show you her foot. In the meantime, you can find me in the office. We'll talk later.

Kitchen   *Sunday, November 15, 8:00 p.m*
The Castle

Julia Connor:

Here, Henry, sit down. I've prepared you a wonderful dinner tonight.

Oh, I fed Pearl earlier and put her to bed. She was tired and should be asleep by now.

See, I've made all your favorites. Roast beef...

Yes, it's bloody, and look at this: buttery mashed potatoes, peas, carrots.

That's right, flowers, too. I just thought fresh flowers would make dinner a little more romantic—give us a nicer atmosphere.

Well, there is a reason behind my spending so much time in the kitchen tonight.... Actually, we do need to have a little discussion, but we can talk after our meal. Here's the knife, you can go ahead and cut it.

Well, nothing too serious, we just need to talk about us, that's all.... Gravy?

Mmmmm! Smells good, doesn't it?

Oh, I just have something to tell you—that's enough meat, thanks.

Henry, I'd rather talk after dinner, but I suppose I can tell you now. Well, you realize we've been involved for months now and practically been living together as husband and wife—pass the salt and pepper...

Thanks. Anyway, you're so good to Pearl and she thinks of you as a father. And you know how much I love you, and I know you feel the same way about me. Well, when two people feel this way...it's....

Henry, don't rush me.... I'm getting to the point. Well, it's just that I think it's time for us to get married.

Because we have nothing standing in our way now that we're both divorced. Besides, well...

I'm not beating around the bush, Henry. It's just that we *have* to.

Because I'm pregnant.

Did you hear me? I said, I'm pregnant.

How could *I* allow this to happen? My God, Henry, *you're* the one who has my legs spread every time we're alone. So don't act like you didn't know this could happen. You've had me upstairs, downstairs, in your bed, in my bed, on the desk, in the closet, behind the counter....

Henry, what are you thinking? Say something...look at me...answer me. This is *your* child, Henry....

Office of Holmes   *Wednesday, November 18*
The Castle

Julia Connor:

Oh, Henry! Why of course I'm still talking to you. It's been three days, and I've missed you terribly, but I realize my news about the baby really took you by surprise. That's why I've left you alone. Darling, I knew you needed time to get over the shock.

So, now that you've had time to think about it, when do you think we should plan to get married?

After an abortion? Is that what this is about?

Henry, this is not a *problem*. It's a baby, our baby.

Why do you want to get rid of our child?

Yes, I know I already have one. Pearl is *Ned's* child. And now I want to have *yours*. What's wrong with that?

And I suppose you're not ready to get married either, are you?

If? If what?

Stop beating around the bush—what you're really saying is you'll marry me if I abort the baby, isn't it? Well, I won't do it—I will *not* have an abortion. As far as I'm concerned this discussion is closed. *You* think about it.

Holmes' Suite   *Thursday, November 26*
The Castle

Julia Connor:

Henry, you know I can't stay angry with you when you touch me like that.

Ohhhh...yes, yes...that feels really good.

Yes, that feels even better. Oh God, it's been over a week since you touched me there.

Of course, I've missed you. I need it every day, you know that.

Yes, I'm ready...right here...on the floor, anywhere...I don't care. Just do it.

Ohhh...Henry, don't stop...of course, I've thought about it. I've thought about nothing else, but let's not discuss that.

Because we are trying to satisfy my insatiable appetite for you, and I don't want to hear about that abortion now.

No, I haven't changed my mind. Have you?

Quinlan Kitchen   *Thursday, December 17, 9:00 a.m.*
The Castle

Cora Quinlan:

I'm so glad to be home, Momma. Please don't send me back to the farm. I like it here with you and Poppa. I wanta stay after Christmas, okay?

There's no one to play with there, and I have to do chores *every* day. Grandma makes me feed the chickens and milk Bossie. I don't like touching those teats. You have to pull real hard, and when I'm still sleepy Grandma yells at me 'cause I can't make much milk come out.

Know what else? Once the goat chased me 'round the pen when I was tryin' to pet his baby. I got real scared 'cause he tried to butt me with his horns. When I started cryin' Grandma said I shouldn't be so rough with the animals. She didn't even care if Billy Goat killed me.

It *was* so! You would've been scared too and I was *not* being rough.

She's mean and always makes me take my shoes off when I come in the house.

Can I help it if she scrubs the floors everyday? She yells at me all the time. I can't do anything right. I don't think she wants me there, Momma. Don't make me go back. Please let me stay here a little longer. Please... please... puleeeeez?

Suite of Holmes   *Thursday, December 17, 3:00 p.m.*
The Castle

Julia Connor:

Hello, Henry. Brrrrrr...it's freezing out there. Can you help me with my cape and boots? How was your day?

Thank you. Oh, Christmas shopping for last minute gifts. Pull...there, that's better. Anyway, it was so cold and windy, I could hardly see where I was going with that snow blowing in my face. Now, help me with the other one, please.

That feels much better, thanks. Now all I need is a brandy and a nice toasty fire to help thaw me out.

By the way, where's Pearl? Is she still with Cora?

Oh, I'm teaching her embroidery, a very quiet task. This way she won't disturb you at all. You won't even know she's around.

I've seen your raised eyebrows when she begins to get rowdy. Believe me, I know what that means. Ned used to do the same thing.

I felt fine today...no nausea, no weakness. I was able to finish all my shopping and I even found another gift for you, my darlin'.

Henry, no. Must you bring *that* up again?

We don't have to discuss it. I can't bear thinking about it. Now I do feel sick.

I've told you I don't want an abortion. We've been through this a thousand times. It's an awful thing to do. The whole idea makes me feel dirty, guilty. It makes me—you and me—*murderers.*

Well, I meant it to sound cold. Can't you understand? This goes against everything I believe in.

Of course I love you and of course I want to get married. You know I do...more than anything.

I'm too exhausted to argue. I'll think about it. Are you satisfied now?

Pearl's Bedroom, Third Floor   *Thursday, December 24, 9:00 p.m.*
The Castle

Julia Connor:

Yes, Pearl, I'm sure Santa will visit you tonight. You've been a very good girl all year, haven't you?

Well then, there's no reason to worry. I'm sure he'll appear with a big surprise for my favorite little girl.

Oh, probably a new doll and goodness knows what else.

I know you're excited...I can tell. But you really must stop talking now. It's time to go to sleep.

I love you very much...you know that don't you, honey?

Come here. Let me give you a big, big hug. Ooohhh...you're such a sweet girl. Mama is so proud of you. You're the one thing in my life I can count on to always be there for me. I'm so glad I had you.

Remember, we're taking a train to Nana's on Sunday. Uncle Henry will come by in a few minutes to turn out your lamp and tell you goodnight. I'm sure we'll both feel different in the morning.

Goodnight, little one, sleep tight.

Bedchamber of Holmes   *Thursday, December 24, 9:30 p.m.*
The Castle

Julia Connor:

Stop fussing. And don't yell at me. I'll take my sweet time if I want to.

I've been upstairs putting my child to bed. Is that all right with you? It is Christmas Eve, you know. She's just a little girl and doesn't understand all the attention you demand of me.

Yes, I'm irritable. Wouldn't you be if you were about to do something you really didn't want to—if someone were pressuring you into committing an act that was against all your moral beliefs?

Oh, come on, Henry. Surely, you're not that callous.

Well, you can continue to believe this is a necessity for our happiness or you can face the truth and admit that your selfishness is behind the whole thing.

Don't even mention the word *love* to me. You don't love me at all. If you did, I wouldn't be going through this.

The only reason I'm doing this is because I want to get married. You've worn me down, Henry. I'll take your *damn* medicine.

Ooohhh...it's bitter.

Henry, it's working already. I need to sit down. Am I supposed to feel so dizzy? My arms...my legs...I'm numb...I...can't breathe...Oh God, help me.

The Castle   *December 24, 1891*

Dr. Frank Noland
Norristown Insane Asylum
Norristown, Pennsylvania

Dear Franklin:

What may seem like bad news to you, especially on this cold Christmas Eve, is quite good news to me: An hour ago, Hatch snuffed out the lives of Julia Connor and her daughter, Pearl. "No more problems from them," Howard said. Trust Howard to say the most gruesome things in the same tone used to request the passing of salt at dinner.

My original plan was to give Julia, who was pregnant with Henry's child, an abortion. But Hatch has no patience with children, and I, quite frankly, don't want the responsibility of two additional consumers.

"You'll find the little girl dead in her mother's bed upstairs," Howard said. "She's still warm for you know what." On questioning him, I found that the mother's guts had been ripped out and thrown away into the basement furnace, along with the fetus. She's still on the dissecting table, but much too repulsive for loving—even Henry wouldn't want her now.

We had to do something about Julia because she insisted on marriage after she became pregnant. She knew too much about my ways of doing business and would have done everything she could to stop my affairs with other women. For that alone, Henry wanted her dead.

The child had to go because I didn't want the burden of spending money to feed, clothe, and educate her. She was sweet; a sad—no, a mournful—smile had developed after her parents' separation. She was like a pink rosebud that had difficulty growing in the perpetual shade of her loss.

She's gone now, but Henry's here, just walked into the room, wanting to pay her a visit. He'll drive me crazy if I don't go.

Merry Christmas,
Holmes

1892

Basement   *Wednesday, January 6*
The Castle
H.H. Holmes:

Watch your step going down—I won't pay for your expenses if you fall.

Thanks, but I don't smoke, Mister Chappell.

Charles, then.

Yes, it stinks. Quite a mess, I agree.

A woman.

Train hit her. I did the postmortem a week ago.

Look, don't ask questions. I'll give you thirty-six bucks to finish stripping the corpse and to articulate the bones.

Let's shake on it then.

Don't bother. A man named Pietzel will drop off the corpse in a trunk later tonight.

Sure, if you do good work, I'll give you more bodies as they come in.

Could happen anytime. I never know. Have a good night, Mister Chappell.

Charles, then. Right.

Outside of City Jail   *Sunday, January 17*
Terre Haute, Indiana

Ben Pietzel:

I've never been so glad to see the sun, Henry. I never knew how dank and smelly the inside of a joint could be.

Kee-ryst, it coulda happened to anybody. That's the risk we take forgin' those damn checks. Hell, that's the reason we came here in the first place, 'cause we was afraid they was catchin' up to us in Chi-town.

All right, all right. So maybe I do have a slight problem with the bottle. Tell ya what—from here on in, whenever we're doin' a job, I'll lay off the stuff, okay?

Well, this time I do mean it. There ain't no way I want to be goin' back into one of those anytime soon.

Now that ya mention it, that was pretty quick 'n easy, I 'spose. So, just how'ja manage to spring me so quick?

Ha, ha, ha. You've got to be kiddin' me, Henry, that's a hoot! An absolute hoot. Here I am, doin' time for forgin' some checks, and here you come and not only forge your signature on the bail, but ya use a Goddamn congressman's name ta boot. You're either a genius or a Goddamn fool, that's what you are. Jesus, Henry, don'tcha think we better get the hell outta Dodge now while the gettin' is good?

I dunno, prob'ly ten to fifteen years in this podunck town. Why?

Look, ya just sprung me on a forgery charge by forgin' their U.S. congressman's name, and now ya want ta ride outta this place on stolen horses? That's insane, Henry, and you know it. Not now, not this time. Let's just go over to the train station, buy us two one-way tickets to Chicago, and get back home. I'm really sick of this town, and I don't wanna get thrown back in the slammer. I'm just not up to it this time, okay?

Shit, Henry, sometimes I just don't get you.

1220 Pulaski Street   *Saturday, March 5*
Chicago, Illinois

Ben Pietzel:

Ah, Henry, you're right as rain. Okay, okay, I'll go. I'll go because I know it's 'fectin' my work, but I'm mainly goin' for Carrie and you.

Y'know I wanna lick this thing as bad as anyone. You think I enjoy takin' a few hours every mornin' to get the cobwebs outta my eyes? Do you think I enjoy yellin' 'round here every other night, gettin' you and the children all upset?

You both just don't understand how hard it's become. I'm sayin' no all the way up to opening that first bottle. And it's the same way for the next few. I just keep sayin' this'll be the last one. Then 'fore I know it, I've had six, eight, ten, and then we're fightin' and then I'm wakin' up the next day with a splittin' headache, wanting to stay in bed. And now with another baby on the way...no, this Keeley Institute is just the ticket for me, and don't think I don't 'preciate all the expense you're going through, Henry. I know it's not cheap. But I promise you both I'll lick this thing, and I promise you, Henry, to pay you back for all this.

No, no, I mean it.

Okay, we'll see. Well, I hope you got enough to eat tonight. Sure you don't want that piece of pie?

Carrie, why don't you at least refill his coffee—Henry, before she gets back, don't forget we need a name for me while I'm up there, just in case.

You have? What is it? C'mon, tell me.

Oh, nuthin', Pigeon. Henry was just sayin' he's got to get going after all. But it's not a total waste—you can refill mine.

G'night, Henry, and thanks again. See you Monday.

1220 Pulaski Street   *Sunday, March 6*
Chicago, Illinois

Alice Pietzel:

Move over, Nellie, you're hoggin' the covers.

Dessie, you still awake?

Then tell Miss Sniffles here to move over.

Thanks. That's better. Dess?

Whatcha think 'bout Uncle Henry?

I don't know. Don'tcha think Daddy's startin' to look like him? Why's that?

Yeah, I guess so. I wish Daddy didn't have to work such long hours at the Castle. All he wants ta do when he comes home is drink. Whatcha think he does for Uncle Henry?

Oh, Nellie, the Castle's not that spooky. It helps if you think of it like a big game or maze.

That's only 'cause you got lost on the second floor. I wanna go back again. Everything's so nice there. Dess, have you gone lately?

Rats, I knew I shoulda gone with you that day instead of stayin' here helpin' Momma. What new things has Uncle Henry bought?

Nellie, stop it. Why don'tcha go to sleep?

Well, Dess, she's doin' it on purpose. Who'd ya see there?

I don't like Mister Quinlan—he's creepy. Didcha know he once tol' me I had to kiss him?

Whatcha think? I ran back into Uncle Henry's office.

Uncle Henry asked what scared me so bad, and I told him. Then he sat me on his lap and started patting my knee. He told me Mister Quinlan only wanted to kiss a pretty lady. 'N you know what Uncle Henry did next?

He kissed me on the lips.

It was kinda nice. Haven't you kissed a boy?

Not even Robert?

I jes' thought you had.

Oh, you've had plenty of chances. What 'bout that time he was over 'n Momma sent him out to the back porch to get some more wood for the stove? You tellin' me you didn't kiss him when you went to see if you could help?

Well, I felt a little warm, you know, kinda like when you're gettin' a fever. 'N I kept my eyes open the whole time. He had his open, too. I mean, it weren't nuthin' like Daddy kissin' me goodnight. It was how he sometimes kisses Momma before they go to bed, 'n they don't know we're watchin'. Uncle Henry even put *his tongue* in my mouth.

Why? What's he ever done to you?

I thought I was the only one he made sit on his lap. Does he bounce you up 'n down?

He doesn't? I guess it is our *special* game.

He calls it a horsy ride. You know, sometimes he has me straddle both legs while we play. He says I'm gettin' too big to ride only one leg. Doesn't he do other things that seem odd? You know, things that make you feel...

Nellie, shut up. You don't even know what we're talkin' 'bout, 'n I didn't ask you. Besides, you're goin' to wake Howard up.

I'm sorry, Dess, but she bothers me. Anyway, does he put his hand over your chest to see if your heart's beatin' fast enough? Then he tells me to draw in a deep breath 'n hold it while he puts his head on my chest 'n listens.

Yeah, that too. Has he ever squeezed your behind to see if it's firm enough?

Didcha know he makes me run in place while he watches?

Yeah, me too. You haven't said nuthin' to Daddy or Momma 'bout this, have you?

Me neither. I don't wanna worry them. Besides, he's always buyin' everyone stuff. Daddy seems to like that.

I guess. You're probably right—I'm jes' bein' silly. Dess, what'd Uncle Henry buy you this time?

Aw, come on. I'm not talkin' 'bout your lace collar. I saw him give you sumthin' in private. What was it?

Nellie, go to sleep. Why'd he give you *those*, Dess?

That's strange. You sure he wants to marry you in a few years?

'Cause he told me the same thing.

Good, then we won't have to fight over him. Do you know who I could never

stand to marry? I'd even become an old maid first.

His weird janitor. Mister Quinlan's always leerin' at me. Hey, I've got a great idea—let's never get married. I could become a scientist, 'n you could, too.

I know it's crazy. But we'd have fun. We'd do experiments all the time 'n maybe we'd find sumthin' to help Daddy stop drinkin'. Wouldn't that be great?

Yeah, you're right. One day, we'll both fall in love 'n marry 'n live borin' lives like Momma. I guess we'll each have at least four kids.

All right, good night.

Nellie, quit stealin' the covers.

Keeley Institute
Dwight, Illinois   *Thursday, March 10*

Emiline Cigraund:

Bonjour, you must be Monsieur Phelps. Welcome to ze Keeley Institute. I'm Emiline Cigraund, Doctor Keeley's assistanté. You look very tired. Let us sit down on ze couch and we will finish ze paperwork so you can lie down before dinner.

Comfor-ta-bal?

Zer is nussing to be nerrvous about. We are 'ere to 'elp you, Monsieur Phelps, with your *little* drinking probl`eme. Now, let me ask you zees questions and zen you will be able to relax more. First, I need your full name.

Good, and 'ow old are you?

No, you cannot be. You look so young for your age. Now, let us see, do you 'ave any family—a wife, little ones...?

You poor man. You 'ave tried to fight zis battle wizzout any—how you say—support? I know zis is difficult, but now you will find many people to 'elp you.

Ouí, including me. Now, ah...we can finish zees forms in ze morning. Come, I will show you where you will sleep. Dinner will be served at six. It is ze same every evening.

Usually, no, but since it is your first night here, I will make an exception. I shall meet you in front of ze dining 'all at a quarter of six.

Keeley Institute
Dwight, Illinois   *Friday, March 11, 9:00 a.m.*

Ben Pietzel (*alias* Robert E. Phelps):

I'm tellin' ya, Doc, it's not like that at all. Look at my hands—they're as steady as a rock. Physically, I'm fine. It's just that I can't control myself after I've had

a few drinks. If I could just stop at two or three beers...but I can't. Before I know it, I'm chasing the beers down with whiskey—sometimes right out of the bottle itself.

The next morning is when it's worse. That's when I don't feel like getting out of bed. But it's not like I'm reaching for a drink then either. In the mornings, the last thing I want is a drink. I just want to sleep.

Really, I never even think of having a beer during the day. Strange, isn't it? But as soon as that sun starts going down, then I start thinking 'bout hittin' that bottle.

I don't know. The first few just taste so good, and I love that initial feeling. But then it's like I have to keep on drinkin' to keep up with that feeling, and before long, the wife and I are fightin', the kids are cryin', and I go stormin' out of the house looking for a bar.

Oh, it's not that way every night. More like two to three nights a week. Some nights I'm able to control it better than others and stop with just the beer. If I stick to beer, I can usually stay away from the fightin'.

I honestly don't know why. Some nights I can, some nights I can't. But why is it that I never drink during the day? Why is it I don't even think about alcohol during the day?

That's why I'm here, Doc. I'm going to give it my all.

Ideally, I would like to be able to have a few drinks and stop. Is that possible?

Well, let's get started.

Keeley Institute   *Friday, March 11, 6:45 p.m.*
Dwight, Illinois

Emiline Cigraund:

A stroll was a wonderful idea, Monsieur Phelps. You will love ze gardens.

Ouí, all ze flowers are very fragrant, but zees are my favorite smell. I wish I could bottle zis fragrance and sell it to ze world.

Monsieur Phelps, you should not say such things, but I thank you anyway.

Either one—all paths lead to ze gazebo. Doctor Keeley wanted zees gardens to be like a little slice of 'eaven.

Ouí, especially when ze company is as nice as you. 'Ow was your first session?

See, I told you zer was nothing to worry about. You just did not believe me. Come, let us 'urry so we can sit and watch ze lighting of ze torches.

It is fascinating. Zey send several young boys out one at a time and each one 'as to wait until ze torch before 'im is shining brightly before 'e can light 'is own. 'Ere—we can see everything from zis cushion. What treatment 'as ze doctor decided on?

Oh? I am sure 'e will let you know tomorrow.

About three years. 'E 'ired me after I 'elped him one day when his regular assistanté did not show. He is a *wonderful* man—very smart— charming. I love working for him.

No, no, nothing goes on between me and ze doctor. I just enjoy my work and I will always be indebted to him.

Because he cured my papa.

As long as I can remember. At least until three years ago, but I don't like to talk about it. I...oh look, zey are starting ze light procession.

Ouí, it is very beautiful.

Keeley Institute, the Gazebo   *Saturday, March 19*
Dwight, Illinois

Emiline Cigraund:

Would you like a breast?

No? You 'ave never tasted one so plump?

'Ow sad. But I forget, you 'ad no woman in your life for so long.

Ouí, you can 'ave anything you want. Zis is our celebration of your first week of sobriety.

I am glad you like my surprize, Monsieur Phelps...I mean, Rob`ere.

My grandmama taught me 'ow to cook when I was a small child. She was afraid that Papa would not be able to care for me properly.

I enjoy it very much. Only Doctor Keeley keeps me too buzy to do it often.

You think so?

I never really thought about it, but I doubt I shall ever marry.

Look at the men I meet—each 'as a drinking problem like my papa.

Perhaps. It is a sad story—are you sure you want to 'ear it?

Papa was a good man until he drank. With each sip he took, he began to—'ow you say—withdraw into himself. After ze first bottle, he would slap me and my mama around for ze slightest wrong doing.

Oh, but, Rob`ere, I love him. I chose to live 'ere with him instead of with my grandmama in Montreal after Mama passed away. Sometimes I regretted that decision.

Wizzout her to protect me, he beat me constantly. Finally, after our doctor 'ospitalized me, he ordered Papa to get 'elp. Now, do you understand why I could never allow myself to fall in love with a drunkard?

Shhhh, our picnic is too nice to ruin with such talk. 'ere—let me wipe off zat juice. Zat is better. Now, for ze piece de resistance.

Keeley Institute, Dwight, Illinois   Monday, March 21, 1892

Henry,

Received your missive earlier today. I'll do everything I can to get that photo before I leave here. I'm telling you, this Emiline Cigraund is the most lovely creature God has ever sent down to this green earth. I am totally smitten by her, but I'm afraid she has no romantic inclination towards drunks like me.

Besides her beauty, she is just so kind and graceful. When she walks into a room, it's as if time stops. Her elegance and style overwhelms this place. You would be doing her a huge service to get her out of this hell hole. It disgusts me the way some of these sots in here leer at her when she passes by. But she doesn't seem to notice how they undress all six feet of her. Sometimes I have to stop staring at her eyes so as not be like them.

I tell you, Henry, as beautiful as Julia was, this girl is twice the woman Julia could ever hope to be. Whereas Julia was a bit tawdry (sorry— your words, not mine), this girl reeks of class. Whereas Julia had slight facial flaws, this angel has none. Not a single blemish to mar this truly wondrous creature. But enough of this pining on my part. Suffice to say you will see all this yourself some day.

As for me, I have now been here over one week, and I think they'll be letting me out this weekend. This place was made for a man like me. I haven't felt this good in years. I really think I've got this drinking problem licked. And the best part of getting Emily (I'm the only one around here who gets away with calling her that) to the Castle, if you can, is that she'll be around to keep me on the straight and narrow. I don't think I could even look at a bottle with her around. I can see the hurt in her blue eyes when she has talked to me about how alcohol ruined her father; about the times her father beat her and her mother when he was on a drunken spree. I suspect her father did even worse things to her, but she has never been able to get past telling me of the beatings before those magical eyes give way to an ocean of tears.

Well, I'll be seeing "Nurse Nightingale" in fifteen minutes, so I had better close. I'll let you know later this week when I'm getting out of here for sure. When I do, I'll be staying an extra day or two to case out the town. Perhaps you can come down here yourself to pick me up. That way, we could not only check out Dwight, but I could also introduce you to Emily. Think about it.

Ben

Keeley Institute, The Gazebo
Dwight, Illinois

Emiline Cigraund:

Oh, Rob`ere, you do not know 'ow much I am going to miss our nightly strolls now zat Doctor Keeley 'as released you. Do you feel ready to go?

I am so proud of you. Not many men could do what you 'ave in two weeks. Just do not forget about me and zis place.

I am going to 'old you to zat promise. 'Ere, I want you to 'ave zis picture of me. I 'ad it taken when I went into town yesterday.

Thank you. Rob`ere, will you write and let me know 'ow you are doing?

What do you mean you want me to work for *you*?

But I 'ave worked so long for Doctor Keeley, and he would be lost wizzout me.

What if we did not get along? Your partner could already 'ave someone else for ze position. I would be all alone in such a large city with nothing and no one to support me. Besides, I am visiting my grandmama for at least a month zis summer.

Rob`ere, I cannot decide right now. Now, be quiet and let us enjoy our last night together wizzout any worries about ze future.

Train Depot
Chicago, Illinois

Emiline Cigraund:

Rob`ere, 'ow I 'ave missed you. You are looking wonderful. Ouí?

And your drinking?

I knew you could do it. You are ze only man I ever met zat I thought would beat ze cruel addiction of liquor.

Monsieur 'olmes, 'ow very nice it is to finally meet you. Rob`ere mentioned you briefly in 'is letters. I am glad to be working closely with ze two of you, especially since you were so considerate in giving me ze month of June off.

Those two bags over zer. Rob`ere, were you able to locate a place for me to live?

Perfect. I am sure I will love living in your Castle, but first I want to eat. Monsieur 'olmes, you will not mind taking my bags with you so I can steal Rob`ere for a few 'ours. Ouí?

Hallway, Third Floor   *Saturday, April 30*
The Castle

Emiline Cigraund:

Monsieur 'olmes, 'ave you seen my pussy?

No? Zen she is 'iding again in one of ze rooms. Would you 'elp me look for 'er?

Rob`ere is so lucky to 'ave you as a partner. Do you 'ave a light? It is dark down zis 'allway.

Monsieur 'olmes, what are you doing?

She is not 'iding zer! I would know.

Monsieur 'olmes, I tell you stop. Look, zer is Rob`ere.

I am very glad to see you. Monsieur 'olmes is leaving to meet with a client, Oui?

Good. Now, Rob`ere, will you 'elp look for my pussy?

Train Depot   *Monday, May 9*
Englewood, Illinois

Ben Pietzel (*alias* Robert Phelps):

Phew, that was a close call. I thought for sure I'd miss the train.

Well, thanks again for seeing me off, Emmy.

The seventeenth. Maybe we can have dinner together?

Until, mon cherí.

Emiline Cigraund's Room   *Tuesday, May 17*
The Castle

Emiline Cigraund:

Rob`ere, you are 'ome? Let me look at you. Do you want sumzing to eat?

I ate earlier with Monsieur 'olmes, but I can make you anything you desire.

Oui, 'e takes me to dinner almost every night.

Perhaps 'e is, but I am more interested in someone else. It would be better for everyone if 'e concentrated 'is feelings elsewhere. Now, sit 'ere with me and tell me 'ow successful your trip was.

Zat is most wonderful. Monsieur 'olmes will be thrilled to 'ave zat new contract. You are such a brilliant man, Rob`ere. Even if you spoil my surprise.

I cook you a wonderful meal tomorrow night, and I would wear my new dress.

Very pretty, but since you've already eaten...

You *rrreally* want to see it zat bad?

Oui, oui, I will run and change, but keep talking—I miss our talks.

What?

Rob`ere, I cannot 'ear you. You need to come closer.

Zat is better. So, what shall we do tonight?

The Pietzels' Kitchen   *Wednesday, May 18*
Chicago, Illinois

Alice Pietzel:

Daddy! I'm so happy to see you. You were gone a long time.

Well, it seemed like it. Momma's been wonderin' when you'd come home. Oh, Daddy, I've missed you so. Maybe you can do somethin' with Howard.

He's been such a pest the past coup'la weeks. Last Saturday he poured ink on Nellie's hair. She was so funny-looking. Dessie 'n I called her the blue ghost. She even went to school that way. Everyone laughed at her 'n it took Momma almost three whole days to get Nellie's hair color back. I'll tell you a little secret, she even had to use some of that color that comes from a small bottle 'n stinks like a wet dog. Oh, Daddy, that reminds me, can we get a puppy? I promise to take care of it. *Pleeease...*

Why not? I saw some in an alley near the Castle.

But we could get the money somehow. Couldn't you ask Uncle Henry for more money? I know he gave Momma some the other day when we went to the drug-store.

We had to get the fake hair color. Uncle Henry even let her have an old bottle at a discount.

He's come by a coup'la times 'n Momma's sent Dessie 'n me to the drugstore whenever we needed somethin'. So, where were you?

Really? Why can't we move into the Castle?

Yeah, I wouldn't wanna be 'round Mister Quinlan every day. I don't like him.

Hey, Daddy, guess what? I received a high mark on my history lesson, 'n in science I mixed two kinds of chemicals together, 'n it formed this weird gas.

Well, my spelling has been down a little, but Dessie's been helpin' me in the evening. My reading marks were a little poor on the last test. Hey, Daddy, why don't *you* help me! Wait right here 'n I'll go get my speller.

Out of my way, Howard, I need to get my book.

First Floor Office of Holmes   *Wednesday, June 8*
The Castle

Emiline Cigraund:

I am sorry, Mademoiselle Dessie, but I cannot 'elp you. No one works 'ere by zat name.

He is very busy. Perhaps you should go 'ome and wait for your father zer.

Maybe if you describe 'im I could 'elp you better.

Oh, Monsieur 'olmes, I am glad you finish your meeting. Zees two young girls...

You know zem?

I keep telling zem no Ben Pietzel works for you, but zey insist zer father is your partner.

I thought Rob`ere was your partner?

Zen I will wait until dinner when you can tell me who all your partners are.

Train Depot   *Monday, June 13*
Englewood, Illinois

Emiline Cigraund:

Rob`ere, I will miss you. Are you sure you will not come with me? Grandmama would love to meet you.

No, no, I understand. Are you sure Monsieur 'olmes 'll keep my position?

Perhaps when I get back, we can arrange a few business trips together. You need someone to 'elp you when you are traveling and...zat's ze final call, I must be going. Do you promise you will write?

And no drinking?

Oui, one *little* kiss so you will crave its taste instead of ze whiskey.

Mon Cheri,   *Sunday, August 21, 1892*

Have I ever told you how much I hate Minneapolis? I hate it even more now that it means being apart from you. I still treasure the last night we spent together under the moonless sky. I swear, like you, I have never seen stars so bright.

As I look out my hotel window tonight, I can see the one we named Emmy. I trust you can see it, too, as I write.

I hate Holmes for not allowing you to come on this trip. But I promise, the next one I take, you will be at my side. My affections for you grow daily.

Well, mon cheri, I must turn in early as my big deal is tomorrow. In fact, I will be meeting with a relative of Holmes' wife. It involves a land deal worth quite a bit of money.

See you September 1. In the meantime, write me here.

> *Amour,*
> *Robere*

P.S. Still sober after all these months, thanks to you, my Nurse Nightingale, my Angel.

My dearest Carrie,   *Sunday, August 21, 1892*

Trudging along and getting it done in Minnie. Hopefully I will be able to get out of here like I initially hoped for by early to mid-September. These deals sometimes just seem to take forever.

Trust all is well with you and the children. I sure do miss them.

Please be kind and sociable to Holmes. He does mean well, and he certainly has been kind to the children. He really does enjoy the Uncle roll.

Going to sign off for now as I haven't eaten all day. Kevin's Bar and Grille is just around the corner, and they serve the best fish fries in town. I promise to keep the drafts to a minimum.

> *Love and kisses to you and the kids,*
> *Ben*

Train Depot   *Tuesday, August 30*
Englewood, Illinois

Emiline Cigraund:

Bonjour, Monsieur 'olmes, I am so 'appy to be back. Where's Rob'ere?

Bah, shame on you. I know Rob'ere is not drinking again. His letters were too full of tenderness. Why are you 'ere instead of 'im?

Oh, at least now you're being truthful with me.

I only brought this smaller one. Ze rest is being shipped. So, I am ready whenever you are.

Ouí, Grandmama is doing much better. I want to say 'ow thankful I am you allowed me to stay longer than ze month intended. She really needed my 'elp. Monsieur 'olmes, where are we going? This is not ze way to ze Castle.

What? Where am I going to stay?

No, no, I realize you 'ad to let my room, but do I even still 'ave a job?

Ouí, it's very confusing. I wish Rob'ere was 'ere. Is this new place very reputable?

What? But we're *not* married.

Oh, I guess I understand if you are sure zat it is ze only way to get a room.

No, I'm going to stay in tonight and rest.

Second Floor Office of Holmes   *Monday, October 31*
The Castle

Emiline Cigraund:

Monsieur 'olmes, I was going over ze inventory list today and we are missing several items.

Zey are very big items. I've asked Rob`ere about zem, but he doesn't remember.

Two desks and three small safes.

Zen where did money go?

No, I checked ze account and zer 'as been no new transactions in over four months.

What other set of books are you talking about?

Of course I will not tell anyone. Rob`ere told me about some of your...how you say...not-quite-so legal practices.

No, no, 'e was not betraying you. 'E was only answering my questions.

Before I visited my grandmama.

I'm only 'elping you more when I know everything. You wish me to take over ze second set of books?

Ouí, you can trust me.

Jenny Iron's Lodging House, Room 8 *Monday, November 28*
Chicago, Illinois

Emiline Cigraund:

Rob`ere, I'm going to 'ave to leave you.

No, I don't want to, but Grandmama is worse. She needs me.

Ouí, and I need you, too. But I must go. Zer is no one else to care for her.

Do not tease me.

Ouí, ouí. Oh, my darling, I never thought you would give up everything you 'ave 'ere and come with me.

Why can't I tell anyone? I want us to spend Christmas with Grandmama. She will adore you.

I know Monsieur 'olmes is infatuated with me, but don't you think 'e will be 'appy for us?

Very well, I will keep our secret from everyone. Rob`ere, you 'ave made me so incredibly 'appy. I will love you to ze day I die.

Holmes' Office, Second Floor *Monday, December 5, 11:45 p.m.*
The Castle

Emiline Cigraund:

Monsieur 'olmes, I thought no one was 'ere.

No, no. I was just going to leave this on your desk for tomorrow, but it can wait.

Very well, it's my resignation. I am leaving in three days to go back 'ome. Grandmama has become worse and I need to be with 'er.

No, I don't believe I'll ever come back.

Rob`ere is going with me. We are to be married.

Of course, I am going to. I know this is a shock for you, Monsieur 'olmes, but Rob`ere and I love each other. 'E...

I tell you zer is nothing zat will stop me from marrying 'im—not even a proposal from you.

What? 'E can't be married!

You're lying to me, I know you are.

No, no, I don't believe you . 'E can't be Benjamin Pietzel.

Where is Rob'ere? I want to see him *now*!

The Castle   *December 6, 1892*

Dr. Frank Noland
Norristown Insane Asylum
Norristown, Pennsylvania

Dear Frank:

I think the most beautiful sound on earth is that of someone faced with the unexpected end of her life, when she must make a primal, uncivilized scream. I like the circularity of the event, beginning and ending human life on the same note. The event is made even more delightful when one is the cause of the scream—when one plots things out in a careful manner, like god, so that he is fully present at the time of his victim's final, desperate act.

A woman died tonight, bless her soul, entrapped in a glass tomb. All in all, she was everything one wants from a French beauty. Her final screams excited me so much that after she died I prayed with her three or four times in different positions. Although she resisted my manipulation of her stiff body, she never resisted my Act of Communion, even in her cool mouth. And though she didn't know it, she gave me everything in her death that she found so sinful and repulsive during her short time on earth. I enjoyed her the more for once having such Puritanical views of love. Strange, isn't it?

> *Rest in peace,*
> *Holmes*

1220 Pulaski Street   *Friday, December 9*
Chicago, Illinois

Alice Pietzel:

Here's another piece of wood, Dess. Do you think that's enough?

Okay, I'll keep choppin'.

No, nuthin's wrong. I...I just overheard some strange things yesterday. Daddy and Uncle Henry.

Well, it was about that pretty secretary of Uncle Henry's. You remember, the real tall one that didn't know our Daddy worked there.

Yeah, her. Uncle Henry was telling Daddy that she had left unexpectedly. He didn't know where she had gone, only that she had put her resignation on his desk when he wasn't there.

But the weird thing was that Daddy was furious. He even grabbed Uncle Henry and pushed him 'gainst the wall.

He didn't hit him. Uncle Henry started whisperin' sumthin' and I fell through the doorway, tryin' to hear them. Daddy set him down, grabbed my arm 'd we came straight home. On the way he told me not to say anything about this to Momma. It just seems strange that Daddy would be so upset when he didn't even know the woman. We'd better hurry—I hear Momma callin'.

Dear Diary,

I must say, Harry certainly has made up for not spending last Christmas at home. I still think he spent it with one of his floozies, but I think he finally broke things off with that one over the past few weeks. For the first time in over a year, I think I finally have Harry all to myself. At least he's certainly acting that way.

Let me start with Christmas Eve. After spending the day shopping with Lucy and stopping for a bite at the Loop, we came back home for some hot cocoa before putting Lucy to bed. Harry was so wonderful with her, reading a story about St. Nick and promising all kinds of wonderful things in her stocking if she got to sleep.

That evening, Harry and I had some eggnog, and then we sat down to exchange gifts. I gave Harry an exquisite gold watch and chain with his initials, HHH, inscribed on the inside. We laughed when I told him with initials like those, he should be in politics.

And then, Diary, it was his turn to give to me. At first I was a little put off after finding only a tiny red lace nightie, with stockings and a garter, in that package. But after Harry assured me there was something else for me to wear that night if I put his first gift on, I went ahead and changed while he opened a bottle of 1872 Dom Perignon.

I must say, I looked very sexy when I caught my reflection in the bathroom mirror. When I came back into the living room and saw Harry's eyes on me, I felt like I used to feel before having Lucy.

When I came back into the room, Harry said: To Christmas '92, my darling, you've never looked lovelier—cheers! And then Harry slipped another package into my hand and said: Go ahead, open it now.

Diary, I still can't believe what was inside that box—the most beautiful diamond necklace I have ever laid eyes on. Harry says he got it

at Cartier's when he was in New York last August. He won't tell me what he paid for it, but I'll bet it was close to $50,000.

Well, anyway, as you can imagine, with that gift I was Harry's for the night. He was so sensuous. He gently lifted the necklace out of the box and let it dangle in the candle and fireplace flames, letting its brilliance and colors light up the room. Then he slowly clasped the jewels around my neck.

He told me to take a look in the mirror, and suddenly I was in one of his trances again, just like old times. Looking down, I couldn't get over the colors it reflected, especially in a room lit only by candles and a fireplace.

When I looked back in the mirror, Harry was behind me, whispering in my ear to keep looking in the mirror while he untied my teddy in the front, letting it slip to the floor.

My eyes were riveted on Harry, on his knees, unhooking my garter and slowly removing my stockings. When his tongue started performing its magic, I became lost. I was incredibly moist when he bent me forward and finally entered me from behind.

Then Harry lifted me up and carried me over in front of the fireplace, where he proceeded to lick champagne off my body. The sensations of those bubbles and his tongue brought me to another orgasm in no time, and it wasn't long before I was returning the favor. By the time we finished that bottle, we were completely spent.

In fact, Diary, we fell asleep right there on the rug in front of the fire, and it was little Lucy at daybreak waking us up. I was so embarrassed for her to see us like that, naked and all. Harry quickly told her to go check her stocking, and while she did, we put on our robes. By the time she started opening her gifts, she seemed to have forgotten all about us. And when she finally saw the rocking horse in the corner under the tree, her eyes grew as big as saucers. She's been playing on it ever since.

Harry insists she doesn't remember seeing us like that anymore. For my part, I tried to act like it was no big deal. The last thing I want is for him to be spending less time around here and giving him an excuse to chase after some other skirt. But I sure do hope he's right about Lucy not remembering. I must be more careful, now that she's four.

Myrta
12/26/92

1893

CHICAGO TRIBUNE MONDAY, FEBRUARY 6,1893

HELP WANTED

FEMALES

WANTED-A PROTESTANT North German girl as chambermaid and seamstress; only a capable and well recommended person need apply; address stating references send to Box 7. MacClellan.

WANTED-CHAMBERMAID and Laundress in a small family spending Summer in country; best references required. Apply between 11 and 1 o'clock, at 28 East 135th-st

WANTED-COMPETENT NURSE to take charge of feeble-minded child; wages, $9 per month; references required. Address Lock Box 222, Englewood, Illinois.

WANTED-TYPEWRITER AND Stenographer. Apply only in person to Harry Gordon 63rd & Wallace, Englewood, Illinois.

First Floor Office of Holmes
The Castle

Tuesday, February 7

Minnie Williams:

Mister Gordon? Hello, I'm Minnie Williams. The agency sent me...about the secretarial position?

Thank you. It's nice to meet you, too.

Yes, it's still blustery and very cold out there, but I'm used to this kind of weather. I've lived in New York and Boston for several years now. Chicago is definitely the windy city, though.

Well, I graduated from the Boston Conservatory of Music more than four years ago with degrees in music and elocution. Since then I've lived in New York and have spent a good deal of time traveling around the States.

No, I'm not married. Sometimes I travel alone and at other times I travel with

a couple of friends. I'm not quite sure what I want to do with my life and I'm still searching—even today.

I know it must seem strange for a single woman to be able to do nothing but travel. But money is not a problem, I assure you.

Because my parents left me a trust fund. They had invested a lot of money in the railroad. They died when my sister, Annie, and I were very young, and we were lucky enough to be raised by caring relatives. I lived with my Uncle Herbert in Dallas and Annie with Uncle Charles, who's a minister in Mississippi.

Uncle Herbert wanted to make sure I'd never have to want for anything, so he left me a nice piece of property in Fort Worth.

Oh, it's worth at least forty thousand.

No, I don't really *need* this job, but I would like to have it.

Really? Just like that? But...you didn't even ask about my qualifications or my experience. Don't you need to know if I can handle this position?

Well...I'm sure I can too, but...

Very well then, tomorrow it is. I'll be here at eight o'clock sharp. Thank you again, Mister Gordon.

Tonight? No, I don't have any plans for dinner.

Why, what a lovely gesture. I'd love to go to dinner with you, Mister Gordon.

Chicago, Illinois   *February 14, 1893, 3:00 p.m*
The Crystal Palace Hotel, Room 223

Dearest Annie,

Sorry I wasn't able to write as soon as I arrived here in Chicago, but by the time I got settled in a hotel, found an employment agency, and interviewed for several jobs, one thing led to another and I just found myself occupied every day until this very moment.

Anyway, now that I can relax long enough to write, I must tell you my exciting news! I have a wonderful job working as a private secretary to the wealthiest, handsomest, most intelligent gentleman I have ever known in all my twenty-four years; and the most startling news is I think I'm in love with him. I know this sounds impossible, but I knew from the moment he looked at me that this man was going to make a big change in my life. There's just something about him that makes me

feel like a young school girl going through her first crush—I can't explain it. Whatever it is, I'm absolutely hooked. Of course, he doesn't know any of this yet. I've only been working for him a week.

My prince, Harry Gordon, lives in a Castle (this is his home, which is a three-story monstrosity of a building with several shops on the ground floor). He's medium height, about 5'8" or so, has chestnut brown hair, and hypnotic blue eyes that make me just want to melt. He has a bushy mustache that enhances his appearance to make him look even more the intellectual.

He's taken me to dinner every night since I began working for him and has behaved like a perfect gentleman. He is very kind and considerate, and in this short time I've discovered we have many of the same interests. He's actually quite intelligent about music, art, and theater. Can you believe we're so compatible? What more could this girl want?

Tonight we're going to dine at a very expensive French restaurant, and I've got to get ready. I'm wearing a new blue silk dress with black fringe—very stylish. I bought it just after arriving here in Chicago. I know you'd like it. Will keep you posted about how things progress with my Mr. Harry Gordon because I'm hoping he is as serious about me as I think I am about him. Hugs and kisses, miss you, and as always....

Love, Minnie

The Versailles Cafe   *Tuesday, February 14, 7:30 p.m.*
Chicago, Illinois

Minnie Williams:

I *love* this restaurant, Harry. The atmosphere is so authentic I actually feel like I'm eating dinner in France. You couldn't have made a better choice for this evening.

Oh, you're absolutely right. The food is superb and good food is one of my real pleasures in life. However, as usual, I'm afraid I've eaten too much. You'd better stop me before I become addicted to these snails and want them every night.

More wine? Oh, I don't know...I've already had, let me think..how many glasses have I had?

That many? Oh well, what's one more? We're here to have a good time, right? Go ahead, pour me another.

Ohhh...that's good. Whew...is it warm in here, or just me?

Probably so.

Chicago? I'm beginning to love it. It's the most exciting place I've ever been. I can hardly wait to see the Fair.

By the way, Mr. Harry Gordon, have I told you how your eyes make me melt? This has been a wonderful Valentine's Day, you know...

Yes, I mean that...

Now how could you possibly make it any more wonderful than this? Oh... Harry, is that your hand on my leg...?

Harry Gordon, you devil, you.... What are you doing? Oh my God, I can't believe you're doing this right here under the table...someone will see us.

I am holding still...I'm paralyzed....Oohhh, oohhh, oh my God, I...can't breathe. Ooohh...if you don't stop...oohhh...soon...I'm going...to...oohhh slide...out of this chair...onto the...oohhh...floor....Oooohhh...oohhh....

Harry, that...was wonderful....

The Castle Drugstore *Friday, March 3*

Charlotte Wild:

Good mornin', Mistah Holmes. Mah name's Charlotte Wild an' Ah'm heah for the stenographer's job.

No, suh. Ah haven't been in Chicago for very long. Only came up 'bout two nights ago. Ah was recently attendin' the College for Young Ladies in South Car'lina.

Oh, we studied how to run a household, the right way to make mint juleps, an' other little things. Ah'd never planned on being a workin' girl, but Ah reckon Ah am now. So Ah figured Ah might as well jump in.

Actually, Ah do know how. Mah father always had me helpin' him when he did the farm books, Mistah Holmes.

You're a doctor? Why, that's wonderful. Ah 'magine you help a good many people.

Why, Ah came to Chicago because...Ah'm not sure whether to tell you or not.

Very well, you seem to be trustworthy. It's a rather long story, but you'll get the short version. Marc Cannen was courtin' me an' Kenny Hawkins—you see Kenny worked for mah daddy, he was a general hand and didn't really have much of a future. Well, he decided he wanted to court me, too. Not that Ah woulda evah taken him seriously.

Why, Kenny Hawkins, of course. He smelt like a dirty cow, an' Marc was such a gentleman, always 'maculately dressed...like you. Well, he was gettin' mighty jealous over Kenny. So, Marc told me one day that he was goin' to ask for mah hand in marriage. Well, Ah wasn't ready to marry yet. Ah'd jest started takin' those classes at the College for Young Ladies. So Ah told him he'd have to wait awhile.

Thank you, Doctor Holmes. That's awfully kind of ya to say. Ah was being a mite rough on Marc. Now, let's see where was Ah at?

That's right. Well, Marc kept on aftah me because he had seen me talkin' with Kenny occasionally. No more than what Ah had to, understand?

Marc didn't. So one day he convinces me to go up to the hayloft with him so we could talk privately.

Yes, suh. Ah know haylofts can be awfully dangerous places, especially since they have spiders, and I can't stand spiders. I've been scared to death of 'em all my life.

True, I shouldn't have, but Marc always had a way with words that a girl never could think straight around him. So Ah followed him up there an' finally convinced him that he was being foolish to be jealous of Kenny. That's when mah daddy came in. He stormed the barn with Kenny trailin' behind him like a whipped dawg. Now mind ya, we wasn't doing anything wrong. We'd only been lyin' down in the hay, touchin'—Ah mean talkin' to each other. But, somehow, Daddy was convinced we was doin' sumthin' else. He wouldn't listen to us with Kenny standin' behind him pointin' out that Ah had straw sticking out of mah dress an' hair. Daddy proceeded to kick Marc off the farm, an' the whole time Kenny's standin' there, grinnin' like a Cheshire. Ah didn't realize at that time he'd made a bet with Daddy.

Oh, aftah a few days, Daddy calmed down. Marc hadn't even been by to see how Ah was doin'. Even though Ah was mad at him for gettin' me in trouble, he could have stopped by an' seen how Ah was makin' out.

Because some vicious rumors were gettin' spread 'round town so Daddy pulled me out of the College for Young Ladies an' said it was high time for me to marry. Ah jest knew he meant Marc, but then he tells me Ah'm s'posed to marry Kenny—that was the bet.

Well, Ah haven't finished. Marc snuck up into mah room that night an' said he still loved me an' had tried to see me, but Daddy wouldn't let him. He convinced me it'd be a good idea to disappear awhile an' when Ah go back we can get married. That's when he mentioned the World's Fair in Chicago, an' Ah thought to myself, now that's a place with a lot of possibilities, an' Ah might find mah destiny there.

Why, in a small hotel near the District.

That bad? What other place would be better?

Truly? But Ah don't think Ah can afford the rent, 'specially since you haven't told me yet whether Ah'll get the job or not.

Ah do? Oh, Doctor Holmes, Ah could jest kiss you.

Longhorn Ranch   *Saturday, March 4, 1893*
Midlothian, Texas

My Dearest Minnie,

How wonderful to hear from you and especially to hear your exciting news about a new job. I'm truly happy for you and glad to know you are doing so well. Everything is fine here—already getting quite hot and humid, but beautiful now that spring is here.

I am still enjoying teaching, although my students are a little restless this time of year, what with Easter coming soon and then summer holidays. Much as I enjoy them, I am already looking forward to other adventures some day—perhaps painting or music, or maybe even marriage and children, if I ever meet the right man.

How were you ever so fortunate to find such an exciting job? I knew you were capable of attracting a good employer, but finding one is the hard part. Chicago is such a big and busy place; it's a miracle you were able to get a job at all, much less so quickly and one you like so well. You must send me more details about your job and what kinds of things you do there.

I also must hear more about your new employer, Mr. Gordon. You certainly make him sound very special, indeed, and I am very curious to know how your dinner date went. Was it a wonderful evening? Was the restaurant nice? Was Mr. Gordon a gentleman? I don't want to meddle, Minnie, but do be careful and use a bit of caution where he is concerned. After all, you have only known him a few days and for all your education and experiences away from home, you are still my little sister and a bit innocent, and I worry about you. Don't go falling in love on me now and beating me to the altar—after all, I am the oldest, and the oldest is supposed to go first!

I'm teasing you, of course, but I do miss you greatly. After being raised so far apart, it was such a wonderful blessing spending time with you again and very difficult parting from you. I hope you will be able to come soon for a visit, unless your Mr. Gordon is an ogre and won't let you leave. In that case, I shall just have to come and get you.

I had a letter from Uncle Charles last week. He is such a dear and worries so about me. He asked about you, and I plan to write and tell him all your good news. We have been very fortunate to have been raised by two very caring and loving relatives, even though it kept us apart for so many years. Things could have been so much worse for us. I am so pleased Uncle Herbert left you the Ft. Worth property, which should be a good nest egg for you. Everything seems to be fine with your inheritance, and I am told it may be worth quite a bit of money one day,

although $40,000 now is no small sum. Do hold on to it as long as you can, though, since we never know what lies ahead for us.

Well, there isn't much excitement to write about here. No new charming boss to take me to dinner in a fancy French restaurant, but I will keep my eyes open for the opportunity. In the meantime, I hope everything continues to go well for you.

Oh, I almost forgot; I want to hear all about the World's Fair. The newspapers here are quite full of stories about the magnificent displays and wonderful shows. Wouldn't it be great fun if I could be there with you to see it in person? Are you very far away from it? The buildings must be fabulous from the descriptions in the papers.

Dearest Minnie, I must go now. It is very late and I must be up very early and off to school. Please take good care of yourself and write me again as soon as you can. I am very anxious to hear more about everything in Chicago. Tell your Mr. Gordon I said he is a very lucky man and a very smart one to have hired you.

> *Your loving sister,*
> *Annie*

Luigi's
Chicago, Illinois

Tuesday, March 7, 8:30 p.m.

Minnie Williams:

Thank you for a wonderful evening, Harry. Dinner was absolutely delicious. I like good Italian food, don't you?

Yes, I really do love to eat. Believe me, I could probably eat my way through Chicago and still never patronize every restaurant in this city. I only wish my sister were here to enjoy this with me.

Oh, she'd love Chicago. Who wouldn't thrive on the excitement in this city?

As a matter of fact, I have written her just recently.

Well, since you've asked, I wrote her about a very kind man who has kept me busy every night since I met him.

I told her he's the most considerate, generous man I've ever known and that, well, he treats me like a princess, and...uh, I'm very impressed with his manner.

Well, she, uh, she seems a little concerned about me.

Because everything is happening so fast. I mean, she's just concerned because of my inheritance.

You know, my property in Fort Worth. She trusts that I'm smart enough to see through a deceitful character, and we both know I don't have to worry about...

My property? Well, yes, it's safe. It's in my name.

Well, what could possibly happen to me?

Of course, if something did happen to me, it would go to Annie.

I've never really thought about it. Well, uh, of course, I'd like to double the value. Who wouldn't?

That's generous of you, Harry, but to handle the whole deal yourself? It sounds a little complicated.

I know you're a good businessman, but are you sure you could double my investment?

Ummmm...and then, what if your plan didn't work?

The *final* phase of the plan? Did I just hear you correctly?

Marry you?

1220 Wrightwood Avenue　　　　　　　　*Friday, March 10, 10:30 p.m.*
Englewood, Illinois

Minnie Williams:

Are we home already? Goodness, that was a fast ride. I feel like we floated home. Oh, dear, my head is really spinning.... I'm not so sure I can stand.

Yes, maybe you'd better help me. I guess I really did have a little too much wine, Harry, as if that weren't part of your plan. I still can't believe what you did. I think that older couple at the next table knew exactly what you were doing.

Because that old man looked over at us several times and then grinned at me when you finished. You are a brazen dare-devil, aren't you?

My key?

Yes, of course you can sit with me for a while, as long as you behave yourself. Is that even possible?

Harry, your shoulder is just perfect for resting my head. If only the room would stop spinning...Harry, Harry...Oh, my God...that feels so good. Your kisses are sooooo tender and sooooo gentle...you're melting me.... Ooohhh...God, I love having my ear nibbled. You're doing all the right things, Mister Gordon....

Yes, I want it...hurry, hurry. Give it to me, Harry...I want you, all of you...now. Hurry, I'm on fire. Ooooooh, oh my God. You feel so good. You're so cold. God, it feels like a big, hard icicle.

Marshall Field's Department Store, Hosiery   *Saturday, March 11*
Chicago, Illinois

H.H. Holmes (alias Henry Howard):

Oh, don't run away, my dear. I don't bite. Here, you dropped your pretty handkerchief.

You're welcome. Are you a regular shopper at Field's?

Franklin, Indiana? I have a close friend in Pennsylvania named Franklin. You
must allow me to help you shop during your stay in Chicago—I know where
all the best clothing is sold at bargain prices.

I know because I own several Chicago stores myself; but my real joy is in a new
copy machine I have a patent on.

Right, there's a fortune to be made if you have a product that's only slightly
ahead of its time.

Why thank you, Miss—?

So you're not married?

I'm glad to hear that.

No, I'm one of those bachelors married to my work. Someday, though.

Well, I like the soft silky feel of women's clothing. These stockings are a great
pleasure to touch. May I say they would look beautiful on your handsome legs?

Bold, yes, but honest, too, Miss Yoke. While I was picking up your handkerchief, I noticed the beautiful shape of your shoes. I bet you have wonderful
ankles.

You needn't be embarrassed. In medical school I specialized in feet.

Michigan.

No, I'm a general MD, mainly connected with the selling of drugs and other
medical products.

Well, the copy machine was something that just came along at the right
moment. If you would lift your skirts a few inches, I'll...

No, I'm not kidding, Miss Yoke. I know a great deal about women's shoes and
stockings. In fact, I have plans to develop both products.

Thank you, I'll only take a few seconds.

Ah, you do have nice ankles. Could you lift your skirts a few inches higher?

Very *nice*, Miss Yoke. Nice color, nice feel. Excellent choice, Miss Yoke. May I
take you out to lunch?

Back Alley
The Castle

Friday, March 17, 6:00 p.m.

Pat Quinlan:

Scad'ja, didn't I? Heh-heh-heh.

Top o' da even' to ya, Mizz Williams. And a very Happy Saint Patty's Day as well. Dats me namesake, y'know—good ol' Saint Patty. We even look alike, wha'd'ya tink?

A'course I'm drunk, <hic>. Have ya already forgotten what day a'tis? Why it's dat blessed saint's day, 'ol Saint Patty h'self, da man who was named for me, heh-heh-heh.

So tell me, lil' Minnie—can I call ya Minnie?

Well den, Skinny Minnie—<hic>—what's a nice lass like y'self doin' gettin' messed up in dese Castle 'fairs? I've been a-watchin' ya from afar, lassy, 'n I'm tellin' ya now for ya own good—git out while da gittin' is good.

Now, why don'tcha 'tach your arm ta ol' PattyQ and 'scort us ta O'Briens? Thassss <hic> where I can tell ya more, wit' out all dese shadows watchin' us.

Well den, Mizz Skinny Minnie, why don'tcha jes' 'tach your mout' ta ol' PattyQ's Dragon if ya gonna be dat way 'bout it. Git your fat ass back 'ere ya lil' bitch 'n lemme intraduce ya!

Dumb 'lil priss, <hic>. Me tinks she be dead 'fore da summer's out. Ah, wha' da hell, I can't saves da world—but I sure's hell can take a squirt. As long as ya out, ol' Dragon boy, do your ting.... Atta boy, spray ya gold'n fire, ahhhhhhh.

The Castle

Friday, March 17, 6:05 p.m.

Minnie Williams:

Harry, open the door. Oh, my God! You won't believe what just happened in the alley.

Yes, I'm out of breath. I...I ran up the steps...two at a time trying...to get away from that...that horrible little man. He was coming after me with...with...

That...that man...you know, uuhhh...Quinlan...Pat Quinlan.

I'll tell you what he did. He scared me to death, that's what he did. He came after me in the alleyway with his...his pants open. He came after me with that...that thing...he called it the PattyQ Dragon. He wanted me to...to, you know. Oh, it was awful.

No, I didn't touch it! How repulsive.

Yes, I know he's drunk. That man is so thoroughly pickled he can barely stand up. He warned me to get out of the castle while the getting's good, he said.

What in the world is he talking about?

Oh, I'm sure it's the liquor talking, but why would he warn me to get out of here in the first place? Why would such a thing be on his mind? I don't understand, do you?

Well, Harry, you don't have to fire him. I don't want the man to lose his job. He does have a family, and I wouldn't want to be responsible for their being thrown out on the street. I got away from him, and he's never said two words to me when he's sober. He just frightened me, that's all. I just don't want him near me again.

Well good, as long as he stays away from me when he's drunk. And you're right, he probably won't even remember what he did.

The Castle   *Tuesday, March 21, 8:00 a.m.*

Charlotte Wild:

Hi, Sandra. Come on in.

Ah'm tryin' to do sumthin' with this awful hair of mine. Howie says he likes it straight.

You know—Doctor Holmes.

Ah like to call him Howie an' aftah last night he told me that Ah can call him anythin' Ah want, includin' dahlin'. What if you pull it over like this?

Thanks, heah's the pins. Ah tell ya, Sandra, he's so good to me, lettin' me have this room at a discount. Oops, Ah wasn't supposed to tell anyone that.

Oh, you, too? Come over heah beside me and sit down. Ah'm fixin' to tell ya sumthin', but ya gotta promise to keep it a secret.

Ah slept with Howie last night.

It was *wonder*ful. Between his hands an' mouth, Ah don't think there's anywhere on mah body that hasn't been touched. Ah've never known anyone like him.

Ah had stayed late to finish typin' some dictation. You know how he's been spendin' lots of time eyein' me an' constantly askin' me into his office. Anyhow, Ah was all by myself in the little room next to his office when Ah saw a light shinin' underneath the doorway. So Ah knocked on his door.

You won't believe this, but Howie was sittin' behind his desk with two glasses of whiskey in front of him. He smiled at me when Ah peeked 'round the door an' invited me in for a drink.

Whiskey's not all that bad. My Uncle Phil makes a moonshine that would cause you to lose your voice. Anyhow, he motioned for me to come inside. It was amazin'. He told me he had come back to be alone with me. He wanted to talk

about our future together. Ah couldn't believe it—he had waited until no one else was around so he could...

He proposed!

Well, he placed his hand over mine. Ah could feel the power of his body surge through our fingertips. Oh, Sandra, he bent his head an' took mah pinkie into his mouth an' started suckin'.

To be honest, Ah wasn't sure what to do. That's when he looked into mah eyes. Ah knew right then that we were meant for each other. He kissed me so gentle like at first, but his kisses grew harder—jest look heah on mah neck at the bruises he left. Ah didn't have this many the time Ah met John behind the barn.

You're right—thank God for high collar dresses. Ah would die if anyone else saw these, even though Howie thinks they're beautiful. Anyway, Ah was lyin' naked on the desktop. Ah could taste whiskey on his lips an' then he was pourin' it all over me an' lickin' it off.

What was that?

Ah thought Ah heard sumthin'.

No, Ah don't see anyone. It could be *Pat*. He's always lurkin' 'round, fixin' to do sumthin'.

Ah know, Pat's so creepy. In fact, Ah was a little scared that he would come in on us, but Howie said not to worry. He had already taken care of Pat. The office was ours for the whole night. He wanted to celebrate our engagement. Sandra, Ah have to ask you...have you evah made love on a desk?

Then you know what it's like to have a hard desk beneath you an' a hard body on top. Ah know we must have ruined at least a dozen letters. Ah'm going in early today so Ah can retype 'em. Ah don't need for the other girls to get hold of 'em.

Dearest Annie,   *March 22, 1893, 9:00 a.m.*

Sorry I haven't answered your last letter. My job is going well. The work keeps me busy during the day and Harry keeps me busy at night. He has wined and dined me every night since I walked into his office and has occupied so much of my time that I haven't had time to catch my breath. Today he is taking care of some business across town; so I'm taking this opportunity to write.

I do have some wonderful news and don't quite know how to tell you except to tell you outright. Harry has asked me to marry him and I've accepted. Now, I know what you're thinking—that I've only known him for a short time; but Annie, he is the most exciting man I've ever known. He's so kind and considerate—he even gave me the afternoon

off yesterday because I was feeling a little tired. He's always surprising me with little presents. The other day he gave me a beautiful diamond brooch. Annie, the man worships me. He treats me like a goddess, so I know I've made a good decision. You'll understand what I mean once you meet him. Please be happy for me and try to understand my decision.

I hope your teaching is going well. I know eight-year-olds must wear on the nerves after a long day. Write me soon. I'm anxious to hear from you, and as always, hugs and kisses.

> *Love,*
> *Minnie*

Second Floor Office of Holmes   *Saturday, April 1*
The Castle

Charlotte Wild:

Here's the papers you wanted, Howie. Ah still don't understand why you bought more life insurance on me.

Yeah, you're right. Ah never thought about it that way. Oh, 'fore Ah forget, they delivered some of the items you requested for the weddin'. Ah told the guys you weren't in, but you said to leave 'em in one of the spare rooms.

No, Ah didn't sign for 'em.

Of course they did like Ah said. Everything's in the spare bedroom on this floor. Ah told 'em we would have the money to 'em tomorrow. So if you'll sign these papers, Ah can run by the bank in the mornin', then swing by Marshall's an' pay 'em.

Ah'm really gettin' excited now. Ah've been through everything they delivered an' it is all so pretty. Ah just wish Ah could invite my father to the weddin'.

Ah know. Well, Ah'm goin' to run on up to bed. Are you comin' soon?

Anything Ah can help with?

A new experiment? Ah thought you'd given up that part of your practice.

Sure. Howie, Ah didn't know you could get to your examining room from in here. Promise me no more secrets aftah tonight.

Good. Now what do you want me to do?

What?

Are you sure bein' tied to an examing table is a legitimate scientific experiment?

Ohhhhh, that kind of experiment. Why didn't you say so?

Howie, that tickles. What are you doin'?

No, Ah can't see or wouldn't be askin'.

Oh my God, what are you doing with that spider?

Get it off me!

Oh, my God, there's more. Please get 'em off me!

Noooooo! Howie, get 'em off. They're crawling inside me. Heeeeelp!

Oh my God, they're all over me...biting me! Quick, get 'em off my face.... Ack! Ah'm...ack...ack...gaggin'...ack.

Longhorn Ranch   *Saturday, April 8, 1893*
Midlothian, Texas

Dearest Minnie,

The news of your engagement has taken me quite by surprise—congratulations to you both! Minnie, dear, I hope you will be very happy and I wish only the best for you. When do I get to meet my new brother-to-be? I hope it will be soon, because I am anxious to see for myself that he is all you say and that this is the right thing for you.

The important thing is I want you to be absolutely sure that this is what you want. If I sound like a worried mother, it is only because I care about you. It's just that this is so sudden—why, you've known each other such a short time. You have been so determined and steady in pursuing your education and career, and then suddenly you want to throw it all away for a man you hardly know. I realize you are no longer a child, but in spite of your years and education, I worry that your Mr. Gordon may be taking advantage of you. Please don't be angry with me for saying this; it's just that I am so far away from you and I have only my imagination and your letters to go by. You are a lovely, smart young lady who also happens to have a nice inheritance. Please be careful.

Well, now that I've preached my sermon (Rev. Bristow would be proud of me—probably invite me up to the pulpit on Sunday!) I hope that you are still speaking to me and haven't thrown this letter in the trash.

Do you still like it, especially now that you're in love with the boss? Does that make it easier, or has it caused difficulties? Do you think you will continue to work after your marriage? I wonder what it would be like working for one's husband? I should think it might be very pleasant, working beside the man you love every day—unless he is an ogre. You probably wouldn't have to worry about getting fired, though. Nevertheless, I must confess to being a little jealous. I would gladly welcome the opportunity to answer all of these questions for myself, but

right now there is no one on the horizon. Perhaps I will come to Chicago and find a Harry of my own!

I am already dreading the hot, dry summer to come. I love Texas, but the summers can be very uncomfortable (you may consider this a piti-ful hint for an invitation to visit Chicago this summer). I may just show up at your front door one day and surprise you!

Well, I still have papers to grade and lessons to prepare, so I'll close for now. Take care of yourself and tell Mr. Harry Gordon he had better be good to you! Almost forgot—when is the wedding?

> *With all my love,*
> *Annie*

1003 Elm Street
Franklin, Indiana

Tuesday, April 11, 5:00 p.m.

Georgianna Yoke:

Yes, Mother, I'm coming.

Oh, Doctor Howard, how nice to see you, but why are you here?

I didn't know you had business dealings in Franklin. Excuse me, I'm forgetting my manners. Mother, this is Doctor Howard—we met about a month ago. Doctor Howard, this is my mother, Mrs. Yoke.

I was about to do that, Mother. Doctor Howard, won't you come inside?

I'm doing fine. How long do you plan on staying?

What a coincidence. That's how long I'll be visiting my parents. Perhaps, we'll be able to ride back on the train together. I know it'll make the trip go quicker.

I haven't heard of any. Are you thinking of buying a business here?

Randall's?

I'm sure it's a good investment since they are the only general store in town. But what about your interests in Chicago?

I don't know if I would trust just anyone with the running of your Castle busi-nesses. If they worked for me, I'd want to know everything that was happening. Aren't you afraid that someone will try to cheat you if you're gone all the time?

Doctor How...

Very well, Henry, I didn't know you traveled every month. What other cities do you have businesses in?

With that many you must be very well off. Who looks after everything in Chicago while you're gone?

I don't believe I've ever met him. Henry, you don't mind if I move a little closer, do you? I feel as though I'm about to fall off the end of this couch. Tell me, how long ago did you buy the Castle?

I didn't realize you were involved in the construction of such a magnificent building. I would really love to see the inside sometime.

You mean it? That's so kind of you, but you must promise to be in town so you can give me a tour of the place. Were you always so wealthy?

How nice for you—I wish I had a rich uncle. What did he do for a living?

How proud he must have been when you became a doctor. Do you have a busy practice?

I'm sorry. I didn't mean to be so inquisitive. I just wanted to get to know you. We've had so few chances to talk. Whenever you've come into the shop, I've had to deal with other customers. And it's rare that you get to come and see me at work.

No, I don't have to work. I only do it because I'm afraid I'll get bored. When I turn twenty-five, I'll come into an inheritance. My grandmother was worried I wouldn't be able to handle all the money sensibly before then.

It's a rather large amount. Nothing like you make I'm sure, but it'll be enough for me to live comfortably, even if I never marry.

I haven't thought of investing it, but maybe you have a good idea. I'll think about your suggestion. Who knows, being business partners might prove interesting.

Why, thank you, Mother. Would you like to sit with us for a few minutes?

Here you go, Henry. Mother makes this tea from herbs she has grown. Oh, will you stay for dinner?

Great. How about a tour of the house while we're waiting. Please excuse us, Mother. As you already know, this is our parlor. I can remember the first time I was ever allowed in here—my seventh birthday. Actually, if you looked under that chair, you can see the stain where I bumped into Father and he spilled his wine.

Across here—here, take my hand—this is the dining room.

Thanks. I wallpapered it myself. Now, this staircase leads to the bedrooms. This is my room. I had it done in white when I turned fifteen.

The lace curtains? Yes, I made those.

Henry, why are you closing the door?

No, I don't think this is the right time for a kiss.

Now...coming, Mother! I guess we'd better leave. Don't worry, there'll be plenty of chances for that later.

Perhaps when you give me a tour of your home and businesses.

You're leaving? But I thought you were staying for dinner?

I understand. I'll give your apologies to Mother.

1003 Elm Street   *Tuesday, April 11, 7:00 p.m.*
Franklin, Indiana

Georgianna Yoke:

Well, what did you think of him, Mother?

He's quite charming. And he's *verrrry* rich. You should see his Castle. It takes up an entire city block.

No, we met at Field's. Here, hand me that cloth. I believe my bread is almost done. You know, at first I thought he was an idiot, the way he kept staring at my feet; but later I discovered what an important man he is.

Don't worry. He thinks my grandmother left me a large inheritance.

He'll never find out that I lied. Here, taste this.

I think it still needs more cinnamon. Mother, I'm so happy he came to Franklin to see me.

I know so. I told him last week I was coming home for a visit.

Quit worrying. I'll go slowly with him. This is one man I'm not letting get away.

THE CHICAGO TIMES-HERALD
MONDAY, MAY 1, 1893

ROOMS FOR RENT

Tourists, enjoy all the marvels of the fair and then relax in the nearby WORLD'S FAIR HOTEL, located on the corner of 63rd Avenue and Wallace Street. Comfortable rooms can be had by the day, the week, or the month. Rates are reasonable; the pleasures unlimited. Ask for Dr. H. H. Holmes, a master provider of heavenly sleep.

1220 Wrightwood Avenue   *Friday, May 5*
Englewood, Illinois

H.H. Holmes (*alias* Harry Gordon):

What we need is a good war, Minnie.

To get us out of this damn depression. Don't you know anything about how the world spins?

Hey, don't overcook those eggs! Are the biscuits done?

A war fills up factories with people who then have money to put in my pocket.

The coffee's good, yeah. By the way, do you have any money I can get my hands on?

I can't do anything with that damn property in Fort Worth. My lawyer says we need your sister's signature on the legal papers.

What I'm sayin' is you need to get her signature—but don't promise her a penny. The forty thousand belongs to us.

Okay, to you then. Look, write to her and invite her to come see the Fair before it's gone forever. Go ahead, do it now before I get mad and send you packin'.

Longhorn Ranch   *Thursday, May 11, 1893*
Midlothian, Texas

Dearest Minnie,

Your letter was the most thrilling one I have ever read. I am so excited at the prospect of visiting you in Chicago, I can scarcely concentrate on my students. Of course I will come—just as soon as school is out for the summer.

I suppose I shall have to be grateful to your Harry for this wonderful treat. I confess, I am looking forward to meeting him and satisfying myself that you are truly happy and he is all you paint him to be. I shall certainly be disappointed if he isn't and may have to tell him so if I think he is mistreating my Minnie! He overwhelmed you so quickly that I think he must be quite the ladykiller.

I simply cannot wait to see the Exposition. I can't believe you live close enough to walk to all that excitement. Can you hear the sounds and sense the thrill of it from where you live? There is so little going on here that I have trouble imagining what it must be like to live in such an amazing place. We will have such a grand time!

It looks as though June 11 will be my arrival date. I am looking forward to my train ride though the countryside. There should be lots of beautiful scenery to help wile away the hours of riding.I have already started planning my packing and will probably be ready to go by next weekend! I can't wait to see you and all of the sights, the smells and the sounds of Chicago. And of course, I am most anxious to meet my new brother, Harry.

Until June, dearest Minnie,

> *Your loving sister,*
> *Annie*

The Castle   *Monday, May 29, 8:00 p.m.*

Pat Quinlan:

Ah, Peeetza-man, ya woulda loved it, I tell ya. Ol' Skinny Minnie was a hollerin' and squeelin' like a pig in heat. An' ol' Holmes was jes puttin' on one helluva show fer me, he was, knowin' I was jes' outside da door peekin' in. Y'know, she got a better body 'n I t'aught. Not bad at all for a five-footer.

He took'r ev'ry which way. I still tink she's a bit shy 'bout him seein' her all naked like dat, but afta a few minutes of da tongue, she was squirmin' all over da place.

Ah, he fucked her good like dat, and den in one motion he flips 'er over like a pancake and starts in from behind. Dats when he turns sideaways, gives me dat wink'a his, and den while he's still puttin' it to'er, picks up a ridin' crop and starts smackin' her on dat round ass o' hers. And dats when she really starts awallerin'. I tell ya, dey musta kept dat up fer five minutes—longer den I was able ta hold out me'self.

Well, maybe dat is disgustin', but your dragon woulda been spewin' too if ya'd seen what I was seein'. Anyway, I haven't gotten ta da best part yet. Right 'bout da time I was a sploogin', dats when he pulls out and flips'r over ag'in. She starts tellin' him no, not dat, anyting but dat. Of course, dats all he needs ta hear, and da next second he's got it buried down her troat and lettin' it squirt all over her face and mout'. And den when it's all over and done wid', y'know what she says?

She says, well it was a lil' bit salty, but udder 'en dat, it didn't taste too awfully bad. Heh, heh, heh, can ya b'lieve dat? A lil' too salty, heh, heh, heh. I had ta take off real quick-like den 'cause I started laughin' me fool head off, and da ol' Dragon was still danglin' in me hand. Whadda sight!

Quinlan Flat
The Castle
Monday, May 29, 10:00 p.m.

Sophie Quinlan:

You been drinkin', haven'tcha?

Well, you been up to somethin', I can tell.

I don't know if I'm gonna get in bed with you or not.

'Cause you're actin' real strange, dancin' 'round here naked, waggin' the drag-on. Hush! You'll wake Cora.

Hush, I said! Come on over here and put it to good use before it falls off.

Not so fast! How 'bout a little somethin' else first. You're always in too big a hurry.

Do what! You're disgustin', Pat. I bet you been watchin' Holmes through that peephole again.

Naw, it's okay. I kinda like it when you been watchin'—maybe I can watch sometime. Whadja think about that?

Yeah? You're kiddin' me! Well, why dont'cha show me 'stead of talkin' 'bout it.

Train Station
Chicago, Illinois
Sunday, June 11

Annie Williams:

Oh, Minnie, it's so wonderful to see you! I didn't think I would ever get here—you look radiant.

Of course, where are my manners? How do you do, Mister Gordon? I have been very anxious to meet the man who swept my sister off her feet.

Why, thank you. How nice of you to say so.

You were right, Minnie, he is quite the *charmer.*

Thank you. Just two large bags and this small one for now. I have a trunk packed and ready for shipment, but that will come later if I find I need it.

We have so much to catch up on—I probably won't be able to sleep tonight from all the excitement of seeing you, dear, and meeting you, Mister Gordon.

Oh, all right, Harry then. Goodness, I believe it's almost as hot here as it is in Texas!

That would be lovely, Harry. A decent meal would be nice after the food on the train.

Is it very far to the flat, Minnie?

Good, maybe I can freshen up a bit and have a cool drink before we go to the restaurant.

Now, you two must tell me everything. I'm dying to hear all about your whirlwind courtship. My goodness, there's so much traffic—how do you manage to get around?

Don't worry, Harry, I won't let you two out of my sight; I would never find you again in all of this. Lead the way!

Dear Diary,

I have been very neglectful of you these past few days, but we have been so busy that I go to bed too exhausted to write. Tonight, though, I decided to stay in and catch up on a few things. I want to write about everything while it's still fresh in my mind. I insisted that Minnie and Harry go out without me tonight—they have been entertaining me so much they haven't had any time alone.

I have seen and done so much, I hardly know where to begin. Chicago is a very exciting city—so big and noisy—I have never seen so many people in one place! My small Texas town will seem dull after this, I'm afraid. There is much to see and do here. The shopping is fabulous! I have several new dresses to add to my wardrobe, and new shoes as well. After all, I want to keep up with the fashions here, and Harry is so complimentary on everything I wear.

We have not been to the Fair yet, but Harry says we will be going there sometime in the next couple of weeks. He is very busy right now at his Castle, as he calls it, and wants to wait until he can spend the whole day there with us.

Harry has been very generous in letting Minnie take so much time off work to be with me. As busy as he is, I'm sure it must be a hardship for him to have her gone so much. He apparently has several young women working for him in different capacities, so Minnie is to take all the time she needs to be with me.

I have been trying to determine my feelings about Harry Gordon. In many ways, he is almost too good to be true. He is much smaller in stature than I had imagined. He is very handsome and has the most unusual eyes I have ever seen. I can understand Minnie's instant infatuation with him—he has that effect on people. I was prepared to mistrust him, but I believe I may have been unjust in my earlier estimations of him.

He has been quite charming in his manner toward me—even a little flirtatious at times (although perfectly innocent, I'm sure). I am surprised dear Minnie hasn't noticed and said something. I'm afraid I would react with more jealousy, but then, Minnie is such an innocent! He has commented several times on my art work. I have been trying to do a little painting in the afternoons when there is time, and Harry insists that I have talent. I just do it for my own enjoyment, but he seems quite excited about it. It would be very easy to fall in love with a man like Harry Gordon, and sometimes I almost feel a little jealous of their relationship. There, I've said it. I really don't mean it, of course, and should not even joke about such a thing! It is just that he has a way of making me feel special and I've enjoyed the attention. Well, it's getting late and I have more sightseeing tomorrow. We may have a picnic in the park and attend an outdoor concert. I will close for now and try to write more tomorrow.

Annie
Saturday, June 24, 1893

The Castle   *Friday, June 30, 6:30 p.m.*

Georgianna Yoke:

Hello, Henry. I've finally decided to take you up on your dinner invitation. It's still open, isn't it?

Good. I'm sure we'll have a delightful evening.

Gracious, this castle's richly decorated. I mean, to look at it from the outside is impressive, but it's nothing to prepare you for the inside. You must have spent a fortune on this place. Henry, I *must* see every room.

Why do I have to wait until after dinner?

That's not a good idea. Why don't we go down the street to that new place? It was finished about a week ago.

No, I'm not scared of you. Well, maybe I'm a little scared of us being alone together, but you can't blame me for that.

It wouldn't be proper. What would someone say if they saw me going upstairs with you?

Truly, you entertain all your guests up there?

Then how could I resist such an offer? Henry, how many more flights do we have to climb?

That many? No, I'm just tired. I've been working since seven this morning, and most of the day was spent standing.... What are you doing? You don't have to carry me!

Ooooh, you're so strong.

Hmmm, and your kiss is so nice, but we must stop.

Because I'm starrrving.

No, not for that. Please, let's have dinner before we do something I might regret.

You're very sweet. Oh, this room is so beautiful. It isn't at all what I expected. I thought when you said your private apartments, you meant your bedroom.

No, that's not a hint. Right now, all I want to see is the rest of this room. I've never seen cushions as red as these. They're so plush.

How charming! I've never eaten on cushions before. Which one's mine?

Thank you. What's under this lid?

Henry, how did you know that I love broiled shrimp?

You actually wrote to my mother? How romantic. What's that?

Mmmmm, that's different—the way it slides down your throat. Tell me, what does one dipped in butter taste like?

Oh, yes, that's even better. Here, try some shrimp.

Henry, what's to drink?

Champagne? What did I do to warrant such treatment?

You're being a very bad boy. We've just started the evening. The champagne is delicious, though. This is such a wonderful meal. I'm glad you convinced me to eat here instead of going out. How's the copier business?

I'm sorry you still haven't found the right investors, but these things take time. Perhaps you should try another city.

Sure, I'll take a refill.

Hehehehe.... You wouldn't try to get a lady drunk now, would you?

Let's wait on dessert. Why don't we talk?

I don't know.... Why don't you—Ouch!

Yeah, I'm all right. When I turned to face you, my shoes pinched me.

I don't know, should I?

Maybe you're right—would you help me pull them off?

Thank you. Untie the knot in the back and the front before unlacing.

I'm afraid that without the two knots, I might trip over the laces. That's it. Ooooh, that feels much better. I can even move my toes now. Here, you need some champagne, too.

Henry, no, I don't have to remove my stockings. This feels good enough.

Very well, since feet are your specialty and you know what's needed to keep them pretty. Where can I take them off?

You want to? I'm not sure....

Well, since you put it that way.

No! You'll just have to unhook the garter by feeling for it. Now, if you'll please help me up.

Uh, I'm just dizzy, all that champagne rushing to my head—I'm going to have to hold onto your shoulders while you're rolling down my stockings. Oooh, you're hands are cold!

That's it. You've almost reached...hehehehe...that's a little too high, Henry.

No, no, none of that. I only want my stockings removed.

Much better. Now then, how's your other businesses going?

Just curious.

You're right. The carpet does feel heavenly. Hey, why are you carrying me over to the table?

Okay, you're the doctor.

Ooooh, they're definitely tender there. What else did you want to know about me?

She left me everything—kinda like your uncle. Ow...that spot's a little too tender.

Yeah, it's funny how my foot fits into the palm of your hand. He*nnn*ry, what are you doing?

Hummm, it feels...it feels...I don't know how to say it. I've...never had my...toes...sucked before.

That's...oh...I don't think you should go any higher.

No, I'm not being mean. But if you keep moving your tongue up my leg, we'll wind up making love.

It would be great, but we can't.

It has to do with my inheritance. Henry, you have to stop. I can't think when you're licking me. My grandmother made a couple of stipulations in her will that I have to follow. Otherwise, I won't get my money.

Oh, about seventy thousand.

I told you before I was going to be an heiress. But in order to get it, I have to be a virgin when I marry and even then I don't get the money for three more years.

No, you can't. My grandmother named a specific doctor to check me out before the wedding night. Your word won't be any good.

I'm sorry, too. I was enjoying what you were doing, but I'd better get going.

No, I can't stay here tonight. If I did, I wouldn't be able to stay out of your bedroom. Just see me to a carriage. Hopefully, the night air will revive me. And, darling, the dinner was magnificent. I can come again, can't I?

Dear Diary,

I have been neglecting you again, but part of the problem is I have been too busy, and part is I have been afraid (or ashamed) to put my thoughts on paper. But if I don't write I won't be able to hold them inside much longer.

I am concerned about my growing infatuation for Brother Harry. He wants me to call him that, although I would prefer just Harry. I love Minnie and would never hurt her, but something is definitely happening between Harry and me, and I don't know what it all means.

I began to notice little things—a gentle hand on the small of my back as we were leaving a restaurant one night, or holding my hand a bit longer than necessary when he helps me from a chair. But in the last few days, the "little" things have been growing into larger things. I really don't think I am imagining this. The worst part is that I am enjoying every minute of it! I feel so disloyal to Minnie, although I would never allow anything to interfere with her happiness. Oh, why do things have to be so complicated?

Thank heavens I have someplace to unburden my feelings. Minnie must never read this, nor Harry. I feel like a silly schoolgirl.

Sometimes when we are left alone for even a few minutes I find him staring at me in a most provocative way—almost as though he is undressing me with his eyes—those wonderful, hypnotic eyes. His touch on my skin when he "accidentally" brushes against me stirs very warm feelings within me. I am beginning to wonder if he is an angel or a devil to cause me such sweet agony. I think it might be a good idea to cut my visit shorter than planned and get out of here, although Minnie would certainly want to know why.

I wish you could talk back to me and tell me what to do. I will try to write more tomorrow. Maybe by then I will be thinking a little more sensibly. After all, I'm very tired tonight.

Annie
Friday, June 30, 1893

1220 Wrightwood Avenue   *Saturday, July 1, 4:00 p.m.*
Englewood, Illinois

Minnie Williams:

Oh, it feels so good to get out of these shoes. My feet are killing me. I bet we walked ten miles today.

Whew...I'm with you. I could use a drink.

I think we wore Harry out, too—my poor baby! He told me he was so tired he was going straight to bed.

I know. I'm going to bed right after this glass of wine. I'm exhausted.

Speak for yourself. You look pretty bad, too. Why did we do all that shopping? Did you have to go into every millinery store we passed? How many hats did you buy? Or, should I say, how many did *Harry* buy?

Four? Oh, God. We're good at spending Harry's money, aren't we? By the way, if you weren't my sister, I'd probably be a little jealous.

Because Harry was really showering you with attention today. I noticed how he held your arm when we crossed the street. I swear he was watching you the entire day with that crazed *look* of his.

You know, the *look* that says, I'm ready to take you right now—so *bend over, honey.*

Oh, don't be so shocked, Annie. I'm sorry to laugh, but I'm not your innocent little sister anymore. Harry has shown me sexual pleasures that I never knew were possible.

Yes, he excites me. That's why I was a little surprised when I saw that look today.

Oh, I'm sure you're right. I know you didn't do anything to bring it on. He probably didn't mean anything by it either. Now, if you don't mind, I'm going to draw a hot bath.

Main Office, 2nd Floor   *Sunday, July 2, 5:00 p.m.*
The Castle

Minnie Williams:

Is it five o'clock already? I'm not even close to being finished with this stack of typing that I came in specifically on a Sunday to complete. It doesn't help that you've given me so many days off lately to show Annie around Chicago.

Oh, Harry, I'm not complaining. I would just like to get out of here sometime tonight. After all, we're going to the Fair tomorrow.

Look, I will probably need another three hours or so to catch up; so why don't you go to the flat and entertain Annie for me.

Just until I get home. I promise I'll work as fast as I can. I wish I could come with you, but you know we have deadlines to meet.

I love you, too. Now, go! Explain my predicament and have fun with my sister.

1220 Wrightwood Avenue   *Sunday, July 2, 6:00 p.m.*
Englewood, Illinois

Annie Williams:

Hello, Harry, I wasn't expecting to see you tonight. Where's Minnie?

Oh, of course, how rude of me—come in, please. I was just thinking about having a glass of lemonade. Could I bring you a glass?

Wine? Wonderful! We'll have some when Minnie gets home.

Don't you want to wait for Minnie?

How late? Oh, Harry, you just can't ask her to work so late tonight with the Fair tomorrow. Why don't we go get her? I still haven't seen your castle, you know. Maybe this would be a good time.

All right, then. We'll have one glass while we wait. I'll go get some glasses.

Oh! You startled me. I didn't hear you come up behind me. Would you like something to eat with the wine? Here—why don't you open the bottle while I...

Harry, you really are being a big tease tonight. You are engaged to my sister, you know. If I didn't know better, I'd swear you were flirting with me.

You're not giving me much room, here. Let's take the wine back into the parlor where we can sit comfortably.

Oh, no. I insist you take the sofa. I'll just sit over here in the chair.

I know there's plenty of room on the sofa, but I...

Very well, if it will make you happy.

The wine? It's very good, I suppose. I'm really not much of a drinker, but it's fine once in a while. Don't you think it tastes a little bitter?

You're right. It does relax one, doesn't it.

Certainly you may remove your coat—it is quite warm tonight. I really don't mind.

Yes, I am looking forward to going to the Fair tomorrow. I'm so glad you feel you have the time to take us for the day. How early do you want to leave?

No, that isn't too early for us—we'll be up and ready.

Well, just a little more—it does relax one, doesn't it?

No, I'm not going to sleep—just feeling very relaxed.

What are you doing?

You really shouldn't, but that does feel wonderful, Harry. You'll spoil me, rubbing my shoulders like that. Another of your many talents. Minnie is a very lucky young woman!

You can stop now, but it does feel nice, thank you.

Please stop, Harry, or I'll be forced to move back to the chair.

Don't be silly. I'm not afraid of you. Should I be? Here, let me pour you a little more wine.

Ohhh, that really is good. If Minnie doesn't get here soon, there won't be any left!

Two bottles? Why, Harry, you must be planning to get us all drunk!

Are you okay?

You are looking at me so strangely, I thought you might be ill or something. You know, you have the most unusual eyes.

Don't say things like that. You know you don't mean it—it's just the wine talking.

No, don't pour any for me, please. I think I'll just move over to the chair...

You shouldn't have done that, Harry. I don't know what to think! No, please don't try to kiss me again or I'll have to ask you to leave.

Yes, I enjoyed—I mean, *NO*, I didn't enjoy it. What's gotten into you? This wine must be very strong—I can't seem to clear my head.

Well, yes, I have noticed that you are very attentive to me, but after all, we will soon be brother and sister.

Please don't say any more. I think you better go now. I do really feel ill.

Yes, thank you, I'll just lie down here for a few minutes. Would you mind if I don't see you to the door?

Don't do that, please, I can't think when you're kissing me like that. Oh, God, what are we doing? Your hands are so gentle. I should never have touched the wine, I can't seem to help myself....

Your hands are distracting me and you shouldn't be touching me like this. I'm going to cry, Harry.

Because we must stop this at once. I feel so disloyal and, oh, please get off me, Harry.

No, you mustn't pull my skirt up like...

Oh, God, your hands...they fee!...

Just a few more minutes.

Yes, yes, I want you.

Now! Yes, oh, yes, Harry.

Ohhhh—

That was unbelievable. What have we done?

But Minnie will be home soon and she'll know.

Handle it how?

I better leave tomorrow—the sooner the better. I can't face Minnie after this.

I'll tell her something came up and I had to return home.

The Fair? How can we go off to the Fair tomorrow and act like this never happened?

Trust you? I don't even trust myself!

Oh! My head! I'm going to lie down in my room. I don't want to be up when Minnie gets home.

No—please don't—you couldn't possibly after that....

You must not be human! No, we have to stop this now! Put my skirt down, please. Ohhhhh—let me up now! I think I'm going to be sick.

No, just leave, please. Goodnight, Harry. We'll handle tomorrow when it comes. Right now, I just want to die.

Chicago's World's Fair   *Monday, July 3*
Chicago, Illinois

Myrta Holmes:

Oh, Harry, I can't believe I'm finally going to ride it! It's all everyone's been talking about. They say it's the greatest ride ever invented.

Isn't this exciting, Lucy? There must be fifty people to a car!

Thank God there's this bar...ooh, is it supposed to rock like this?

Gosh, I sure hope they don't stop us at the top—stop rocking this thing!

Wow, look how much we can see already, and we're just halfway up.

Look at Chicago—which building do you think that is?

Wheeee! Oh, this is so exhilarating! I can't believe how high up we get, and how fast this thing goes. I sure hope it's as safe as the papers say.

Ha, ha, ha.

I see it, I see it! It sure does go by quick. What's that?

Wheeeeeeeeeeeee! Ha, ha, ha.

Uh, oh. It's slowing down. Oh God, it's going to stop on top, I just know it is!

Stop trying to rock this thing this instant, Harry. I mean it. Knock it off!

Well, when you're not rocking it, it isn't so bad...don't you dare! My, look how far you can see at the very top.

Hey, isn't that Bob and Felicia with Gary and Paula? And look, over there, it's Wharton. Who's *that* he's with?

I promise, Lucy, we'll get some candy after this ride is over. Are you sure you have to get going, Harry?

Ah, the ride's coming to an end—we're better than halfway down. Look at the line for this thing, would you?

Well, well, well. If it isn't the slut sisters. What's Quinlan call them? Oh, yeah, Fanny Annie and Skinny Minnie. What in God's name do you see in either one of them?

Don't give me that shit. I know you're at least doing the short, *fat* one.

Geez, give me credit for *some* intelligence.

Hey, I told you years ago, just don't flaunt it. Now don't you dare say a word to either one of them when we get off. I mean it, Harry, not a *word*.

Mr. Charles Williams   *July 4, 1893*
5952 Morningside Street
Jackson, Mississippi

Dear Uncle Charles,

I am sorry to be so long in writing to let you know all about my trip. I was very glad to read in your last letter that your gout was much improved and I hope you are finally listening to Dr. Wilkins' advice. You need to take better care of yourself.

Today is the 4th of July, and I suppose the usual celebrations are taking place in Jackson. I always looked forward to the parade and the big picnic with fireworks. We will be going out later today to a picnic. Brother Harry says there will be a big fireworks display later in the evening over the lake, but after yesterday, fireworks will seem tame in comparison.

We went to the Columbian Exposition yesterday, and it was the most wonderful thing—I wish you could be here to see it. Most people call it the World's Fair, which I believe is a much better name. We rode the giant Ferris wheel. You cannot imagine in your wildest dreams how large it is. It was scary and exciting at the same time. Brother Harry says it is well over 200 feet high and over 2,000 people can ride it at once.

I particularly enjoyed the Art Palace with what seemed like miles of paintings, sculpture, etc. I could have spent the whole day there, but then I would have missed the wonderful gondola ride on a real canal made especially for the Fair. We capped off the evening by watching a

brilliant fireworks display from the roof of one of the buildings. I am planning to write down all of the things we saw and did and describe them in more detail. I will send it to you one of these days along with sketches of some of the buildings and sights.

I have been so caught up in writing about the Fair, I forgot to tell you about Harry, or Brother Harry, as he likes me to call him. He is a very wonderful man and Sister is a very lucky woman to have him. She will certainly never have to worry about money or anything else. He is kind and good and generous to a fault. In fact, he told me just this morning about a trip he has planned for the three of us. He says we will go to Milwaukee and to Old Orchard Beach, Maine, by way of the St. Lawrence River. We'll visit two weeks in Maine then on to New York. Brother Harry thinks I am talented and wants me to study art. Then we will sail for Germany by way of London and Paris. If I like it, I will stay and study art. Brother Harry says you need never trouble any more about me, financially or otherwise. He and Sister will see to me. Isn't that wonderful?

I guess I better close for now and take care of a few other things. I just wanted you to know we are fine and having a wonderful time and thinking about you. Sister sends her love along with mine. I miss you and hope you remember to miss me once in a while—but don't worry about us. We are in good hands.

> *With all my love,*
> *Annie*

The Castle   *July 4, 1893*

Dr. Frank Noland
Norristown Insane Asylum
Norristown, Pennsylvania

Dearest Frank,

I have a very pretty lady screaming inside my office vault. Surprised?

I'm in a jolly mood, dear boy. After all, the only thing standing between me and an easy fortune of $40,000 is the caged Annie Williams, not so smart as she may have thought herself.

Yes, yes, dear Annie, scream on! Can you hear her, Franklin? My, my, the lady doth protest too much.

For her pleasure, I have nothing on but a royal purple bathrobe her sister gave me.

Are you very jealous, doctor? Wouldn't you just love to be with this woman, able to do with her whatever you wish? In a delicious half hour or so, while most other men, including you, are going about your boring, ho-hum lives, I shall enter my slave's tomb and master her without objections. Yes, and I shall know the heaven of a woman's body while the rest of you must be caught up with all the complexities and questions that exist in the relationships between living men and women.

But my slave, my entrapped female, all her delicate feathers now in a flutter, will be mine, all mine.

Oh, yes, on this hot summer night I stand before the cool garden of love, my bride still screaming her passionate demands that I rip down the steel door and satisfy her unquenchable lust.

Oh, my darling, sleep! Sleep, and soon I shall slip into your dreams.

Later,
Holmes

1220 Wrightwood Avenue   *Wednesday, July 5, 7:00 p.m.*
Englewood, Illinois

H. H. Holmes:

Stop cryin', please. You'll ruin my meal with all those tears. Annie's okay, just feelin' bad 'bout herself.

I left her in a nice room located not more than three miles from here. She'll come to you when she deals with her guilt or runs out of the money I gave her.

Twenty bucks.

I told you all about the affair last night. You don't believe me?

It happened fast. We were in the Castle and I was giving her a tour. Damn it, the coffee's cold!

Why go into all the steamy details? We had a wild and passionate fling at each other on my bedroom floor. All the while we were doin' it, I was thinking of you.

Don't put too much butter on the bread. And stop cryin'—I don't like it.

Yes, I'll tell her you forgive her, but she's really ashamed of herself.

Probably a week or two. You forgot to get me a napkin.

The Castle

Pat Quinlan:

C'mon, Peetza-man. We gots to hurry up wid' da' job or else da' boss-man ain't gonna be too very happy.

Youse knows' well as I dat we can't never talk 'bout dat dere blasted infernal furnace. Jes' keep da mout' shut and keep on diggin' Mista Pizza-man before youse too becomes a fixture down here. Heh-heh-heh. I can see da' papers now: Peetza-man baked in oven. Heh-heh-heh.

Quinlan Apartment
The Castle

Sophie Quinlan:

Not now, Pat.

Because I want to talk to you and I can't talk when you're doin' that.

Just wait a few minutes—this is important. I've been tryin' to talk to you ever since you got home this evenin', but you've been too busy to listen.

It's about Holmes and things goin' on in this place.

Weird things—scary things—even more weird than usual.

I saw somethin' today I don't think I was supposed to see.

Well, you can laugh if you want, but I think I saw Holmes burnin' a body—a real body.

I knew you wouldn't believe me.

I know it's wild. I been scared to death ever since.

In the cellar. I was carrying that stack of boxes you said needed to go down there.

I know, I know. I should waited for ya, but I was tired of trippin' over 'em. Ooh yeah, rub my legs—that sure feels good.

Well, I stopped by the door to Holmes' medical room—you know, where he keeps all them doctor's tools and stuff.

No, he didn't hear me. If he'd a turned around I'da died right there on the spot.

Just seein' him burnin' somethin' in that big old stove wouldn't scare me—it was the smell.

Oh, Pat, it weren't like nothin' I ever smelt before.

I started to. I was about to open my mouth to ask where that awful smell was comin' from when he shifted just 'nough I could see what looked to me like a human arm he was pokin' down in the fire there.

I'm not crazy! I tell you I saw him burnin' a body!

Well, what if I'm right?

I tell you it was a body. Whose do you suppose it was?

All right, I'll rub your back if you tell me you believe me. Turn over. I swear I'm tellin' you the truth; I know what I saw. And I ain't felt too good since. I'm scared, Pat. I can deal with the cons and insurance schemes, but this is another matter. Where could the body have come from?

Suppose it was me, or worse yet, Cora?

Well, I'm glad she's stayin' with my parents for a while.

Yeah, I know he needs you around too much to try anything—at least for now. But I haven't told you the scariest part yet.

He was whistlin'.

It sure as hell *was* scary. What kind of man would be whistlin' a tune while he's burnin' a body?

I know you trust him, but for my peace of mind I want you to find out what you can without makin' him suspicious I saw anything.

I don't want to talk about this any more, either. Why don'tcha finish what you started?

Yeah, come on, big boy, I think that dragon's breathin' fire again. Maybe I can douse that flame.

The Castle   *Monday, July 31, 10:00 p.m.*

Pat Quinlan:

Let's draw cards for it. Whaddya say, Peetza-man?

What's da matta? Can't take ya eyes off 'em?

Ah, she'll be jes' fine. Da more she struggles like dat, da more Holmes is gonna stick it to 'er. But if da trut' be told, I tink she kinda likes it rough like dat. I knows da type.

Hey, I t'ought ya quit drinkin'? If Holmsey catches ya takin' a plug like dat ag'in, he sure won't be happy 'bout it.

Well, well. Looks like he's puttin' da finishin' touches on'er. Ya sure ya don't want some of dis here action? Tell ya what, Peetza-man, I'll even letya have at'er next.

Ya sure? Fer Christ's sake, put da bottle down 'fore he comes over here.

Ya git 'er nice and wet for me, Mista Holmes? Heh, heh, heh.

Howya doin', lassie. Ol' Holmsey leave ya high 'n dry? Naw, looks like ya pretty wet down dere, heh-heh-heh. Ya eyes'r lookin' like saucers, hon. Whats da matta', cat got ya tongue, or's dat gag jes' a bit too tight? Heh-heh-heh?

Ah, it's jes' dat ya never seen anyting like da Dragon here, have ya? God, youse all oiled up real good-like. Ya musta pleased ol' Holmsey real well. Now it's time to take care of ol' PattyQ.

Hhh-hhh-hhh-hhh-hhh-hhh—hahh-hahh-hahh-hahh-hahhhhhhhh.

Well, me darlin', I'll go see if da Peetza-man is gonna deliver next, or if ya jes' gonna be stuck with ol' Holmsey the rest of the night.

Tanks a lot. Say g'night ta da Dragon. Hope ta see ya'round.

Dats a real nice lass ya caught dere, Mista Holmes. What's da matta', ain't ya gonna take a run at 'er, Peetza-man?

Yeah, I'll take 'im wit' me. Ya lookin' kinda pale-like, Peetzy. Ya gonna be okay?

Hey, tanks ag'in, Mista Holmes. G'night.

God, I jes' hope he goes easy on'er.

Ya really tink so? Yeah, y'right, he prob'ly will. He had dat look 'bout him, didn't he?

Oh, dat was *his* bottle? Den you're right. Dat can only mean one ting, 'n dat ain't good news for da gal. Ah, now I need a drink. Let's go ta Pete's.

Pete's Bar   *Monday, July 31, 10:30 p.m.*
Englewood, Illinois

Pat Quinlan:

Look, Peeetzy, ya jes' gots ta git ol' Emily offa ya mind. Dats all in da past now.

I know, I know. But ya can'ts beat ya'self ova da head 'bout it. It ain't ya fault dat t'ings turned out da way dey did.

Hey dere, Petey, line us up fer a few shots and a coupla beers.

Ahhhhh. So, when'ja git back ta drinkin'?

Least ways now I knows why ya didn't want no part of dat poor lil' harlot ta'night. Now dat ya mention it, I do see a sorta 'semblance.

1369 Lake Shore Drive   *Tuesday, August 22, 1893*
Chicago, Illinois

Dear Mother,

How are you feeling? Sorry I haven't written sooner. I hope you are taking the medication Dr. Harley prescribed for your heart. You had better take care of yourself because I'm going to need your support more than ever in the next few months. Maybe it's time to start thinking about altering your wedding dress, but more about that later. How is Father? Is he still trying his hand at woodworking? He seemed to be enjoying it the last time I was home. Please tell him, if he can, to make me a towel rack. The last one I bought came apart about a week ago. What have you been doing to keep busy?

Mother, you'll never believe my good fortune. Do you remember meeting Dr. Howard? Well, I finally had dinner with him. It was incredible. We had the most delicious seafood. Thank you for telling him I love shrimp. All of this took place at the Castle—that's his home. The name is right though because it's so huge. It must hold at least 25 bedrooms. I didn't get to see all of the place. He says he rents rooms out to help pay for the maintenance costs. Pretty smart, don't you agree?

Anyway, he's incredibly rich. He probably has more money than anyone else in Chicago. I know he has numerous business interests. He's especially trying to get this copier business going. Even Paul, the old man I'm dating, isn't as wealthy as Henry. And the great part is Henry is young. I think I could actually enjoy my wifely duties if I married him.

I know I've always told you I planned on marrying an old man so we wouldn't have to spend so many years together before I became a rich, grieving widow. All of that's changed since I met Henry. I think I'm falling in love with him. However, I haven't let him know this. He might pressure me for more affection before we're married. And I am going to marry him.

Also, I have a new kitten. He's the cutest little thing. Henry bought him for me. He said it would keep me company whenever I was lonely, and it would remind me of him. I named the kitten Oscar. He's a tawny-colored ball of fur and claws. If you notice any smudges on this letter, please forgive Oscar. He wants to be petted and keeps trying to steal the pen from my hand.

I had better stop for now. Give Father a hug and kiss for me. I love you both.

Love,
Georgianna

Please fill out the following form to apply for insurance with FIDELITY MUTUAL LIFE ASSOCIATION:

Date: September 19, 1893
Person to be insured: Henry Howard Holmes
Address: 38 North John Street, Wilmette, Illinois
Person requesting insurance: Henry Howard Holmes
Address: Same
Health: Perfect
Age: 33
Kind of insurance desired: Optional life
Amount of insurance: $10,000
Name of primary insurance company (if optional insurance is desired): New England Life
Amount of primary insurance: $25,000
Mother's name of person to be insured: Mary Holmes
Mother's age: Mother died at 58, don't remember cause, no acute disease
Father's name: Christopher Holmes
Father's age: Father died at 62 from injury to his foot
Name of beneficiary: Myrta Z. Holmes, wife
Address: Same as mine

1369 Lake Shore Drive   *Thursday, September 28*
Chicago, Illinois

Georgianna Yoke:

Good morning, Henry. How have you been?

How nice—you went on a business trip and didn't even think to tell me good-bye.

I'm not upset. Whatever gave you that idea?

Well, I've only seen you once in the past few weeks. I figured you had moved on to some other *interest*.

No. I'm not putting Oscar down. I need to finish brushing him.

Stop that!

I don't want to. Just leave me alone. Besides, Oscar has been much better company than you've been. He's learned some new tricks, especially since I've had plenty of time to work with him in the evening.

No, I'm not complaining. Only stating facts. Here's your tea.

I said stop it. I don't feel like kissing you. I'm going to go get Oscar something to eat.

Oh, Oscar, how cute. Did you see how he followed me? You've got to admit he's pretty smart to know when he has a wonderful master. Come here, baby.

Not you, Henry, I was talking to Oscar. Here, why don't you pet him?

Oscar, no!

It's only a small scratch.

There's no need for that tone. Oscar didn't like how tight you were holding him. Are you okay, baby? Henry didn't mean to scare you like that.

Henry, wait a minute....

1369 Lake Shore Drive   *Sunday, October 1*
Chicago, Illinois

Georgianna Yoke:

Yes, please pour me some more—I'm so thirsty tonight. Henry, I want to thank you....

Let me finish. It was sweet of you to rush over. You showed how much you care for me, especially since you left your appointment waiting. I wasn't sure you would come after our fight the other night, but I knew I wanted you here with me.

Well, I don't know if I would say we have *officially* made up, at least not yet. Anyway, you were wonderful in cleaning up Oscar's blood. I couldn't have handled it. Henry, who could have done such a callous thing? Why would someone want to cut off Oscar's head and leave it at my front door? Poor, poor Oscar.

No, I promise I won't start crying again. It's only that he was so special to me. Do you realize he's the only thing you've given me?

Really? Can I have it now?

Oh, what a pretty box. I want it!

Give it to me, give it to me. Pleeeeeeeeease, Henry.

Oh my goodness, it's gorgeous. I'll treasure it always. The brooch almost looks like Oscar, and the tiny red rubies for its eyes. Why look at the way the light catches the small diamond collar! How can I ever thank you?

I told you we can't make love or I'll lose my inheritance.

Don't pout. I know of another way I can make you happy and it's almost as good as the real thing. Curious?

Well, for such a beautiful gift, you can do anything you'd like to the top half of my body for twelve minutes, but on one condition—you can only use your mouth. Now be a good little boy and turn around.

Because I have to tie your hands.

No, I trust you in most things, just not in this situation. The temptation to bring those hands into play could become too strong. That shouldn't be too tight. Okay, darling, I'm all yours.

Mmmm, you know I love your kisses, the way you thrust your tongue in and out of my mouth. Yesss, that way.

No, I'm not taking off my dress. You'll just have to figure out a way to get me out of it—at least the top part.

Stop! That tickles! There, that's better.

Well, what do you think?

I didn't realize you liked fairy tales. Remember, you'd better watch the time.

Ohhhh, Henry, your mouth's so hot. Yes, that's it—blow on them. Umm-huh, yes, suck on Gretel...harder. Oh my...oh my...oh dear, yes, don't forget...Hansel. That's it. No, keep on. Ohhhhh....

Oooh, you're so rough. Are you trying to eat me?

I'm glad to know I taste so good. No, no, you can't go lower than my belly. Why don't you come back to my mouth and work your way down again.

Hmmm, you have to stop. Time's up.

No, it's the best I've ever had. But if we continue....

I can't help that you're in pain. You still have to wait. We can play some more another night.

I don't like it any better than you, but it has to be this way. I'll untie your hands when you're outside the door. Give me a moment and let me cover myself.

I guess you can have one more look.

Yes, they're a little sore, but I don't mind. Turn around and I'll get you where you can finish untying yourself.

Goodnight, Henry.

1369 Lake Shore Drive   *Sunday, October 8, 1893*
Chicago, Illinois

Dear Mother,

I'm so thrilled—IT HAS FINALLY HAPPENED. Henry's proposed to me. Can you believe it? I almost can't. He's been visiting me every night since Oscar was killed, and he brings me a new gift each time. I've thanked him as you've suggested and it's worked. You can say you told me so. I've kept him dangling long enough, and now he's dying to marry me. I can't wait. I'll have all the money I could ever want.

He wanted to get married this weekend, but I told him I wanted an actual wedding with all our friends and relatives. Guess what—he's agreed! After we get married, you'll have to give me advice on how to keep him happy and interested. I'm not tolerating any mistresses.

I'm afraid I've fallen in love with him. His money may have been what first caught my attention, but now the man has become more impor-tant. I don't think it would even matter to him if I had an inheritance or not. Don't worry, I haven't told him I was lying about the money Granny left me. He doesn't need to know that we are not quite as well off as he thinks. I'll just have to think of other conditions to the will to keep him from wondering why I haven't received the money, yet. Any ideas?

Sorry if this letter seems a little short, but I'm still in shock from Henry's proposal last night. I haven't asked—how are you and Father doing? I hope both of you are well. I just wanted to tell you my great news. I still can't believe I've gotten what I went after. I know we'll be happy.

      Love Always,
      Georgianna

The Castle   October 15, 1893

Dr. Frank Noland
Norristown Insane Asylum
Norristown, Pennsylvania

Dear Frank:

I have four different insurance policies on the Castle, so I'm going to burn it down to get a new source of money to replace what I've been getting on renting rooms to tourists. I won't be here while it's burning, of course. I have a grunt named Quinlan, a sub-human type, who will do the job if I tell him twenty times how to go about it.

While the flames rise to the stars, I'll be at the World's Fair with my new lady, a rich beauty named Georgianna Yoke. I'll soon marry her, using the name of Henry Mansfield Howard because I'm still married to other women under different names.

I'm still getting what I can from Minnie Williams, but she is beginning to bore me. Everywhere we go, she looks for signs of her sister, Annie, who made her final mark on the world by leaving her footprints in my vault more than three months ago. Remember? If Minnie doesn't shut her mouth soon, I'll shut it for her forever.

In a minute or so, I'm going down the back stairs with Henry, who wants to take a long look at a pretty little girl and her mother. He says they like to walk around in their undies in their room. What are you doing that's exciting this Sunday?

Enjoy your day off,
Holmes

Brutal Slayings End World's Fair

Five murders/one night.

Tragedy follows Mayor slaying

CHICAGO, Nov. 1 —Five teenagers—between the ages of 16-19—were found late last night, bludgeoned to death inside the Chicago World's Fair Fun House. Police on the scene were still investigating at press time and had little to say about the murders.

Following the shooting murder of Chicago Mayor Carter Harrison in his home last week, this latest tragedy has certainly put a pall over all of Chicago.

All five teenagers—three female, two male—were found nude from the waist down, and all had been brutally sodomized. Each had been slashed, and three of the victims had been partially mutilated. A half- empty bottle of chloroform was also found at the feet of one of the victims.

The identity of all five bodies has been withheld, pending notification of next of kin. An autopsy has been scheduled for later in the week.

"This is a most heinous crime," said City Detective G. F. Izzo, Chief of the Homicide Division. "We're obviously dealing with a very sick mind—someone with a subhuman mentality."

As of late last night, police had very little information to go on. The bodies were found by workers cleaning up following the final day of the Fair. Police theorize the teenagers were murdered just before closing, perhaps during the Grand Fireworks Finale that began on schedule at 6 p.m.

The Castle   *Sunday, November 5*

Pat Quinlan:

I tell ya, Sofe, dis here storm jes' ain't natch'ral. It's too late in da year for it ta be stormin' like dis'. Dat last bolt musta hit da Castle itself.

Dis whole place has been kinda dead since da end of da Fair. All dats left are a

few of da reg'lars and da workers, and Holmesy's been layin' 'em off one after da utter lately. Say, ya fine'ly got da beast cooked jes' right–nice 'n rare.

Nah, he ain't gonna git rid a me or Peetzy, but tings will be diff'rent.

Well, I tink he's headed for Texas real soon. And I tink he's takin' da Peetza-man and Skinny Minnie wit' 'im. When dat happens, it'll be gloomier 'n ever 'round here. I really miss all da activity we had when da Fair was in full swing.

Listen ta da rain and da wind, would'ja? Not safe for man or beast out dere t'night.

I wish ya would try it dis way 'stead of cookin' it till it tastes like shoe ledder.

Hey, youse da one keeps tellin' me ta 'span me horizons. Den when I do, ya want me ta go back ta eatin' da way I always did.

If ya tink dis is too rare, ya should see da way ol' Holmsey likes it. I tell ya, blood's jes' oozin' outta it when he gits it da way he likes it best.

Yeah, tanks, but be sure to get it from da center...yeah, dat piece looks perfect. An', Sofe, while your up, how 'bout anudder stout?

FIDELITY MUTUAL LIFE ASSOCIATION:

Date: November 9, 1893
Person to be insured: Benjamin F. Pietzel, Jr.
Address: 1220 Pulaski Street, Chicago, Illinois
Person requesting insurance: Benjamin F. Pietzel, Jr.
Address: Same as above
Health: Excellent
Age: 37
Kind of insurance desired: Optional life
Amount of insurance: $10,000
Name of primary insurance company (if optional insurance is desired): New England Life
Amount of primary insurance: $25,000
Mother's name of insured: Deborah (Gordon) Pietzel
Mother's age: 59
Father's name of insured: Benjamin F. Pietzel, Sr.
Father's age: 69
Name of beneficiary: Carrie Pietzel
Relationship to insured: Wife
Address: Same as above

The Castle   *Friday, November 10*

Pat Quinlan:

C'mon, youse guys. We gotta hurry up wit' dis keer'seen. Make sure ya splash it in da corners, too.

Hey, Mista Holmes says ta be sure we git da t'ird floor, and dats 'zactly what we gonna do.

All right, ready? Here, gimme da matches.

Hurry up! Let's git da fuck outta here!

CHICAGO TRIBUNE MONDAY
NOVEMBER 13, 1893

Arson Suspected in Castle Fire

Two still hospitalized—third released today

ENGLEWOOD, Nov. 12—Police Detective Dan Grogan confirmed today what has been suspect—that the fire that destroyed the third floor of The Castle in Englewood on November 10 was arson.

Dr. H.H. Holmes, the owner of The Castle, expressed disappointment in the Chicago Police Department's findings. Because of the suspicious nature of the fire, Mr. Holmes will not be able to collect any insurance monies. The Castle was believed to be insured for $100,000. Authorities estimate the damage to the third floor to be in excess of $20,000.

Eye witness accounts saw three men leave the building in a hurry, shortly before flames were reported around 11:00 p.m. Three females who were renting rooms were hospitalized for smoke inhalation. One of them, a Miss Julie Shumer, was released today.

The Castle   *November 15, 1893*

Dr. Frank Noland
Norristown Insane Asylum
Norristown, Pennsylvania

Dear Frank,

I just came back from an amusing afternoon with Miss Minnie Williams, who had gained at least fifty pounds since the disappearance of her sister. A delightful Indian Summer day, Minnie thought it a good idea to have a picnic lunch beneath some pleasant falling leaves. She suggested we go to a nearby pond, but I protested that I was full of lust for her and wanted to go deeper into the woods surrounding the pond.

That girl could eat! Her basket was full of sandwiches and fruits, including half a dozen hard green apples. I made her go really deep into the woods, took her clothes off, and rammed myself against her as she stood bent over, facing a thick tree. She soon satisfied me by making some loud screams and moans, and we then settled down to a naked lunch.

I knew Minnie was in trouble when I saw Hatch walking toward us fully dressed. Hatch came upon us suddenly; but Minnie was so busy eating and talking that she took no notice of him, even when he sat down smiling behind her.

Minnie raised an apple to her face, the last she would eat. Suddenly, Hatch grabbed her from behind and shoved the whole apple into her mouth. She struggled in the otherwise quiet shade of the tall noble oaks. Hatch picked up a nearby tree branch to push the thing deeper into her throat. The poor lady died, and Hatch removed her head with the knife she had brought to cut the sandwiches. We buried the rest of her, throwing into the grave the remaining apples, cookies, and other goodies we were unable to eat. I kept the basket, of course, to take home the souvenir.

> Got a train to catch,
> Holmes

Second Floor Office of Holmes   *Saturday, November 18, 10:00 p.m.*
The Castle

H. H. Holmes:

That's right, Howard—sulk, as usual. I see Herman has joined you.

Oh shut up, Henry, I'm in no mood to go pop the bitch. Besides, the way she's demanding things, only the act of rape could get us between her legs—and I lack both the energy and desire to do so. It would be like fucking a tornado.

Haven't seen Hatch since Monday. Maybe he's trapped inside a locked casket in Hell. Why—you don't think we can handle this situation without him?

DENVER POST   SUNDAY, NOVEMBER 19, 1893
ENGAGEMENTS

DENVER, Nov. 19 —Mr. and Mrs. Elmer Yoke announced the engagement of their daughter, Georgianna, to Mr. Henry Mansfield Howard of Englewood, Illinois. Miss. Yoke graduated from Denver High Academy a few years ago. The groom is a medical doctor with his own practice in Chicago. The couple will be married in Denver on January 17. They will honeymoon in Ft. Worth, Texas, where Mr. Howard is developing a large horse ranch.

Anna Gorky's Bedroom Closet   *Wednesday, November 22*
The Castle

Cora Quinlan:

Anna, close the closet door so we can hide. Ooohh, it's dark in here. Wait...we'll be able to see in a few minutes.

I like it dark. It's good for hiding...and, for telling secrets. No one will know we're here if we talk real soft. Where's your Momma?

Mine's busy, too.... She's baking pies.

Poppa? Oh, he's pro'bly downstairs. I never see him much anymore. 'Cause Mister Holmes always has him cleanin' that old basement all the time. He never even gets to eat dinner with me and Momma.

He acts really queer around Mister Holmes.

I don't know, just kinda quiet and spooky, I guess.

You wanna know somethin' else? Sometimes I hear them talkin' bout secret stuff.

Oh, I know it's secret 'cause they always talk real soft. But once I was playin' in my room and they was standin' outside my door and I heard 'em talkin'.

About money, and Mister Holmes told Poppa if he wanted more money he'd better keep his mouth shut and help him cut up the stuff in the basement.

I don't know what stuff, but maybe we could go down there and find out.

Oh, Poppa tol' me I 'm never s'posed to go there neither 'cause it's dark. He says I might get hurt. But I still wanna' go see what's there. We can pretend we're on a secret adventure. Besides, Momma says I shouldn't be ascared of the dark. I'm almost ten, you know.

Well, then, let's sneak down there sometime. Poppa will never know. We'll walk real soft and we'll go when no one's around. We're not fraidy-cats, are we?

Kate Gorky's Bedroom
The Castle

Monday, November 27, noon

Anna Gorky:

There's a window on a wall, Cora, in the room where that pretty Miss Kitty stays and you can see right through it.

Take your shoes off and hop up on the bed with me. My mother won't be back for another hour.

Mister Holmes was havin' another fight with Mama, and I was lookin' for a place to hide. I was runnin' down the hall on the third floor and saw one of the office doors open and so I run fast in there to get away from their bad words.

When I shut the door I couldn't hear them much, but I put my hands over my ears and cried and cried until I just had to wipe my nose. They were still fightin' so I went into a smaller office in the back of the big one. It was dark and cold and I couldn't hear them no more.

I went to sleep on the floor.

I don't know how long, but I felt better when I woke up.

I looked for some paper to wipe my face and that's when I tripped over a rug and hurt my knee. When the rug moved, I saw a small door in the floor with a latch on it.

Sure, I was afraid, but I knew that I would never leave that room without lifting up that door.

It wasn't too heavy.

Stairs, and a stale, wet smell like the kind cellars have with dirt floors.

No, 'fraidy cat, I didn't run away.

It was dark and there's a brick wall on the side of the steps. I went down them real slow so's I wouldn't fall into a deep hole or somethin' worse.

When I reached the bottom, I still couldn't see nothin'. The brick wall was still there, so I crawled on the floor next to it until I saw the window with light.

In Miss Kitty's room.

She was readin' a book.

Of course I knocked on the window, but she couldn't hear me even when I yelled out her name.

Somethin' ran over my shoe so I crawled back to the stairs as fast as I could.

That's all I saw, honest Injun.

Train Station   *Sunday, December 24*
Englewood, Illinois

Georgianna Yoke:

Oh, Henry, do you really have to spend Christmas in Wilmette?

It just doesn't seem right that you have to work on Christmas Day. Couldn't you catch the late train tomorrow night? My parents would love for you to come, and I was even going to fix you a special dessert.

I know, I wish you could, too. I've got an idea. Why don't I go to Wilmette with you? I could even get a hotel room next to yours, and when you aren't meeting with clients, we could have our own Christmas celebration.

Well, at least I can finish some of the wedding plans while I'm there. Can you believe it's less than a month away?

I can hardly wait. Then we'll never have to spend another Christmas apart.

Mmmm, kiss me once more. Are you sure you don't want your Christmas gift early?

Very well, hold onto mine until we're together again.

No, I'm not sure what day I'll get back. It should be right after New Year's unless I decide to go to Denver to visit some relatives. Let me go—that's the final boarding call. Take care, darling. I'll dream of you every night.

1894

The Denver Heights Hotel   *Wednesday, January 17*
Denver, Colorado

H. H. Holmes:

Dear God, in case you exist, please hear my prayer. There's a woman undressing for me in the bathroom of this expensive hotel in snow-bound Colorado. I know, I know, she's not the only apple of my eye. In fact, she's one of my Trinity. Oh Lord, help me to be strong, to draw the line, to stop my employment of another Justice of the Peace. Sweet Jesus, forgive her her sins, for you'll never forgive mine. Most of all, do the impossible: Keep me faithful to this woman, Georgianna—although only among the living. My attentions to the dead don't count because no one gets hurt, neither the dead nor their former friends. In a strange way, making love to the dead brings me closer to Mom and Dad. It's my way of honoring them, just as you, the Almighty, have commanded. I think the buxom bride is coming—now wish me luck. Amen.

The Ft, Worth Fortress   *January 28, 1894*
Ft. Worth, Texas

Dr. Frank Noland
Norristown Insane Asylum
Norristown, Pennsylvania

Dear Frank:

Can you picture me in a huge hat and black boots? I'm here in Ft. Worth to gobble up as much cash as possible from these good ol' country boys who walk as if they were still on horses.

I may have told you of Miss Minnie Williams, whose dear sister died in my office vault last July. Minnie made the mistake of turning over some Texas property to me, and now the poor lady is missing, last seen in the company of Hatch.

I'm with my new bride, the former Georgianna Yoke, now fast asleep after the two of us wore out the hotel bed earlier this evening. Next door is my drunken slave, Ben Pietzel, who is registered as Benton (i.e., he has bent) T. (the Truth) Lyman (and thus is a lying man).

Unfortunately, I had to tell Georgie a damn lie, too, something I hated to do. I told her that the Ft. Worth property was an inheritance from an uncle in Tennessee; but because some damn desperate squatters were insisting on their right to possess my land, I needed secrecy to deal with them. Thus, you will note that the envelope for this letter has a return

address listed under the name of H. M. Pratt—can you guess its meaning?—who is a co-owner, along with Lyman, of the property: a vacant lot in the best part of town.

Tomorrow we will use the property deed to establish credit to build another 3-story wonder (like my former castle) and furnish it with good Texas furniture. Once I have the place built and furnished by the excellent bankers and businessmen of Ft. Worth, I'll sell it back to them for a few hundred thousand. It thrills me to know I can outfox these Southern cowboys. And outfox them I will, stressing my Northern roots everytime I deal with them. In a year or so I'll mail them a letter postmarked from New York, sending them my condolences for their loss to me.

> *Need some sleep,*
> *Holmes*

Second and Russell Streets
Ft. Worth, Texas

Wednesday, February 14

Ben Pietzel (*alias* **Benton T. Lyman**):

These Texans may be big, but they sure are dumb—even dumber'n some of those Chicago boys.

Ha, ha, ha. That last bank scam was one of your best ones yet, Henry. And look at these young boys out here, sweatin' away in the Texas sun, pourin' the concrete for Castle Two. That older one over there asked me just before you got here when he was going to get paid. When will they ever learn? Ha, ha, ha.

Ah, c'mon, Henry, you've got to be kiddin' me.

Nah, I know you're bullshittin'. You got rid of 'er before ya picked up Georgie, fer Chrissakes.

Ironic? It's sick! Henry, if you really brought her skull all the way down from Indy just to bury it here, you are a sick bastard.

You really find this funny. Why should anything you do surprise me?

I don't wanna hear any more about it. Tell me where we're at with ol' Lawyer Crockett.

Hell, I say let's go for the full twenty thou. How much longer do you think it'll take?

Great! In the meantime, I'll work a few more of these bankers. We should be up fifty grand by the end of the month.

Yeah, well I still think it was a dumb thing to do. You've really started taking

some big chances. What if Georgie or someone else had seen it? They're all so inbred 'round here, someone mighta recognized her. And I can't imagine her kin finding her head under all this concrete quite as amusing as you do—'specially considerin' you swindled this land from her in the first place.

Well then, let me leave so you can pay your last respects. I've got to take care of some business.

Santa Fe Railroad *Thursday, March 15*
Amarillo, Texas

Georgianna Howard:

Ben, why did we have to leave Fort Worth so quickly?

You can go ahead and tell me. Don't worry, he's asleep.

I can't believe Henry let those squatters run him out of town. I mean, that's his land legally. They had to be related to the law. No one who knows the two of you would believe that you were capable of horse stealing.

I'm angry and disappointed. I couldn't wait to buy all the furnishings for the new Castle. Now I guess it's back to the old one.

Yeah, I guess I could persuade Henry to let me redecorate. I only wanted something that Henry and I could call our own.

Oh, these train seats are so hard after awhile. How long to Saint Louis?

That long? What's Henry planning?

No, he only tells me what false name to use in a new city and then leaves me to entertain myself until nighttime. I never realized that doing business could be so dangerous. You know, I wouldn't mind traveling at night if you could see something of the landscape, but when you look outside everything seems so distorted and unreal.

Tell me, have you heard from Carrie lately?

She must be a very strong woman. I don't know if I could go that long without seeing Henry.

Oh, you're awake.

No, Ben and I were just talking.

Ben, why don't you pass that flask over here? Mmm, this stuff is strong—it sure warms you up.

Henry, not in front of Ben!

Stop it!

I'm not joking, Henry. No games here. You'll just have to wait.

Then get a sleeper next time.

635 *Carondelet Street*   *Friday, May 11, 1894*
St. Louis, Missouri

My Dearest Carrie,

Arrived in St. Louis over the weekend, but didn't find this place until Wednesday. Everything is all set for you to come on down next Friday. Your train arrives at the station here at noon. I'll be there to pick all of you up. God, how I've missed you over these past six months.

Henry and I are working on one more BIG deal. I'll tell you all about it after you get here. When this is over, we will have enough money to strike out on our own. Henry is planning on going to Europe for an extended time with Georgie, so this time I really do mean it, my little Carrier Pigeon.

This place isn't the greatest, but it is a fully furnished three-room flat located at the south end of town. (We made some pretty good money in Texas.) There's also a really nice park called Carondelet Park just a few hundred yards from here that the kids will love. And the river is just over a mile from here. I can't wait to take you on a few moonlit walks along the Missouri R.

I need to get this off before noon to make sure you get it early next week. Please give kisses to all the children. I anxiously await our reunion.

> *Missing you terribly—lots of love,*
> *Ben*

Train Station   *Friday, May 18*
St. Louis, Missouri

Carrie Pietzel:

There's your father, children. Wave to him. I think he sees us!

No, Howard, you have to wait until the train stops—just a few more minutes.

Dessie, Alice, help me with the little ones. Watch where you're goin', Howard.

Benny, Benny, I can't believe we're finally here. We've missed you so much!

Don't strangle your father, children. Everybody gets a hug and a kiss, includin' me.

Ohhhh! What a hug! Benny, you're making me blush—people are starin'!

Yes, it was a very long trip—hot and dusty. But we're here and that's all that matters, love.

Oh, the children were fine. Wharton was a little fussy, but Alice and Dessie were a big help with him, and Nell entertained Howard.

Yes, I think we have everything. How far to our new home?

Then I guess we'll need a carriage. Is that one by the lamp for us?

Come on, children, we're goin' home.

Benny, I can't believe you've been gone so long. I know you must have a lot to tell me about your trip. I was sure glad you wrote as often as you did. I was so lonely, I reread your letters every day. Did everything go all right? Did you get the money?

All right, Benny, we can talk about it later. Right now, I just want to see our new home and get the kids put to bed...and then...?

St. Louis Cardinal, Suite 312   *Monday, May 21*
St. Louis, Missouri

H. H. Holmes:

I will be as rich as Vanderbilt, maybe as rich as the Pope. We'll have a house as big and beautiful as the Cardinal. Bigger, better, if Lady Luck stays friendly. For now, though, hold up a bit on your spending, Georgie.

Well, six pairs of shoes are enough for any woman. Even the Queen of England doesn't have—

Yes, I counted them in your closet: a red, two browns, and three blacks. I know your whole damn wardrobe, from the shoes to the three ribbons you use in your hair.

Yes, I know what colors they are. By the way, don't buy any more whites. Your virgin bride days are over. Buy black.

That's right, black. It's my favorite color next to blond hair. And that reminds me—you need to take out an insurance policy.

No, not on me. On yourself. And make me your beneficiary. Tomorrow I'm going to be doing the same for you.

Okay, Wednesday then.

Anywhere but Fidelity Mutual.

The Prudential is fine, yes.

Thirty thousand.

Good girl. Now, let's have breakfast in bed.

St. Louis Cardinal, Suite 312   *Friday, June 15*
St. Louis, Missouri

Georgianna Howard:

But, Henry, I don't understand why I can't meet her? Ben is your partner, isn't he?

Then it's only right we have Carrie and him over for dinner.

It wouldn't be that hard. We can have dinner here in the suite. I'll call in the morning and let the staff know what to prepare. Tomorrow night would be perfect since you don't have any meetings scheduled.

Well, you could give him a raise, and I could take Carrie shopping. She sounds like a very nice woman. Besides, I wouldn't mind looking for a new wrap myself. And before you say we can't do it because of their kids, I've already thought of a solution. The older girls can baby-sit the little ones.

I am serious about this. Darling, it's one time you're going to have to put me ahead of your work.

You have and I love my new onyx ring, but I want someone to talk to. During the day I get so bored. At least when I could shop it was bearable, but you've even stopped that.

Henry, you're only here at night.

The hotel *is* beautiful, but not when you're working. I'm beginning to wish I could sleep all day and only wake up when you come home.

No, I don't want any of those pills. I want some friends. I want us to socialize.

Nothing I can do will change your mind?

Oh, what?

I don't know. You got too rough last time—I had bruises that made it hard to sit for a week after that.

Well, instead of you punishing me for being a *naughty* girl, why don't I punish you?

Because I know you've been a very, very bad boy. Now, pull down your pants and bend over my knees.

635 Carondelet Street   *Tuesday, July 17*
St. Louis, Missouri

Ben Pietzel:

I love you so much, my little Carrier Pigeon.

Don't stop. That feels nice.

All right. Why is it you never feel my weight until after you climax?

Where you going? Get back here!

Oh, right. We certainly don't want any more pregnancies, now do we.

Hurry up, would ya?

Come to Papa Benny. Mmmmm-smooooch.

Well, it's finally time for me to tell you about the deal to end all deals. But don't tell a single soul.

I mean it. Not even the kids—promise?

Okay, well it's like this. Remember that ten thousand dollar insurance policy on me that names you as the beneficiary?

Here's how we're gonna be ten thousand bucks richer. Actually, it'll be more, but let me explain it from the start. The insurance policy is with a company called Fidelity Mutual in Philly. So, we—me and Henry that is—are goin' to Philly where we'll stage my *accidental* death.

Ah, ah, ah. Lemme finish. By doin' this in Philly, Henry'll be able to expedite matters much more quickly. I'll be goin' there under the name of B.F. Perry. Once we're there, Henry'll find a look-alike corpse for me from some doctor friend of his from way back in his medical college days.

Anyways, we'll fake an explosion, Henry'll I.D. the body as that of Ben Pietzel, and we'll be all the richer.

Now, now, shhhhsh. Carrie, this is fool-proof. The only drawback is I'll have ta lay low for awhile after we collect on the insurance.

Six months, tops. I Promise.

Carrie, be quiet. You'll wake the kids. Now list'n ta me. I know you can't stand Henry—*never* have liked him—although with all he's given me, the kids, and especially you, I'll never understand why. But this is our chance to start over with a lot of money. We'll move back home if you like, or anywhere you desire. And the best part is that there'll be no more Henry.

Don't you see, Pigeon, this is our ticket to freedom. We'll be our own bosses and we'll have plenty of money.

Because in addition to the money we make on this insurance deal, we'll also be investing back into some of those real estate deals we closed in Fort Worth...which reminds me. After Henry turns over the money to you—it should

be seventy-five hundred—you need to...

Honestly, Carrie. Obviously he needs to make some money on the deal. I think it's pretty decent of him to give us three-fourths of it, 'specially since it was his idea to begin with.

Because we've been partners and friends for a long time and because for the thousandth time he's going to Europe with Georgie and he won't be around any longer to keep me in his employ. It's his way of rewarding me for my loyalty all these Goddamn years. Anyways, out of the seven 'n a half, you need to wire five thousand to Fort Worth as soon as you can so we don't lose the property we have down there.

The land's worth more than twenty thousand, and it's vital that you wire the five grand to them right away, understand?

Don't worry, I'll write all the details down before I leave.

Everything'll work out. Just think—we'll be rich, living back home, and you won't have to deal with H.H. Holmes anymore. It's a winner all around.

Oh, yeah—when you read about *my* death, don't you worry. I might not be able to get any word to you for a while, but Henry'll keep you informed as to my whereabouts and how long it'll be before I can come back. Now, remember, not a word of this to anyone. I mean it! And be sure you don't let the kids see the newspaper story. No, on second thought, maybe they should. Hmmmm.

Well, let me think about that one. In the meantime, turn over, I'll even give you that back rub you're always askin' for.

St. Louis City Jail, Receiving Room   *Thursday, July 19*
St. Louis, Missouri

H.H. Holmes (*alias* Henry Mansfield Howard):

Thanks, but I don't smoke, Mister Carter.

I'm sorry to interrupt you, sir, but can we get down to business?

Last month I bought a drug store here in Saint Louis, buying the mortgage with a three hundred down payment.

The man's name was Winston or Winestone, I can't remember. Anyway, I stocked the store with supplies on credit I got from the Merrill Drug Company. A Mister Lawrence Brown then bought the store from me— here's the bill of sale—two weeks before I was to pay off the mortgage. But this man Brown sold all the inventory and then skipped town. When I didn't pay up on my credit account, the Merrill Company had me arrested for fraud.

I'm willing to give this Whitstone his store back, but I'm no longer the owner of it. Brown's his man, not I. In fact, I'm out two hundred on this deal because Brown gave me only a hundred down on the place.

Mister Carter, you also need to speak to the Merrill Company. They need to go after Brown—he's the true fraud, a sly fox on the lookout for naive sheep like me.

Right, I'm the victim, not the perpetrator. You're the attorney—get me out of here.

635 Carondolet Street *Saturday, July 21*
St. Louis, Missouri

Ben Pietzel:
Oh, hiya, Dess, <hic>, what'reya still doin' up?
Thass a ba-you-ful dress you're makin'. My lil' gal's so tal'ted.
Where's Mama?
Good, good. She deserves 'er sleep. She works so hard 'round here all time.
Well, my lil' Dessie, I need ta tell ya sumpthin', but ya gotta promisssss me you won't be tellin' no one else. Promisss your ol' Pappy, 'kay?
I'll be leavin' 'bout another week fer Philly. I'm goin' there under <hic> name of Beee Efffff Parreeee.
Trus' me. I got my reasons. Now, I'm 'fraid ya might see sumthin' in the papers that might upset you.
Sumpthin' 'bout my bein' dead.
Honest, Bugaboo, thass all I can say fer now. But 'member, if ya read 'bout my bein' dead in the papers, or if ya overhear Mama and Unca' Henry talkin', jes' 'member I'm really still 'live. As ol' Huck would say, accounts of my death've been greatly...'za-ggerated.
Thass all I <hic> say 'bout it fer now.
Don't look at me so. I might've had one er two too many...ha, ha, ha.
Two too many. Not bad, huh? Well, I bes' be gittin' ta bed, and so shou' you. Don't stay up long, 'kay?
Night-night, Dess. Give ol' Pappy a big hug 'n kiss. And not a word of this to anybody.

The St. Louis City Jail   *Monday, July 23*
St. Louis, Missouri

H.H. Holmes (*alias* **Henry Mansfield Howard**):

It's an honor to meet ya, Mister Hedgepeth. I've been followin' your career for years.

H.M. Howard, a businessman.

H for Howard, *M* for Mansfield. Real estate, prescription drugs, copy machines, human skeletons—anything that sells. Made lots of money, but never in the same direct way as you.

I mean that I've never held up a bank, blew up trains, or robbed people in coaches like you and Jesse James do. Must take a lot of nerve, Mister Hedgepeth, like...

Marion, then.

Like Ahab.

A character in a story.

He was a sea captain, fought whales, especially a giant one, bigger than this jail.

No, he didn't get it. It got him and most of his crew.

You're Ahab. The law is your whale.

Well, you're in its belly now.

This cell.

Okay, what would you like to talk about?

I've been rearrested for fraud against a drug company, but they'll never be able to prove it.

I'm several steps ahead of them. I've outwitted much bigger, richer companies than theirs, especially the life insurance giants. In fact, I've a surefire way to get ten thousand from one of them now.

Fidelity Mutual.

Because I need a lawyer who would be willin' to do things my way.

Lie, yes. Know one?

Five hundred.

Just give me a name and address, and if he agrees to my terms you'll get five hundred big ones as soon as the deed's done.

A fellow who works for me will fake a mortal accident. The insurance company will pay his wife the ten grand, and then I'll take my share of it.

It's easy, Marion, but unlike your way of doin' things, it's indirect.

Let me give you an example, then, of how I got twenty thousand from a Boston insurance company.

Right, we have plenty of time in here. Wanna hear my story?

Good. Well, one night after I registered in the Cleveland Hotel, I hung 'round the lobby for hours, making small talk with everyone who works there. The next morning I did the same thing. Then, after lunch I told everyone I was gonna take a nice, long nap because I wasn't feelin' well. No, thanks, I don't smoke. I went up to my room, unloaded my trunk, changed my clothes, put on a fake mustache and beard, wore a set of glasses, and went downstairs and out the front door.

I hired a buggy and took a nice ride out to the country, where I changed my clothes, put on a new mustache and beard, and wore a wig.

Yes, I kept the same glasses. No one would remember them. Could you guess what I was doin'?

Neither could anyone else. That's why I ended up with the twenty grand.

I went back to the hotel after the dinner hour and asked the manager if I could see a Mister Herman Mudgett, the name I had registered under. Eventually, since I, as Herman, was unable to open the door for me and the others, the manager agreed to use his extra room key to let us in. We found poor Herman dead on his bed. Somehow, he had burned his face in an accidental explosion he had caused by mixing chemicals in his room. Later on, it was established that Herman was a scientist; so the explanation was plausible.

You're still wonderin', aren't ya? My way of makin' money is really indirect, just the opposite from yours.

See, I had brought a corpse in my custom-made trunk, keepin' the thing covered in ice. On the day I went up to take a nap, I put the corpse on the hotel bed. Its face had been burnt earlier to make identification difficult.

Well, I had made sure that its height and general body size were similar to mine. It was wearin' the same clothes I had worn that morning in the hotel lobby.

A check was sent to my wife, Myrta, who turned it over to me when I told her it was a mistake that I would correct. She's beautiful and bright.

Yeah, you give me the name of a lawyer I can count on, and I'll tell you how I'm gonna bilk the lifers.

Howe? What's his first name?

The St. Louis Ciry Jail   Wednesday, July 25
St. Louis, Missouri

H.H. Holmes (*alias* Henry Mansfield Howard):

Good news, Marion—my wife Myrta is bailin' me outta here. Too bad ya can't get one of your beautiful ladies to unlock this cage for you.

Right, no bail for murderers. Use one of your women to blackmail a judge then. All women are slaves.

I won't forget. As soon as Mister Howe helps me to get the money, you'll get your five hundred.

Yeah, I'll give my wife a few shoves for you. I'll even have her call me Marion all night and won't even charge you for it, ha ha.

You're welcome, pal. I believe in stayin' in touch, ha, ha.

635 Carondolet Street   *Sunday, July 29, 8:00 a.m.*
St. Louis, Missouri

Ben Pietzel:

Nope, there's nothing like a Sunday breakfast with family to let you know all is right with the world. Do you have any strawberry preserves?

Thanks. I'll sure be missing this type of service and food for the next several months.

Now, now, Carrie, don't be gettin' all teary-eyed on me already. Save it for when I walk out that door if you must.

Kids, remember to pitch in and help Mama while I'm gone. She's going to need all your help. And, Howard, now's the time to show you're the man of the house for awhile, okay? Don't tease your sisters, and be sure to pick up after yourself. My, you're getting to be such a big boy. Don't grow too much while I'm gone.

Is there any more of that apple pie left?

Yes, for breakfast. It'll be the last piece of homemade pie I'll have for a long, long time.

What? Haven't any of you seen a man eat apple pie at nine in the mornin'?

Ha, ha, ha.

Okay, kids, gather 'round your ol' Pappy one last time. Stop that, Carrie. I'm gonna eat you up, Howard, chomp, chomp, chomp. Alice, Nellie, mind your mama. Dessie, I know I can depend on you. Keep Mama strong. Wharton, my little man—all of you be sure to help with the baby.

Now, kids, excuse us while I say good-bye to your mama.

Carrie, you've got to be strong about all this. Be sure to write me as Perry, and remember, when you read about my death, act the part of the grievin' widow. I won't be far from your dreams, I promise. Oh, and be sure to throw away my letters to you.

There, there, let me kiss those tears away. There's no need to cry, Pidgeon. Six months'll be gone before you know it. Then it's a new life for us all. And be

sure to take care of that property matter. I can't stress that enough. You have all the information?

Okay, okay. Well, this is it. Wish me luck. I'll be sure to write as soon as I find a place in Philly. Until we meet again....

The St. Louis City Jail, Exercise Yard   *Sunday, July 29, 2:00 p.m.*
St. Louis, Missouri

H.H. Holmes (*alias* Henry Mansfield Howard):

It's not really funny, Marion. They think Myrta's bail papers are fake, but they're not.

She just made a stupid mistake, so I'll be outta this furnace in no time. You still in the same cell?

Fritz Richard's Bar   *Monday, July 30*
Philadelphia, Pennsylvania

Ben Pietzel (*alias* B.F. Perry):

Howdy, Mac, let me try one of those Dock Streets.

Thanks. Nice place ya got here. How's the burgers?

Make it rare—blood-drippin' rare. By the way, my name's B.F. Perry. You can call me Ben.

The Fritz Richard—like the name on the sign? Real nice ta meet'cha.

Just got ta town 'bout 'n hour ago. Figured I'd knock the dirt off my throat and grab a bite to eat. By the way, that hit the spot pretty good. Lemme have another draw.

Saint Louie. Thanks. You pour a nice mug, Fritz. So, ya know of any places to rent cheap?

Oh, I don't know. A few weeks, a few months, perhaps a few years. Depends on how business is. I'm into patents—I buy 'n sell 'em. Basically what I'm lookin' for is a room to hang my hat and a front room to do business in. Once business is up and running, I'll get a bigger place and send for the wife and kids.

Five now— three girls, two boys. The youngest is just two. How 'bout yourself?

You don't say? Well, if this ain't my lucky day. Out of a town of thousands, the first person I run into has a sister who just happens to run a lodging home 'round the corner from here. Ha, ha, ha. Here's to you, my friend.

Er, how 'bout another draw?

St. Louis City Jail   *Tuesday, July 31, 2:00 p.m.*
St. Louis, Missouri

H.H. Holmes (*alias* Henry Mansfield Howard):

Hey, guard, do me a small favor, will ya?

Will a dollar change your mind?

Good. Listen, when you go by Hedgepeth's cell, tell him that Howard —that's me—was released on bail by his wife Georgianna. He'll get a kick outta that.

St. Louis Cardinal, Suite 312   *Tuesday, July 31, 4:00 p.m.*
St. Louis, Missouri

Georgianna Howard:

I still don't understand why your business is so dangerous, Henry.

You've said that before, but how many people could know about that patent? Now move so I can finish packing your shirts.

Yes, I'm upset. Here I am in this strange city with no family or friends, and I'm told my husband has been put in jail. Luckily, I was able to find someone to buy that bracelet you gave me or you would still be there.

I don't want a new one. It's just strange that we had to leave Fort Worth in the middle of the night and now we have to leave Saint Louis the same way.

Stop that. I'm getting a really bad headache and I want to finish packing so I can lie down.

I said no! If you want to be helpful, fasten these bags.

Exclusively Bonnets   *Friday, August 3*
Lake Bluff, Illinois

Georgianna Howard:

Elizabeth, I'm so happy Henry decided I needed a break from all the traveling. Hasn't it been wonderful to be back together, just like when we were in college?

Oh, no, I wouldn't want to be single again. Henry's a wonderful man and a great provider. Here, try this one on.

Well, he's a bit mysterious. No, I don't like that one—it looks like you're wearing a big grape on your head. He has a lot of business ventures. I don't even know about half of them. He's very wealthy, but he doesn't like me to spend that much money. Oh, won't he be surprised when he gets the bills from this trip!

I'm going to spend as much as I want. Besides, I'm still a little angry with him. What do you think about this blue one?

We haven't made up from our fight, yet that's the best part. You wouldn't believe how many ways that man can think of to make love. He even wanted me to do it on a train with him.

Well, it would have been fine if we had been in a sleeper car, but I wasn't about to do it with his friend sitting across from us. Let's talk about this later—those old women over there are listening to us.

Henry's not that old.

Seriously, I thought I told you.

I'm sorry. Henry's not the older gentleman friend I had been seeing. He's only about ten years older than me. Very intelligent, has wonderful blue eyes and dark brown hair, and treats me like a princess. In fact, before I got on the train, he gave me a gold comb and brush set. But then he's constantly surprising me with little pieces of jewelry or clothing. Here's a green bonnet that matches your dress. Let me buy it for you.

Yeah, I guess I did catch a good one.

Oh, I'm sure he wouldn't cheat on me.

Because I keep him satisfied.

Yes, I'm serious. I still don't know whether I should get the black bonnet with the flowers around the brim or this blue one. I know—I'll get them both.

38 North John Street
Wilmette, Illinois

Saturday, August 4

Myrta Holmes:

This is so unlike you, Harry. I just don't get it. Why are you taking so many chances?

That's crazy! Just because you spent a few hours in some cell with some so-called famous train robber is no reason for you to be blabbin' all your ideas to him.

And just exactly who is this Howe guy? Some shyster lawyer you've never dealt with. Good Lord, Harry, can't you see what's happening here? You're involving too many people in on your scheme—people you don't even know. It's bad enough that you dragged Ben into this, but these other two guys? C'mon, you know that's just plain stupid.

Well, there's a reason I've never nagged you before. That's because you've never done anything so dumb. Cut your losses now while you still can. Hell, it's only ten thousand. That's peanuts compared to some of the jobs we've pulled.

Count me out of this one completely. You're making this way too complicated. This makes no sense at all, and you know it. It's become some kind of Goddamn game to you—a game I want no part of.

Go to hell!

Leave then, damnit!

Yeah, Merry Christmas to you, too, asshole.

Oh, Lucy, what are we going to do? He's changing so. It's as if I hardly know him anymore.

1905 North Eleventh Street   *Sunday, August 5*
Philadelphia, Pennsylvania

H.H. Holmes (*alias* Henry Mansfield Howard):

Georgie, dear, rub my foot.

Please, right. Please?

Ah, that feels good. A little lower.

You know, I should have been a foot doctor. Much of my inner life is made up of ankles, heels, and toes. I'm in love with high arches.

Years ago. My father had small, delicate feet like a woman's. The odd thing is that he used his feet to beat us, and my mother would sometimes lift her skirts and give us a swift kiss of a pointed shoe.

Out of anger, I guess. A strange glow would enter their eyes as they did it, as if the anger were a flame of hate inside them, forever burning in their desires to be rid of us.

He was a farmer who sold his soul to the Christians in our hometown of Gilmanton, New Hampshire. Sometimes I think I'm the price he paid for his hypocrisy.

She just went along with whatever he ordered. Both were despicable.

Ah, you rub so well! Listen, before I forget, I'm gonna be in and out of here for the next few weeks.

Making money, my dear! I have several big companies interested in the patent letter copier we have for sale. If sold, we'll have both our feet rubbed by four young girls.

Okay, two boy slaves for you; two full-breasted slaves for me.

1316 Callowhill Street
Philadelphia, Penn.

Monday, August 6, 1894

Dear Carrie,

You would all hate this place. I know I do.

I'm beginning to think you were right about this whole thing. I don't know what I'm doing here anymore. Henry is supposed to get here on Wednesday, and I'm going to tell him then that if he can't speed this up, I'm heading home. Some things just aren't worth the money.

Trust all is well with you and the kids. Carrie, I really am sorry for all the bad times over the years. I honestly don't know how you have put up with me. I pray to God that I get one more chance to prove myself to you and the children. If I am never able to do anything else, I do want so badly to provide for you and the kids. I want you all to live long, comfortable lives. If that is the only thing I can provide for you, then my life will have been worth living.

But enough of this talk. Please give my love to all the kids. I'll write again soon. Don't forget to take care of this letter.

Your loving husband who misses you terribly,
Ben

Adella Alcorn's Boarding House
Philadelphia, Pennsylvania

Wednesday, August 8

Georgianna Howard:

Good morning, Doctor Alcorn.

Very well, Adella, but please call me Georgianna.

No, only Henry calls me Georgie. Would you pass me one of those biscuits, please? So, what are your plans for the day?

I'm not sure either. Would you like to go for a walk after breakfast? I think the fresh air might do me some good. These rolls are delicious. How did you fix them?

I've never been very good in the kitchen. Luckily, we've been traveling so much that I haven't had to worry about cooking for Henry.

Oh, I think we'll hire a chef and maid once we find a place to settle down. So, are you up for that walk? I hate going by myself.

Good, we can go before it gets too hot.

No, I don't have a headache so far today. I think your home remedy did the trick.

I keep trying to tell Henry that, but he doesn't believe all the traveling could be causing them. We've seen so many towns I could barely name them all.

I believe he's in Saint Louis until the middle of next week. I miss him so much, but I don't think I could have made the trip. How long were you and your husband married?

Thirty years! Henry and I have a while before we reach that. We've only been married eight months. Well, I'll go change so we can be on our way.

The Pickwick Restaurant   *Thursday, August 9, noon*
Philadelphia, Pennsylvania

Ben Pietzel:

Why, thank you, Henry. Mmmmm, that's a mighty fine cee-gar to top off a mighty fine lunch.

Excuse me, waiter.

Ah, no dessert for me. That meal was an elegance of sufficiency. But I'll have another Dock Street.

I tell ya, Henry, you should try one of these local brews. They're excellent.

Ah, shit, I'm not drinkin' all that much. Hell, I've only had two for lunch.

Frankly, I'm gettin' fed up with this whole thing. You have no idea what it's like livin' in that hell-hole all alone. It's only been a week and a half, but it already seems like a month. We really need to get movin' on this. Can't you get your doctor friend to hustle up a body?

You gotta be kidding me! I don't know if I can hang on that long. I told Carrie to expect to see the notice within a few weeks, not a few months.

If you really think it won't be till late August at the earliest, then I'm definitely gonna need more money.

I gave Carrie seven hundred. I had to lay out fifty bucks up front for that rat-infested dump, and then, uh, there was the train ticket, and then, um, some other 'sorted odds and ends.

No, I still got about one-fifty left from the grand. Geez, what do you take me for?

My God, I completely forgot!

Henry, say something. It's just that I got caught up in saying good-bye...and then all that travelin'—it's not like I forgot to send the premium in on purpose. Would you say something?

Yes, you're right! There was at least a one-week grace period. And there's a Western Union right across the street. We'll wire a money order back to Chicago today.

Fidelity Mutual Insurance Company   *Thursday, August 9, 1:00 p.m.*
Chicago, Illinois

Fidelity Clerk Chris Hargrove:

Hey, Andy, get a load of this one. See this telegraphic money order for one-fifty-seven-fifty?

Check the date.

Now, check this B.F. Pietzel—number zero-four-four-one-four-five in our records.

Isn't that amazing! Two more hours 'n he would've missed his grace period. Now *that* is one lucky stiff.

Fritz Richard's Bar   *Friday, August 10*
Philadelphia, Pennsylvania

Ben Pietzel (*alias* B.F. Perry):

Hey, Fritz. Better line me up a shot to go with that beer. Tough day to go with 'n even worse yesterday.

Thanks.

Ah, hell, I almost blew a business deal with my partner. As it is, I was down to my last few dollars and had to get a loan on a big deal we got goin' down. God, how I hate to beg. 'Specially him. Sometimes he just pisses me off. Ya better just bring the bottle and another beer.

Henry Howa, er...Campbell. Our biggest project together is with a copier company. But we do a lot of other deals. Can I pour ya one?

Does life ever get you down to the point where you wonder if it's worth livin' anymore?

Yeah, like right now. I mean, what's the point? Ya bust your ass all day, catch shit from half the people—hell, this is my only 'joyment.

Hey, thanks, ya read my mind—and the perfect head. Sure ya don't wanna shot of whiskey?

Suit y'self.

Henry? Nah, he don't drink much. Don't think he'd care much for this place, Fritz. He's not like us. At times he's like no one. That's why I haven't mentioned him to you before.

Keep a secret?

This's goin' down too smooth t'night. Cheers. Ahhh.

Well, lemme tell ya a lil' story 'bout ol' Henry that you'll prob'ly think is bull-shit, but sure as shootin', it's the God's honest truth. One day after buyin' a res'trant with no money down, he buys a whole buncha furn'ture for it. The next night the supplier stops by ta collect on the stuff. What's Henry do? He sets the fool up with drinks, treats him ta dinner, fixes'm up with a fine cee-gar, and then sends the man off laughin' at one of his stupid-ass jokes with a promise ta pay him his due the followin' week. Within thirty minutes, Henry and his wife are loadin' up that furn'ture, and 'fore the week's out they've not only sold it all, but they've also backed out of the res'trant deal. Henry pockets five grand and never lays out one red cent.

Honest. Next day he tells the cops he got cold feet 'n that's why he not only backed out of the mortgage, but also had the supplier take all the furn'ture back. It's his and his wife's word 'gainst the supplier's. An' jes' in case, he's also got a fancy lawyer ta boot.

Hell, Fritz, that's jes' one of a thousand stories I could tell ya. I prob'ly should-n't've told ya that one. It's jes' that he pisses me off, 'n I 'spose it don't much matter no more whether you heard that story or not. It was years ago anyways. Ancient his-tor-reee.

Yeah, yeah. Go take care of 'em. Um, 'fore ya go though, how 'bout two more draws 'n a burger. And Fritz, don't go repeatin' that story, 'kay?

1316 Calloway Street   *Friday, August 17, 1894*
Philadelphia, Penn.

Dear Carrie,

Happy birthday!

I'm so sorry I'm not there with you today to celebrate your 34th! Trust you have gotten the dress and hat I picked up for you here in Philly. It's the latest style on the East Coast. Hope you don't find them too immodest for either yourself or for the Midwest.

You were certainly right about this whole deal, my love. How I wished I had listened to you. But in the end, when you collect all that money, I hope all this will have been worth it.

I would also like to take this time to again apologize for all the agony I have put you through over the years—from the time I seduced you and you became pregnant with Dessie to all the times I became violent and drunk. I'm especially sorry that I hit you. But remember, my Carrier Pigeon, I was drunk on each occasion. Pappy was right about one thing—I have been a no-good drunk. Alcohol is the root of all evil.

I really thought I had shook it after Keeley, but I now find myself finding solace in the bottle more and more everyday. I've barely drawn a sober breath since I arrived in Philly. Even as I write this, I find I must have my liquid companion. God, how I hate myself and what I have done to us.

If God will only give me one last chance, I promise to make all of this up to you and the kids—and to myself. That's all I want is one more chance. That is why I must hang on for a while longer. I've come this far, and Holmes keeps reminding me that he has also stuck his neck out. So, one last time, and then I promise, never again.

Remember why I'm here and think about what life will be like in the near future. Please give a big hug and kiss to each of the kids, and don't forget to you know what.

I love you and miss you ever so much. Keep me in your prayers.

Ben

1316 Callowhill Street   *Wednesday, August 22*
Philadelphia, Pennsylvania

Ben Pietzel (*alias* B.F. Perry):

Mister Smith, nice to meet'cha. My name's Ben...Ben Perry.

All right, Eugene, then. So, Eugene, how can I help you?

Sounds interesting. Let me take a look at it.

Let me get this straight. This is the part of the sharpener where you put the handsaw?

Didja bring a dull blade with ya?

Great, lemme see it.

Yes, Eugene, it's dull, very dull. Well, show me how it works.

That's all? Just four strokes? Lemme see it now.

Ouch. I can't believe you got it that sharp with just four strokes. I think you just might have a winner here.

Now, who could that be coming in without ringing the bell?

Oh, would you excuse me for a moment? Make yourself comfortable. That was, um...my...um, my business partner—I'll be right back.

Holmes, what are you doing here?

A Mister Smith—Eugene Smith. He's got a great invention. With just four strokes...

All right, all right. I'll get rid of him. Hey, it's not my fault you came boundin' in like that. If you don't wanna be seen 'round here, you should knock first before...

Jeez. Okay, I'm goin'!

Ah, Eugene. I really think you have something here. If you don't mind, I would like to look it over, and, um, discuss it with my business partner— you know, get a feel for it. Like I said, I really think you have something.

Saint Louis. Been in the patent business on and off all my life—set up shop here 'bout three weeks back.

Trust me, Eugene. I really do need to hang on to it a few days. I'm sure any patent dealer would tell ya the same. But I also have ta get back upstairs. So, if you don't feel right about leavin' it here, take it somewhere else.

Tell you what. I'll write out a receipt for you, 'kay? And we'll store it right over there in the back room.

Well, yes, on the floor. I've been meaning to build a counter, but I just haven't had the time....

Really? All right then. Tell you what, you come back day after tomorrow—ah,

better make it next Monday. You come back Monday to build that counter, and I'll have an answer regardin' that patent. Here's your receipt. See you Monday.

He's gone. Now, Henry, what's this all about? What's so goddamn important that you have to run off one of my customers?

I really don't think he saw you, but so what if he did? Sometimes you get so worked up about the littlest things. Now, what's going on?

No shit. Really?

Oh that's great, Henry, really great news. I must admit I've been having second thoughts about this whole business. But knowing that the stiff is on its way—when can we do it?

This is what I've been prayin' for. Nothin' personal, but I just couldn't take this any longer. I've been away from Carrie too, too long. I guess I just wasn't cut out for this type of business the way you are. You live for these moments. But when this deal goes down and you leave for Europe, that'll be that for me. I'm going straight after this, Henry, you hear me?

I tell ya, I really do miss her. Bein' away all this time has gotten me to thinkin'. I've been real bad to her. But after we score on this deal, I'm gonna make it all up to her, I tell ya. I really am. How's Georgie doin'?

See, that's my point. You always have one of your gals nearby. Ya jes' don't understand how lonely a man like me can get. Well, get back to her and tell 'er I said hey.

Oh, Henry...ah...I'm still a little short on cash. Can you either give me a bit more of my share on the Texas deal or float me a loaner 'til that other deal goes down?

Hell, if you wuz all 'lone like me, you'd be drinkin' a bit, too. I'm swearin' off the bottle after this is all said and done. That's 'nother one of my promises to Carrie that I intend to stick to. But until you get that corpse down here...

Hey, thanks a lot, Henry. I'll pay you back, I promise.

Adella Alcorn's Boarding House, Outdoor Garden   *Saturday, September 1,*
Philadelphia, Pennsylvania   *8:00 p.m.*

Ben Pietzel (*alias* B.F. Perry):

Don't do this to me, Henry. I told you the other day I can't take this anymore.

It's been one excuse after another. This is the third time that for some reason or 'nother the cadaver hasn't shown up. What's this guy doin' up there?

Well, then, that's it. I'm out. Forget the whole deal. I'm goin' home to Carrie, and that's that.

You sonuva bitch. That was a *long* time ago. Anyway, for every one thing you

have on me, I've got a thousand on you. And don't think I won't. You tell any-one about that, Henry, and I'll squeal like a pig.

Well, then, don't be talkin' that shit. We've been through too much together. Why can't you just for once understand my side of things. I'm sick and tired of all this. I can't take it anymore, don't you see that?

Don't ask me to stay. You know how hard it is for me to say no to you. Hell, I don't think I ever have. But this time I just have to say no. I'm going home, you hear me?

All right, all right. But this is the last time. If there's no body by Monday, I'm going back to Saint Louie. I've taken all I can take. I'm not feelin' too awfully good 'bout myself, and stayin' in this town another day is jes' gonna make matters worse.

Okay, I said. I'll stay 'til Monday. That is if you give me a few more bucks.

You only gave me twenty. Give me another twenty now, and I'll be goin' back to the shop. If you don't, I'm headin' straight to the train station.

Thanks.

I told you I'll stay! If nothing else, you can count on that.

No, I won't be doin' a thing tomorrow. But I'd just as soon you not stop by—unless you have a body.

Good-bye, Henry.

Fritz Richards Bar   *Saturday, September 1, 10:00 p.m.*
Philadelphia, Pennsylvania

Ben Pietzel (*alias* B.F. Perry):

Life's the pits <hic> and then ya die. How's a 'bout a nudder round, Fritzzzy?

Ah, hell, ya ain't seen nuttin' yet. T'night's the night I've been waitin' for. He won't have his stoolie ta kick 'round no more, yessiree.

Why 'ol Henry the Sca-neevin' Heathen, that's who. Who'dja think I've been talkin' 'bout all night long? The one 'n only. The man who's made my life a livin' hell these past five, six years.

Ah, you're right as rain, Fritz. Yeah, it wasn't always <hic> such a bad time. Hell, I think there wuz even a time I kinda liked the sonuva bitch. But no more, I tell ya, no more.

Hey, bring me anudder beer 'n pour us both a shot—I'll tell ya a leettle, bitty secret.

Ah, here's to you, Brother Fritz. The only man in this here godforsaken town that's worth a shit.

Promise not ta tell a soul?

'Kay. The man's really not a man at all.

Shhhh. No, he's not. Ya wanna know what he is? He's the devil 'imself, that's what he is.

No, no, you don't understand. I mean, he really is the devil. I used ta think he was just bad, y'know, a bit of a thief, 'n on ocassion, a bit of a killer. But these past few weeks here in Philly, it's all become quite clear. The man's Satan 'imself. Now, whaddya think of that?

Goddamnit, Fritz. You're not listen'n ta me. Shit, no one listens ta me. It's like I'm not even here. Well, I might as well not be. Tell ya what. Get me a couple a pints of whiskey 'n cash me outta here. Oh, 'n one of them there fine cee-gars of yours.

Thanks, Fritz. For the most part ya been a real pal. I'm gonna miss ya.

Whaddya care? Ya won't even listen ta me when I try tellin' ya 'bout my friend from Hell. Like I said, I might as well not even be here. No one listens ta me— my life ain't worth a shit. Naw, I'm goin' home 'n I ain't comin' back, 'n that's that.

My Dearest Carrie,　　　　　　　　　　　*Saturday, September 1, 1894*

The bewitching hour is near, and my damned, tortured soul is soon to be released to Satan, who I am now convinced is the brother of Holmes. When you read this letter, I will probably have been dead for several days. Though it pains me to write this through my alcohol crazed mind, I must continue.

Being here in Philly has given me time to reflect on my pitiful life. What I now realize is in order to set us both free, I must sacrifice my life (what's left of it), to give us both a chance.

After you read this letter, you must remember to destroy it. Neither Holmes nor the authorities should ever see it. For my part, when this letter is finished, I will place it in an envelope addressed to you in a saw sharpening invention that a Mr. Eugene Smith brought in to me last week. As soon as he hears of my death, he will be sure to come pick up his machine. If all goes well (and if you are reading this, then all did indeed go well), Mr. Smith will mail this on to you.

Forget what I told you earlier about taking $5,000 and putting it into that Texas land deal. I now know that Holmes will never give me my real cut on that deal. Instead, take the entire $10,000 (or what's left of it after the lawyers get their cut) and keep it. Be strong, Carrie. Tell Holmes you are keeping the money (remember, it is made out in your name—you are the only one who can cash it). Tell him he can keep all of my share in the Texas deal, and put the insurance money straight in

the bank. Hire an attorney yourself. Check with Joe DiMeglio—he has always seemed to be an honest enough Joe. The best thing about all this is that neither one of us ever has to lie again. The authorities will find my real body, the insurance company will cut the check, and you and the kids can live out the rest of your lives on the $10,000. I know Holmes will do his best to make this look like an accident because I'm sure he will be looking to take at least half of the money, if not more. The greatest revenge I and you can hold over him is to keep all the insurance money away from him. In the end, after you tell him he can keep the Texas money and you will never bother him again, I should think he might go rather quietly. All you need do is hold him off for a few weeks. After that, he will be leaving for Europe with Georgianna with all his thousands from the Texas deal and any other scams he pulls between now and then.

Always remember I love you, Carrie, and know that I died bravely for you, the kids, and myself. I pray that God takes pity on my soul and that someday we can be together again. If nothing else, I leave this world knowing that I have finally provided for you and the kids.

In eternity,
Ben

Holmes,   Sunday, September 2, 1894

I write my final letter to you as the clock strikes midnight. An appropriate ending for my life, wouldn't you agree?

As you have noticed by my quite dead body, I could no longer take you, the lies, and more than anything else, myself. Just think, I saved you the trouble of having to owe your doctor friend anything else. There is a real live (or should I say dead?) body upstairs, and it is quite obviously mine. All you need to do is make sure it looks like it was an accident.

If you have any shred of decency left in you, and if you have any real feelings in regard to our relationship, then please allow Carrie to keep most of the insurance money. In return, she will not press you at all for the Texas money due me. She's never had much, Holmes. This is the least we both can do for her. Please allow me this final moment of gallantry for my wife.

Good luck to you and Georgianna, and I hope you all have a great life in Europe. May God have mercy on both our souls. I suspect we shall meet up again in Hell.

Pietzel

P.S.
I have left two shots of whiskey from the two pints I bought earlier this evening. Have a toast in my honor.

Adella Alcorn's Boarding House   *Sunday, September 2*
Philadelphia, Pennsylvania

Georgianna Howard:

Henry, what are you doing back so early? I didn't expect you 'til this evening.

Oh my goodness, what's wrong?

Dear, you're sweating like crazy and you're so pale. What's the matter? Should I call a doctor?

Slow down—I can barely understand what you're saying.

Henry, we can't leave with you looking like this. Please lie down for a little while. We can catch the late train.

There's no reason to get that tone with me. I won't finish packing until you tell me what happened at that meeting. And if you don't, I'll go see Ben and have him tell me.

Yes, I'm serious. You're frightening me, Henry. Now sit down in this chair and tell me what's gotten you so riled. I've never seen you like this.

Why don't you sell the patent to that copier? Obviously, there are too many people who know about it and are trying to steal it from you. It's not worth all this. You will kill yourself if you keep this up.

Darling, I just want you to be like you used to be.

I've already told you, we're not leaving 'til you get some rest.

All right, I'll make a deal with you. If you will lie down and rest, I'll finish packing and then we can leave. Here's a cold compress—now hand me your jacket and shirt.

Yes, dear, I'll hurry. When I'm finished, I'll wake you.

Stubbins' European Hotel, Room 12   Wednesday, September 5, 1894
Indianapolis, Indiana

Dear Mother and Father,

Hello. How are the both of you doing? Mother, I was sorry to hear you had caught a cold. I hope by this time you are feeling better. Please tell

me Father did not get it, too. I remember last year when he was sick with the flu, and you were so tired from waiting on him. Both Henry and I are doing fine, except I am still suffering with my migraines from time to time.

As you can tell, we are no longer staying with Dr. Adella. She is a very nice lady, but Henry said it was time for us to move to another city. I will be thrilled when we are finally able to stay in one place. I know I have always said I wanted to see the world, but I never meant for it to be done this fast. It seems like we have only just arrived before we have to leave again. Adella said this probably causes my headaches.

Otherwise Henry has been quite the perfect husband. He has bought me so many little gifts, mainly jewelry. Last night he gave me a gold bracelet. It was so shiny—I wish you could see it. He bought me some new books, too, which he sometimes reads to me.

Well, I must be going. The innkeeper's wife, Mrs. White, is coming to check on me, and she can post this letter. Henry has gone to St. Louis for a few days. He is always working.

We miss you and will try to come for a visit soon. Take care.

Love Always,
Georgianna

The St. Louis Star Thursday, September 6, 1894
Patent Dealer Found Dead

Body believed to be that of B.F. Perry

Death of mysterious origins

PHILADELPHIA, Sept. 5—The body of B.F. Perry, a patent dealer at 1316 Calloway Street in Philadelphia, was found dead this past Tuesday. It is believed Mr. Perry died sometime early Sunday morning.

Mr. Perry's body was found on Tuesday by Eugene Smith, a client of Mr. Perry's.

There are two theories as to how Mr. Perry died. The coroner who performed the autopsy, Dr. William Mattern, has ruled the death was a result of chloroform poisoning. The police, however, have theorized that Mr. Perry died as a result of an explosion caused by carelessly lighting his pipe too close to bottles containing a volatile mix of benzine, chloroform, and ammonia.

At an inquest held yesterday afternoon, the jurymen's verdict covers a range of possibilities—that Mr. Perry died from "congestion of the lungs, caused by the inhalation of flame, or of chloroform, or other poisonous drugs." The question of whether his death was accidental, suicidal, or a result of foul play has been left open.

As of this writing, police still have not been able to locate any next of kin. The only one who seems to have known Mr. Perry, who apparently came to town just last month, is Mr. Smith. Police are continuing to investigate the matter.

635 Carondelet Street   *Thursday, September 6*
St. Louis, Missouri

Carrie Pietzel:

Hello, Mister Holmes. Won't you come in?

No, I'm afraid we're not doing very well at the moment. Please excuse my appearance, but we're all a little upset right now. Dessie saw the death notice in the paper a little bit ago.

The death notice for B. F. Perry—and they all know I been gettin' letters from Ben under that name. They think their Papa's dead.

Of course, Ben told me what to expect, but I have this terrible feeling. Are you sure he's okay? When did you see him?

I'll run in the kitchen and let the children know that he's all right...

Why not?

But nobody would question the children, would they?

If that's what Ben says...

How long before I can see him?

We can't wait that long!

You don't understand. Ben hasn't sent us much money and what little I have left has to go to buy food for the children. I've got a sick baby and no money for a doctor or...

That would be a relief. I'll get Dessie.

Dess, honey, go fetch the doctor for Wharton.

No, it's okay. Mister Holmes will take care of it. Now, run along quick!

Thank you—Wharton has been so sick, and I didn't know what to do.

'Preciate your concern.

Yes, the policy's in my bureau drawer. Do you want me to get it now?

But I don't know if Wharton'll be well enough by tomorrow to....

I suppose Dess and Alice could handle him. Where do I take it?

Jep..tha Howe, Es..quire. Am I reading this right?

No, I've never been in the Commercial Building, but I know where it is. Does Mister Howe know about...uh...everything?

Good. I'll gladly let him handle it. No, I won't lose his card—I'll do my best to go tomorrow. I want to hurry this up as quickly as possible so Benny can come home.

I'm glad you stopped by. Please let me know as soon as you hear from Ben.

Jeptha D. Howe's Law Office   *Friday, September 7, 10:00 a.m.*
St. Louis, Missouri

Carrie Pietzel:

Mister Howe?

I'm Carrie Pietzel. Mister Holmes said I should come to see you about my husband's insurance policy. He said you'd tell me what I need to do.

Yes, I have it right here along with the newspaper clipping. I thought maybe you might need that, too.

What kind of letter?

If you'll help me. What should I say?

All right, it will only take me a few minutes for that little bit.

There. Do you think that's okay?

Now, how long do you think it will take to get the money?

Okay, I'll wait until I hear from you. I'm glad you and Mister Holmes are takin' care of this. I don't know much about business.

Fidelity Mutual Insurance Company   *September 7, 1894*
Commercial Building
St. Louis, Missouri

Dear Sir,

I wish to inform you that the person described in the enclosed newspaper article, Mr. B. F. Perry, is my husband, Benjamin Freelon Pietzel, who is insured by your company under policy number 044145 in the amount of $10,000.00.

I would greatly appreciate it if you could handle this claim as quickly as possible as my children and I have no money for food or clothes.

> *Thank you for your help.*
> *Mrs. Carrie A. Pietzel*

38 North John Street   *Thursday, September 13*
Wilmette, Illinois

Myrta Holmes:

Yes, I'm Myrta Holmes. And whom might you be?

Inspector Cass? Inspector of what?

And just what would the manager of Fidelity Mutual want of me?

No, I don't believe I will invite you in, Mister Cass. I'm very busy today, and I really don't have the time to be—what is it, Lucy?

As you can see, Mister Cass, I really am very busy. Go ahead, honey, and help Denise dry the dishes while I finish with this gentleman.

As for my husband, he has seldom been at home lately, if you must know. He is a very successful businessman, as you can see from this home and the maid who greeted you. We do, however, correspond regularly, and if you have any messages for my husband, I will be sure he gets them.

Fine, I'll make sure he gets all of these questions. Anything else?

Okay, and this article from the—*The Chicago Report* as well.

Sorry I couldn't spend more time with you, Inspector Cass. But as you can see, I really do have to get going. Good luck in your investigation.

Good-bye.

Jesus, Harry, you're an idiot. I told you this whole insurance scam was a mistake from the start. This just wasn't your style. You've had too many damn people involved, and now look what's happening. Fidelity Mutual knows something's up. Here.

And don't forget the goddamn newspaper story. Although what could possibly be so important about a newspaper story from Chicago is beyond me.

A trick? What do you mean?

Shit, they really are on to you. Why else would he have wanted me to show you that story about the body being in Chicago. They're trying to trip you up, don't you see? That could have been so easy for you to have told them you would meet them in Philly, when the article says the body's right here. Then they would have known for sure your involvement.

Just be very careful. And remember, if the heat gets too hot, take off for awhile until things cool down. I mean, it's only a lousy ten thousand dollars we're talking here. It's just not worth getting thrown in jail over.

Now then, before you sit down and start answering all those questions, why don't you come upstairs with me and rest awhile?

Denise, could you be a dear and take Lucy to the park while Mister Holmes and I rest a spell.

Okay, dear, I do believe it's my turn to pick the fantasy. Now, upstairs—on the double.

Stubbins' Hotel, Room 12   *Friday, September 14*
Indianapolis, Indiana

Georgianna Howard:

Who's there?

The big bad wolf? Is it really you, Henry?

No, dear, come in. I've missed you so much.

What took you so long in getting back? Did things go well?

That's wonderful. I can't wait to decide where we can settle down—here, let me hang up your jacket. Hopefully, Europe will be different. The hotels have to be of a better quality. This one's pitiful, Henry. There's barely enough room for me to turn around, much less entertain anyone. When do we leave?

That soon? Thank goodness, I've already got the bags packed. What's that box you're holding?

Dear, it's gorgeous! I've always wanted a heart-shaped locket. Here, fasten it around my neck. Ouch! Not so tight.

That's better. Oooh, I love it.

Yeah, I guess you're forgiven. You know, the one good thing about this room is the huge clawfoot bathtub and I just filled it. Do we have time for a bath?

Oh, even enough time for a story. Let's see then—once upon a time....

Train Station   *Tuesday, September 18, 6:20 p.m.*
St. Louis, Missouri

Jeptha D. Howe:

The straw seat by the window is all yours, Miss Alice. Gee, you're awful pretty!

Wow! What a cute little smile, and your face is now red as an apple!

It is! And to tell ya the truth, I'm as red as a McIntosh myself.

I'm not too old for you! Just old enough and man enough to take care of a little kitten sweet as you. Want somethin' to drink?

Now look, don't ya worry 'bout what ya have to do in Philly. I'll be at your cute little side all the time, makin' sure no one gets his paws on ya. So you gonna be my little sweetie?

I mean, hold on to my hand, cute stuff! It's gonna be a long ride.

Train Station
Washington, D.C.

Wednesday, September 19

Jeptha D. Howe:

Okay, honey, what do you wanna see? We've got two hours 'til our next train leaves for Philly.

C'mon, doll face, don't be like that. There has to be something you'd like to see.

Well, good ol' Jep's got somethin' he can show ya!

Ouch! Whadja do that for? I was only kiddin'. C'mon, let's walk over there and check out some of the sights.

Don't be such a spoil sport. It'll be fun.

You know, if you keep acting up like this, we're never getting married.

Sure ya do, you just don't know it yet. I've got big plans for us once we get back from this trip.

Oh, I'll take care of your mother. You just worry about takin' care of ol' Jep. You scratch my back, I'll scratch *anything* you want!

Ouch! You're gonna have to stop doin' that. While we're on the subject, I can arrange for a sleeper car on the next train if you'd like. You just say the word and I'll.... Ha! Missed me that time.

C'mon, sweetie, we better get movin'—lots to see and not a lot of time to do it.

Cor. Filbert & 11th sts.,
Philadelphia, Pennsylvania

September 20, 1894

Dear Mamma and the rest:

Just arrived in Philadelphia this morning and I wrote you yesterday of this. Mr. Howe and I have each a room at the above address. I am going to the Morgue after awhile. We stopped off at Washington, Md., this morning, and that made it six times that we transferred to different cars. Yesterday we got on the C. and O. Pullman car and it was crowded so I had to sit with some one Mr. Howe sit with some man we sit there quite awhile and pretty soon some one came and shook hands with me. I looked up and here it was Mr. Howard. He did not know my jacket, but he said he thought it was his girl's face so he went to see and it was me. I don't like him to call me babe and child and dear and all such trash. When I got on the car Tuesday night Mr. Howe asked me if I had any money and I told him 5 cents so he gave me a dollar. How I wish I could see you all and hug the baby. I hope you are better. Mr.

H. says that I will have a ride on the ocean. I wish you could see what I have seen. I have seen more scenery than I have seen since I was born I don't know what I saw before. This is all the paper I have so I will have to close & write again. You had better not write to me here for Mr. H. says that I may be off tomorrow. If you are worse wire me good-bye kisses to all and two big ones for you and babe.

> *Love to all,*
> *E. Alice Pietzel*

Grand Hotel, Suite 140   *Thursday, September 20, 1894*
Indianapolis, Indiana

Dear Mother and Father,

How are you both feeling? Henry is doing fine, but he is traveling again. I cannot keep up with him on the many overnight trips he has to make in a week so he has rented this suite. I have been in bed most of the time, partly due to my migraines and partly because of boredom. However, I have had some nice talks with the owner's wife, Mrs. Rodius. She has been very gracious and comes to visit me frequently throughout the day. That helps some, except she is constantly asking me questions about Henry. She barely caught a glimpse of him, but now she wants to know everything about him. I keep warning her that she had better stay away from him when he returns.

The only other things I have to do are shop and read. I have already bought your Christmas presents and many of the others. I have not told Henry yet because he tends to get upset when he thinks I am spending too much money. It is his own fault, though. If he had been here, he could have kept me occupied.

I am beginning to wonder if Henry and I will ever lead a normal life. I realize I sound ungrateful, but I think Henry should spend more time with me. We have not even had a real honeymoon, yet. Hopefully, after two more cities, he will be finished and we can go to Europe. I cannot wait.

> *Love Always,*
> *Georgianna*

Fidelity Mutual Life Association   *Friday, September 21, 10:10 a.m.*
Philadelphia, Pennsylvania

Jeptha D. Howe:

Yes, Mister Fouse, old Ben Pietzel was using the name of B.F. Perry to carry on his business interests.

Well, because he was in trouble doing business in Tennessee a while back. He didn't want to draw attention to his real identity.

I really can't tell you much more of relevance, except for a physical description.

He was kinda tall, I guess. Good build, muscular.

Well, his face was sort of handsome. Strong jaw. He had a mustache. Starting to go bald in front. I recall that some teeth were missing. That's it, I think.

Yeah, I'm sure. No, wait a second! He had a wart of some kind on the back of his neck—I remember seein' it when he was walking away from me.

No, nothing more. See ya tomorrow morning then.

Imperial Hotel   *September 21, 1894*
Eleventh, above Market Street
Hendricks & Scott, Propr's.
Philadelphia, Pennsylvania

Dear Mamma and Babe:

I have to write all the time to pass away the time.

Mr. Howe has been away all morning. Mamma have you ever seen or tasted a red banana? I have had three. They are so big that I can just reach around it and have my thumb and next finger just tutch. I have not got any shoes yet and I have to go a hobbling around all the time. Have you gotten 4 letters from me besides this? Uncle Henry said he would mail them the day I gave them to him. Are you sick in bed yet or are you up? I wish I could hear from you but I don't know whether I would get it or not. Mr. Howe telegraphed to Mr. Beckert and he said that he would write to you tonight. I have not got but two clean garments and that is a shirt and my white skirt. I saw some of the largest solid rocks that I bet you never saw. I crossed the Patomac River. I guess that I have told all the news. So good bye Kisses to you and babe,

> *Yours loving daughter,*
> *Miss E.A. Pietzel*

If you are worse telegraph to the above address. Imperial Hotel, Eleventh above Market Street.

Imperial Hotel   Friday, September 21, 1894
Eleventh above Market Street
Hendricks & Scott, Propr's.
Philadelphia, Pennsylvania

Dear Dessa:

I thought I would write you a little letter and when I get to Mass. you
must all write to me. Well this is a warm day here how is it there. Did
you get your big washing done if I was there you would have a bigger
one for I have a whole satchel full of dirty clothes. I bet that I have
more fruit than all of you. Dessa I guess you are without shoes for I
guess they don't intend to get me any. H has come now so I guess I have
to go to dinner.

Dessa take good care of mama. I will close your letter and write a little to Nell and Howard next time so good bye love to you with a kiss.

Dear Mama:

I was over to the insurance office this afternoon and Mr. Howe thinks
there will be no trouble about getting it. They asked me almost a thousand questions, of course not quite so many. Is his nose broken or has
he a Roman nose. I said it was broken. I will have to close and write
more tomorrow so good bye to all with kisses to all.

        Your loving daughter,
        E. Alice Pietzel

My dear Patty,   Sunday, Sept 23, 1894

I know how much you lust after the Pietzel girls, drooling whenever I
describe them for you. Now, devil that I am, I have ripped out the vir-
ginity of the young Alice.

I'm on a train with the sweet child now, just outside Philadelphia as we
head towards Detroit, where I will take her every chance I get. In fact,
I have my left hand between her legs even as I'm writing this letter, rubbing her dry, dirty little crotch. The poor dear has no panties now
because I left them all torn up underneath the mattress where I spread
apart her thighs time after time during our mad search for the new garden of Eden last night.

This child can't help but get a little wet from my fingers playing with
her tight little pussy. And I bet she's thrilled by reading every word of

this letter as I write it. Yes, Patty, little Alice with the wet cunt is now reading about her seduction.

I seduced her yesterday, the day she identified her father's dead body at potter's field! I repeatedly raped this young lady at a Philadelphia rooming house run by a fellow physician, a Dr. Adella Alcorn, now retired from our bloody profession.

I was especially interested in taking advantage of the poor girl's vulnerability. After all, the last thing the child would want to do after the terrible ordeal of seeing her father's corpse was to give up her maidenhood to old Uncle Henry—a man she does not even like or trust.

And now, dear Patty, the sweet little thing is rubbing my exposed and erect cock as I continue to do my own rubbing of her own contribution to the world. It's true that I will break her fucking neck if she doesn't rub me. Patty, Patty, I have a great urge to shove myself into her hot little swamp right now—to just stop this nasty letter you will destroy right after you jerk off—and get on top of her in front of the three or four other people riding on this train. (They can't see the seduction.)

Oh, Patty, I'm losing control of myself—I think I will now have the little lass lower her head to where her hand is now so that I might enter the garden a totally happy man. Oh, my dear man, besides the little girl has a soft moist mouth and a hot wet tongue. Oh, Patty, Patty, I am slipping into heaven!

> *Good night,*
> *HHH*

Stubbins' European Hotel *Monday, September 24, 1894*
One square north of Union Dept
on Illinois Street
Indianapolis, Indiana

Dear Ones at Home,

I am glad to hear that you are all well and that you are up. I guess you will not have any trouble in getting the money. 4, 18, 8 is going to get two of you and fetch you here with me and then I won't be so lonesome at the above address. I am not going to Miss Williams until I see where you are going to live and then see you all again because 4, 18, 8 is afraid that I will get two lonesome then he will send me on to school. I have a pair of shoes now if I could see you I would have a nough to talk to you all day but I cannot very well write it I will see you all before long though don't you worry. This is a cool day. Mr. Perry said that if you did not get the insurance all right through the lawyers to rite to Mr.

Foust or Mr. Perry. I wish I had a silk dress. I have seen more since I have been away than I ever saw before in my life. I have another picture for your album. I will have to close for this time now so good bye love and kisses and squesses to all.

> *Yours daughter,*
> *Etta Pietzel*

P.O. I go by Etta here 4, 18, 8 told me to O Howard O Dessa, O Nell O Mamma, O Baby. Nell you and Howard will come with 4, 18, 8, & Mamma and Dessa later on won't you or as Mamma says.

> *Etta Pietzel*

Quinlan Apartment,
The Castle   *Tuesday, September 25*

Sophie Quinlan:

What's this business about Ben Pietzel?

I mean, is he really dead or what?

You know exactly what I'm talkin' about. He and Holmes are up to somethin', I know. Have you washed up? Dinner's almost ready.

Hurry it up, then. I wanna know about Pietzel.

Well, I overheard Holmes talkin' to somebody in his office about it—somethin' 'bout an insurance scheme and that Pietzel.

Somebody named Frank.

No, I never heard him or saw him—just Holmes talkin' to him. Who is he, anyway?

Are you sure you don't know? I thought you knew everything goin' on around here.

I know Holmes is queer and there's been a lot of strange things happening here. I've been a little worried about me and Cora.

I know she ain't here now, but what about when she's home for a visit?

Well, what about those Williams sisters last summer? And that woman and little girl that disappeared two years ago?

I know nobody could prove nothin', but nobody's ever seen' em again, have they?

S'pose me and Cora disappeared? How'd ya feel then?

I don't think that's very funny, Patty Quinlan.

Well, if I was Carrie Pietzel, I'd be askin' some question: but that poor woman's got so many children they must not do much talkin'. Old Ben must be better in bed than he looks.

635 Carondelet Street   *Wednesday, September 26*
St. Louis, Missouri

Carrie Pietzel:

Hello, Mister Holmes. Please come in.

A little better, thank you. But I'm still awful tired.

Oh, Wharton is much better, thanks to you. He's sleepin' right now. I want to thank you for gettin' that doctor for us. It was real nice of ya.

I was expectin' Alice would be with ya. Why didn't she come home?

Long story?

Would you like some coffee or something?

No, but it won't take long to fix it. Why don't you come into the kitchen with me and tell me all about it. Nell, you and Howard run outside with Dessie for some fresh air.

It is *not* cold outside. Just 'cause the sun ain't shinin' real bright, you think it's cold. If you're cold, put on your sweater. Now run along. I want to talk to Mister Holmes.

My children are good, Mister Holmes. But they miss Ben, and so do I. When's he goin' to be comin' home? And where is Alice?

Oh, I can't sit down. I'm too nervous, that's all.

Yes. But you don't know what it's been like for me these past weeks havin' to worry about everything by myself. What with Ben bein' gone and me not knowin' what's goin' on, and me and Wharton so sick, I was scared of what would happen to my children if anything happened to me. Milk and sugar?

You're welcome. So what about Alice? When's she comin' home?

I don't understand why that's necessary. I need her here with me. We miss her.

Of course I want to see Benny. If he can't come home, we'll go to him.

Cincinnati?

Well, we'll just go meet him there.

What authorities? Why would they be checkin' on me and the kids?

I s'pose so, but I'm confused.

My parents?

But I don't have money to be takin' the kids to Indiana for a visit.

Fifty dollars should be enough.

Why do you want to take Howard and Nell?

But no one's goin' to pay attention to a sick woman travelin' with four children. Besides, we'll use a different name.

I don't know about this, Mister Holmes. I've already got one child gone. Now you're askin' me to send two more of my babies away.

But even a couple of weeks is a long time away from your kids.

Ben's idea?

I just wish I could talk to him about it. I'm so tired I'm not thinkin' real straight. You know, Alice sent us a letter from Washington! She was havin' a real good time—said Mister Howe was real nice to her. I 'preciate you takin' care of that.

All right. I'll get them ready by Friday. At least Alice will have them with her and won't be so lonely.

A letter? From Alice? Let me see what she says?

She sounds okay. Doesn't say too much about bein' homesick. She needs shoes and a warm coat soon—the weather's startin' to turn.

Okay, if it'll help get my family back together, I guess Nell and Howard can go.

Oh, you don't need to pick 'em up. I'll see they get to the station on time.

I don't know why you're so set on my takin' the other two to my parents in Galva, but if it's that important....

I said I would go, didn't I?

Until Friday then. Goodbye, Mister Holmes.

Train Depot   *Friday, September 28*
St. Louis, Missouri

Carrie Pietzel:

Watch where you step, Howard. Don't mess up your shoes.

I know they're old, but they have to last a while longer. Nell, do you see Mister Holmes anywhere?

Oh, yes! On the platform. It looks like Mister Howe with him. I wonder....

Hello, Mister Holmes.

Yes, Mister Howe, I *am* surprised to see you here. Are you goin' with Howard and Nell?

Oh, I see.

Really? Oh, Mister Howe, that's wonderful! When will I be able to get the money?

That soon? Then why is it necessary for Howard and Nellie to leave? Won't everything be all right now?

Yes, I know we still have to be careful. It's just that I hate turnin' loose two more of my children—even if it *is* for only a few weeks.

Oh, please, just a few more minutes. I didn't think it would be pullin' out this soon.

Nellie, now remember everything we talked about. You mind Alice, and help watch out for your brother.

I'm gonna miss you, too, sweetheart. And remember that Dessie, Wharton, and me will be in Galva with Grandpa and Grandma for a couple of weeks, then we're comin' to meet you in Cincinnati.

I promise we'll all go to Galva when you're all back home. Howard, sweetheart, you be a good boy for Alice and Nell, ya hear?

Now give Mama a big hug, both of you...mmmmmmmmmmmmmmmmmmm.

Oh, please don't. You're makin' me cry, too. Now write us every day and— Nellie, you got that lunch I packed?

You be good, and mind Mister Holmes.

Take care of my babies, Mister Holmes. Oh, Lord, I hate to see 'em go. I'm sorry, Mister Howe, to be blubberin' so.

Yes, I'm ready now.

Papers? What papers? I'm sorry. I guess I wasn't payin' much attention to what you were sayin'.

All right, I'll come in whenever you say.

Next Tuesday? I'll be there, Mister Howe. Thank you for waitin' with me 'til the train left. And thank you for the five dollars just now.

The Bristol House, Room 6   *Saturday, September 29*
Cincinnati, Ohio

Alice Pietzel:

Wha...What's the matter, Uncle Henry?

No, I was sleepin', but I'm sure Howard's been in this bed the whole time. Why?

He couldn't have done that. See, he's sound asleep.

Can't we talk 'bout this in the mornin'? I'm so tired.

No, I don't think it could've been Nellie, either. Why don't we let both of 'em sleep? We'll find out tomorrow who moved your trunk to the other side of the room.

I'm sure they didn't open it, but I promise I'll ask them first thing in the mornin'.

No, I don't want nuthin' to drink. Uncle Henry, what are you doin'!

There's no room for you here!

Please, keep your voice down or you'll wake the others. Can't we do this some other night?

I'm sorry, I know you're in pain, but I can't with them in the room.

Uncle Henry, you *wouldn't*! Nell and Howard are too young. Please don't even think it.

No, please, don't touch 'em.

Fine, I'll do what you want.

Yes, anythin'—just don't wake them, please?

Circle Park Hotel, Room 312   *Monday, October 1*
Indianapolis, Indiana

Georgianna Howard:

Who's there?

Henry, is it really you? Did you come in on the afternoon train?

Well, you're here now and that's all that matters. Oh, darling, you look so tired. Let me help you with your coat. Can I get you something to drink? You look like you could use a week in bed.

Be serious, I'm talking about sleep. Here you go. Why don't you tell me about your trip while I massage your shoulders?

The meetings lasted over three hours at a stretch? That's ridiculous! How long are you going to put up with these people stalling and trying to get every cent for themselves? I think you could easily find another buyer.

Henry, you're going to have to do something. I'm getting tired of staying in strange hotels in different cities every other night, some of them not even good ones.

But you promised me.

I'm thinking about going to stay with Elizabeth for awhile.

Only until you get everything settled and can devote more time to me. I'm so *bored*.

I know it's an old argument...

Okay, I'll ease up. I was only thinking about visiting her until we can take our honeymoon.

Hennnry, you promised me Europe!

Living there? What about your investments and my parents?

Well, I guess you're right, it could be done. I just didn't know you were planning this. You really should tell me these things.

I don't know if I can forgive you. This is something *very* big.

Yes, even bigger than your friend. Why don't you come with me to the bedroom? I've thought of something new to try. I call it the "Georgianna Teaser."

Circle House, Room 222   October 1, 1894
Indianapolis, Indiana

Dear Mamma,

We was in Cincinnati yesterday and we got here last night getting that telegram from Mr. Howe yesterday afternoon.

Mr. H. is going to-night for you and he will take this letter. We went us three over to the Zoological Garden in Cincinnati yesterday afternoon and we saw all the different kinds of animals. We saw the ostrich it is about a head taller than I am so you know about how high it is. And the giraffe you have to look up in the sky to see it. I like it lots better here than in Cincinnati. It is such a dirty town Cin.

There is a monument right in front of the hotel where we are at and I should judge that it is about 3 times the hight of a five story building. I guess I have told all the news so good bye love to all & kisses. Hope you are all well.

   Your loving daughter,
   Etta Pietzel

Circle House   October 1, 1894
Indianapolis, Indiana

Dear Mamma, Baby and D.

We are all well here. Mr. H. is going on a late train to-night. He is not here now I just saw him go by the Hotel He went some place I don't

know where I think he went to get his ticket.

We are staying in another hotel in Indianapolis it is a pretty nice one we came here last night from C.

I like it lots better than in C. It is quite worm here and I have to wear this warm dress becaus my close an't ironet. We ate dinner over to the Stibbins Hotel where Alice staid and they knew her to.

We have a room right in front of a monument and I think it was A. Lincolns.

Come as soon as you can because I want to see you and baby to. It is awful nice place where we are staying I don't think you would like it in Cincinnati either but Mr. H. sais he likes it there.

> *Good bye your dau.*
> *Nellie Pietzel*

Jeptha Howe's Office, Commercial Building   *Tuesday, October 2, 10:00 a.m.*
St. Louis, Missouri

Carrie Pietzel:

I hope we don't have to wait too long. Wharton was fussy when I left and Dess might have her hands full. I'll really be glad when all this is over.

I think I *have* been patient, Mister Holmes. You just wouldn't understand. Besides, I've had this feelin' that somehow this isn't goin' to work out like we planned.

I hope you're right, I.... Hello, Mister Howe. Nice to meet you, Mister Harris.

Fine.

Well, maybe just a glass of water, please.

Thank you. I'm real anxious to get the money in the bank.

Expenses?

Well, certainly, Mister Howe, we expected you to charge us a fee. How much is it?

I...I...I wasn't thinking about it bein' that much. Are you sure?

I can't believe this! Twenty-five hundred dollars, plus expenses, out of ten thousand? Talk to them, please, Mister Holmes. This can't be right.

I know, but we've been countin' on this money—it's all we have comin' in. My children and I need it to live.

Oh, I don't care anymore. I don't want any part of this.

No, I just want to go home. This isn't worth it. Everyone's tryin' to cheat us.

Yes, but....

Very well, Mister Holmes. I'll sign the check so these thieves can get their share. Then can we leave?

You just can put what's left of the cash here in my bag. I'll be goin' straight to the bank anyway.

You needn't show me to the door—I know the way. Good day!

First National Bank   *Tuesday, October 2, 11:15 a.m.*
St. Louis, Missouri

Carrie Pietzel:

Yes, Mister Holmes, I *am* relieved to be getting the money. There's so many things we need—I don't know what to buy first. As you can tell by the number of times this skirt has been mended, I could use a new one. And heaven knows the children need clothes. It seems strange to be carryin' around this much money. I was so afraid on the way over here something would happen to it.

Lots of things. Like maybe someone would snatch my bag, or I'd drop it from the carriage.

Well, I'm just glad we arrived safely at the bank. I guess I'm still upset over the meetin' with the lawyers this mornin'. I don't think Ben knew they would charge so much. Twenty-five hundred dollars is a lot more than I expected to pay. It just doesn't seem right.

Well, that's that, then. You're more familiar with this kind of business than I am. Let's just get this over with quickly so I can get home to my children.

Yes, Dessie's very capable, but I don't like to be gone too long with Wharton bein' so little and still a little sickly.

The loan? Oh yes, Bennie told me about the loan.

He told me it would be five thousand dollars. That's a lot of money, but Ben says it's what we should do. I sure wish we could just keep the money.

Oh no, I didn't mean anything by that. Benny would really be mad if I made him lose that property. I just hate to give up so much.

I think this is right—you might want to count it again. Five thousand dollars is a lot of money. I certainly hope this property is worth it. I'll just sit over here and wait for you.

That didn't take long. What is this?

Prom—Promise what?

Promissory note? What is it?

I see.

Yes, I have a safe place to keep it. Does this mean everything's paid up now?

Can we go?

Your expenses? What kind of expenses?

I see...how much?

Mister Holmes, you can't be serious! Fifteen hundred dollars! Why, that's practically all I have left. I don't understand.

Yes, I know you had some expenses in helpin' with this, but I....

No, I'm...I'm just a little surprised—I mean I wasn't expectin' to have to pay you quite so much.

Another hundred? What on earth for? This isn't fair! It isn't turning out anything like I expected. I....

No, I understand there are expenses in carin' for my children. I guess I just didn't realize how little would be left, especially after the lawyers and now you. It really hasn't been worth it, has it? I'm so tired of it all, I don't even care anymore. I just want to go home now, please.

Well, my parents are expecting us on Friday.

Okay. I'll wait until I hear from you. I don't have much choice, do I? Will it be long, do you think?

I guess a letter is better than nothing.

Well, if you don't mind waiting, I guess I could write a quick note. I don't have any paper or a pen.

That will do just fine, thank you. This won't take but a minute. I'll be so glad when I can see my children instead of having to ask you to deliver my letters. I'll make this one very short.

Western Union Office
St. Louis, Missouri
Tuesday, October 2, 2:30 p.m.

Pres Levi Fouse <stop> Fidelity Mutual <stop>

Visited Lawyer Jeptha Howe today <stop> He earned $2500 on $10000 check <stop>

Insp W Gary

Circle House, Room 222   *Friday, October 5*
Indianapolis, Indiana

Howard Pietzel:

Alice, I'm not scared.

Am not. I jes' want you to light a lamp so Nellie won't be scared.

Shut up, Nellie. Don't listen to *her*, Alice.

That's better. I can see you. What's that noise?

Don't let him in! Please, Alice, keep him outta here. He'll ruin everythin'.

Alice, don't blow it out. You don't have to obey him. He's not really our uncle.

It's too dark. I wanna go home. Alice...Alice...where you goin'?

Don't leave me here alone.

You don't count, Nellie. You can't protect me from the night crawlers. Alice, please stay! I'll be good.

But why do you have to go with him?

Can't I come with you?

But I don't wanna stay here. It's scary.

Promise?

Hurry up then.

Nellie, wanna come over here?

I wish Uncle Henry'd take us back home. I miss everyone. How long do you think we'll have to stay with him?

Circle House, Room 222   *October 6, 1894*
Indianapolis, Indiana

Dear Mamma, Grandma and Grandpa:

We are all well here. It is a little warmer to-day. There is so many buggies go by that you cant hear yourself think. I first wrote you a letter with a crystal pen, but I made some mistakes and then I am in a hustle because Mr. H. has to go at 3 o'clock I don't know where. It is all glass so I hafto be careful or else it will break, it was only five cents. Mr. H. went to T.H. Indiana last night again. Their was a poor boy arrested yesterday for stealing a shirt he said he had no home the policeman said he would buy him a suit of clothes and then send him to a reform school. The patrols are lots different here than they are in St. Louis & Chicago. they couldnt get away if they wanted to. We hafto get up early

if we get breakfast. We have awful good dinners pie fruit and sometimes cake at supper and this aint half. They are all men that eat at the tables we do not eat with them we have a room to ourselves. They are dutch but they can cook awful nice. Their is more bicycles go by her in one day than goes by in a month in St. Louis. I saw two great big ostriges alive and we felt of their feathers they are awful smooth 1/2 they are black with white tails they are as big as a horse. Why have buffaloes got big rings in their noses for I want Grandma and grandpa to write to me. Is the baby well and does he like coco I want you to all write why don't you write mama. I will close for this time goodby write

Yours truly,
Nellie Pietzel

Alices eyes hurts and she just don't feel good so she wont write this time.

Circle House, Room 222   *October 7, 1894*
Indianapolis, Indiana

Dear Mamma,

We are all well except I have got a bad cold and I have read so much in Uncle Tom's book that I could not see to write yesterday when Nell and Howard did. I am wearing my new (ders) dress today because it is warmer to day. Nell Howard and I have all got a crystal pen all made of glass five cents a piece and I am writing with it now. I expect Grandma and Grandpa was awful glad to see you. The hotel we are staying at faces right on a big wide bulvard and there is more safties and bugies passing than a little bit and how I wish I had a safty. Last Sunday we was at the Zoological Garden in Cincinnati, O. And I expect this Sunday will pass away slower than I dont know what and Howard is two dirty to be seen out on the street to-day. Why dont you write to me. I have not got a letter from you since I have been away and it will be three weeks day after tomorrow. It is raining out now quite hard. Nell is drawing now. The hotel is just a block from Washington Street and that is where all the big stores are. There is a shoe store there And there has been a man painting every day this week. They give these genuine oil painting away with every $1.00 purchas of shoes with small extra charge for frames. You cant get the pictures with out the frames though I wish I could get one you dont know how pretty they are. We go there every day and watch him paint. He can paint a picture in 1 1/2 minutes aint that quick. Nell keeps joring

the stand so I can hardly write I mad half a dozen mistakes on the other side because she made me. This letter is for you all because I cant write to so many of you I guess I have told all the news so good bye love to all and kisses

Your loving daughter
E. Alice Pietzel

P.O. *Write soon Howard got a box of collars and took one out and lost box and all the contents.*

Dear Chief of Police: Sunday, Oct. 7, 1894

When H. M. Howard was in here some two months ago, he came to me and told me he would like to talk to me, as he had read a great deal of me, etc.: also after we got well acquainted, he told me had a scheme by which he could make $10,000, and he needed some lawyer who could be trusted, and said if I could, he would see I got $500 for it. I then told him that J. D. Howe could be trusted, and he then went on and told me that B.F. Pitezel's life was insured for $10,000, and that Pitezel and him were going to work the insurance company for the $10,000, and just how they were going to do it; even going into minute details; that he was an expert at it, as he had worked it before, and that being a drug-gist, he could easily deceive the insurance company by having Pitezel fix himself up according to his directions and appear that he was mortally wounded by an explosion, and then put a corpse in place of Pitezel's body, etc., and then have it identified as that of Pitezel. I did not take much stock in what he told me, until after he went out on bond, which was in a few days, when J. D. Howe came to me and told me that man Howard, that I had recommended him to, had come and told him that I had recommended Howe to him and had laid the whole plot open to him, and Howe told me that he never heard of a finer or smoother piece of work, and that it was sure to work, and that Howard was one of the smoothest and slickest men that he ever heard tell of, etc., and Howe told me that he would see that I got $500 if it worked, and that Howard was going East to attend to it at once. (At this time I did not know what insurance company was to be worked, and am not sure yet as to which one it is, but Howe told me that it was the Fidelity Mutual of Philadelphia, whose office is, according to the city directory, at No. 520 Oliver Street.) Howe came down and told me every two or three days that everything was working smoothly and when notice appeared in the Globe Democrat and Chronicle of the death of B.F. Pitezel, Howe came down at once and told me that it was a matter of a few days until we would have the money, and that the only thing that might

keep the company from paying it at once, was the fact that Howard and Pitezel were so hard up for money that they could not pay the dues on the policy until a day or two before it was due, and then had to send it by telegram, and that the company might claim that they did not get the money until after the lapse of the policy; but they did not, and so Howe and a little girl (I think Pitezel's daughter) went back to Philadelphia and succeeded in identifying and having the body recognized as that of B.F. Pitezel. Howard told me that Pitezel's wife was privy to the whole thing. Howe tells me now that Howard would not let Mrs. Pitezel go back to identify the supposed body of her husband, and that he feels almost positive and certain that Howard deceived Pitezel and that Pitezel in following out Howard's instructions, was killed and that it was really the body of Pitezel.

The policy was made out to the wife and when the money was put in the bank, then Howard stepped out and left the wife to settle with Howe for his services. She was willing to pay him $1,000 but he wanted $2,500. Howard is now on his way to Germany, and Pitezel's wife is here in the city yet, and where Pitezel is or whether that is Pitezel's body I can't tell, but I don't believe it is Pitezel's body, but believe that he is alive and well and probably in Germany, where Howard is now on his way. It is hardly worth while to say that I never got the $500 that Howard held out to me for me to introduce him to Mr. Howe. Please excuse this poor writing as I have written this in a hurry and have to write on a book placed on my knee. This and a lot more I am willing to swear to. I wish you would see the Fidelity Mutual Life Insurance Company and see if they are the ones who have been made the victim of this swindle, and if so, tell them that I want to see them. I never asked what company it was until today, and it was after we had some words about the matter, and so Howe may not have told the proper company but you can find out what company it is by asking or telephoning to the different companies....Please send an agent of the company to see me if you please.

Your Resp., etc.
MARION C. HEDGEPETH

Circle House, Room 222   *October 8, 1894*
Indianapolis, Indiana

Dear Mamma,

Just got a letter from you saying that the babe was cross and Dessa and Grandma was sick. How is Grandpa I hope you will all feel better I thought you would not be home sick at all when you got there but it seems as thought you are awful homesick Who met you at the depot did you get there Saturday or Sunday. I dont like to tell you but you ask me so I will have to. H. wont mind me at all. He wanted a book and I got life of Gen. Sheridan and it is awful nice but now he dont read it at all hardly. One morning Mr. H. told me to tell him to stay in the next morning that he wanted him and he would come and get him and take him out and I told him and he would not stay in at all he was out when he came. We have written two or three letters to you and I guess you will begin to get them now I will send this with my letter that I wrote yesterday and didnt send off Hope you will all keep well.

I have just finished Uncle Tom's Cabin and it is a nice book. I wish I could see you all. This is another cold day. We pay $12.00 a week for our room and board and I think that is pretty cheap for the good meals we have Yesterday we had mashed potatoes, grapes, chicken glass of milk each ice cream each a big sauce dish full awful good too lemon pie cake dont you think that is pretty good. They are Germans. I guess I will have to close so good bye, love to all and kisses. Write soon keep well.

         Yours Truly,
         E. Alice Pietzel

Western Union Office   *Tuesday, October 9*
St. Louis, Missouri

Pres Levi Fouse <stop> Fidelity Mutual <stop>

Spoke to St Louis Police Chief Harrigan today <stop> Shown amazing letter from train robber Marion Hedgepeth <stop> Claims Ho plotted to defraud us <stop> Interviewed in city jail <stop> Letter confirmed <stop> Got portrait of Ho <stop> Known in jail as H M Howard <stop>

See you tomorrow <stop>

Insp W Gary

2 Union Ave.   *October 10, 1894*
Irvington, Indiana

Dr. Frank Noland
Norristown Insane Asylum
Norristown, Pennsylvania

Dear Frank:

I'm writing in a house of death. Yesterday, young Howard Pietzel finished his supper and stared out the front window, taking in his last look at the world. The sunset covered him with a red glow, and I wanted to see him naked. After sitting down on one of two chairs in the room I asked him to give old Uncle Howard a big hug.

When he turned towards me, his eyes were full of tears.

The boy resisted my attempts to remove his clothes, but his struggles and screams drove me mad with desire. Poor kid, I soon had him on my lap, both of us without our pants.

Do you know how nice it is to conquer little boys, to have them aroused and fearful at the same time? The lad was mine, all mine.

Then Hatch appeared, coming up from the cellar, to sit across from us in the other chair.

"Give me the child," he said. Not wanting to stop what I was doing, I not only ignored the demon but quickened my movements.

Suddenly, just before I had fully satisfied myself on the boy, Hatch put his large hands around the child's neck. Soon the boy hung between us, a flaming stick of flesh. I had one end of him and Hatch had the other.

The boy choked to death as I made my final strokes. The whole thing was really marvelous because the sunset continued to fall on our bodies like a warm mother while the boy shuddered for what seemed like an eternity before he died. The sexual thrill was the best I ever had.

A few hours ago I cut up the body and Hatch stuffed the pieces into a coal oven I had installed in the barn yesterday morning. Hatch disappeared. I'll shove the boy's remains up the chimney later.

So tired,
HHH

Midwest Line   *Friday, October 12, late evening*
Heading to Detroit, Michigan

Georgianna Howard:

Henry, dear, what are you doing here? I thought I was supposed to meet you in Detroit.

No, I'm glad you're here. Where did you board?

Oh, that's why I didn't see you get on. Did you come through the second-class?

There were two of the cutest little girls back there. They said their uncle was traveling with them. I asked the porter to let me know if they needed anything. Did you know they've been....

Oh, I'd love to see our compartment. What are we waiting for?

This is great. Here let me unfasten those pants for you. I've really missed our special friend. Ooooh, he's missed me, too.

Well, I could blow on him like this...or maybe I could lick him very slooowly like this...or maybe I could use my teeth to barely glide over him...or what about if I just rub my tongue back and forth over his head, barely touching him...or I could suck on him.... Which do *you* like best?

Western Union Office   *Friday, October 12*
St. Louis, Missouri

Pres Levi Fouse <stop> Fidelity Mutual <stop>

Perry and I failed to find Carrie P in St Louis today <stop> Neighbor James Becker saw photo of Ho <stop> Becker says Ho visited CP many times in summer and fall <stop>

Insp W Gary

Western Union Office   *Saturday, October 13*
Chicago, Illinois

Pres Levi Fouse <stop> Fidelity Mutual <stop>

Myrta Ho in Wilmette revealed nothing <stop> Next talked to Ho business partner Frank Blackman <stop> He evaded us too<stop> Talked to Chicago detectives <stop> Say Ho is wanted in Ft Worth <stop> Defrauded many businessmen there <stop> Stole train load of horses <stop>

Ho fast-moving Ho<stop> Need Pinkertons <stop>

Insp W Gary

New Western Hotel, Room 11   *Saturday, October 13, near midnight*
Detroit, Michigan

Alice Pietzel:

Shhh, there, there, it's okay, Nellie. I promise. You'll be okay.

Yeah, I know it hurts, but you've got to quit cryin' or Uncle Henry will come back. Then, we'll have to do it all over again.

Hush now, it's goin' to be all right. I promise it'll be fine. Trust me. I've never lied to you.

No one needs to know nuthin' about this. There's no tellin' what he might do if someone found out. Now let's dry those eyes.

Nah, you didn't do nuthin' wrong, but it needs to be our secret. I ain't tellin' no one, and you have to cross your heart that you won't say nuthin'—not even to Momma.

Good.

Of course it hurt—it was your first time. You need to stand—you think you can do that for me?

It's okay, Nellie. We're only goin' as far as the washstand to get you cleaned up. Let's take off that torn chemise. Hush now! He loves to hear you cry. Shhh, it's only a little blood.

Here—wash yourself. You see, it comes right off. No one would ever guess what happened tonight.

I'll clean up after you go to bed. See what a pretty nightgown I found for you to wear.

Yeah, it's new. Uncle Henry bought it for me, but I haven't worn it yet.

Uh-uh. Tonight wasn't the first time I've done that with him, except it was only me and him before.

You knew? How?

I was prayin' you didn't. Here—wash your face. Now, let's get ya tucked in. Shh, don't start crying again.

Yeah, I wish Daddy was here, too.

Carriage from Train Station to Hotel   *Sunday, October 14, 10:30 a.m.*
Detroit, Michigan

Carrie Pietzel:

The streets are so muddy—must've had a lot of rain here.

I know your letter said to come Wednesday, Mister Holmes, but I just could-
n't wait any longer. I'm so anxious to see Bennie and the children.

Well, I'd rather wait here than there. How are my children? I haven't heard
anything from them in over a week. Are they okay?

School? Where?

Indianapolis? I thought they would be here. Who's taking care of them?

What's the name of this widow?

You don't know?

I can't believe you left my children with some stranger in Indianapolis whose
name you don't even know. Where did you find her?

How well do your wife's parents know this woman? Are they sure she can
be trusted?

Patient! I'm getting tired of this—I want to see my children! Here, Dessie, let
me take Wharton for a while—he must be gettin' awfully heavy.

Okay, but if he gets too heavy, let me have him. He was so good on the
train—slept most of the way. Is this our hotel already? That certainly didn't
take long. Geis's European Hotel? Sounds like they're givin' themselves
airs—European hotel, indeed.

I'm sure it'll be fine—it's only for a few days. As long as the beds are clean
is what's important. Let me get out first, Dessie, and I'll take Wharton—you
help Mister Holmes with our things. Watch out for this mud—mind you
don't slip.

Now, Mister Holmes, about my children....

New Western, Room. 13   *October 14, 1894*
Detroit, Michigan

Dear Grandma and Grandpa,

*Hope you are all well Nell and I have both got colds and chapped
hands but that is all. We have not had any nice weather at all I guess
it is coming winter now. Tell mama that I have to have a coat. I nearly freeze in that thin jacket. We have to stay in all the time. Howard*

is not with us now. We are right near the Detroit River. We was going boat riding yesterday but it was too cold. All that Nell and I can do is draw and I get so tired sitting that I could get up and fly almost. I wish I could see you all. I am getting so homesick that I don't know what to do. I suppose Wharton walks by this time don't he I would like to have him here he would pass away the time a goodeal.

> *Hugs and kisses to all,*
> *Alice Pietzel*

Albion Hotel, Room 66-F   *Monday, October 22*
Toronto, Canada

Alice Pietzel:

Nellie, quit knockin' the table so much.

Because I'm tryin' to write a letter. Why don't you go read the rest of that book I gave you?

I said to stop it. I'll play with you in a few minutes.

I'm writin' Mister Howe.

I'm askin' him why he hasn't written me like he promised.

No, I don't think he's gotten another girlfriend.

I just don't. Stop buggin' me about him.

Nellie, I've already told you, Uncle Henry said he would take us home after this last stop. He has to tie up a few loose ends and then we'll get to see Momma. I can't wait to get home and taste her potato soup again.

18 St. Vincent St   *Wednesday, October 24*
Toronto, Canada

Tom Ryves:

Keep on knockin' and ya'll break the door down!

So, what's the matter?

Well, my name's Ryves. Glad ta meet ya, neighbor Holmes.

A house for the sister, huh? Awful nice of ya. Must be loaded, huh?

A spade for diggin'? Sure, I got one. What ya need it for?

Well, pataters grow nice in the cellar this time of year. The spade's 'round back,

so just go help yerself to it.

Take yer time with it. I'm not goin' anywheres. If your sister's good-lookin', tell her to return it! Ha ha!

Henry Street   *Thursday, October 25, 4:00 p.m.*
Toronto, Canada

Joe Flannagan:

Top 'o the mornin', Miz Nudel.

Giddyup!

Funny, I never even wondered what was in that there box, ol' Nellie. Just like a woman though ta be askin' 'bout a crates' belongin's. As if that were all one had time to be thinkin' 'bout.

Ahh—that hits the spot—bet you'd like a bit of the nip as well, eh Nellie?

Giddyup!

Top o' the mornin', Miz Fischel.

54 Henry Street   *Thursday, October 25, 6:30 p.m.*
Toronto, Canada

Janice Nudel:

Can you believe that old sot Joe Flannagan?—Is that meat warm enough, Frank?

He has no idea what's in that trunk parked out in front of our porch on Saint Vincent Street. You'd think he'd at least take an interest in what he's droppin' off—the drunk.

It *is* our business. The really weird thing is he said the trunk was coming from Detroit, and yet Mister Holmes himself told me last week that his widowed sister and her two daughters were coming in from Hamilton.

Well, I'm beginning to have my doubts about that Mister Holmes, too—stop feeding the dog. He was so nice and cordial when we first met, but stayin' out all night, every night—his comin's and goin's during the day—and now that darn trunk. I have a mind to go over there after dinner and give it a shake or two.

How would he know, he's never home!

Coach   *Tuesday, October 30*
Outside of Burlington, Vermont

Georgianna Howard:

Henry, why do we have to be in Burlington tonight?

I'm tired. Couldn't Ben have come with you?

Is everything all right between the two of you? I haven't seen him since the beginning of September.

I just wondered, that's all. Do you realize I never did get to meet Carrie when we were in Saint Louis?

It was nice of you to give him a vacation, but I wish you had waited until after we left for Europe.

Then *he'd* be the one on this dreadful coach. I swear that driver couldn't hit more bumps on the road if he tried.

Stop that, Henry. I'm not in the mood.

On a train in Burlington, Vermont   *October 31, 1894*
Dr. Frank Noland
Norristown Insane Asylum
Norristown, Pennsylvania

Dear Frank,

Don't fall over, but Hatch just told me how he killed two young kids, little girlfriends of Henry.

Last week we went by train to Toronto, trying to escape the damn Pinkerton mob, now following me as if I were the monster, not Hatch. I had my third wife, Georgie, in one hotel; I had the two deflowered girls, Nellie and her pretty sister, Alice, in another hotel; and I kept the girls' mother, older sister, and younger brother in yet another hotel. You know how Herman is about wasting money—well, I'm the same way— but with Pinkertons on my ass I had no choice.

Anyway, I had to rent a house on St. Vincent Street in Toronto because moody Howard was going crazy with so many people in our lives. I no sooner rented the place when he demanded I borrow a shovel from a neighbor to dig a nice resting place for himself in the dirt cellar. Little did I realize then that Hatch was behind the scene, using death-loving Howard to push me into his horrible plot to kill the kids.

Things then happened quickly, much too fast for me to stop the killings.

Hatch must have ordered the large trunk to be delivered to the St. Vincent address on Thursday, October 25th. The next day Henry and I picked up the girls from the Albion Hotel and Henry secretly played with their thighs as we rode toward the rented deathtrap. I left Henry alone with them in the house while I brought in the trunk and other things that had been dropped off by the express driver. Meanwhile, Henry was playing with the girls, grabbing their private parts, sometimes handling them both at the same time as they screamed for my help. I figured that Henry was Henry; once he wanted sex from these girls, there would be no stopping him. And so he did have sex with them, demanding that the one girl stay in the same room while he took the other. At one time, I'm almost ashamed to admit it, I joined the orgy and spent myself upon the younger girl. Later, while I was sleeping, Hatch entered the house and ended their lives.

My stop is up ahead.
Holmes

MEMORANDUM

TO:Inspector William Gary
FROM: Chester Harris, Pinkerton Agent
DATE: November 1, 1894

As requested, we followed Holmes to Ogdensburg, New York. He took a room with a woman—his wife?—on Saturday, the 25th. Next day, Holmes visited Carrie Pietzel staying with daughter Dessie and son Wharton at the National Hotel in Ogdensburg. Three days later, Holmes and wife traveled by train from Niagara Falls to a station just outside Burlington, Vermont. Then, after taking a carriage into the city, they stayed overnight at the Burlington Hotel. Yesterday they registered as the Halls in Ahern's Boardinghouse. Two hours later, Holmes as J.A. Judson rented a furnished house at 26 Winooski Avenue. He told real estate agent that the house was for his widowed sister, a Mrs. Thadeus Cook. Do you want us to turn him over to police for the Fort Worth warrant?

Clara's Living Room   *Monday, November 5*
Tilton, New Hampshire

Clara Mudgett:

I still can't believe you're finally home, Herman.

Of course, I've missed you. It's been so long. Where have you been?

Well, I guess you can tell me later. Do you realize you haven't even asked about Harry? He's practically grown now—you wouldn't even recognize him. Then again, maybe you would. He's beginning to look like you in the face. He even has your eyes. Darling, I need to get up.

Well, I hate being out of your arms, too, but I want to show you something. This is a sketch of your son. One of the girls he knows did this and gave it to me. You'll be so proud of him. I can't wait for him to get home. He's going to be so happy to see you.

Herman! We can't do that right now. We'll have to wait until tonight.

Harry will be home any minute, and your being here will surprise him enough. He doesn't need to come home and find his mother on the floor with a strange man.

Western Union Office   *Thursday, November 8*
Concord, New Hampshire

Insp William Gary <stop> Fidelity Mutual <stop>

Agree use telegraph <stop> Tell us when to arrest <stop>

Morn Nov 1 Ho went to train station <stop> Met nobody <stop>

Afternoon met Carrie P at station <stop> Took her and 2 kids to Winooski house <stop> Took 3 hour walk with daughter Dessie <stop>

Later bought chemicals in town drugstore <stop> Left wrapped package at Winooski house <stop> No one home <stop>

Today Ho arrived at Gilmanton NH farm owned by Mudgett family <stop> Who are they <stop>

Chester Harris

Clara Mudgett's Home   *Monday, November 12, 8:00 p.m.*
Tilton, New Hampshire

Herman Mudgett:

Clara, darling, I've fallen in love with you all over again. Forgive me, the biggest scoundrel on the face of the earth.

Here then, take this knife and put it through my heart!

Then say you love me, your eternal lover, the father of the wonderful boy you have raised.

I swear I'll return to you in April.

I'll set up a home for us in Gilmanton, and we'll start all over again.

I can't stay here now, Clara. You see, I married another woman last year.

Just let me explain. I was in a train accident in Denver, and when I awoke in a hospital I no longer had a memory of who I was or of what my former life had been like. Then a beautiful and kind hospital volunteer, a Miss Georgianna Yoke, spent a month helping me get back on my feet. We fell in love and I married her.

I know it sounds almost too amazing to be true, but Georgianna hired a great doctor who worked on my brain.

Not even a month ago my entire memory returned. And you, my darling, were the first person to enter my mind.

Well, I promise to get an annulment from Georgianna now that I've found my first and only love!

Clara Mudgett's Bedroom   *Monday, November 12, 9:30 p.m.*
Tilton, New Hampshire

Clara Mudgett:

Herman, I wish you could stay. Couldn't you just write this Miss Yoke and tell her that you've remembered everything and are staying here with me? You don't really have to see her.

I guess so. I'm just going to miss you. Mmmmm...*what?*

I thought you already bought your return ticket.

Well, I've got a little bit saved up. How much do you need?

But, Herman, that's almost all the money I have. What if something comes up with Harry?

Okay, I keep forgetting you're going to be taking care of us again. We can stop by the bank tomorrow morning before you leave.

Mmmmm. Promise me you'll be coming home soon.

Adam's House   *Thursday, Nov. 15, 1894*
Boston, Massachusetts

Dear Carrie,

I want you to meet Benjamin on the 22nd, in Lowell, Massachusetts. I'm enclosing a few dollars for the train ticket and a bit for some free spending.

Oh, yes, do me a favor. While you and Dessie were out shopping, I put a very expensive bottle of chemicals behind the coal bin downstairs in the basement. But now I'm afraid the heat might ruin the mixture.

As soon as you read this letter—and do destroy it, dear, to keep the damn Pinkerton from finding me and Ben, who will be put in a prison if found—go fetch the bottle and hide it in a cool spot in the attic somewhere until I get back to Burlington to deal with it.

Thanks, doll. In a short week from now you'll be in the strong arms of your hubby. He misses you as much as you miss him. Until then,

> *Sweet dreams,*
> *H.H. Holmes*

Western Union Office   *Friday, November 16*
Boston, Massachusetts

Insp William Gary <stop> Fidelity Mutual <stop>
Gilmanton small farm town <stop> Thanks for info on Mudgetts <stop> Family reunion over yesterday <stop> Ho in Boston today at Adams House <stop> Mailed letter then went to some steamship offices <stop> Plans to leave country <stop>

Chester Harris

Western Union Office   *Saturday, November 17*
Boston, Massachusetts

Insp William Gary <stop> Fidelity Mutual <stop>
Nabbed moment he came out <stop> Now in Boston jail <stop>

Chester Harris

Police Headquarters   *Saturday, November 17, 2:00 p.m.*
Boston, Massachusetts

H. H. Holmes:

I, Henry Howard Holmes, on this 17th day of November, 1894, so solemnly swear that I and Mr. Benjamin Pietzel did deliberately defraud the Fidelity Mutual Life Association of Philadelphia of $10,000. To carry out our deception, I was given a corpse by a friend and fellow physician in New York City. The corpse was selected for its physical similarities to Mr. Pietzel. On Sunday, September 2, 1894, Pietzel placed the corpse in a second-floor bedroom at 1316 Callowhill Street in Philadelphia. Then he set up the corpse as directed by me so as to make it appear to be a victim of an accidental explosion while lighting up a pipe to smoke. Therefore, Mr. Pietzel is still alive, hiding from the law. I myself had seen him several times in various cities on several different days for almost two months. I last saw him in Detroit a month ago. Such is the truth, I swear by God.

Police Headquarters   *Saturday, November 17, 4:00 p.m.*
Boston, Massachusetts

H.H. Holmes:

Gentlemen, I don't know where the Pietzel girls are, but you will find them when you find their father.

A month ago, as I said, I saw him drunk in Detroit. I gave him five hundred dollars so that he and his children could escape from you folks.

New York, then Europe or South America—even Australia was mentioned. Who knows?

The girls—Alice, Nellie—and little Howard had been with me for a month or so.

We knew the Pinkertons were after us. So we kept switchin' locations to throw off their search.

No, Carrie Pietzel didn't know. That's why I kept the three kids away from her.

After leavin' the corpse behind in Philly, Pietzel went to Cincinnati to hide. Meanwhile, I went to Saint Louis to get Nellie and Howard and then all three of us went to Indianapolis where I was keepin' Alice.

Cincinnati. Carrie, Dessie, and Wharton were to join us a few days later. I had wanted to rent a hotel room downtown so that Carrie and Ben could have a moment together before he went South for the winter.

Neither parent knew where I was roomin' the kids. Then one day Ben must have followed me back to the hotel and broke in on us when the kids were havin' cookies and ginger pop.

Dessie and Wharton were with their mother at the time. I had just rented rooms for them in their own place.

Cincinnati, yeah. I thought it best to keep everybody apart to throw off the Pinkertons.

Now Ben took Howard to Detroit and I soon followed with Alice and Nellie, dressin' up Nellie as a boy to keep the Pinkertons confused. In Detroit, I heard that the police in Fort Worth were lookin' for Ben and me in Chicago. That's when I turned the girls over to Ben and gave him the five hundred.

Yes, it's the God's honest truth. I'll swear on a Bible if you have one handy.

Winooski Avenue
Burlington, Vermont   *Monday, November 19, 11:30 a.m.*

Carrie Pietzel:

What is it, Dessie?

Has the mail come already? Must be a little early today. What do you have there?

From Alice?

Oh, him. Here, keep an eye on this pot of beans while I read what he has to say, and mind you don't let 'em stick. Just keep stirrin'—I'll only be a minute.

Oh, no! Not again! I'm not goin' one step further. I can't believe this.

Now he wants to send us off to Lowell, Massachusetts. Dessie, I'm so worried. Why doesn't he just bring Alice and Nell and Howard here? I'm gonna tell him so.

I don't care if I do make him mad. We've been sent all over the place, with never a word or a sign from them except for what he tells us. Besides, it's not fair draggin' you and Wharton everywhere; and Lord knows if Alice and Nell are in school or if he's just tellin' me that.

No. We're goin' to stay right here and wait until he brings them back. Are you watchin' those beans?

No, he doesn't say nothin' else...except for something about some chemicals. Let me read it again. Oh, he says he hid some valuable chemicals behind the coal bin and wants me to get them to the attic for him. Now what do you suppose that's all about?

Well, it doesn't make much sense to move 'em from the basement to the attic. If they're so valuable, why doesn't he just come and take 'em? Here, let me have that spoon; you can set the table. It's about time for Wharton to wake up.

The Silver Express   *Monday, November 19, 3:05 p.m.*
Philadelphia, Pennsylvania

Detective Thomas G. Gordon:

Let me get this straight, Mister Holmes. You're going to hypnotize me so that
I'll take the handcuffs off and then look the other way while you make your
escape?

Oh, that's right. I left out the five hundred dollars, which you promise to drop
off to me at a later time.

Well, you see, Mister Holmes, hypnotism has always spoiled my appetite. I'm
afraid the five hundred dollars is no inducement when weighed against possible
dyspepsia.

Dining Room   *Monday, November 19, 3:05 p.m.*
Silver Express bound to Philadelphia

Georgianna Howard:

Ma'am, is there something I can do for you?

Oh, Missus Pietzel, I didn't even recognize you. What's the matter?

Please stop crying. Henry will work everything out. You'll be back with your
children in a few days.

What do you mean? Ben's alive.

Yes, he is. I saw him when we were in Philadelphia the last time.

It was right before Henry and I left. In fact, we left so quickly that we didn't
even have a chance to say good-bye to him.

He can't be dead, Missus Pietzel. Henry told me Ben was taking a vacation.

There, there. I'm sure Henry knows exactly where Ben is.

What three children?

Henry didn't have any children with him. He's been traveling with me most of
the time. I mean, there's been a few days he's been gone, but he...couldn't have
been taking care of any children, could he?

Oh, Carrie, I didn't mean to make you cry more. Shhh, it's going to be okay.
We'll straighten all this misunderstanding out somehow, I promise.

New York Times Tuesday, November 20, 1894

CHICAGO BUSINESSMAN ARRESTED IN BOSTON

Indicted for Insurance Fraud

Death of Partner B.F. Pietzel Suspicious

PHILADELPHIA, Nov. 19—The Grand Jury this afternoon returned true bills of indictment against Herman Mudgett, alias H.H. Holmes, who is under arrest at Boston; Jeptha D. Howe, a St. Louis lawyer; and Mrs. Carrie A. Pietzel, for fraudulently obtaining $10,000 insurance from the Fidelity Mutual Life Association of this city upon the death of B.F. Pietzel. Immediately following the finding of the indictments, which charge "conspiracy to cheat and defraud," the life insurance association received word of the arrest in St. Louis of Howe and of the capture in Burlington, Vt., of the woman who is the widow of the victim, and who to-day confessed to the conspiracy. Steps have already been taken to extradite the accused. While the indictments do not charge murder, the authorities suspect it will be shown at the trial that Pietzel was done away with by the accused, either intentionally or otherwise.

BOSTON, Nov. 19—Mrs. Carrie Pietzel, wife of the man whose life was insured for $10,000, was found in Burlington, Vt. , and came to this city to-day with a Pinkerton detective and Inspector Whitman. She is held on the charge of conspiracy after the fact. When she arrived at Police Headquarters she realized for the first time that she was under suspicion, her trip to Boston having ostensibly been made for the purpose of meeting Holmes. She fainted dead away, but later recovered her composure and told the officers what she knew of the case.

To the best of her knowledge, she believes that her husband is alive, but of this she is not certain. Neither does she know the whereabouts of three of her five children. All she knows is that Holmes has repeatedly told her that she would meet Mr. Pietzel and her three children in different places, only to be disappointed when she went there. She has not seen one of her daughters, Alice, since either Sept. 18 or 19 when she left her home in St. Louis to go to Philadelphia with Holmes to identify the supposed remains of the young girl's father. Two other children, Nellie and Howard, have not been seen since by their mother since late September.

It is these suspicious things that make the police tend to the theory that Holmes has done away with Pietzel, and that he has been deceiving Pietzel's wife in the matter all along.

HOLMES'S CAREER IN CHICAGO.

He and Pietzel Swindled Many Firms of House Furnishings.

CHICAGO, Nov. 19—The police, fire insurance men, and those who deal in store, hotel, and house furnishings and in material for construction of houses, would like to see again in this city H.H. Holmes, who is a prisoner in Boston on the charge of conspiring to defraud the Fidelity Mutual Life Association out of $10,000, for which amount he had insured the life of B.F. Pietzel. Holmes and a woman named Lucy Belknap, who lived at his house as his mother-in-law; another woman who went by the name of Williams, and Pietzel, swindled numerous supply firms and furniture houses out of several thousand dollars by means of getting houses built in the name of Mrs. Belknap, who was represented as a rich widow. When a house was finished and furnished on credit, it would burn, and the victims would have nothing to show for their confidence. Of course, the house would be well insured, and the policies were paid.

Before the Fair opened, Holmes and his confederates swindled numerous merchants and hotel furnishers out of several thousand dollars' worth of goods by various schemes. It is now alleged that Holmes built his entire "Castle" located on 63rd and Wallace Streets without spending so much as a dime. One of his largest victims, the Tobey Furniture Company of Chicago, is now readying to take action against Holmes and his confederates.

New York Times   Thursday, November 22, 1894

PIETZEL WAS ONCE A DETECTIVE

ST. JOSEPH, Mo., Nov. 21—Four years ago B.F. Pietzel, who figures in the Philadelphia insurance swindle for which H.H. Holmes is now locked up, was a resident of this city. Under the name of John Carpenter, he operated a detective agency and made a number of clever captures. Pietzel worked up a puzzling case at Garden City, Iowa, and arrested one of the citizens who set fire to a building and killed an officer while escaping. He left a large number of bills unpaid after he left.

1316 Callowhill Street   *Wednesday, November 28*
Philadelphia, Pennsylvania

Eugene Smith:

Yes, Mister Geyer, Mister Perry...

Sorry, Mister Pietzel was livin' on the third floor of this house. Took rooms during the summer and was expectin' to stay here to the end of December.

I'm the manager, yes. Mister Towers owns the house, and I do all the rentin' and fixin' of the place.

Maybe. Don't think they ever met though.

Mister Perry—I mean, Mister Pietzel was interested in somethin' I made to sharpen handsaws. He was gettin' a patent for me—said I would be as rich as Rockefeller. Smart man, that Mister Perry.

Mister Pietzel, right—sorry.

Yeah, I met Mister Holmes, in late August, I think.

At Perry's office.

I guess he was a silent partner of Perry's. Strange man, that Mister Holmes. Gave me the creeps.

His eyes were cold as a fish. Looked right through ya. In one second I felt he knew everything 'bout me, 'specially the bad things in my life. Scared the hell outta me.

Like I says, first time I saw Mister Holmes was in Perry's office last few days of August.

Yep, he came once or twice to the house.

Nope, never saw him in Mister Pietzel's rooms.

What else would he be doin' here?

Tipped his hat and went up the stairs.

Twice.

Well, I wanted to see Mister Perry 'bout my invention. So I went to his office on Monday.

Don't know.

Okay, on September Third.

The office was open, but no one was there.

No typewriter, no clerk, no one. Never did hire any office workers. Said he could do all the work hisself.

Yes, sir, I called out his name lotsa times, but he was gone.

Next day. Still no one there.

On the Fourth, yeah.

What else could I do? I went home and later decided to check up on him in his rooms. Thought he might be sick or somethin'.

After lunch.

Twelve thirty or so.

Knocked on his door, then turned the knob. The door opened and the moment I stepped in I knew there was trouble.

The stink. Somethin' was dead.

I found his body in the bedroom above us. His face was all putrid and decayin'. Glass all over the floor.

Yeah, met Holmes 'bout three weeks later in the Fidelity Building, not far from here.

On a Saturday mornin'—in the big chief's office.

Mister Fouse.

Agent Perry, who invited me to look at the body, the daughter of the dead Mister Pe—Pietzel! Gosh, I don't know if I'll ever get the names straight.

Someone else whose name I don't know—but he was a lawyer 'cause he spoke like one. Had somethin' to do with the girl.

Was holdin' her hand or had his arm 'round her waist all the time we were there.

He was the last to show up. Soon as he walked in the office I felt I had met him before, but I couldn't place him.

Maybe it was the glasses. He was wearin' specs this time.

He shook hands with all the men and whispered somethin' to the girl.

Well, we rode over here to the city morgue, just behind us, to pick up two doctors. Then we took some more streetcars until we got to Potter's Field.

Yeah, we talked for a short while—on the final ride, when I had a chance to sit next to him.

I asked him what he did for a livin'. Told me he was a patent agent, just like Mister Pietzel. I asked him if he maybe wanted to do somethin' with my invention.

He made me feel that he wasn't interested.

Yeah, I asked him why the insurance company had him comin' to view the body. He said it was really none of my damn business, so I shut up. But that's when I knew he was Holmes 'cause that's when I saw them cold eyes of his lookin' right into my own.

I didn't say anything to Mister Fouse or others who later asked because I was afraid I might be wrong. I talked myself into sayin' nothin'. You're the first to know the truth.

At Potter's Field I identified the body. So did Holmes and the girl. Then we went our separate ways.

Only unusual thing happened was Mister Holmes takin' over the job of the coroner. He was soon turnin' the body all different ways and tellin' us where to find different marks on the body. The way he spoke, I didn't understand a lot, not being a doctor and all.

Just a letter addressed to his wife.

Found it with my invention.

Holmes took it. Said he would deliver it in person.

Never opened it.

Sure, I'll show you exactly where I found the body upstairs. Wanna go now?

Holmes' Office   *Monday, December 24*
The Castle

Myrta Holmes:

Would you hurry up, Quinny, and unlock his office? I don't have all day. I promised Lucy I'd be home in time to take her to six o'clock Mass. Here it is, Christmas Eve, and we're lurking around like thieves in my own husband's office.

Did he ever tell you what the combination numbers were, and why he chose those numbers?

Well, I 'spose at this juncture it doesn't matter much, does it? The four here stood for the letter *D*, eighteen stood for *R*, and the eight here then stood for...

Very good—*H*. You're not half as dumb as you look sometimes. Now then, guess what the letters—*holy shit*—look at these two huge dents in this door.

Oh, Christ, Quinny, I don't wanna know—and wipe that stupid look off your face. C'mon, help me with this money. Load it into these bags. I'll start going through the papers. But first, let's put this chair here in the doorway, just in case.

Keep putting it in those bags. Now listen, when the authorities start asking questions, act neutral towards Holmes—and whatever you do, don't mention a thing about tonight.

Basically, just don't offer too much information. They can't pin a thing on you if you keep your mouth shut. But if you or that wife of yours starts talking, then you both'll wind up 'longside Holmes himself.

Shoot, I know you're loyal as hell. It's just, well, just be careful, that's all. And be sure about Sofie. I'd hate to see either one of you doin' time.

All right, these are the papers I'm taking home with me, and these are the ones we burn.

Here, right now. Get that trash basket.

C'mon, light it. I want to get this over with.

1895

38 North John Street   *January 1, 1895*
Wilmette, Illinois

My Dear Handsome Harry,

*It's noon on the first of the year and I haven't said "Happy New Year"
to anyone yet. What a terrible way to start '95.*

I still can't believe you're behind bars. I hate to say I told you so, but...

*The stories I continue to see regarding your alleged marriages break my
heart. For the most part, I regard most of the stories as rubbish. But I
can now no longer doubt that you were married once before me, and
as much as this especially pains me to write, once after me.*

*But I also have no doubt that when you get out, you will return to your
proper spouse and place in society.*

*Still, I fear that as hard as all this has been on me, it has been even hard-
er on Lucy. A day does not go by that she doesn't ask questions about
her daddy. I'm afraid some of the kids in school are beginning to say
things to her. She's very perceptive and sensitive.*

*I talked again with Wharton the other day. He says not to worry about
a thing on the business end. I was able to get all of your business
papers to him. So now they are in his safe-keeping.*

*The only thing left to worry about is getting out of your current
predicament and back to Wilmette.*

*In the meantime, I thought I'd send you a little fantasy of mine that I
thought of when I was over at your office. This is meant only to help
keep you warm during the upcoming winter months. I know it has kept
me HOT!*

*I meet you in your office at six o'clock. I'm dressed like one of the
dance hall girls, and when I tell your secretary that I had an appointment with you, she tells me you're not in. So, I dash past her and enter
your office. I tell you that she told me you weren't in, and you fire her
on the spot.*

*You then ask me if I would be interested in a secretarial position. I tell
you it depends. You open up a bottle of fine champagne and ask me
what it depends on. I tell you it depends on how good the champagne
tastes. We laugh and have a toast.*

*After some more pleasant exchanges, a few more toasts, and some
serious flirting, we start to dance. Slowly, we move our hands along
each other's backs and steal our first kiss. I bring my fingers to your
face and start tracing your nose, your lips, and then on down to your
chest where I begin opening your shirt one button at a time. I remove
your pants, shoes, socks, and now we are dancing again, you wear-*

ing nothing but an unbuttoned shirt, my fingers lightly playing with your chest hairs.

When you attempt to lower my dress straps, I back away and tell you to wait. I move back and start moving your shirt off your shoulders. When I get your shirt down to your hands, I bind them together behind you and gently push you onto your chair. I move to your door to be sure it's locked. You ask me if it's locked. When I tell you yes, you reply, "Well, then, I guess I'm your prisoner."

Smiling, I move toward you, and bending, I start teasing you with my tongue, first on your lips, then to your ears, your neck, and on down your chest to your stomach, and to your legs. Eventually, I take you in my mouth, and work you up almost to an orgasm before backing away. Now I start a slow strip tease for you. Your eyes show me how hungry you are for me, your binds remind you that you are at my mercy.

With just my garter, stockings, and heels on, I approach you again, and straddling you, I gently lower myself onto you. When you enter me, we both shudder. Our rhythm is slow at first, and I bury your face between my breasts. As our pace quickens, I bring your face to mine and our tongues find each other. You want so badly to hold me, but your binds prevent you. Knowing you are mine to do with as I please excites us both all the more, and soon our frenzied pace brings us both to climax.

Save the story, my love, and enjoy it throughout the long cold months. Hope to act this out for you real soon.

> Love and kisses,
> Myrta

Moyamensing Prison   Wednesday, May 29

Dear Det. Graham:

As we discussed yesterday, the last time I saw Howard was in Detroit, Michigan. There, I gave him to Miss Williams, who took him to Buffalo, New York, from which point she proceeded to Niagara Falls. After the departure of Howard in Miss William's care, I took Alice and Nellie to Toronto, Canada, where they remained for several days. At Toronto, I purchased railroad tickets for them for Niagara Falls, put them on the train, and rode out of Toronto with them a few miles, so that they would be assured that they were on the right train. Before their departure, I prepared a telegram, which they should send me from the Falls if they failed to meet Miss Williams and Howard. I also carefully pinned inside Alice's dress four hundred dollars in large bills, so Miss Williams would have funds to defray their expenses.

They joined Miss Williams and Howard at Niagara Falls, from which point they went to New York City. At the latter place, Miss Williams dressed Nellie as a boy and took a steamer for Liverpool, whence they went to London. If you search among the steamship offices in New York, you must look for a woman and a girl and two boys and not a woman and two girls and a boy. This was all done to throw the detectives off the track, who were after me for the insurance fraud. Miss Williams opened a massage establishment at Number Eighty Veder or Vadar Street, London, I have no doubt the children are with her now, and very likely at that place still.

Although it pains me to realize you do not believe this story, I can prove to you it is true. Long ago, Miss Williams and I worked out a secret code that allows either one of us to get in touch with the other through an advertisement.

The code is based on the word "republican." When capitalized, the word corresponds to the first ten letters of the alphabet, when lowercased the word corresponds to the next ten letters. The remaining six letters are uncoded.

For example, my name would be coded as follows:

H o l m e s

C b e p B a

The adv. should appear in the New York Sunday Herald, and if some comment upon the case can also be put in the body of the paper stating the absence of children, it would be an advantage. Any words you may see fit to use in adv. will do. Only one sentence need be in cipher as she will know by this that it must come from me as no one else knows this code. Besides using her real name in the newspaper's personal column, I would also add the names of Adele Covelle and Gereldine Wanda, as these are two aliases she has employed from time to time.

The New York Herald is (or was a year ago) to be found at only a few places regularly in London.

Very respectfully,
H.H. Holmes

New York Herald
Sunday, June 2, 1895

In Search Of: MINNIE WILLIAMS, ADELE
COVELLE, GERELDINE WANDA—
AplbcnRun nb CBRc EBLbcB 10th
PREeB cBnucu PCAeUcBu Rn buPB...
CbepBA, Address George S. Graham,
Philadelphia, Penn., U.S.A.

Kings Hotel   *Thursday, June 27*
Cincinnati, Ohio

Frank Geyer's Notes

Cause i was sure to get the assignment the dis att had me makin the interview
on Monday with the mother and next day with suspect Holmes in jail the mother Carrie Pietzel is in an awful mess poor woman with the three kids gone im
havin a bad time keepin the eyes from startin in cause Martha and Esther are
gone wiped out in minutes from my own life and so thats why they say you
need to get the most out of things since you never know old Holmes is a
smoothie and his kind is the scum of the earth he seemed almost like i knew him
before though strange that i should feel that way cause i never met him she
could be my own mother but thats how i feel bout most older ladies takin care
of their kids like they should anyway somethin in his face is so damn familiar
like the eyes, maybe the mouth might have been a kid i knew as a child anyway theres no part of his story where you can say this is where hes lyin rather
you can't trust the whole thing even though each part seems really detailed he
gives us dates names locations times every thing else we ask for but deep down
inside i know hes pullin my leg im sure he killed not only the father but the 2
girls and boy he will never get away with these crimes cause i wont stop til i nail
his ass good met detective John Schnooks what a name tonight at headquarters
said Dietsch will assign him tomorrow to help me with trackin down the clues
anywhere in the city its late but i got a hard on maybe downstairs in the bar
might be somethin sweet to eat tonight

Kings Hotel
Cincinnati, Ohio

Friday, June 28

Frank Geyer's Notes

Schnookums and i went knockin on the doors of Cincis hotels and boarding houses found 2 Atlantic House and Bristol Hotel where Holmes took rooms for himself and 3 kids all identified by photos interesting that he used HH Cook same one he used to check in Mrs Pietzel in Burlington hotel cause Holmes had a pattern of rentin houses we then interviewed real estate agents after more than 50 interviews we talked to George Ramsey of the J.C. Thomas Agency who recognized photos of Holmes and Howard but Ramsey couldnt open safe in Mr Thomas office to find location of rented house Ramsey only knows that Thomas lives somewhere in Cumminsville we checked out lead but no dice i was too tired to whack on any dame tonight just wanted to get days activities down and go to bed

Kings Hotel
Cincinnati, Ohio

Saturday, June 29

Frank Geyer's Notes

Schnookie doesnt like to talk bout pressin against the warm wet parts of women so were all business im always on the lookout for something good to eat or be eatin by even when Martha and Esther were alive i had to have a good whore or 2 on the side well Schnooks and i went back to the Thomas real estate agency and i showed Mr. Thomas my photos he recognized Holmes and the boy $15 was paid in advance for a vacant house at 305 Poplar St we might want to talk Thomas says to Miss Henrietta Hill who still lives next door to the rental property this afternoon she said a moving van soon arrived after the man she identified as Holmes and the boy she identified as Howard went into the house it was strange she said that the van driver delivered a huge stove and nothin else she saw it all while standing on her front porch next day Holmes knocked on her door and said she could have the stove since she showed such an interest in the way it was delivered Holmes and the boy left an hour later in a one horse cab after Schnooks and i shook hands goodbye i went to a show downtown Cinci where you can peep on men and women doin it in mauve rooms then after dinner i went to a red light house where i really pressed all the juice out of a little plum so much so im still sore

Torelli's Hotel
Indianapolis, Indiana

Sunday, June 30

Frank Geyer's Notes

Arrived after 7 last night and went straight to headquarters spoke to Capt Splann then to Super Powell who assigned det Dave Richards to assist me here in Indy today we checked out all the hotels and lodgin houses around Union Depot and the Circle neighborhood a clerk at the Hotel English identified photos of suspect and children Holmes rented rooms for kids on last day of Sept 94

and then checked them out next morning Oct 1st we went everywhere in the city but found zero Richards then said we needed to talk to an owner of a hotel that probably was open last fall but not now

Torelli's Hotel   *Monday, July 1*
Indianapolis, Indiana
Frank Geyer's Notes

Richards and i spoke to loud jew Herman Ackelow a saloon owner who once ran Circle House on Meridian St in Sept 94 he remembered Alice Nellie and Howard they had been kept inside their hotel room for days Ackelow recalled that Holmes several times said he couldnt stand the boy wanted to be rid of him rid of him asked Ackelow yeah said Holmes put the whining bastard in a home kids were taken out of Circle on 12 Oct 94

Sunrise House   *Tuesday, July 2*
Chicago, Illinois
Frank Geyer's Notes

Really bothered bout what happened to the childrens trunk acordin to Holmes he last saw it at a hotel on West Madison St det John McGlinn assigned to help me in search of hotels we never found the trunk but near the corner of Madison and Ashland we talked to landlady Jennifer Irons who recognized Holmes in my photo as Harry Gordon who spent 3 months comin in and out of her lodgin house at end of 92 Mr Gordon she said introduced his new bride a very pretty woman named Emiline info no good to me now but may be of use later since only bride of Holmes we know is woman Georgianna caught with him in Boston after McGlinn and i split up i took out my anger on a kid prostitute hope now she got some help i puffed up her face and think i broke her nose

Sunrise House   *Wednesday, July 3*
Chicago, Illinois

Frank Geyer's Notes

McGlinn and i met the strangest man in the strangest place ive been outside horror shows of freaks in cages i wanted McGlinn just to let me see the famous castle of Holmes the place even the outside is like a nightmare dark and secrets everywhere all the windows closed and covered with torn bedsheets didnt look like anyone could be home Pat Quinlan was second floor he didnt invite us in stood behind door opened just enough to see half his face and body and fingers of one hand he said he hadnt seen any member of the Pietzel family for over a year said lots of bitter things bout Holmes all opinions no use to us asked if he would show us around the building he made a weird sound meant to be a laugh never said yes or no said all the doors locked i have no key hee hee hee i think the guy is nuts thanked him and left

Chicago Tribune Thursday, July 4, 1895

CASTLE CARETAKER DEFENDS HOLMES ON MURDER CHARGE

Quinlan Comes Clean on Archfiend's Audacious Scams

(Philadelphia)—The archfiend's legend continues to grow; his audacity is unsurpassed.

Following a three-hour meeting between Detective Frank Geyer and Harry H. Holmes' number one confidante, Patrick Quinlan, yesterday, this reporter caught up with the former janitor of Holmes' Castle (63rd and Wallace Street, Englewood). Holmes is currently awaiting trial on the charge of murdering his life-long business accomplice and friend, B.F. Pitezel.

Quinlan, called to Philadelphia to answer questions regarding Holmes and the murder, seemed to be in an almost playful mood following his return. Responding to one of my questions, Quinlan replied, "I'll give you a sample of what that man is like. Nearly every board laid in this building, nearly every nail and coat of paint, nearly every brick was gotten on credit and never paid for.

"One day he has furniture sent to his restaurant, and that night the dealer comes to collect. So what's Holmes do? He buys the man dinner and drinks, they share a laugh, and he promises to pay next week. The next day he sells the furniture to another restaurant in town and keeps the money. Then he reports the furniture stolen, tells the dealer it wasn't insured, and then cashes in on the insurance company. A month later his restaurant is fully stocked with new furniture, which he again doesn't pay for."

According to Quinlan, Holmes also did the same thing with his household furnishings, even going so far as sealing off rooms to hide the furniture, insisting to the dealer that the furniture was never delivered. Once the dealer left, Quinlan and Pitezel would install new doorways.

But Quinlan's favorite tale this day came in reference to a safe the size of a walk-in bank vault. After the vault was delivered, Quinlan and Pitezel reduced the size of the entry way.

When the safe company sent four men to retrieve their vault, Holmes, writing a letter and never so much as looking up, told them, "Go ahead and take the safe. But if you even so much as scrape the doorway, my lawyer will have to file a ruinous lawsuit against your company." The vault, although today severely dented on the inside, never left the room.

Quinlan added that Holmes had a lawyer as a backup to keep him out of trouble should he need it, "but he also had Ben Pitezel, who could glower over any man and back him down should Holmes tell him to. Holmes didn't need to use his lawyer very often, but he sure as heck used Pitezel a lot. Now you tell me—does that sound like a man you would murder—a man who is at your command and who would back away almost any challenger?"

Hotel Normandie   *Thursday, July 4*
Detroit, Michigan

Frank Geyer's Notes

Hit Detroit after 6 pm tired from the ride went to headquarters got det Joe Tuttle assigned to me funny thing back at the hotel i found G Howell and wife registered in handwriting of Holmes Oct 12 last year great roast beef mash potatoes peas vanilla ice cream on cherry pie in hotels dining room upstairs here i thought bout makin love to 2 nice older women with dirty mouths made both beg for my big dick before i came real messy into my hand

Hotel Normandie   *Friday, July 5*
Detroit, Michigan

Frank Geyer's Notes

Joe Tuttle and i started off the morn on a visit to the office of the Fidelity Mutual Life Ass to get help from its investigation of Holmes they had name Bonninghausen a real estate agent who had rented a place to H in Oct 94 later B said H made $5 advance for vacant house on E Forest Ave said H had a boy bout 9 or 10 with him Bons clerk Moore confirmed Bs story next went to dozens of places before we ran into PW Cotter owner of New Western Hotel Cotter showed us entry of Etta and Nellie Canning who checked in Oct 12 the boy Howard not with girls said he couldnt be absolutely certain but if right what happened to boy on trip from Indy to Detroit i think H got rid of kid somewhere in Indy based on letter by Alice who dated and gave name of places in all her letters we visited Lucinda Burns at her boardinghouse at 91 Congress St said the girls no boy with them never left their room always readin or draw-

in we worked our ass off now checking out every goddamn hotel in the city nothin new found so tired i went off like a light right after big dinner later woke up and wrote these notes

Hotel Normandie   *Saturday, July 6*
Detroit, Michigan
Frank Geyer's Notes

From early morn to night Tuttle and i searched out all Detroits boarding-houses almost dusk we talked to Mrs May Ralston owner of rooming house at 54 Park Place she examined my photos and said H and nice looking lady probably his wife Georgianna based on Ralstons description stayed 2 nights the liar H told her he was an actor the boy and girls not with them as expected by us dead tired after dinner still no hard on difficult enough just to jot down these words

Hotel Normandie   *Sunday, July 7*
Detroit, Michigan
Frank Geyer's Notes

In my June interview of Carrie P she said that H had placed daughter Dessie and boy Wharton in Geis European Hotel on Oct 14 so we went there talked to Miss Minnie Mulholland a housekeeper she identified Mrs P photo but said she knew her as Mrs Adams a broken hearted woman this European Hotel is only a short walk from Lucinda Burns house at 91 Congress St where H the creep was probably fuckin the two daughters of the poor mother almost close enough to hear her girls clothes being torn off by him in the night cause i was headin up to Toronto tomorrow Tuttle and i went out to the E Forest Ave house Mr Branum the current occupant said he found a hole in the cellar soon after he moved in late Oct he had to fill it in it was so big about 4X3X3 maybe even 4 ft deep i think H had dug this grave for the boy but somethin happened to spoil his plans perhaps for the second time we now decided to interview people who might know bout the childrens trunk we talked to hackmen, liverymen, freight depot workers others at omnibus companies express companies even undertakers but not one ounce of luck

Albion Hotel   *Monday, July 8*
Toronto, Ontario
Herbert Jones:

Thanks, Detective, but I don't smoke—makes the teeth dirty. Your name again? Well, Mister Geyer, I—
I've been working here five years; started when I was sixteen. The owner's the

father of a school boy chum of mine. The Albion's real class, best hotel in Toronto, great place to stay if you're interested in seein' the city.

On October twentieth, last year, I was here, yeah.

I was the only one on duty that night.

I meant of the clerks. October is still a busy time for us, the trees still in color and people wanting a good look before winter settles in.

Two bellboys and Dugan, the elevator operator, were on duty, too. Marie, our cleaning lady, was doin' some dustin'.

At exactly six-fifteen the coach arrived with hotel guests from the station. I know 'cause I always check my watch to make sure the coach is on time.

It was.

I'd been reading a good piece on makin' some bucks on rentin' houses when the coach stopped right out there, where it always stops. I checked my watch again and went out the door to meet the new guests.

Five of 'em: one older gent—

Over forty, I'd say. Nice hat but the heels were showin' some wear.

Four women. Well, two women, two girls. The women were with the guy, a lawyer from Detroit. Nice city, Detroit.

The one was his wife; the other, her sister.

The girls were dressed poorly. Nice figures on both of 'em, and the older one knew how to use hers, turning this way and that, just enough to give ya a good look, a different angle to think about.

Well, like I said, I went out to meet the coach, to open the door and help the guests step down. People remember little things like that—makes 'em wanna come back.

I helped all the ladies down. The girl called Nellie came down first. She wore brown woolly gloves with holes in the fingers. Alice came next. She gave me a big smile and held onto my hand a bit longer than necessary. She gave it a quick, gentle squeeze before lettin' go and then moved on with her sister into the hotel lobby.

They were sitting down, right in these same chairs, matter of fact, when I came in with the other guests. Alice had taken off her gloves and was rubbin' her hands together to get 'em warm. Nellie was starin' into the fire, quiet and disturbed about something, holdin' an old umbrella 'cross her lap.

You like some coffee, Detective? It's three-eleven. In four minutes one of the serving girls will bring me my afternoon drink. I could send for another cup.

Black?

Horace, tell 'em to bring two black coffees, one for Mister Geyer here.

After I registered the Henderson party, Alice came up to my desk at six twenty-four and told me that she and her sister wanted a room that would be paid by

their father in the morning. I had no reason not to believe her, so I put them in Room Six, our smallest room with one bed.

Canning.

The next day they had a late breakfast, and then Mister Canning, or so he called himself, showed up to pay the hotel bill for the previous night and the night to come. He took the girls on a rented buggy and didn't come back till after supper. He kissed the girls goodbye—a rather long kiss of Alice I thought—and left the hotel.

Ah, the coffees are here, and a minute early. Sugar?

Well, yes, I think Mister Canning was actually Mister Holmes. I've seen some newspaper pictures and drawings of Mister Holmes, and he's a dead ringer for the Mister Canning who came here.

Every day for five days, and always did the same thing 'cept for Day Five, of course.

Well, on the fifth day he didn't pay for their room 'cause he was takin' 'em to a new home—or at least that's what he told me.

He seemed nice, very polite, good to the girls. But I think he had somethin' goin' on with Alice.

Gosh, I can't tell ya how I know—I just do. He was too nice to her, if you get my drift. Liked to put his arm around her waist. Squeezed her hip. One afternoon I was looking at myself in that tall mirror over there to adjust my collar, and I could see him rubbin' her back as he kissed her square on the lips.

Nellie? She was just standin' around, looking a little jealous by all the attention her sister was gettin'.

No, he didn't talk much. Seemed to be in a hurry most of the time.

Would say hello, tip his hat, say goodbye at night.

Yes, October twentieth till the twenty-fifth.

Not at all. Hope I've been of some help. Say, where do you buy your shirts?

Rossin House   *Monday, July 8*
Toronto, Canada

Frank Geyer's Notes

Arrived by train this morn went directly to headquarters got det Alf Cuddy to help me begin a long run thru this city lucky us in a few hours we tracked down 2 hotels used by the wife of Holmes Georgianna first the Walker House on Oct 18 and then with H in the Palmer House on the 20th same day H put Carrie Dessie and Wharton into Union Hotel and not too far away he used his Canning name to register Alice and Nellie in the Albion he must be quite a chess player the two girls were taken out of the Albion on the 25th and never seen

again so my strong feeling is H took the girls to a rented room somewhere in Toronto and killed them

Rossin House   *Tuesday, July 9*
Toronto, Canada

Frank Geyer's Notes

Needed to take the day off get back in touch with myself sometimes i feel im on the run and cant stop since the deaths of Martha and Esther who else do i have for Christs sake no mother no father an orphan in more homes than i can remember left on the steps of hospital in New Hamp by who or rather by what kind of woman who didnt want to be my mother i have to assume that NH is my birthplace do i have brothers and sisters uncles aunts cousins was or is my father a doctor lawyer teacher maybe even a detective probably they were poor or even more likely i represented some sort of scandal so they decided to get rid of me do they ever think of the hurt and anger and worst of all the terrible feeling of loneliness their decision has caused in me their son i dont know what i am Irish French German am i supposed to be Catholic or Baptist Methodist Congregationalist without my work i would gladly put a bullet in my head who cares at my graveside the other detectives will yawn look at their watches want to get home to be with their families the only people i can feel at home with now are whores and prostitutes who are also no good throwaways no one wants for more than half an hour and yet i always do bad things to them always beat the hell out of them even the nice ones cause i dont want them they are just fuckin bastards just like me

Rossin House   *Wednesday, July 10*
Toronto, Canada

Frank Geyer's Notes

Det Cuddy and i used a city directory to write down names and locations of every real estate agency in Toronto someone rented a house to H not knowing it would supply a gravesite for 2 little girls who were given to a devil by their foolish mother at the end of the day we didnt have one goddamn lead but still had a long list of real estate agencies to visit Cuddy said use the papers how i asked have them come to your room and tell them what youre doin give them a look at your photos they will have all of Canada talkin bout your search tomorrow headquarter notifies some Toronto reporters they came they heard they ran out of here half an hour ago

Rossin House   *Thursday, July 11*
Toronto, Canada

Frank Geyer's Notes

Sure enough every Toronto paper smothered their front pages with H now interviews went fast cause agents had read the news wanted to help find the

girls nothin found on the road back at headquarters a message left from an agent he had rented a house to someone fitting H description at Perth and Bloom a house that stands in the middle of a field surrounded by a fence taller than 6 foot Cuddy although dark we found the house now occupied by old couple and their son 19 the old man had the kid get us a lamp then led us beneath the house to a crawl space we found a pile of loose dirt Cuddy and i took turns diggin up 4 feet of soil but got nothin after 2 hours

Rossin House　　　　　　　　　　　　　　　　　　　　*Friday, July 12*
Toronto, Canada

Frank Geyer's Notes

Somethin we should of done yesterday talk to Robert Izzie the real estate agent with the Perth and Bloom rental this guys nothin like the fella i gave the keys to Izzie said today cant really blame him our own damn fault for runnin off diggin up zero without checkin the source my backs killin me now cause for those 2 hours i couldn't stand up straight in the crawl space the rest of the day we talked to train ticket agents to find H next move now we ran into luck H killed the girls in Toronto im sure of that then took a little honeymoon trip with his recent bride the bastard

Rossin House　　　　　　　　　　　　　　　　　　　*Saturday, July 13*
Toronto, Canada

Frank Geyer's Notes

Took train to Niagara Falls just across the border went around to various hotels and found H as Gordon and Wife in the registry of Kings Imperial Hotel no kids with them as expected the way H kept shifting his 3 chess pieces around keeping each piece in the dark about the movements of the other pieces i feel sure that his wife didnt have any part in the madness of her devil husband i then returned to Toronto and without Cuddy went to the big newspaper offices to check out all advertisements for house rentals in Sept and Oct 94 lots of houses were rented by private people but we have no choice must find this house

Mapleleaf Hotel　　　　　　　　　　　　　　　　　　*Sunday, July 14*
Toronto, Canada

Frank Geyer's Notes

Just finished off a woman old enough to be my mother she knew what to do with a dick and did it so well in so many ways that i let her off with a good hard spanking shes gone now and i am faced with the absolute nothing i am without a search for killers my life has no meaning no substance no depth no pleasure i am the devil chasing other devils who are probably more honest than i am cause they live on the other side of the law where all of us devils belong i am the devil with the badge

what a goddamn laugh i think my fellow devil H saw right thru me when i interviewed him he surely knows a brother when he sees one

54 Henry Street   *Monday, July 15*
Toronto, Canada

Janice Nudel:

Yes, I'm Missus Nudel. And you?

Well it certainly is a pleasure meeting you, too, Detective Geyer...

Okay, Frank...won't you please come in and have a sit?

I tell you, what a beautiful day it is today. Care for some tea?

Why yes, it is him. This is definitely the same man who rented the Saint Vincent Street house last October.

Let's see. He only rented it for a few days, certainly less than a week. There were plenty of odd things about him....

That's right, Holmes was the name.

Well, for one thing, he gave a whole month's rent up front, and then, like I say, he didn't even stay a full week. Just disappeared without a trace. And so did that trunk.

Well, that was another really strange thing. I remember one afternoon last October a trunk was delivered there in the middle of the day. And it just sat on the porch for a couple of days. The delivery man told me the trunk had come from Detroit, and yet Mister Holmes had told me earlier that he was expecting some family connection coming from Hamilton. Anyway, after he had been gone a few days—vanished really—I went in the house and everything he had brought, trunk included, was gone. For some reason that trunk just gave me the willies.

Not at all Detective—I mean, Frank—that's the same name as my husband, you know. What's this Holmes done, anyway? I hope he didn't do anything to those precious little girls of his.... No, wait, they were his nieces, I think. That's right. The relative that was s'posed to be comin' to visit from Hamilton was his sister. I think he said they were her kids.

Oh my God! You can't be serious. Now I remember reading something about this case. I just can't believe something so horrible would have happened at one of my rentals. I can't imagine anything like that at all.

The Armbrusts live there now. I know he works during the day, but she should be home now, what with it being almost supper time. Would you care to stay for dinner? I know my husband would be very interested in talking with you.

Well, best of luck. If I can be of any further help...

Rossin House
Toronto, Canada

Monday, July 15

Frank Geyer's Notes

We nailed the bastard good today that fucker will be sorry he was ever born one less devil will roam the world one more monster will be whipped into its waiting cage and it is i who cracked the whip on him the morn began with Cuddys grin headquarters had received a note from Mr. Thomas Ryves he said that near the end of Oct last year someone who looked like H described in the newspapers had rented the house on 16 St Vincent St next door to his own the man had two girls with him but when he left suddenly one week later the girls were not with him when i consulted my long list of private rentals i composed from classified ads i soon found that a Frank Nudel at 54 Henry St had placed an ad for rentin the St V house lets go talk to him first Cuddy said if only to avoid some unnecessary digging in a damp cellar when we called on Mister Nudel he confirmed that his wife had rented the house last Oct to someone who kept it for a week and then left that all he knew his wife could probably give us the details since she handled the people end of their rentals she would be back in less than an hour Cuddy and i couldnt wait of course we hurried over to 18 St V to talk to Ryves the old guy could only identify the photo of Alice said the young feller had borrowed a spade from him so as to dig a place in the cellar to grow spuds for his sister said the girls were his sisters daughters that same afternoon Ryves saw the new neighbor move a mattress an old bed and a large trunk into the house my mouth began to water so much i had to spit several days later he saw the renter haul away the trunk before the noon hour i then took a good look at the 2 story house nice front porch pretty yellow and white flowers on vines on both sides of the steps such a quiet peaceful lookin place Cuddy pulled on my arm and we went back to Henry St to talk to Mrs Nudel who immediately recognized the photo of H as the St V renter he gave her a sawbuck in advance for months rent and promised to pay balance at their next meetin said he stayed only a few days not a week we got the name of the current tenants the Armbrusts and their kids and off we went back to St V old man Ryves was sitting on his porch wanting to help us i asked him if he still had the shovel used by H he dragged himself to the shed in back of his house returned with the tool i felt odd the moment it was placed in my right hand it was as if i had H by the neck the bastard was mine at last i would soon dig his grave Mrs Armbrust almost fainted when we told her what we were lookin for she had to sit down and catch her breath then took us into the kitchen where she uncovered a trap door on the floor i lifted it and could see nothin in its darkness she got us a coal lamp now Cuddy and i went carefully down a wooden staircase until we stood on the damp solid earth of the cellar Cuddy followed me with the light while i looked with the shovel for a soft spot i found it in the far corner and after Cuddy and i exchanged nods i began to dig a little way down the earth stunk of hidden decay a few minutes more i struck the bone of a human

arm its flesh falling off from the contact with the shovel the stink was horrible both of us sick from it i threw some dirt over the arm and we went quickly up the stairs and closed the door we agreed we needed to inform Cuddys boss Insp Stark we found a telephone in the telegraph office on Yonge St he suggested we get the undertaker Mr Humphrey to help get the body or bodies out of the cellar Mr Humphrey lived on a nearby street he listened to what we discovered handed us some rubber gloves to wear and asked his asst to take 2 coffins to the St V house Alice and Nellie were naked their little legs wrapped around each other when we lifted Nellie up from off her sister the top of her head and hair slid back onto the face of Alice Mrs Armbrust gave us 2 sheets to carry the bodies out to the wagon that had brought the coffins Humphrey took the bodies to his funeral house reporters neighbors strangers all thankin me smilin shoutin while im feelin little more than disgust my nose full of dirt snot the foul smell of our stinkin fate

Hotel Normandie　　　　　　　　　　　　　　　　*Sunday, July 21*
Detroit, Michigan

Frank Geyer's Notes

So it looks like im a big hero in good peoples eyes what a laugh if they only knew how im surely the devil himself i feel like hell inside the only way to keep me from turnin into ashes is to feed the hidden flames with the handcuffed bodies of icemen killers like Holmes or uncarin fuckers like the bitches who suck my cold cock for dimes so here im back in Detroit in the same goddamn room i had on independence day free once again to track down the dead boy Pietzel

Hotel Normandie　　　　　　　　　　　　　　　　*Monday, July 22*
Detroit, Michigan

Frank Geyer's Notes

Met Tuttle at the station just before dawn we ate pancakes at the Downtown Diner and plan was made on what to do Tuttle stuck me again for the bill 2 cents for the coffees 2 bits for the stacks we went back to real estate agent Bonninghausen who now remembered zero about rentin out the vacant house on E Forest A and the clerk Moore said maybe 6 times when we asked him to identify photos of Howard P 3 times Moore said maybe its him maybe its not so not havin any luck we went out to 241 E For A looked over the whole damn place nothin in barn shithouse chicken shed but the cellar had huge furnace and the 4 foot hole with nothin in it same size and depth as Toronto grave for girls i feel sure H dug it told Tut he asked for the boy the girls or all 3

Torelli's Hotel   *Wednesday, July 24*
Indianapolis, Indiana

Frank Geyer's Notes

Again Richards assigned to me we went dutch on eatin breakfast back here at Torellis Nina didn't mind usin one of her tables to write up a list of every real estate agency we could find in city directory hey youre on the front page of todays paper she said when we were almost done yes i said while starin at her pretty open mouth yes the whole world is waitin Richards told her

Police Headquarters   *Friday, July 26, 11:00 a.m.*
Chicago, Illinois

Pat Quinlan:

'Dose? 'Dats my key ring.

I'm Holmes' caretaker, so course I gots to have all 'dem keys. How else can I get in 'da rooms?

I'm innocent, I tell ya. All dese people you say was murdered, yeah I knowed most of 'em. And when dey left, as how Holmes' says, I laugh 'cause I find it funny. But now you say I helped him wid' da' murders, and now I no longer tink it's so funny. I'm innocent I tell ya, innocent.

No, I never saw no kind of monkey bidness goin' on 'round 'dere.

Oh yeah, sure, Mista Holmes had his way with da women folk, if youse guys know what I mean. But I swear 'dats all 'da monkey bidness I ever saw. Ya got ta believe dat.

Leave me wife outta 'dis. She got nuttin' ta hide. She don't even know 'bout 'da girls. So just leave her outta dis, I tell ya.

I don't believe she'd say 'dat. How could she talk 'bout somethun' like 'dat when she didn't know nuttin' 'bout no fire insurance scam.

Why in God's name would I torch 'da place where I work and sleep? I tell ya, I know nuttin' 'bout no fire insurance scam neither.

The New York Times
Sunday, July 28, 1895

A LETTER TO QUINLAN

Holmes Says He Is Willing to Have the Truth Told

CHICAGO, July 27—A search of the apartments of Patrick Quinlan, the ex-janitor, made by police yesterday, resulted in the finding of the following letter, written by Holmes to Quinlan:

June 18, 1895

Dear Pat: Among their other fool theories they think you took the Pietzel body to Michigan and either left him there or put him out of the way. I have always told them that I never asked you to do anything illegal, but they are bull-headed. Oct. 19, I saw you at the factory, I think. Can you show where you were all the rest of the month? If they question you or threaten to arrest you, tell them anything there is to tell about this or any other matter. They may want to know if you were in Cincinnati or Indianapolis about Oct. 12. It is well for you to be able to know where you were working. I am awfully sorry, Pat, for I have always tried to make things easy for you. When Minnie killed her sister, I needed you the worst way, but would not drag you into it. If the detectives go to New-York, as I want them to, they would find where Minnie W. took them by boat. I have done no killing, Pat. One by one they are finding them alive. Minnie will not come here as long as there is any danger of her being arrested. A Boston man knows where she is, and her guardian (Messie H. Watt) will, at the proper and safe time, go to her. Let your wife write me anything you wish not oftener than twice a month, directing H.H. Holmes, County Prison, Tenth and Reed Streets, Philadelphia. I cannot write many letters to you. I am doing all I can for all. Expect to hear shortly from you. Give my love to your wife and Cora. Tell her I have her picture in my room and thank her for it. I have a tame mouse and spider to keep me company. My feed is the worst part here. Clarence Phillip's restaurant at its worst would

be fine compared with it. I only eat once a day. Shall be out of it sooner than you expect. They kept Mrs. P. shut up here six months when we would have let her out on bail. Made a fool of her. Write soon and free. Ask any questions you want to. Georgianna is visiting her mother. Went about two weeks ago. With regards to all,

H.H. Holmes

The following memorandum in pencil is added: "If you see Tiedt, tell him I am much obliged to him."

The foregoing is an exact copy of the letter, with the exception of three lines, which Chief Badenoch carefully erased before exhibiting a copy of it. It is written in ink on two scraps of common manila wrapping paper. Quinlan did not tell the police he had the letter, and he does not know yet that it has been found, but nevertheless it looks remarkably as if it were written on purpose to be found, or, if not, with the knowledge that it would eventually be discovered and read by the police. The man Phillips mentioned in the letter has been summoned to appear before the Chief and Inspector and tell all he knows about the case.

Chief Badenoch said to-day: "I think I will be able to wrest a confession from Quinlan before long. I do not intend to let him turn State's evidence, if I can help it, although I believe he is weakening to such an extent that should such a suggestion be made to him he would grasp it eagerly and at once."

The police also suspect that Quinlan can help them find a missing girl named Miss Wild, a Chicago girl, who has not been seen or heard from for two years, and whose name police have been keeping from the press. She was employed as a clerk for Holmes about two months before her disappearance. She was sixteen years old then—in the Spring of 1893—and left her home one day to go to work, and never returned. She was pretty and Holmes affected to be surprised when told of her disappearance.

The Chicago Inter Ocean
Sunday, July 28, 1895

Reports of Second Nightmare House False

Myrta Holmes, Wife Number Two, Makes Statement

Wilmette, Ill., July 27—Earlier today I toured the house located at 38 North John Street, here in this city. The house is owned by Harry and Myrta Holmes, the former who is being held in Philadelphia for the murder of his business partner, Ben Pietzel.

Following recent grisly discoveries of human bones and remains at Mr. Holmes' Castle in Chicago, several reports have been filtering that a second "Nightmare House" was located here in this city.

Admitted graciously to the house by Mrs. Holmes, a tall, stunningly attractive woman with light hair and strikingly beautiful blue eyes, I was seated in the front parlor where I met the Holmes' equally fair-haired, sweet-faced six-year-old daughter, Lucy. Before the interview began, Lucy was ushered out by the family maid to play with her dollies.

I was very much moved by Mrs. Holmes' agonizing situation. Polite and obviously well-bred, Mrs. Holmes regularly attends the nearby Episcopal Congregational Church with her daughter, Lucy. In my view, Mrs. Holmes has been more cruelly persecuted and misrepresented than any other woman alive. She has been hounded by would-be detectives, reporters and vulgar curiosity seekers. At all hours of the day and night, they have gone to her home. Because they were refused admittance, many of them hurled oaths at her and made all kinds of threats. Many went so far as to claim a second "Nightmare house" was located here.

Well, here is a simple statement of truth. This house does not contain a single mysterious feature. The articles which have been "secretly removed" during the past two weeks were vegetables, a child's hat, two boxes of glass, and an old stove. The "grave" in the garden is a cess-pool, and the statement is authorized that anybody can explore it who wishes to.

The house itself is a very attractive, two-story, red-framed dwelling, located in the finest part of town. Mrs. Holmes,

along with her mother, who has recently come to live with her daughter during these trying times, and the family maid keep the house meticulously clean.

During our interview, I was particularly struck by Mrs. Holmes' devotion to her husband. The following is a verbatim transcript of what Mrs. Holmes told me about Mr. Holmes:

"Naturally I know a great deal of Mr. Holmes' business. I do not intend to be interviewed again about it, for it is his business and no one else's. I have no doubt he will clear himself of all accusations if given a fair opportunity. Every businessman has enemies, and Mr. Holmes has some who would like to overwhelm him.

"In his home life, I do not think there ever was a better man than my husband. He never spoke an unkind word to me or our little girl, or my mother. He was never vexed or irritable, but was always happy and seemingly free from care. In times of financial trouble or when we were worried over anything, as soon as he came into the house everything seemed different. His presence was like oil on troubled waters, as mother often said to him. He was so kind, so gentle and thoughtful that we forgot our cares and worries. It is said that babies are better judges of people than grown ups, and I never saw a baby that would not go to Mr. Holmes and stay with him contentedly. They would go to him when they wouldn't come to me. He was remarkably fond of children. Often when we were traveling and there happened to be a baby in the railway car he would say, 'Go and see if they won't lend you that baby a little while,' and when I brought it to him he would play with it, forgetting everything else, until its mother called for it or I could see that she wanted it. He has often taken babies that were crying from their mothers, and it would hardly be any time until he had them sound asleep or playing as happily as a little one can. He was a lover of pets and always had a dog or cat, and usually a horse, and he would play with them by the hour, teaching them little tricks or romping with them. Is such a man without a heart?

"As for having another wife, I do not believe it. I have the utmost confidence in him. Our domestic relations have been pleasant, and so far as there being any separation I have never heard of such a thing. Mr. Holmes left the first of January. He has been here twice since then on brief vis-

its, and I was with him during the winter on one of his business trips to the South. We have one child, a little daughter, and have been married about nine years. Mr. Pietzel was his business partner at one time, I believe. I hear from my husband two and three times a week, and he continually sends me money for my needs and wants. That does not look like there being trouble between us, does it? And as for other matters, Mr. Holmes can answer for himself. I have nothing to add."

It was at this juncture Mrs. Holmes lost her composure for the only time that day. Through tears, she continued, "Ambition has been the curse of my husband's life. He wanted to attain a position where he would be honored and respected. He wanted wealth. He worked hard, but his efforts failed. He was involved. Temptation to get money dishonestly might have overwhelmed him once or twice. I suspect he might have even defrauded one or two people. But he did not commit murder. He has been accused of crimes which happened on the same date in Chicago, Canada, and Texas. Will not people see the absurdity of charging to him all crimes that cannot otherwise be accounted for?"

Now sobbing, Mrs. Holmes finished by exclaiming, "Mr. Holmes is a human being. He is not supernatural!"

Torelli's Hotel
Indianapolis, Indiana

Wednesday, July 31

Frank Geyer's Notes

All week we swam thru an ocean of sweat every goddamn day near 100 no rain no clouds just the naked sun pressin itself against us we had to drink water at almost every stop we made Indy is full of real estate agents half the population must be sellin land with or without buildings cause we kept on comin up with no luck the newspapers kept on pushin our story toward the back pages maybe im all wrong bout H killin the boy in a rented house maybe he killed him in a dark alley or quiet graveyard the man is nuts so why am i treatin him as if a house is the only place to look given all the evidence i have he had to kill Howard somewhere between Indy and Detroit the child was never seen in Detroit rooms but on Oct 12 H took all 3 P kids out of jews Circle House and on same night only the 2 girls were checked into New Western Hotel in Detroit if we dont come up with somethin tomorrow the boss might pull me back to Philly

New York Times

Friday, August 2, 1895

HOLMES AND QUINLAN

How Much Did Janitor Know?

Mrs. Quinlan Also Questioned in "Sweat Box"

CHICAGO, Aug. 1—In a case where the twists and turns have become as common place as the secret tunnels in Holmes' Castle, two shadowy figures have emerged as possible accomplices. However, as of this writing, both have been released on their own recognizance.

The two suspects are Patrick Quinlan, the janitor of the Castle, and his wife, Mrs. Quinlan.

The Quinlans first surfaced in newspapers when authorities initially suspected that Holmes had murdered the Quinlans' eleven-year-old daughter, Cora Quinlan. But on July 20, Inspector Fitzpatrick received the following telegram from an N.S. Taylor, a Justice of the Peace in Lakota, Mich.:

Cora Quinlan is at Johnson's, and has been for about two weeks.

The Johnsons referred to are the grandparents of the little girl. It is a result of this discovery that Mrs. Quinlan, who has all along maintained an air of crafty reserve, was forced to admit that she had lied to the officers on at least one point, and this had the effect of weakening her considerably. Although officers have refused to divulge much information, as incredible as it may seem, it is believed that an insurance policy was cashed in on the body of one Cora Quinlan for $10,000.

Patrick Quinlan also spent much time in the "sweat box," and both were initially held at length. In fact, at one point last week, Chief Badenoch decided to formally hold them both for trial on the charge of being implicated in various other insurance swindles. The Chief also believed at one time that both were guilty of the crime of assisting Holmes, if not directly at least indirectly, making away with some of his victims.

At another point during the interrogation, Mrs. Quinlan was

forced to admit that she had impersonated a dead woman, representing herself as the beneficiary of a fire insurance policy in order to gain the money that eventually found much of its way into Holmes's pocket.

But as the police were believed to be narrowing their nets around the Quinlans, Chief Badenoch announced to the press that Holmes had corrupted Quinlan, who was "known as an honest man before he met Holmes." Quinlan worked for Holmes as a laboring man, and latterly drew $2 a day, but he never did any labor, and acted more as a confidential agent. This is the only real ground for belief that he knew that his employer was committing murder. It has been daily expected that Quinlan would make a confession that would implicate both himself and his wife, but now suddenly, the police seem to be backing away from the Quinlans as prime suspects.

"Mrs. Quinlan was very much affected during her examination," said Chief Badenoch. "She not only wept throughout the whole interview, but she said: 'I call on God to witness that I know nothing more of the murder than I have already told. If Pat says I know anything more about it, he simply lies, and that's all I know.'"

This remark was called out by the decoy statement given to her that her husband had confessed "everything." According to a police stenographer, Quinlan told Chief Badenoch the following:

"In my opinion, Miss Cigraund, Mrs. Julia Connor, and her daughter Pearl, and Minnie and Annie Williams are all dead, and Holmes killed Pietzel so as to prevent any telling of his crimes, which I was aware of to some extent.

"As to whether Pietzel participated in any of the murders, I know nothing. I do believe that after Holmes killed Pietzel, he felt it necessary to dispose of the dead man's children, and Alice, Nellie, and Howard Pietzel were all killed by Holmes. As to Miss Van Tassel, I know nothing and never saw her.

"Miss Cigraund, Mrs. Connor, Pearl Connor, Minnie and Annie Williams probably all came to their death in the Castle. One day while I was away Mrs. Quinlan saw Holmes poking into a red-hot stove in his office, and saw something that looked like a portion of a human body. The Mrs. also said that a horrible odor was emanating from that room. That night, after Holmes left, I went looking into that room

and found a bottle of chloroform in the steel vault. That was July 5, 1893, and that was the last night I saw either of the Williams' girls."

After the Quinlans had endured the "sweat box" for a third consecutive day, Holmes himself was moved to say, "This talk about Quinlan making a confession and implicating me in all these horrible crimes is the veriest of nonsense. Quinlan will never confess anything, and his wife does not know anything to confess. Even if Quinlan did know some things about me, he is not the kind of a man to shoot off his face to these infernal fools of police, and the fact that he cannot tell them anything makes my mind much easier. I don't fear Quinlan, and whatever confession he makes to the police cannot injure me. Finally, if the police want me to believe any of this nonsense, they should at least have Quinlan say things he is capable of saying. Quinlan wouldn't know the word emanating from urinating, which about sums all this up."

Perhaps there is some truth to what Holmes has to say, for shortly after his statement hit the papers, the Quinlans were released. Chief Badenoch now says that the Quinlans will not be put back in the "sweat box" anytime soon.

Mrs. Strower's Laundry   *Friday, August 2*
Chicago, Illinois

Mabel Strower:

Oh! A detective are ya?

Yes, I knew Mister Holmes—oh, Mabel Strowers, sir.

It's nice to meet you, too, Detective Geyer. Oh my, I don't believe I've ever met a real live detective before. It must be a very excitin' job. Do you get to arrest many murderers? Oh, I would just be terrified, I'm sure!

Oh my job ain't near as excitin' as yours, Detective. I'm in the launderin' business. Don't sound very excitin', I know, but I do a good job, if I do say so myself.

Yes sir, that's how I got to know Mister Holmes. He used to bring me his laundry—him and that tall pretty woman—now let me think, what was her name? Oh yes, Conners I believe. Sometimes they would both come by and sometimes just one of 'em, usually Mister Holmes. I just can't believe all this terrible stuff in the papers about that man—he was always the perfect gentleman around me. He was sure enough handsome!

Well, as a matter of fact, there was one incident that kinda bothered me a

little.

No, no—nothin' like that. The thing is he wanted me to take out this life insurance policy on myself. He made it sound like a pretty good thing, too. He said if I was to take out a ten thousand dollar policy, with him as beneficiary, he'd see I got six grand right away.

Yes sir, that's right, six grand. That's a whole lot of money, I don't mind tellin' ya.

Well, he said it was a good deal for us both. I could have some money now when I really need it, and he would get it back when I died, assumin' he lived longer than me. But it just made me feel real funny—I wasn't so sure I wanted somebody waitin' round for me to die.

Yes, I did kinda say somethin' like that to him.

Oh, he just laughed. Told me he gets big commissions on those policies.

Well, ya know, that was the really strange part. It didn't seem to bother him a bit when I told him I wanted to talk it over with my friends. He just stared me right down with those eyes of his—you ever seen his eyes, Detective?

Well, they sure can give a person the willies, I'll tell ya.

No, he didn't look mean at me—just stared real hard and told me not to be afraid of him. Well, if I hadn'a been afraid before, that did the trick right there! I decided right then I didn't want any part of his offer. I wasn't sure I even wanted to do his laundry.

No, except for that one time, he never mentioned it to me again.

I expect you're right, Detective. I am a lucky woman to be alive. I reckon if I'da taken that policy, I might not be talkin' to you right now.

It was my pleasure. Do you think they'll hang him? I still can't believe he done all those things they're sayin' in the papers! Such a nice man.

Sunrise House *Friday, August 2*
Chicago, Illinois

Frank Geyer's Notes

DA Graham sent telegram yesterday said a small human skeleton was found by Chicago police in Castle cellar still frustrated in not finding a damn thing in Indy i came here to have a good look not only did i see one skeleton but many other bones in huge furnace and 2 chemical vats H has a big bloody table and several large knives and saws hangin on the walls near the table cause hes a doctor no one will get him for murder charge doesnt matter if he had a room full of skeletons and bones now another telegram from DA wants me back in Philly to start workin with William Gary from Fidelity Mutual he says Gary has been chasin Holmes for almost one year

Sanborn Hotel   *Friday, August 9*
Chicago, Illinois

Frank Geyer's Notes

Agent Gary and i put our heads together for 3 days after i went back to
Philly he is sharp as a new nail and all business we figured we would first
check out some long shot possibilities and then focus on Indy and all the
towns around it our aim is to find the P boy today we talked to Pat Quinlan
and his wife to see what they know the Qs are a strange couple especially the
husband he doesnt seem to have a tight fit upstairs kept on makin little
laughs no matter how serious our questions and she kept on sayin she didn't
know where any kids were must have said it 30 times even if we asked a question like when was the last time you saw Mr Holmes i dont know where any
kids are she would say

Longansport Inn   *Sunday, August 11*
Logansport, Indiana

Frank Geyer's Notes

We spent day checkin out every inn boardinghouse hotel and real estate agent
in this small hot city Gary never complains just keeps a small cloth in his hand
to wipe off the sweat i admire the way he carries himself a real gentleman
always nice to people every question to the point no stone left unturned

Moyamensing Prison   *Tuesday, August 13*
Philadelphia, Pennsylvania

Pat Quinlan:

Hey, I know youse'd never woulda hurt 'ol Peetzee—jes' like ya never woulda
hurt 'ol Patty Q 'imself. But ya gotta stop talkin' like dis. You've been in udder
fixes 'afore, but we've always managed.

Yeah, I understand. I promise ya dis time I'll finish 'er off real good-like. They'll
be no jes' third-floor fire—the whole Castle'll be gone—poof.

On my word, Mista Holmes. If ya don't get outta dis mess, I'll be sure to get
with Myrty and we'll leave one helluva treasure buried somewhere in dat smol-
derin' basement.

Heh, heh, heh, yeah, I'd love ta see da look on whoever finds it.

Wade's Hotel   *Tuesday, August 13*
Peru, Indiana

Frank Geyer's Notes

Moved twenty miles of Logansport yesterday checked out Perus hotels inns and
boardinghouses no success today visited all the real estate agents but nobody

can place the boy and H together at the same time Mrs Wade flashed her bedroom eyes at me tonight at dinner but agent Gary waved his index finger in the air and shook his head no so looks like the lovely Wade and i will never test out one of her comfortable cots together unless she comes aknockin on my door tonight

---

New York Times
Tuesday, August 20, 1895

THE HOLMES CASTLE BURNED

Chicago Firemen Say the Fire Was of Incendiary Origin and Was Accompanied by Three Explosions

CHICAGO, Aug. 19.—The row of buildings at Sixty-third and Wallace Streets, Englewood, burned this morning. This row constituted the "Castle," in which H.H. Holmes, the confessed insurance swindler now awaiting sentence in Philadelphia, is popularly supposed to have concocted many of his crimes and committed numerous murders.

Firemen who were early on the scene unhesitatingly declared the fire was of incendiary origin, and it is generally supposed the intention was to destroy it and any evidence it might yet contain relative to the Holmes case.

The fire started in the rear of the structure of the first floor, in the southwest corner of the building, and the first known of it was when Thomas Rogers, the watchman at the railroad crossing, heard a muffled explosion. A moment later smoke issued from the north windows of the building. A small crowd gathered, but were frightened away by a series of three explosions similar to the first. Then, in an instant, the whole building was in flames, and the work of destruction was well under way before the fire engines could get to work.

Marshal declares there is ample evidence of incendiarism, as do members of the first fire company that reached the scene. It is said the explosions were caused by kerosene oil. The fire started in rooms behind a confectionery store that changed hands a few days ago.

Davis's drug store, on the corner, is a complete wreck, as is also the confectionery store. The total loss will not exceed $15,000.

Kevin Knussman found a can half filled with gasoline underneath the secret stairway on the second floor. Two men were seen to enter the building between 8 and 9 p.m. Half an hour later they came out and walked rapidly away. It is believed the men placed the oil there and attached a slow fuse.

This marks the second time in the past year that a fire of mysterious origin has occurred at the "Castle." Last year's fire was also believed to be started by kerosene. That fire destroyed only the third floor of the building.

Police are expected to bring back Patrick Quinlan, the former janitor of the "Castle," for questioning. He has spent much time recently in the "sweat box" regarding the Holmes case.

PHILADELPHIA, Aug. 19.—W.A. Shoemaker, attorney for H.H. Holmes, laughs at the idea that the fire in the "Castle" at Chicago was of incendiary origin. He said: "Such a theory is ridiculous. Holmes has no reason for having the Chicago building destroyed. There was nothing in the place that could convict Holmes of any crime. That has been shown long ago by the Chicago police. They hunted the place from cellar to roof, and what did they find? A lot of fowls' bones and other refuse that was thrown away from the restaurant that was in the building during the fair. I am becoming sick and tired of these reports that are being circulated about the man. Most of them are emanating from the vivid imaginations of a lot of detectives. They have no case; but what's the difference? The boys do not often have a chance of going on a junketing trip and having their names heralded through the breadth and length of the land."

Torelli's Hotel
Indianapolis, Indiana

Friday, August 23

Frank Geyer's Notes

Agent Gary and i have been on the road together since Aug 9 a full 2 weeks and not one new goddamn clue we have checked out places in Ohio Michigan and at least 50 towns surrounding Indy after finishin off Indy itself the only place left is small town Irvington bout 10 miles from here i convinced Gary to take a 3 day break to go back to his family in Philly you live in the city too dont you he asked but i told him i was too bushed to do any more travelin little does he

know i just got to get to a Indy whorehouse before i burst at the seams havent
had any since Mrs W

Torelli's Hotel   *Tuesday, August 27*
Indianapolis, Indiana

Frank Geyer's Notes

Almost midnight but need to get down these notes can't sleep anyway agent
Gary returned last night took room next door i had pounded on 4 or 5 girls
over the weekend felt more relaxed than any other time in past 3 months
Gary was feeling better than ever too this mornin i flirted with Nina while
Gary and i ate huge plates of ham and eggs cool breeze blew thru windows
gray clouds covered the miserable sun i read sports page while Gary poked
his teeth with pick as we rode trolley to nearby Irvington our last hope in
Indy area after getting off in center of town we checked out Irvington Inn
and 5 boardin houses zero then lets try real estate people Gary said our luck
struck a bell when we walked thru the door of Albert Browns office old Al
smiled all the time i asked him if anyone wanted to rent a house for his widowed sister 10 months ago then gave him my worn out photo of Holmes yep
he said this guy was in here 10 months ago like you says said Dr Thompson
had left the key with me Al went on to say the house was not one of his own
rentals Doc rents out his own house but leaves a key with me in case hes out
of town wow my mental bell was ringin so loud i had to sit down a few
mintues later Al took us to docs home not far doc looked at photo then said
the man in photo rented his house just outside main area of town right off
Union Ave last Oct i asked him if a boy with man no he said but you might
want to talk to my young helper Elvet Moorman who was cleanin up the
house for me on the day the stranger moved into it now all 4 of us went to
Moormans house the boy 15 was soon sayin the words i wanted to hear and
there was a young kid with him the cellar of Union Ave house looked undis-
trubed we next went outside to small barn found zip then walked back
toward side porch thats when i saw object under porch the object semed out
of place perhaps hidden on purpose we all looked thru attached latticework
and saw a somewhat curved piece of wood lyin up gainst bottom of house
after i assured doc he would be conpensated for damages we tore out porch
and i went under and dragged out a large piece of trunk a small patch of blue
calico was glued to a seam the calico had a pattern of white flowers now we
searched for more clues almost 3 hours later over 100 curious people came
to see what we were doin i feared the crowd might damage evidence we
might need later but since nothin new had been found Gary and i agreed to
call it a day and go see real estate agent who made first listing of rental Mr
Crouse said H paid 1 month advance on Thompson house for widowed sister a Mrs Cook the Cook name was a favorite of H we felt great but where
was boys body our break came when girl called from office of Indy Evening
News said Dr Thompsons partner Dr Sam Barnhill was waitin for us at

office Barnhill dumped out his doc bag full of burnt pieces of human skull and leg he said that after we left Union Ave house 2 boys snuck in and found bones in stove pipe near chimney in cellar we now took carriage back to house to stop people cause sharp lawyers will say amateur detecs had planted evidence in house to make H look guilty took almost half hour to get jerks outside then we knocked down chimney and used a window screen to sift out ashes and soot first found a complete set of teeth and small jaw bone then found remains of someones stomach and intestines at last our search is over i can sleep way past noon tomorrow

Philadelphia Court House   *Saturday, November 2, 4:00 p.m.*
Philadelphia, Pennsylvania

Judge Michael Arnold:

Gentlemen of the jury. After listening to all of the facts of this case, I find that while you could find this defendant guilty of second-degree murder or manslaughter, this is a case in which there should be a verdict either of murder in the first degree or a verdict of acquittal.

Because there were no witnesses to Mister Pietzel's death, the testimony offered is known in law as circumstantial evidence, as distinguished from direct testimony, or the evidence of an eye witness to the offense. Of this kind of testimony I will say that many of the most important cases are provided by circumstantial evidence only.

The word circumstantial leads some persons to believe that the evidence is inconclusive and imperfect, but this is not so. The difference between circumstantial and direct evidence is that direct evidence is more immediate, the evidence of the eyesight, generally, and requires fewer witnesses than a chain of circumstances which leads to but one conclusion.

Suppose while walking along the street, you hear something behind you that sounds like a pistol shot. You turn and find a man running past you, with others in pursuit. You join in the chase and see the man arrested. You walk back with him under arrest, and on the way back you find a pistol with a chamber discharged, and yet warm and smoking. Further on, you come upon a man who has been killed by a pistol shot. What is the inference that you draw from those facts? Is not that inference irresistible? Yet, you did not see the pistol fired.

Now, in cases of killing by means of poison, experience shows that nearly all such cases are proved by circumstantial evidence only. Poisoning is generally a secret act, and unless the party using the poison has someone to assist him, who afterwards confesses and testifies, direct evidence cannot be obtained.

In the present case, the defendant is accused of killing Benjamin F. Pietzel

by means of poison. Three questions must be considered and determined and answered by you in order to reach a verdict of guilty of murder as charged in the indictment.

The first question is: Is Benjamin F. Pietzel dead? The second is: Did he die a violent death? And the third is: If he died a violent death, did he commit suicide or did the defendant kill him?

In all criminal cases, gentlemen, it is essential that the defendant shall be convicted by evidence which persuades the jury of the guilt of the prisoner beyond a reasonable doubt. If, after considering the testimony, you are unable to come to the conclusion that he is guilty; if there is a doubt in your mind about it and you hesitate, or if you are not fairly satisfied by the evidence of his guilt, then he is entitled to the benefit of the doubt and should be acquitted.

Consider this defendant's case calmly, considerately, patiently. I have no doubt that if you will do that, if you will adhere to the evidence, you will have no trouble in reaching a righteous verdict.

Philadelphia Court House   *Saturday, November 2, 8:45 p.m.*
Philadelphia, Pennsylvania

Foreman Linford Biles:

Your honor, we find the defendant guilty of murder in the first degree.

Chicago Herald
November 3, 1895

HOLMES RESPONDS TO GUILTY VERDICT

Master Criminal Surprisingly Composed

Swears His Innocence to Almighty God

The following is a written statement by Herman Mudgett, alias Harry Holmes, following his guilty verdict yesterday in Philadelphia for the murder of B.F. Pietzel.

PHILADELPHIA, Nov. 2.—It is not safe for a man in my position to criticize the verdict which has been rendered concerning me. Many able lawyers who have followed this trial have declared that the evidence is not sufficient to convict. I, who know my own inno-

cence of the charge brought against me, know of course that no evidence could be brought. I know that I am innocent and, while lack of time and money to prepare my case have brought about this temporary defeat of justice, I know that I shall be acquitted and vindicated in the end.

I have been told and I have been warned that for me to tell the truth would be dangerous. A plain denial, I was told, would be more convincing than any explanation, however truthful. I believed, however, as I still believe, that an innocent man cannot be convicted under our laws and that he could certainly not be convicted for telling the truth.

I am aware that a higher tribunal must pass upon my sentence before it can be confirmed. I know that this higher tribunal must, in the face of my innocence, give me a new trial. At this new trial I shall have had time, at least, to prepare my defense and to refute the web of false contortions spun by the ambitious lawyers who have prosecuted and persecuted me.

I did not murder Pietzel. He committed suicide. I am innocent of the charge against me. I cannot possibly be condemned for a crime which I did not commit.

Early in my life I was thrown much into the company of an old man, upon whom I grew to look at almost as an oracle. Often he would say to me: "He that seeks sympathy receives ridicule." Bearing this in mind, and in no sense wishing to appear before the public as a martyr, yet more for the sake of others than myself, I ask that for a time at least I be dealt with leniently, for in the name of Almighty God and in the names of those who are near and dear to me, I state that I have not taken a human life.

Moyamensing Prison *Thursday, Nov. 21, 1895*

Dear Mama:

It is Thanksgiving Day. It finds me in my cell with the feeling strong upon me that I have nothing to be thankful for, not even my life. I took my chances and failed, and my principle regrets

are the suffering and disgrace upon you and all others. I do not think I have to ask you to disbelieve the murder charges—I expect a two years' sentence, but if I were free today I should never live again as in the past, either with you or anyone else, as I will never run the chances of degrading any woman further. In a little time I will write you about the property; only one-half page letters are allowed. Direct care of the superintendent if you wish to write.

H.

Moyamensing Prison, Death Row   *Tuesday, December 24*
Philadelphia, Pennsylvania

Herman Mudgett:

Dear Father, forgive me, for I have sinned. This is my first confession as a Roman Catholic.

Father, many of my problems are the product of a miserable childhood. My parents didn't want me; my father beat me daily while my mother turned her head pretending all was well.

Father, I'm no good—a liar, a cheat, a murderer. I lost my way so long ago that I have no clear idea of who I really am. I never wanted to murder people, but my own life was taken over by three dark demons: wild-man Henry, black-souled Howard, and especially the despicable Hatch. These three devils have destroyed whatever life I had in the name of Holmes, not that Holmes was an

angel. While Holmes was concentrating on making a living for himself and his families, his three awful companions took advantage of his weaknesses and led him into acts of horrible depravity.

Dear God, I have no clear idea of who or what you are. But I do believe you exist as a merciful being, one who will forgive me, whoever I am, the worst of the worst.

1896

The Philadelphia Inquirer
April 13, 1896

HOLMES CONFESSES TO MANY MURDERS

The Most Fearful and Horrible Murderer Ever Known in the
Annals of Crime

FIRST AND ONLY COMPLETE CONFESSION

The Most Remarkable Story of Murder and Inhuman
Villainy Ever Made in Public

CONVICTION LIES IN EVERY LINE

The only way to describe it is to say that it was written by
Satan himself; or one of his chosen monsters

PHILADELPHIA, April 12.—The following statement was
written by me, H.H. Holmes, in Philadelphia County Prison
as an exclusive with the Hearst Papers. This is a true and
accurate confession in all particulars. It is the only confession of my fearful crimes I have made or will make. I write it
fully appreciating all the horror it contains & how it con-
demns me before the world.

A word as to the motives that have led to the commission of
these many crimes and I will proceed to the most distasteful
task of my life, the setting forth in all its horrid nakedness
the recital of the premeditated killing of twenty-seven human
beings...thus branding myself as the most detestable criminal of modern times—a task so hard and distasteful that,
beside it, the certainty that in a short time I am to be hanged
by the neck until I am dead seems but a pastime.

Ten years ago, I was thoroughly examined by four men of
marked ability and by them pronounced as being both men-
tally and physically a normal and healthy man. Today I have
every attribute of a degenerate—a moral idiot. Is it possible
that the crimes, instead of being the result of these abnormal
conditions, are in themselves the occasion of degeneracy?

Even at the time of my arrest in 1894, no defects were not

able under the searching Bertillon system of measurements to which I was subjected, but later, and more noticeably within the past few months, these defects have increased with startlingly rapidity, as is made known to me by each succeeding examination until I have become thankful that I am no longer allowed a glass with which to note my rapidly deteriorating condition.

I am convinced that since my imprisonment I have changed woefully and gruesomely from what I was formerly in feature and figure. My features are assuming a pronounced Satanical cast. I have become afflicted with that dreaded disease, rare but terrible, with which physicians are acquainted, but over which they have no control whatsoever. That disease is a malformation or distortion of the osseous parts. My head and face are gradually assuming an elongated shape. I believe fully that I am growing to resemble the devil—that the similitude is almost completed.

In fact, so impressed am I with this belief, that I am convinced I no longer have anything human in me.

Now, before I proceed any further with my full confession, I would like to take a moment to commend and praise the work of three men: Assistant District Attorney Barlow, Detective Frank Geyer, and Inspector O. Le Forrest Perry. It seems almost impossible that men gifted with only human intelligence could have been so skillful.

Now, to my confessions of murder:

A friend and former schoolmate, Dr. Robert Leacock of Baltimore, whose life I had insured for $40,000, was my first victim. Until hitting him over the head with a spade and then dumping his body in Lake Michigan in 1886, I had never sinned so heavily by thought or deed. Later, like the man-eating tiger of the tropical jungle, whose appetite for blood has once been aroused, I roamed about the world seeking to quench my desires.

Still, it was several years before I took the life of my next victim, a Dr. Russell, who fell behind in his rent payments while living at the Castle. During a heated exchange, I struck him to the floor with a heavy chair, whereupon with one cry for help, his life ended in a groan of anguish and he ceased to breathe. It was here I began the practice of selling the corpse to an old college acquaintance, who still works for that medical college, for anywhere from between $25 and $100.

Alive with murder, that Christmas Eve (1892) I took the lives

of my mistress, Julia Connor, and her four-year-old daughter, Pearl. Julia died to a certain extent as a result of a criminal operation. The death of Pearl was caused by poison. It was done as I believed the child was old enough to remember her mother's death.

With my next three murders performed in the Castle, I moved east ward for my next victim, a Mr. Rodgers, a fellow tenant at a boarding house in Morgantown, West Virginia, where I spent several weeks on one of my frequent business trips. Learning that the man had money, I induced him to accompany me on a fishing trip. I ended his life with a single, sudden blow to his head with an oar. After taking several hundred dollars that he was carrying on him, along with his watch and diamond ring, I weighted his pockets and then dumped him overboard. I must admit it was a thrill watching his body slowly sink to the bottom of Cheat Neck Lake.

A fatal blow was also used to do in victim number six, a Southern speculator named Charles Cole. But this time I was aided by an accomplice who was actually the one to hit the unsuspecting Mr. Cole with a gas pipe. The blow was so vicious that Cole's skull was damaged and I was unable to unload the corpse as a medical specimen. This was the first time in which I knew my accomplice, Hatch, had committed murder, though in several other instances he was fully as guilty as myself, and, if possible, more heartless and bloodthirsty. I have no doubt he is still engaged in the same nefarious work, and if so is probably aided by a Chicago businessman.

Number seven was a girl by the name of Lizzie, who I employed in the Castle's restaurant. Unfortunately, my janitor, Pat Quinlan, had become infatuated with her. Fearing he might make a tragic mistake and run off with this girl, I thought it wise to end her life. I did this by calling her to my office and suffocating her in the vault. She holds the distinction of being the first one I murdered in such a fashion. I must admit that this method worked so well that many others met their fate the same way. Hers was also the first corpse to fetch $50 (for some reason, the women always seem to go higher). But before I sealed her in, I had her write letters to her relations and to Quinlan stating that she had left Chicago for a Western state and would not return.

Something snapped in me after killing Lizzie the way I did,

and within a few days I took three more lives in the same manner. A Mrs. Cook and her niece had access to all the rooms in the Castle by means of a master key. While I was upstairs preparing Lizzie's body for shipment to the medical college, the door suddenly swung open and Mrs. Cook and her niece stood before me, their mouths agape. It was time for quick action, rather than words of explanation on my part, and before sounds could come from their mouths, they were both sealed tight inside the fatal vault, so lately tenanted by the dead body.

Ah, you say, "I thought he said three lives." Well you see, what makes this particular crime all the more vile was the fact that Mrs. Cook was in her ninth month of pregnancy.

Now, where was I? Oh, yes, victim number eleven, truly one of my most despicable acts. You see, Emeline Cigraund, a most beautiful creature who came my way at the behest of my good friend, Benjamin Pietzel, had become engaged to another man. This attachment was particularly obnoxious to me, both because Miss Cigraund had become almost indispensable in my office work and because she had become my favorite mistress. When she had stopped by to say good-bye for the final time, I told her I had some securities and bonds that I wanted to give to her as a wedding gift, and asked her to step inside the vault to retrieve those papers. After locking her inside, I told her I would only let her out if she would write a letter to her fiancé indicating that she was calling off the wedding and ending the relationship. She was more than willing to do this under the circumstances, as you could well imagine. It was not until after she completed the letter that she realized the door would never again be opened until she had ceased to suffer the tortures of a slow and agonizing death. Like Julia, at nearly six feet, her body commanded a hefty sum from the medical school.

To celebrate my dozenth victim, I went for a triple murder—three teenage girls who were staying at the Castle. This was during the early stages of the Chicago World's Fair, and although I bungled this attempt, it gave me the idea of stealing from several more Fair patrons, and murdering any who got in my way. That these women live today is only due to my foolishly trying to chloroform all of them at the same time late one night. By their combined strength they overpowered me and ran screaming into the street, clad only in their nightgowns. Perhaps the most sobering experience of all this

was that I was arrested the next day. But with some quick talking and an excellent lawyer, I was back at the Castle before nightfall. I vowed thereafter to be more careful.

The beautiful Rosine Van Jossand, whom I poisoned with ferro-cyanide of potassium after she told me she no longer wanted to be my sex slave but rather my wife, has the honor of finally being that twelfth victim. She also has the honor of being the first victim I buried in the Castle's basement.

My thirst for blood was now overpowering, and my next victim, a Mr. Robert Lattimer, who worked for Mr. Quinlan as a janitor, received a most gruesome death sentence. Mr. Lattimer made the fatal mistake of trying to blackmail me after finding out about certain insurance schemes. His own death and the sale of his body was the recompense meted out to him. I confined him to a secret room and slowly starved him to death. Finally, needing the room for another reason, and because his pleadings had become almost unbearable, I mercifully ended his life. The partial excavation of the walls in this room found by the police was caused by Lattimer's endeavoring to escape by tearing away at the solid brick and mortar with his unaided fingers.

I went much easier on Miss Anna Betts, a Fair-goer with whom I had a brief affair and whom I poisoned by substituting a drug that she filled in the Castle pharmacy. Gertrude Conner, the sister-in-law of Julia, also died in a similar manner after she came back to the Castle looking for Julia. I sent her away pregnant and with medication. I knew this would be the perfect murder as it took over a month for that medication to work its magic.

A young woman from Omaha with valuable real estate holdings in Chicago was introduced to the vault and became victim number sixteen; of course, not before I got all of her real estate holdings plus $20,000 in cash.

It will be remembered that the remains of a large kiln made of fire brick was found in the Castle basement. It had been built under the supervision of a Mr. Warner of the Warner Glass Bending Company for the purpose of exhibiting his patents. It was so arranged that in less than a minute after turning on a jet of crude oil atomized with steam the entire kiln would be filled with a colorless flame, so intensely hot that iron would be melted therein. It was into this kiln that I induced Mr. Warner to go with me, under the pretense of wishing to obtain certain minute explanations of the process; and then stepping outside, as he believed to get

some tools, I closed the door and turned on both the oil and steam to their full extent. In a short time not even the bones of Mr. Warner remained.

For my eighteenth victim, I again employed the assistance of my lunatic friend, where together we tortured a wealthy banker from Wisconsin named Rodgers, alternately starving him and nauseating him with gas in that secret room. Disoriented and nearly mad, we forced him to sign over checks and drafts totaling $70,000. My friend administered the chloroform while I added $35 to the grand total by selling his body to the medical school.

Chloroform also did in victim number nineteen, a wealthy young lady who was spending a week at the Fair. For the life of me, I cannot remember her name, although I can still remember every crevice of that magnificent creature; as well as the $5,000 in cash she "lent" me.

Without exception, the saddest and most heinous of any of my crimes were the murders of my twentieth and twenty-first victims, Annie and Minnie Williams. What has been said about Minnie by her Southern relatives regarding her pure and Christian life should be believed, and I am eternally sorry for the wrongs I have heaped upon her name. Also, prior to her meeting me in New York in 1888 as the mysterious Edward Hatch (the same Mr. Hatch that newspaper men all around the country have been so busy writing about), she was a virtuous woman. After coming to work for me in 1893 in Chicago, I induced her to give me $2,500 in money and to transfer to me by deed $50,000 worth of Southern real estate; a little later I convinced her to live with me as my wife, all this being easily accomplished owing to her innocent and child-like nature, she hardly knowing right from wrong in such manners. It was during this time that I also learned that she had a sister, Annie, who lived in Texas and who also was an heir to some property. So I induced Miss Minnie Williams to have Annie come to Chicago for a visit.

Shortly after Annie came to the Castle, I seduced her, then blackmailed her into signing over to me all that she possessed. After that, I forced her into the vault, and it is the foot-print of Annie Williams that police found imbedded into the vault's door, a foot-print made during her violent struggles before her death. Later, I took Minnie on an afternoon picnic where I poisoned her and Hatch choked her to

death by stuffing an apple down her throat. Eventually, I interred her skull in the foundation of my second Castle in Texas, a property that was legitimately hers, and has since been taken over by that State.

I wasn't yet finished with the Williams family, but before I could attend to one additional family member, a man whose name I no longer remember, came to the Fair and rented a room at the Castle. I was determined to use this man in my various business dealings, and did so for a time, until I found he had not the ability I had at first thought he possessed, and I therefore decided to kill him, after which I buried his body in the basement.

After I killed Minnie, I found among her papers an insurance policy made out in her favor by her brother, Baldwin Williams of Leadville, Colorado. I therefore went to that city early in 1894 and, having found him, took his life by shooting him, it being believed I had done so in self-defense.

Because of the spotless life Minnie had led before she knew me, because of the large amount of money I defrauded her of, because I killed her sister and brother, because, not being satisfied with all this, I endeavored after my arrest to blacken her good name; for all these reasons I would like to state again that this is without exception the cruelest and most heinous of all my crimes.

Now my friends, this brings me to my twenty-fourth victim, the crime for which I will be hung. From the first hour of our acquaintance, I intended to kill Mr. Benjamin Pietzel and his entire family. All of my subsequent care of him and his, as well as my apparent trust in him by placing in his name large amounts of property, were steps taken to gain his confidence and that of his family so when the time was ripe they would the more readily fall into my hands.

It seems almost incredible now as I look back that I could have expected to have experienced sufficient satisfaction in witnessing their deaths to repay me for even the physical exertion that I had put forth on their behalf during those seven long years, to say nothing of the amount of money I had expended for their welfare, over and above what I could have expected to receive from his measly little life insurance policy. Yet, so it is.

After I set things up in Philadelphia, I forged letters from Mrs. Pietzel to her husband that made him increasingly despondent. When he became a hopeless drunk with noth-

ing left to live for, I made my move, stealing quietly into his apartment and to the second-story room, where I found him insensibly drunk, as I knew I would.

Only one difficulty still presented itself: It was necessary for me to kill him in such a manner that no struggle or movement of his body should occur, otherwise his clothing being in any way displaced it would have been impossible to again put them in a normal condition. I overcame this difficulty by first binding him hand and foot and having done this, I proceeded to burn him alive by saturating his clothing and his face with benzine and igniting it with a match. So horrible was this torture that in writing of it I have been tempted to attribute his death to some more humane means—not with a wish to spare myself, but because I fear that it will not be believed that one could be so heartless and depraved.

The least I can do is to spare my reader a recital of the victim's cries for mercy, his prayers, and finally, his plea for a more speedy termination of his sufferings, all of which had no effect upon me. Finally, when he was dead, I removed the straps and ropes that had bound him and extinguished the flames and a little later poured into his mouth one and one-half ounces of chloroform. I placed it there so that at the time of the post mortem examination, which I knew would be held, the coroner's physician would be warranted in reporting that the death was accidental.

Unfortunately, the chloroform drove from his entire body tissue, brains, and viscera, all evidence of recent intoxication to such an extent that the physicians who examined the body did not believe the man was drunk at the time of his death, or within twelve hours thereof.

Because of Detective Geyer's discoveries, which we could not at that time in any way refute, it would have been but a waste of my counsel's energies, and of my own, to have tried to convince the most impartial juries that this was a case of suicide and not murder. What difference would it have made? Even if I had been found not guilty of this crime, I surely would have been found guilty of the murders of the Williams' girls, as well as the Pietzel children, my final victims, numbers twenty-five through twenty-seven, the first of which was little Howard Pietzel.

Howard was strangled to death around 6:00 p.m. on October 10 in Irvington. As soon as he ceased to breathe, I

cut his body into pieces that would pass through the door of the stove and by combined use of gas and corncobs proceeded to burn it with as little feeling as though it had been some inanimate object. To think that I committed this and other crimes for the pleasure of killing my fellow human beings, to hear their cries for mercy and pleas to be allowed even sufficient time to pray and prepare for death—all this is now too horrible for even me, hardened criminal that I am, to again live over without a shudder. Is it to be wondered at that since my arrest my days have been those of self-reproaching torture and my nights of sleepless fear? Or that even before my death, I have commenced to assume the form and features of the Evil One himself?

Alice and Nellie were exterminated on the afternoon of October 25, after I took them to the St. Vincent Street house and compelled them to both get within the large trunk, through the cover of which I made a small opening. Here I left them until I could return and at my leisure kill them. At 5:00 p.m. I borrowed a spade from a neighbor and at the same time called on Mrs. Pietzel at her hotel. I then returned to my hotel and ate my dinner, despite the children's cries, and at 7:00 p.m. went again to Mrs. Pietzel's hotel, where I aided her in leaving Toronto for Ogdensburg, N.Y., all the while assuring her that her three children were in good hands. Later than 8:00 p.m. I again returned to the house where the children were imprisoned, and ended their lives by connecting the gas with the trunk. Then came the opening of the trunk and the viewing of their little blackened and distorted faces, then the digging of their shallow graves in the basement of the house, the ruthless stripping off of their clothing, and the burial without a particle of covering save the cold earth, which I heaped upon them with absolute fiendish delight. Many of you will think the deaths of these children were my cruelest crimes of all, both on account of their ages and the terribly heartless manner in which it was accomplished. However, I tend to believe the worst crime I committed against these children was the taking of their innocence—or as District Attorney Graham might have said, the way I "ruined" Alice. I admit freely here and now that Alice was not the only Pietzel child I "ruined."

As to the questions of whether Benjamin Pietzel abetted me in any of my murders, or even knew of any of my previous murders, I answer that he neither knew of nor was a party to

the taking of any human life. The worst acts he ever participated in were dishonesties regarding properties and unlaw-
ful acts of trade, in which he aided me freely. So, what is to
be said of all my crimes?

As I mentioned at the outset, I will soon be going to the gallows as one of Satan's minions. If I could have one request
as to how I should die, I would ask that I be hung from a
cross, upside down. That is a fate befitting a man whose
physical appearance is changing by the hour to that of the
devil himself—so apparent that an expert criminologist in
the employ of the United States Government who had never
previously seen me said within thirty seconds after entering
my cell: "I know you are guilty."

It would now seem a very fitting time for me to express regret
or remorse. To do so with the expectation of even one person
who has read this confession to the end believing that in my
depraved nature there is room for such feelings is, I fear, to
expect more than would be granted.

Moyamensing Prison   *Friday, April 17, 1896*

Dear Mama:

The hangman cometh in three weeks, and unless Governor Hastings grants me executive clemency (which I have no reason to believe he will), I suspect my date with destiny is secure.

Enclosed you will find a check for $7,500, which is what I received from old man Hearst for that ridiculous "true confession" story. The media sure ate that up, although I suspect now most people will believe it is true despite the fact that a dozen of those "murdered" individuals have already come forward to state they are not quite dead yet. As Twain would say, "Events of my death have been greatly exaggerated."

Speaking of which, I still think I may have an ace up my sleeve if Hastings doesn't come through. After talking with Plummer, I think I will be able to place the sale of what remains of my property on Sixty-third Street into escrow for Carrie. She deserves something for all the wrongs I have committed against her. The only catch is Plummer doesn't think all this can be accomplished until the eighteenth of May, which means Carrie would have to intercede on my behalf with Hastings in order to delay the execution.

Finally, I have still been wrestling with one other dilemma. As you know, Hatch killed the children and I am beginning to think I should lead Detective Geyer to this evil man before I am hung from the gallows. Lately, the thought of him laughing at my death has become more of a bother than trying to be honorable to an old accomplice.

Give my best to little Lucy, and know I love you both dearly.

    H.

P.S. Thanks for your letter yesterday. I think that one was the "hottest" one yet. Keep them coming, my love.

The Yoke's Parlor
Franklin, Indiana

Wednesday, May 6

Georgianna Yoke:

Elizabeth, I am so glad you could come. I don't know what I would have done without you.

Mother and Father have been wonderful, too. Neither one mentions his name, and Father finally got that one pesky reporter to quit aggravating me.

No, I'm just tired. All we did those last few months was travel. Sometimes it's still hard for me to believe he was the same man who swindled so many people and murdered so many others.

I guess I'm lucky. Why was he such an evil man?

Well, shouldn't I be angry? Henry—Herman—whoever—left me nothing, except the gifts he gave me during our months together.

Oh, Elizabeth, you should have told me you wanted the amethyst bracelet before I sold it. In fact, I've sold all the jewelry except this heart-shaped locket with our pictures inside. Do you want it?

Good! That's one more thing for the fireplace.

No, leave it alone. I want to see if the gold melts. It probably isn't real anyway.

I wish you could have been with me during the trial. I think that was the hardest thing I ever had to do, but everyone was very nice.

Yes, Detective Geyer was extremely helpful. He tried his best to shield me from all the newshounds.

Actually, he's better looking than his picture. Why? Are you interested in meeting him?

I don't know. He wired me the other day to see how I was doing and to invite me back to Philly.

Yes, I'm serious, Elizabeth.

I'm not sure. Maybe I'll go. What do you think?

The New York Times
Friday, May 8, 1896

HOLMES HANGS FOR MURDER

Under the Noose He Says He only
Killed Two Women

HE DENIES THE MURDER OF PIETZEL

Slept Soundly Through His Last Night on Earth and
Was Calm on the Scaffold

PRIESTS WITH HIM ON THE GALLOWS

Prayed with Him Before the Trap Was Sprung—
Dead in Fifteen minutes, but Neck Was Not Broken

PHILADELPHIA, May 7.—Murderer Herman Mudgett, alias H.H. Holmes, was hanged this morning in the County Prison for the killing of Benjamin F. Pietzel. The drop fell at 10:12 o'clock, and twenty minutes later he was pronounced dead. He was thirty-six.

Holmes was calm to the end, dying as he had lived— unconcerned and thoughtless apparently of the future. With vivid recollection of the recent confession which he admitted the killing of a score of persons of both sexes in all parts of the country, his last public words were nevertheless a point-blank denial of any crimes committed except the deaths of two women at his hands by malpractice.

"Gentlemen, I have very few words to say," began Holmes. "I would make no remarks at this time were it not for my feeling that by not speaking I would acquiesce in my execution by hanging. I wish to say at this instant that the extent of my misdoing in taking human life consists in the killing of two women. They died at my hands as the result of criminal operations. I only state this so that there shall be no misunderstanding of my words hereafter. I am not guilty of taking the lives of the Pietzel family, the three children or the father, Benjamin F. Pietzel, for whose death I am now to be hanged. This is all I have to say."

Holmes then bowed politely to the audience and briefly embraced his court lawyer Rotan, who fled the gallows in tears. Next, Holmes, who converted to Catholicism in April, knelt briefly between his priests, Fathers Dailey and MacPake, while they administered last rites. After this, he stepped upon the trap door and held his hands behind him so they could be handcuffed. A black satin hood was placed over his head, followed by the hangman's noose.

"Make it quick, Richard," Holmes whispered to Assistant Superintendent Taylor and with a signal, the trap was sprung. Beyond a few incidental post-mortem details, the execution, which terminated one of the worst criminal stories known to criminology, was ended.

New York Times
May 9, 1896

HOLMES IN A TON OF CEMENT

The Murderer's Body Buried—
Mrs. Pietzel's Claim on His Estate

PHILADELPHIA, May 8.—The body of H.H. Holmes, which was imbedded in cement in a pine box yesterday after the hanging and then placed in a vault in the Holy Cross Cemetery, was this afternoon buried in a grave ten feet deep. The Rev. Father MacPake, who was one of Holmes's spiritual advisers, and who remained with him to the last, conducted the services of the Roman Catholic Church at the grave. The box, with the body imbedded in cement as a result of Holmes's final wish, weighs over a ton. The grave diggers, aided by a mason, and under the supervision of Lawyer Rotan, piled a layer of cement two feet thick upon the box.

The material was packed about the sides and ends of the novel sarcophagus, and when the job was finished the remains of Holmes were pronounced safe from grave robbers for all time.

Lawyer Thomas A. Fahy, the legal adviser of Mrs. Pietzel, stated to-day that he would shortly confer with Lawyer Rotan and District Attorney Graham with the view of locating any cash or property left by Holmes that could be attached, in order to satisfy the claim of Mrs. Pietzel. The latter wants restitution for the insurance money she was swindled out of by the bogus promissory note which Holmes represented as having been signed by her husband.

Mr. Fahy further said: "I have been given to understand that Holmes died intestate, although I did believe that he would leave a will devising the one-third interest in whatever estate he had to Mrs. Pietzel. I fear now that he did not make any provision for the widow of the man he yesterday denied killing, and unless he had given instructions to his attorney as the matter of restitution, I will have to proceed upon different lines. I will attach anything I can find, for no one will deny that the first claim upon Holmes

property is that of Mrs. Pietzel. However, I now suspect that a Mrs. Myrta Holmes is the sole recipient of all that Holmes left behind."

1914

Look at Life Magazine
October 1914

HOLMES' MYSTERIES PUT TO REST
by Howard Abrams

Perhaps now, nearly twenty years after Herman Mudgett was convicted and hung for the crime of murder, can America finally lay to rest the restless spirit of one H.H. Holmes.

As many of you might still remember, Mudgett, who went by the alias of Holmes, as well as nearly fifty other names, was a prosperous business man who resided in Chicago—Englewood to be exact—during the 1893 World's Fair.

It was also during this World's Fair that Holmes has been alleged to have taken up to 200 young women into his notorious "Castle." And it is also alleged that after seducing these young ladies, some still in their teens, he would slowly torture them to death using various methods, from poisons to suffocation in his infamous "vault." Often times, he would then strip the flesh from their bones and sell the skeleton to a local medical college for cash.

While Holmes was enjoying the flesh of these young ladies, he was also married to as many as five different women at the same time and was defrauding countless insurance companies out of thousands of dollars.

In September of 1894, Holmes slipped up and was convicted a year later in Philadelphia of murdering his business partner of many years, Benjamin F. Pietzel, in the hopes of receiving a $10,000 life insurance settlement from the Fidelity Mutual Insurance Company. Immediately following the murder of Pietzel, Holmes led his bride, and several of Pietzel's family split into three distinct groups, around much of America, keeping each group separate. It was during this time he murdered Pietzel's three young children, one by one.

Following his capture two months later, Holmes told one story after the other, none appearing to be the truth according to one of the lead detectives in the case, Frank Geyer. Finally, a year later, Holmes was found guilty and was hung in May, 1896, for the crime of murdering B.F. Pietzel. Within hours of his death, per his request, Holmes was buried in a ton of cement so that no one could steal his body.

Unfortunately, there was nothing to keep his spirit from returning to earth.

For immediately following his death, strange and unexplained events began to take place against almost anyone who had anything to do with Holmes.

The first such incident befell Dr. William K. Mattern, the coroner's physician who testified against Holmes, and who mysteriously died from blood poisoning.

Immediately thereafter, in quick succession the following misfortunes occurred: Coroner Samuel Ashbridge and the presiding judge of the trial, Michael Arnold, were stricken with life-threatening diseases on the same day, June 3, 1896; Anthony Perkins, the Superintendent of Moyamensing, the prison that housed Holmes, committed suicide just two days later when he hung himself in his prison office; the father of one of Holmes' mistresses, Emiline Cigraund, who met her fate in the vault, received third degree burns from an unexplained gas explosion on July 15; and while investigating that explosion two days later, Detective Geyer was overcome by a mysterious illness from which he never recovered.

Despite all these coincidences, the theory of Holmes having an "evil eye" or was of an "astral" entity did not firmly catch on until the next incident, which occurred August 17. On this date, the office of O. LaForrest Perry, the claims manager for Fidelity Mutual, was completely destroyed by fire—or should I say, almost completely. For despite the fire destroying all of the furnishings and valuables, three items, and only three items, did manage to survive the fire: the original copy of Holmes' arrest warrant, and two separate photos of Holmes. "The Holmes Curse" was now on the lips of every resident from Chicago to Philadelphia.

"The Holmes Curse" seemed to take a holiday until All Saints Day, when the body of Father Henry J. MacPake, the Roman Catholic priest who gave Holmes his last rites, was found in the backyard of St. Paul's Academy on Christian Street. "Uremia" was listed as the official cause of death after the coroner could not explain away heavy bruises on the priest's face and head, blood stains on the fence, and unknown footprints on the soft ground where the priest's body was found.

Perhaps Holmes' curse was forever assured when Linford Biles, the jury foreman for the Holmes trial, was electrocuted, along with his son, on his roof that Christmas Eve, thus ending for the year a startling string of strange occurrences.

"I read in the papers where Holmes said he was starting to look like the devil," said Mrs. Crowell, a neighbor of the Biles. "Now I'm thinking he didn't just look like the devil, but really was one."

Another one to meet the curse was Marion Hedgepeth, a famous train robber of his day. It was Hedgepeth who, after befriending Holmes in a St. Louis jail, turned state's evidence against Holmes in the hopes of receiving a reprieve. However, Hedgepeth's hopes of early release backfired, and on the day Holmes was executed, Hedgepeth began serving a twenty-five year sentence. After being released in 1906 for good behavior, only to go back to jail a year later for another robbery, Hedgepeth was released again in December of 1910 because he was dying of tuberculosis. Within weeks, Hedgepeth had rounded up another gang, and while holding up a saloon on New Year's Eve just blocks from where Holmes' "Castle" had once resided, he was shot to death by a policeman who happened to walk in upon the robbery. A newspaper article accounting Holmes' hanging was found in his wallet.

Which brings us to 1914 and the reason for this particular story. Earlier this year, on March 7, a short article graced the pages of The Chicago Tribune with this blaring headline: Holmes "castle" secrets die.

The story was in regard to Pat Quinlan, who was Holmes' former janitor of the Castle, and a serious suspect for months in regard to all of Holmes' misdeeds. Although police had Quinlan interrogated time and again, and were often on the verge of arresting him, he somehow managed to come out of the trial unscathed—that is until March 5 of this past year when Quinlan took his own life by taking strychnine.

His daughter, Cora, did not find his body on their Portland, Michigan, farm until the next day. In his hand was a suicide note that said the following: I have been haunted day and night by voices and faces for longer than any human should ever have to endure. Although as of this writing it may seem that the mysteries of the Holmes' Castle will stay just that—mysteries forever, rest assured my friends, the memory of those mysteries will indeed be resurrected someday.

So, you might ask, what is the big deal about a former crony being haunted by bad dreams and eventually killing himself? Police have recently confirmed that the suicide note was penned in the handwriting of one H.H. Holmes, a man who has been dead for nearly twenty years, on paper yellowed by time.

ODE TO HOLMES

Holmes, Howard, Mudgett, all the same man,
he killed pretty girls by the score.
He'd use whatever was closest at hand,
chloroform, gas, knives and more.

"Come into my parlor, I'll show you around"
was the line he would use very often.
And the girls, young, naive, and quite new in town,
would find themselves starting to soften.

Like lambs to the slaughter, they followed his lead,
as he lavishly wined them and dined them.
He lured them to bed to fulfill his great need,
and the next day, no one could find them!

A few of the girls, those with an estate,
he would toy with until they resigned it.
Their estate would be his, but how sad their fate—
they'd be dead as soon as they signed it!

"My vault door is open, please do look inside,"
he would say as the ink was still drying.
"Fetch me those papers, you'll soon be my bride."
The door would slam, and then they'd start dying.

He schemed with Ben Pietzel on an insurance deal,
that cost poor Ben Pietzel his life.
Then he murdered Ben's children, with hardly a squeal.
Then went after Ben Pietzel's wife.

Holmes married three women without a divorce,
and claimed to love each of the three.
And maybe he did have a little remorse,
'cause they all lived longer than he!

The policemen had followed all of their clues,
so they finally put him away.
Justice won out and Holmes paid his dues,
when he swung from the gallows in May.

U.S. Five is a professor, Bob Stanton, and four of his students at Jacksonville University—Sandi Branum, Gary F. Izzo, Dedra Torelli, and Nina D. Wade.